Where The Truth Lies

MJ LEE
WHERE THE TRUTH LIES

CANELO

First published in the United Kingdom in 2018 by Canelo

This edition published in the United Kingdom in 2019 by

Canelo Digital Publishing Limited
57 Shepherds Lane
Beaconsfield, Bucks HP9 2DU
United Kingdom

A CIP catalogue record for this book is available from the British Library.

Print ISBN 978 1 78863 418 2
Ebook ISBN 978 1 78863 316 1

Look for more great books at www.canelo.co

Printed and bound in Great Britain by Clays Ltd, Elcograf S.p.A.

Chapter One

10 March 2008. Chorlton, Manchester.

'I always bites the heads off babies. Dunno why. The orange ones first, then green, red, pink and finally yellow. Always save the yellow for last, I do. Never eat the purple ones though.'

Sergeant Mungovan put the head between his teeth and carefully bit down, avoiding the arms. 'What about you?'

'Never touch them, Sarge.' PC Tom Ridpath tapped the top of the steering wheel, staring through the windscreen at the road. The wipers swept across once, clearing the light drizzle from the glass. It was one of those Manchester days when it was either raining, thinking about raining or had just finished raining and was about to start again. The sergeant popped the remaining torso of the jelly baby into his mouth, searching in the white paper bag as he chewed. 'They all have names, you know. Now this one, the purple one, is called Big Heart.' He held the body of the jelly baby between his large, nicotine-stained fingers. 'Ugly brute, isn't he?' The windscreen wipers cleared the glass once more.

'If you say so, Sarge.'

They had parked up in front of Turner's newsagents on the corner of Withington Road. Sergeant Mungovan went there every day at eleven o'clock when he was on the morning shift. It was the only place selling his jelly babies out of a jar. The Sergeant bit the head off a bright fluorescent-green baby. 'Look, I told you this morning, it's either Doc or Sergeant. I can't stand "Sarge". Makes me think of Bilko.'

'Who's he, Sarge… Sergeant?'

'Before your time, son.'

'And you can call me Ridpath. I hate Thomas or Tom, they're so bloody Victorian.'

The Sergeant shifted his bulk as he peered into the white paper bag. Years of sitting in police cars, eating sweets, bacon butties and Greggs' Cornish pasties had taken their toll.

'You can have the purple ones, Tom, if—' Before he had finished the sentence, a large white van turned sharply right in front of them without any indication, causing another motorist to stamp on his brakes, bringing his car to a screeching stop. Sergeant Mungovan folded the top half-inch of his paper bag. 'Right, our kid, time to pop your cherry. Looks like you've got your first collar. Let's get after him.'

Ridpath leant forward to switch on the siren and lights of the Vauxhall Astra, only to find his hand slapped away.

'Sergeant's privileges. Didn't they teach you anything at Sedgeley Park?'

The whoop of the siren erupted from above Ridpath's head and the light cut through the gloom of March in Manchester. He put the car in gear and raced after the white van, now 200 yards ahead and moving fast. Sergeant Mungovan spoke into the radio. 'In pursuit of a white Ford Transit, licence plate FB05 TBY, along Wilbraham Road, over.'

The van was ignoring the siren and the flashing lights, over-taking a slow-moving car and racing down the road. A spike of adrenalin surged through Ridpath's body as he stamped on the accelerator. So this is what it felt like – a police chase just like those on *Miami Vice*, except he was involved and he was in charge. After a short lag, the Vauxhall leapt forward, belying its age. At least the engine was well looked after. They were gaining rapidly on their prey, the van ahead boxed in by the traffic.

'Slow down, Stirling Moss. I want to nab this one with me in one piece.'

Up ahead the van was turning right, again without any indication, past a large Morrison's supermarket. Ridpath followed it round the corner, accelerating to within 50 yards. The noise of the siren was louder now, echoing off the buildings on either side, the flashing light more intense. As if raising a white flag, the driver of the van slowed down, signalling to pull in. Ridpath stopped behind him, parking the regulation five yards away so he could see both sides of the vehicle, exactly as he had been taught in police training school.

The driver of the van was sitting in his seat, not moving, staring straight ahead.

Sergeant Mungovan picked up the radio again. 'Anything on the status of the van? Over.'

Static, followed by the voice of a male dispatcher. 'Nothing yet, computers are a bit slow this morning, Doc. Over.'

Mungovan switched off the radio. 'Aren't they bloody always?'

Up ahead the driver was still behind the wheel of his van and still not moving.

'You wait here till dispatch gets back to you on the status of the van.'

'Yes, Sergeant.'

The experienced copper placed his cap on his head and opened the door of the Vauxhall. As he shifted his bulk to get out of the car, the springs squeaked and the car rocked in complaint. He stood up, pulled down the stab vest over his stomach and closed the passenger door, keeping his eyes fixed on the driver of the van.

The car instantly felt lighter, more spacious. The radio emitted a squeak of static and then went silent again.

Sergeant Mungovan walked slowly, deliberately, towards the van, stopping for a moment to check a broken rear light. The driver side door opened and a middle-aged man wearing glasses and blue overalls stepped out. Long strands of hair coated the top of his head in the classic Bobby Charlton comb-over.

3

Static crackled from the radio. Ridpath looked down at the noise coming from the speaker. He didn't know why he did that. It was a sound, not an image; why did he look down?

'Proceed with caution, over. Driver of Ford Transit FB05 TBY wanted for questioning regarding abduction of prostitute from Moss Side...'

Ridpath looked up.

The man was standing over Sergeant Mungovan, his fist raised as if to strike downwards. The fist lashed out at the same time as the sergeant jumped backwards.

Ridpath watched it all as if in slow motion. The fist arcing through the air, the look of surprise in the sergeant's eyes, the man's hair flopping in the breeze, the fist striking the top of the stab vest where it was fastened across the shoulders. The sergeant falling backwards, arm stretched behind him.

The windscreen wipers sang across the glass, clearing the rainwater.

The man's fist was raised again, the white knuckles clearly visible against the grey Manchester sky.

Ridpath fumbled with the latch of the door. It caught his sleeve then swung open. He stood up and shouted. He didn't know what he said but it stopped the man.

Sergeant Mungovan was lying against the rear tyre of the van, his left arm raised to ward off the coming blow.

Ridpath shouted something again. It could have been 'Stop, police' but he didn't know the words he used.

The man looked across at him, arm suspended in mid-air, a red wildness in his eyes. For a short moment, they stared at each other as if daring the other to act first.

Ridpath slammed his car door shut and the moment was broken.

The man hesitated for a second, eyes darting left and right, before running down Albany Road away from the van.

Ridpath rushed over to Sergeant Mungovan lying next to the rear wheel, his right arm hanging loosely at his side. He knelt down and placed his fingers on the Sergeant's neck.

'What the bloody hell are you doin'?'

'Checking for a pulse, Sarge.'

'Does it sound like I'm dead?'

'No, Sarge. Are you OK?'

'Of course I bloody am. Get after the bastard – I'll call it in.' He fumbled for his radio with his left hand.

The man was already 60 yards ahead and moving with a speed which surprised Ridpath. Should he leave the sergeant?

'Get the bastard,' shouted Mungovan, pointing with his unhurt arm.

As if on automatic pilot, Ridpath found his legs obeying the order and running down the street after the suspect. Behind him, he could hear Sergeant Mungovan calling for backup on his radio.

The man was a hundred yards ahead and moving pretty quickly for a middle-aged, overweight bloke: his head tilted back, his arms pumping and the strand of hair flopping in the wind.

He wasn't going to stop for anybody.

Ridpath was running strongly despite the tight stab vest and heavy boots. He was proud of how healthy he had managed to keep himself despite spending two years stuck behind a desk and a computer in that insurance office.

Two mind-numbingly boring years of his life.

Wasted.

But police training school had soon sorted him out. Most of the others moaned like donkeys when they went on another cross-country run. Not him. For him, it was pure joy to feel his chest sucking in air and his legs splattered with mud. Anything, even cross country running in the middle of an English winter, was better than sitting behind that desk.

The suspect was already crossing Brantingham Road and heading towards Unicorn, the co-operative grocery. Ridpath had been in there once with his wife when she was on her 'organic vegan, just eating fish, no milk' week. A strange place with an even stranger smell. A mixture of turmeric, cumin, sour milk and just a whisper of self-righteousness. Luckily the vegan week had only lasted four days before a pork *char siu bao* called his wife's name.

The man stopped at the kerb and looked over his shoulder, seeing Ridpath still running after him. He darted across the road, narrowly missing a cyclist and bringing a white Mercedes to a screeching halt.

The rain still drizzled down, forming a thin wet film over the smooth paving stones. Ridpath slid to a stop at the edge of the road, feeling his legs slide from under him. He put his arm down to stop his fall and jerked himself upright, shouting, 'Stop him!', but his words were lost in the noise of the traffic.

A student must have heard because he reached out to grab the man, only to be shoved off his bike viciously. The man stamped on the student's hand before doubling back up Barlow Moor Road and swinging right down a narrow lane past an Indian fruit and veg shop, its wares displayed in crates across the pavement.

Ridpath stopped for a moment, hearing the sound of sirens in the far distance. The cavalry was on their way. He clicked his radio. 'In pursuit of suspect on Barlow Moor Road opposite the Unicorn Grocery, over, heading west towards Chorlton Library, over.'

The radio crackled like it was clearing its throat. 'Message received, over. Vehicles dispatched, over.'

He waited for a gap in the traffic but none appeared: a never-ending flow of cars, trucks and bikes. Ridpath took a deep breath before sticking out his hand and slipping between a bus and another Mercedes. He dodged between the other cars accelerating towards him and managed to reach the other side of the road, hearing the screech of tyres on asphalt to his left, followed by a shouted, 'Bloody idiot!'

The student was lying on the ground holding his left hand across his chest. An old woman with a shopping trolley was bending over him, asking how he was.

Ridpath ignored both of them and ran up the road, past the oranges and mangoes outside the shop, turning right to follow the suspect.

Nothing.

The man had vanished. 'What the…?'

He ran down the lane. At the bottom, a mound of grass-covered earth blocked the road. Ridpath leapt up on top of it. On the other side two rows of lock-up garages formed a short street. Right at the end the suspect was fumbling with a bunch of keys, trying to open the door at the side of one of the garages

Ridpath reached for his radio. 'Suspect at corner of Claridge and Oswald Road lock-ups. Over.'

'Message received. Over.'

The sirens were louder now, the high-pitched squeal modulating with all the harmony of a scourge of banshees.

The suspect had seen him, and redoubled his efforts to get the door open, searching through the keys looking for the one that would fit.

Should he tackle him alone or wait for backup?

Ridpath ran down the other side of the mound of earth and up between the garishly painted garages. One was sprayed with a sign in big bold letters: 'Free Benny'.

Who the hell was Benny?

The suspect had the door open. He vanished inside and the door began to close. Ridpath threw himself at it, feeling his shoulder crash into the wood. The next moment he was falling into blackness as the door crashed open, throwing the suspect backwards onto the floor.

A jolt of pain shot through Ridpath's shoulder as he tried to push himself off the floor.

The man scrabbled for a hammer lying on the ground next to his head. Ridpath threw himself on top of him, grasping with both hands the arm that held the hammer.

His shoulder screamed in pain as he struggled on the floor, seeing the hammer above his head, the dull metal ball ready to strike down.

7

The man was much stronger than he looked. He pressed down harder, leaning all his weight into the hammer, forcing his arm forward.

Ridpath could feel his arm shaking, the shoulder shrieking, the metal getting closer to his head. He rolled away, hearing the swoosh of the hammer as it swung past his head, seeing the sparks ricochet off the floor as it struck the ground.

The man swung the hammer back towards him, backhanded now, curving it round in an arc. Ridpath jumped backwards, grabbing the arm as it curved through the air.

His opponent fell forward, off balance.

Ridpath swung the man's arm against the leg of a metal desk, hearing the wrist crack beneath his hands.

The hammer tumbled to the ground.

Ridpath grabbed the back of the man's head and smashed it into the metal edge of the desk. He pulled the man's head back, ready to strike the forehead against the desk again.

For a second, the man's eyes flared with fear. Ridpath grabbed the thin blond hair and thrust the head forward once more.

Again, the head struck the desk with a sickening thud.

The man recoiled for a moment before sinking down to his knees. Ridpath ignored the pain in his shoulder and punched downwards, connecting with the man's head just below the ear, the momentum of the blow propelling him across the man's body.

He pushed himself off and brought his fist back.

The man raised his hands to cover his face, not fighting back any more, just protecting himself. 'Don't touch me, don't touch me!' he screamed, hiding behind his hands.

He slammed his fist into the side of the man's head where it wasn't protected, feeling the crunch of his knuckles against the man's temple. Then he hauled the man's body around and fumbled for his handcuffs, wrenching the man's arms up and behind him, snapping the steel jaws onto the wrists.

Behind him came the screech of tyres, the slamming of doors, the welcome sound of police boots on tarmac.

'In here,' he shouted pushing himself off the man and sitting back on the floor, his breath panting in short sharp gasps.

Voices outside the lock-up.

'In here,' he shouted again.

As the door slowly, cautiously opened, the grey light of a Manchester day crept into the garage, gradually reaching to the rear wall.

Ridpath stared up. 'Oh, my God,' he said.

Chapter Two

Present day

Ridpath stood outside looking up at the acres of plate glass covering the building and shivered. Why was he so nervous? This was his place, his patch; he knew every inch of police headquarters.

He took another long drag on his cigarette. He wasn't supposed to smoke, the doctors had told him many times, but he was sick of them and their rules. He laughed to himself. Only he could be sick of doctors.

He took one more life-giving suck on the Marlboro Red and threw the butt into the drain on his right. It had been nine months since he'd been inside this place. Nine months is a long time. A lot could have changed. A lot probably had changed.

As his DCI, Charlie Whitworth, always used to say; 'Listen, Ridpath, the only constant with the police is change. A new chief constable and we change. A new government and we change. A new policy and we change. Only the job remains the same. We catch the bad guys and we put them away. Remember that and you'll go far in this job.'

Well, he had remembered it and he had gone far.

Until nine months ago.

He pulled his jacket tighter around himself. 'Come on, lad, get on with it,' he said out loud, adjusting the tie his wife had given him to wear. It felt strange to feel the noose of the tie around his neck, touching his Adam's apple. You'll get used it, he thought. You always get used to it.

He launched himself up the whitewashed steps, stopping in front of the glass doors, waiting to be buzzed in.

The door opened and he strode into the reception area. Well, at least this hadn't changed. There were still the same old fading police notices on the wall with their fading messages:

'Look out, there's a thief about.'

'Don't be blind to the signs.'

'Look her in the eye and tell her a little drink never hurt anybody.'

And there were some new ones, clean and crisp in their colour and design:

'Help free the UK from modern slavery.'

'Hate crime. Tell the Manchester Police about it.' Beneath this one somebody had written in biro: 'Because nobody hates crime more than the Manchester Police.' He thought he recognized the handwriting.

Just two people spoilt the pristine emptiness of the reception area: a wrinkled woman and a young, burly man, both sitting forlornly on the row of plastic seating screwed to the floor. Probably waiting for someone to be released after a night in the cells. Another drunk driver.

A sergeant he had never seen before was standing behind thick glass, looking like a clerk at a post office except for the blue uniform. A muffled voice through the microphone. 'How can I help you, sir?'

'An appointment with Detective Chief Inspector Charlie Whitworth at 10.30.'

The sergeant checked his diary. 'Nothing in here, sir.'

Just then the door to the inner sanctum of the police station opened. 'Well, I never. Ridpath, it's great to see you.'

'Harry Makepeace, skiving off as usual.'

'You know me too well.' Makepeace scanned him up and down. 'You're looking well.'

Ridpath stepped back and waved his hands. 'Feeling great. Raring to go.'

'You here to see the boss?'

He nodded.

Harry held open the door. 'I'll take you through...'

'But there's no appointment...' The tinny voice of the sergeant sounded feeble through the speaker.

'No worries, Martin. This is Detective Inspector Tom Ridpath. Used to work here.'

'Still do.'

Harry Makepeace turned slowly towards him. 'Aye, I suppose you do. Come on.'

He stepped through into the back office. Behind him the voice of the sergeant was calling, 'Can you sign the book?'

They both carried on walking down the corridor.

'Been a few changes since you were here.'

'Have there?'

'Me for one – I've been promoted.'

'Congrats, Detective Inspector Makepeace, it's been a long time coming.'

Harry looked across, checking for irony. 'Aye, too bloody long.'

'Charlie's still here though. Still running the Major Incident Team?'

'Aye, nowt's changed there. John Gorman's officially in charge, but he's so snowed under by management meetings, Charlie does the day-to-day.'

They entered the CID office on the right.

The place hadn't changed at all. The same beige walls with the marks of ancient posters staining the government-issue wallpaper. The same mismatched desks. The same ancient desktop computers due to be mothballed a year ago but still being used. And the same grey, coffee-stained carpet that always gave him an electric shock every time he touched his desk.

That detectives' office.

His detective's office.

Most of the workstations had detectives sitting at them, tapping away at their keyboards or just staring at the screen, their tabletops strewn with papers and coffee cups. Others were on the phone, their shoulders hunched as they tried to take notes and ask questions at the same time. Two young men rushed past him without saying a word, hastily grabbing jackets and coats.

As he stood in the entrance, a few people discreetly looked up from what they were doing and smiled. One or two waved. But nobody came forward to say hello.

There was a buzz about the place Ridpath missed, something magical in the air. That invisible current of energy running through the room when something big was happening.

'Busy time, a murder. Charlie's expecting you,' said Harry.

He pointed to the far side of the room which was blocked off at the end by a curved glass wall. For as long as Ridpath could remember, this place was called 'the Bubble'.

'See you later, for a...' His hand wobbled in front of his mouth. The universal sign language for a beer, the fuel of choice for any modern police force.

Ridpath nodded, turning towards the Bubble. Inside, he could see Charlie Whitworth staring at a computer screen. He crossed the floor and knocked on the door.

The detective chief inspector frowned and glanced up from his computer, before his face cracked a large smile and he stood up from his desk.

He pushed open the door.

'Great to see you again, mate.' Charlie Whitworth advanced with his hand held out.

'Great to be back, boss.'

The piercing blue eyes stared directly at him as they shook hands, examining him carefully. Finally, his hand was let go.

'Take a seat.'

Ridpath had barely settled in the chair facing Charlie Whitworth when the question he had been dreading came with all the subtlety of a kick to the head.

'How's the cancer?'

Chapter Three

'Don't hang about do you, boss?'

Charlie Whitworth reached forward to touch a beige folder on his desk. 'You know me. I was never one for small talk.'

'What can I say? I'm in remission after six months of chemo. The cancer's not spread and all the doctors say I'm as fit as a butcher's dog.' He reached forward to tap the wooden table.

The gesture wasn't lost on Charlie Whitworth.

'But you know – it's all in the report in front of you. What's more, the doctors have certified me as fit to return to work and it's been signed off by HR. Been through so many rounds of "assessment"' – he formed quotation marks with his fingers – 'I feel like I've been prodded and poked more than a hooker in a room of blind men.'

Charlie Whittaker opened the report and pretended to read it. 'True. Says it all here, but—'

'But what, Charlie?'

'But…you collapsed in the middle of an important investigation. What if it happens again? And what about the stress? This job isn't famous for being an easy ride.'

'Stress didn't cause my myeloma, Charlie. The illness had nothing to do with the job. It's just one of those things.'

'A bit shit for someone who's 35.'

'You said it. But I'm OK now and raring to get back to the job. You don't know how boring it is sitting at home all day with the wife fussing around and *Cash in the Attic* on bloody telly. If I see another Paul Martin with another bloody toby jug, I'll shove it where the sun don't shine.'

Charlie Whitworth chuckled. 'I can imagine.' Then the smile vanished as suddenly as it had appeared. 'How's Polly handling it?'

'Wants me to get back to work. Jesus, Charlie, I've been prowling round the house like a caged lion for the last three months. She'll be happy to get rid of me.'

Charlie Whitworth closed the file and placed it on the desk in front of him. He licked his lips and the moustache sprouting beneath his nose like a tangled vine. 'I'm gonna lay my cards on the table. The deputy chief isn't keen on you coming back—'

'But—'

He held his hands up to stop Ridpath from speaking. 'But John Gorman and I had a chat with him and we've found an answer.'

'Go on.'

'We're going to give you a job where we can monitor your performance and your health for three months.'

'What's the job?'

'It's an important job for us. We need somebody to sort it out, and quickly.'

'What's the job, Charlie?'

'Coroner's officer.'

'Coroner's officer? You've got to be joking, Charlie. It's a job for the deadbeats and the terminally stupid. I thought Jim Howells was doing that job?'

'He was.'

'He was, but what?'

Charlie Whitworth sighed. 'He was, but he screwed up big time. Taking early retirement. Listen, it would help us out and it's only for three months. The deputy chief would owe you one. Three months, that's all, then John and I can move you back into the squad when the coroner finds a full-time replacement. The bloody woman wants somebody with a medical background.'

'Not a copper?'

'Not any more. Apparently, the job is changing according to her.'

Ridpath thought for a moment. 'I can retain my rank?'

'Of course, you're still a probationary detective inspector. Have to start again though. The clock's gotta be reset. Rules, I'm afraid.'

'And you'll take me back onto the squad after three months?'

'Listen, Ridpath, you're a bloody good copper, who wouldn't want you back on their team? And for us it kills three birds with one stone.'

'It's two birds, Charlie.'

'Not in this case, Ridpath. Relations between the coroner and the deputy chief are a little strained at the moment.'

'Jim Howells?'

'You got it.'

'He always was a bit of a twat.'

'That's just the half of it. Anyway, the deputy would like you to use your undoubted charm to smooth things over, build up trust with the coroner, show her how cooperative and useful the police can be. You know, the usual crap.'

'Because the deputy is never going to make chief constable if the local coroner has been bad-mouthing him to the Ministry of Justice.'

'You got it in one. You can be his eyes and ears.'

'I'm no snitch, Charlie.'

'Never said you were. A watching brief. Show us you can do the job.'

'I dunno…'

'Look, I'll be honest. The only other available job is in dispatch.'

'Stuck behind a desk wearing a headset listening to you lot doing the job? You think I'd like that?'

The DCI shrugged his shoulders and smiled. 'What's your answer?'

'I don't have a lot of choice, do I?'

'Not a lot – we never do.'

The looming presence of Harry Makepeace appeared through the glass of the Bubble, followed by a knock on the door.

Charlie Whitworth waved at him to enter.

'Boss, the initial post-mortem report is in on the unknown vic.'

The DCI stood up instantly, picking up a sheaf of notes from his desktop. 'You'd better attend this briefing, Ridpath. It can be the first step in our new policy of openness with the coroner.'

'What's the case?'

'A strangling. Body found yesterday morning.' The DCI strode towards the door, followed by Ridpath hastily rising from the chair to follow his boss. The DCI stopped abruptly just as he left the office. 'If you want get back with us, don't screw this up.'

Ridpath looked down to see a finger prodding him in the chest.

'You haven't told me when I start.'

The cornflower-blue eyes stared back at him. 'She's expecting you at 2 p.m. You start this afternoon.'

Chapter Four

'Right, you lot, listen up.' Sarah Castle looked across as Charlie Whitworth entered the room and the noise quietened down.

Ridpath took a seat in the rear beside the door, watching Charlie weave his way through the detectives to join Sarah Castle at the front.

He remembered her from before his illness. One of the fast-track mob, parachuted in from some management course and already racing up the promotion ladder. Now here she was, telling some senior detectives to be quiet.

She looked to Charlie, waiting for the nod before she could begin.

Detectives were taking out their notebooks. Next to Ridpath, a young detective constable was neatly writing a row of headings across the top: time, date, name of investigation, call sign, location and his role.

He must be new, thought Ridpath, just out of training school.

Sarah Castle coughed twice, silencing the last of the gossipers amongst the detectives. 'To recap: victim found yesterday morning at 6.45 a.m. on the towpath of Bridgewater Canal next to Stretford Marina, by a man walking his dog.'

'Didn't know Stretford had a bloody marina. Sounds a bit posh...'

'It's on the canal, Harry – you work out how posh it is,' said Dave Hardy, one of the senior detectives.

Sarah Castle continued speaking despite the interruption. 'Name of victim unknown as of this moment. No identification found with the body. Fingerprints taken but no record on IDENT1. We've asked the Interpol AFIS to check, plus her prints have been sent to EURODAC in case she's an asylum seeker. SIS II isn't online yet but as soon as it is, we'll tap into the database.' She took a breath and looked around the room, then carried on. 'Age approximately 25 years old, dyed blonde hair, originally brunette—'

A murmur of amusement ran around the room, quickly silenced by a stern look from Charlie Whitworth.

'...tattoo of a swan on the inside of the right arm. A specialist search team is still at the scene checking forensic evidence and a team of divers from the marine unit is arriving in' – she checked her watch – '42 minutes, to begin dragging the canal. The crime scene manager is Katie Green, who will be the liaison between the underwater and forensics teams.'

She walked over to the desk and picked up a clipboard with a printed form attached. 'The pathologist has come back with some initial findings. The victim was struck on the back of the head by a blunt instrument, followed by multiple stab wounds to the torso and blows to the left side of the head. A ligature was also found around the neck. The pathologist is still trying to ascertain the cause of death, but the victim had been dead for at least two days before she was found. Full report will be available to us as soon as possible, once the post-mortem is completed.'

Sarah Castle let the clipboard drop to her side and stepped backwards to allow Charlie Whitworth to take over the rest of the meeting.

'Thank you, DS Castle. I'll call the pathologist myself and give him a kick up the arse to speed him up.' The other detectives laughed but Ridpath noticed Sarah Castle went bright red, the colour in stark contrast to her blond hair.

Next to him the young detective was scribbling furiously in his notebook, taking down everything that was said.

'We're treating this as a murder inquiry. You all know what that means. The canal path is on the dog walkers' daily route. If our vic has been dead for two days but only just found, it means the body was dumped recently. Harry, I want you to pull in all the CCTV from the area, checking on cars and vans. The body must have been transported to the site somehow. Dave…?' The older detective sergeant raised his hand. 'I want you to continue with the house-to-house of the local area. Check if anybody saw anything or anybody acting suspiciously.'

'Will do, boss.'

'Chrissy… Where's Chrissy Wright?'

A tiny woman stepped out from behind a burly sergeant wearing a Manchester City scarf around her neck.

'Can you get on HOLMES? I want to know if any there have been any similar crimes on the database anywhere in the last year.'

Chrissy simply nodded her head.

'Sarah, I want you to check missing persons. The tattoo is the one clue to this woman's identity. You'll also be the FLO when we discover who she is.'

Family liaison officer – the worst job in cases like this. Staying with family and making sure they were kept informed of the investigation. Ridpath didn't envy Sarah; it was always a nightmare, with little thanks and lots of hassle.

'I'll get on it, boss,' she answered without a trace of annoyance in her voice.

A clipboard was passed to him. On it each detective had signed their name, rank, department and mobile number. For a second, Ridpath was tempted to add his name to the list but he didn't, passing the board on to the detective constable with the copious notes.

'Any questions?'

Harry Makepeace raised his hand. 'The local toms sometimes do their business beside the canal. I wonder if our vic could be one of them? Or maybe one of them saw something?'

'Good, Harry. Can you follow up? When the pictures come in of the girl and of the tattoo, you might want to show it to the toms and see if they recognize her. Get Bob to help you.'

Harry looked back at the young detective sitting beside Ridpath. 'Will do, boss.'

'One other question, sir.' It was Sarah Castle who spoke. 'A blow to the back of the head followed by stab wounds to the torso and more blows to the head is consistent with the MO of James Dalbey…'

'And?'

'I just thought it was worth a look at the case files.'

The DCI ran his fingers through his thinning hair. 'James Dalbey, aka the Beast of Manchester, has been locked up inside Belmarsh High Security Unit for the last eight years. In fact, we have the man who caught him sitting at the back of the room. Stand up, Ridpath.'

He stood up slowly, like a reluctant singer in a karaoke bar, and nodded. The detectives all turned and stared at him before returning their gaze to Charlie Whitworth.

'Ridpath's just come back to work after a long illness. He'll be the coroner's officer for the next few months, liaising on this case and others.'

Why was Charlie singling him out? Could it possibly mean he was back on the team? He sat down again.

'To get back to your point, Sarah. Do me a favour; call Belmarsh when this meeting is over. Check the bastard is still tucked up all nice and cosy in his cell.'

A chorus of laughter around the room, led by Harry Makepeace. Sarah Castle went an even brighter red.

'Right, you lot. Get a move on. Chrissy will give you all the logon details plus case numbers for the overtime. John Gorman has assured me all available resources will be targeted at this. No bloody austerity on this case. He wants it solved, and solved quickly.'

A buzz of approval went round the room. There would be overtime and more until this case was done.

'I don't have to tell you to keep schtum. The papers have picked up on it already but none of the details.' He stopped for a moment for emphasis. 'I want to keep it that way. If any of you are thinking of earning an extra bob or two from the reporters, don't. If I find out somebody has sold details of this story, I'll personally grind their balls with my teeth. Is that clear?'

'Yes, boss,' chorused the seated detectives.

'Get a move on, then – there's lots of work to do.'

Ridpath watched as the room was filled with movement. He loved the buzz of a major inquiry. The total focus on the job: sod the hours, sod the time, sod the weather, sod everything and everybody. Just get the job done and find the bastard who did it.

He got up slowly and walked out of the room without talking to anybody.

God, he missed this job.

Chapter Five

Would he be pleased with her?

Lesley hoped he would. It hadn't been easy enticing her into the car. He'd said the third would be harder than the first two. This one seemed to be more wary, more skittish. Had the news that girls were going missing already been circulated by the tom-toms of the concrete jungle?

'I don't do none of that kinky stuff. Strictly a meat and two veg girl.'

'I just want to have a chat.'

'Why? Why do you wanna chat with the likes of me?'

She remembered his words. Be open, smile a lot, remember the story. All these girls need money to feed their habit.

Before she'd driven up to the girl, she'd practised the smile in the rear-view mirror. It always felt strange to her, smiling, as if her face didn't have the correct muscles in her face. As a child she hadn't smiled much – never felt the need.

She had followed his instructions precisely to choose the girl. Go during the day. The ones desperate for money will be on the streets then. After dark, there are more girls and a greater likelihood of being spotted. The ordinariness of daylight is your friend, not your enemy. Drive up the road twice and look for a young girl on her own. One that's thin and scrawny, with no friends around her. She'll be the one desperate for money. Better if she has an accent, somebody who's not local.

After driving down the road twice as she was told, she found the one she wanted on her own away from the others, standing at the corner next to the waste ground. A young girl wearing a blue nylon shirt which had seen better days and a short fake-leather miniskirt which showed off her thin thighs. The girl was hugging her body against the cold wind of a Manchester March.

She turned left at the bottom of the road, deciding to loop round and come back for a third time, hoping and praying the girl would be still be there when she returned.

This one was perfect.

She turned left again at the lights, coming back to the top of the road, accelerating past a white Volvo parked in a side street, a single man sitting in the driver's seat. A woman's head rose from his lap, wiping her mouth, as she drove past.

Why did men do this? What pleasure was there in it? What good did it do them?

He was right. This shouldn't be happening.

Not here.

Not now.

Not ever.

She stomped on the accelerator, feeling the surge of power taking her away from all the dirt and decay and disgust.

The girl was still there. Smoking a cigarette now. Trying to keep warm with each inhalation of smoke.

She brought the car to a stop beside her and opened the window.

The girl approached her slowly, checking with rat-like eyes if anybody else was in the car.

'Are you up for business?' That's what he told her to say this time.

The girl leant forward. She could see down the silk shirt to where soft breasts nestled in a purple bra. The rat eyes flickered from her face to the rear seat and back again.

'I don't do no kinky stuff. Strictly a meat and two veg girl.'

The accent was Scouse or something like that.

Perfect.

24

She flashed the smile she had just practised in the rear-view mirror. 'I just want to have a chat.'

'Why? Why do you wanna chat with the likes of me?'

'I'm a writer, doing a piece on the local girls. I only want ten minutes of your time.'

The girl looked in the back of the car and then down the empty road. 'You just want ten minutes?'

She brought out the twenty-pound note. It was crisp and fresh, making a rustling noise as she held it in her fingers. 'Twenty now and twenty when we've finished talking.'

She watched the girl's eyes fasten on the note, seeing in it all she needed to feed her habit.

'We'll just go round the corner and chat. I've even got some hot coffee.' She held up the flask and shook it so the girl could hear the liquid sloshing inside.

That was the clincher, as he said it would be. She remembered his words: 'On a cold day, always make sure they see the coffee. Open it if you have to so they can smell the warm aroma. Put yourself in their place. What would you do? Sit in a warm car with a free cup of coffee or stand out in the cold hoping against hope some bloke with a swollen dick is looking for a blow job?'

The girl snatched the money out of her hand and shoved it into the top of her purple bra, marched round the bonnet of the BMW and climbed into the front seat, the miniskirt riding up to reveal purple knickers against thin white thighs.

'My name's Lesley,' she said, holding out her hand, 'what's yours?'

The girl ignored the hand. 'It's Suzy. Just ten minutes and no more. And don't use my name. I don't want you to use any names.'

'No worries. No names, no pack drill.'

'What?'

'Nothing. Something my father used to say. He was in the army.' She was following his instructions exactly. Tell them something about yourself. It will put them at ease.

She put the car in gear, signalled and pulled away.

The girl didn't fasten her seat belt.

She drove slowly. Take your time, there's no need to rush now.

'You mind if I smoke?'

The girl reached over and pressed the cigarette lighter on the dashboard, bringing out a crumpled pack of Rothmans. 'I always smoke these. They're a bit more expensive but they don't give you cancer like the others.'

The cigarette lighter popped out and she brought the glowing end up to the cigarette. 'Days like this you need the warmth of a fag. God knows what I'd do without them. Always have a pack at home and one in my bag, just in case. You never smoke?'

She changed down and signalled left, pulling out onto the empty road.

'Where we going? I don't want to go far. Those thievin' bitches will nick my patch.'

'We'll stop here, if that's OK?' She turned left up a dilapidated street and then right to park behind an advertising hoarding. The nearest terraced houses were all dark and desolate, the windows either boarded up or broken.

He had chosen this area specially. An 'improvement area' under renovation for the last three years.

'Would you like some coffee?' She shook the flask.

The girl blew a long trail of light–blue smoke through her reddened lips. 'Has it got sugar in it? Cos I can't take no sugar – trying to lose a few pounds.' The girl took hold of a handful of flesh through the silk shirt.

The woman could see that even though the girl was thin to the point of emaciation, flesh still sagged off her. 'There's no sugar in it. Can't stand the stuff myself.'

'But I still have my chocolate. A bar of Cadbury's Fruit and Nut every day. Even when I got no money.'

For a moment, she tried to work out how the girl could afford chocolate when she had no money, then gave up. No point in understanding these women. They sold their bodies to men. What worth were they?

She poured out the coffee into the plastic cup and handed it to the girl.

'You drink all this down, it'll warm you up for the rest of the day.'

The girl cradled the cup in her fingers. 'Coffee and a fag. Just what a girl needs on a day like today.' Then she drank a long draught of warm coffee, following it with an even longer suck on the cigarette. 'Feels better already,' the girl coughed.

She took out her notebook and wrote 'Girl 2' at the top of the page. Have to keep up the pretence. Mustn't spook her now.

Not now.

'What you wanna ask me? You ain't no social worker or nothin'?'

'No, I'm not, but I do take care of people. You could call it my hobby.'

'Which paper you work for? I hope it ain't the *Sun*. Can't stand the *Sun*. I'm from Liverpool.'

'I work freelance, with one other man, taking care of people.'

'Oooh, that fag has gone straight to my head.'

She took the plastic cup and the cigarette from the girl, who tried to protest but no words came out of her mouth. She threw the cigarette out of the window and poured the dregs of coffee back into the flask.

'You just relax and have a good rest, that's my girl.'

The girl didn't answer. Her mouth lay open, spittle drooling out of the corner, sliding over her chin to cover the sores from drug use. Inside her mouth, a black gap showed where a couple of teeth used to be.

She reached over to fasten the girl's seat belt. 'Clunk, click, every trip – remember?'

Shame it was going to be this girl's last journey.

Chapter Six

It struck him he was wasting too much of his life outside buildings smoking cigarettes.

This time, it was the East Manchester Coroner's Court in Stockfield. He had arrived early and, not wanting to sit in reception like a desperate pillock waiting for people to drift back from lunch, stood outside smoking his third cigarette of the day.

Three more than he was allowed.

The Coroner's Office was in a Victorian building in the centre of Stockfield. Another city decimated by progress instituted by the town planners of the sixties and seventies from the comfort of their Edwardian mansions in Hale and Alderley Edge. A few buildings had survived their contra-flow diagrams, traffic management systems and usage pie charts. The Coroner's Office was one of them. It had the air of a Victorian schoolroom occupied by a modern-day Wackford Squeers, but lacking the humanity and empathy of that celebrated teacher.

Ridpath checked his watch: 2 p.m. Time to go in and face the music. He hoped it wasn't going to be something from *The Rocky Horror Picture Show*.

The reception desk was still empty, silently guarding the offices behind it. Ridpath walked past and shouted to the deathly quiet interior. 'Hello, anybody there?'

No answer.

He was sure he heard the echo of his voice off the eau-de-Nil painted walls. Why are all government buildings painted in this colour? Had the civil service somehow issued a memo in

1958 that all walls were to be painted an ugly pastel green and nobody had found the time to revise it? Or had the government bought a job lot of paint in 1962 and was still trying to use it up? The latter was the more likely reason.

He called again, 'Helllooo...'

A tap on the shoulder, followed by: 'You must be the coroner's new officer?'

He turned round to face a young, attractive woman whose dark clothes seemed to come from the same era as the paint.

'The name's Ridpath. Detective Inspector Tom Ridpath.' He held out his hand.

She took it as if she were holding a wet fish. 'A detective inspector? We are honoured this time.' She brushed past him. 'Come this way. Margaret's waiting for you.'

As she walked away from him, he noticed her blonde hair was wound into a tight chignon and held in place with four shiny grips, each one carefully placed at the side of her head.

She stopped outside a large Georgian door. 'Margaret's office is in here. I don't think Jenny is back from lunch yet, so I'll take you through.'

'Jenny?'

She pushed open the door. 'Office manager and general factotum. She does everything, but don't ask her to make the coffee.'

'She doesn't see it as part of her job description?'

A tiny smile crept into the corner of her mouth. 'Noooo, she just makes terrible coffee.'

They were in a compact office. At one side, a desk with a computer even older than the ones down at the station was surrounded by an array of cute dolls: Hello Kitty, a bear from Bavaria, three versions of the Smurfs and a troupe of what looked like plush versions of garden gnomes.

'If you ever travel abroad, you have to bring one back for Jenny, otherwise you'll find your paperwork gets eaten by one of the trolls.'

She knocked on the door.

A curt 'Come' came from inside.

She rolled her eyes and pushed open the door. Behind an expansive oak desk sat a nest of long grey hair surrounding thick black spectacles. The head rose to reveal a woman with the clearest skin Ridpath had ever seen. It was like cream with just a few flakes of raspberry rippling through it.

'Margaret, this is Detective Inspector Tom Ridpath, our new coroner's officer.'

He stood there, uncertain whether to advance with his hand out or stand at attention. He ended up doing neither, simply slouching in the doorway.

'Thank you, Carol.' She placed the forms she had been working on in a neat pile to the left of her desk and stood up. She was far taller than he expected, at least six foot, the grey hair now neatly framing a face showing only the faintest signs of her age. Either she used some of the most expensive face creams known to woman or she looked after herself incredibly well.

She walked around the desk towards him. 'Good afternoon. You're on time.' Her hand came out. The fingers were long and the nails expertly polished and shaped.

He was surprised at the strength of the grip as she shook his hand. 'I make a habit of it – being on time, that is.'

'Good.' A curt nod towards the person who had escorted him into the room, whom he now knew was called Carol. 'Thank you, we have a meeting about the Rattigan inquest at four, do we not?' It was a not very subtle dismissal.

'We do, Margaret. I'll prepare the papers.'

'Good.' Margaret Challinor closed the door as Carol left. 'Take a seat.'

There was only one chair in front of the desk. It was a bent-wood chair, more often found in schoolrooms than in offices.

The woman sat behind her desk as he made himself comfortable in the uncomfortable chair.

'You're a detective inspector?'

'Probationary. Still in my first year.'

The grey eyebrows rose above the dark, slightly tinted spectacles. 'Normally, they send us a constable, or at most a sergeant. The deputy chief must be trying to butter me up.'

'I wouldn't know about that, ma'am.'

'It's Margaret, Mrs Challinor or Coroner, not ma'am. I'm not the Queen. Well, not yet anyway.' There was no smile on her face. The hands came up to interlock in front of her nose. It almost looked as if they were fighting each other. 'Why you?'

'Why me... what?'

'Why did they send you?'

'I was told the last coroner's officer had retired—'

'Did you know him?'

'Jim Howells?'

She nodded, still staring at him through the darkened glasses. On her left, the April sun shone through the large picture windows, highlighting a photograph of Mrs Challinor surrounded by two girls in their late teens. There was no man in the picture.

'What did you think of him?' she asked quietly.

Ridpath knew his next answer was crucial. He had conducted enough criminal interviews to know the early questions were always the most important. Personally, he used the rule of three: two questions to get a witness talking, then the most important question as the third. The coroner used a slightly different technique. Three or four personal questions to unsettle and discomfort the interviewee, then ask a question to which you already know the answer.

As with any interview, he had five options. He could tell the truth. He could be diplomatic. He could lie or he could dissemble.

He used the fifth: play for time.

'What did I think of Jim Howells?' It was classic stalling technique. Simply repeat the question and wait for the interrogator to explain herself, giving him more time to think.

Margaret Challinor just nodded her head, without removing her gaze from his face.

No more options now, he would have to answer. He chose the first option. 'The man was a waste of oxygen. Should have been kicked out of the force years ago.' When all else fails, tell the truth. Or as much of the truth as was humanly possible.

'You could have dissembled,' she said.

He shrugged his shoulders. 'What was the point? You worked with him.'

'I did have that misfortune. He was a lazy, good-for-nothing shyster who spent more time and effort avoiding work than he ever did doing it.' She smiled like a cat who had seen a mouse. 'So why you?'

The truth will set you free. 'I'm a good copper, Mrs Challinor, a very good copper. Nine months ago, I was diagnosed with myeloma – bone cancer – I embarked on a course of chemo in Christie's and took a new drug they were trialling. Six weeks ago, I was finally given the all clear. The cancer is in remission.'

'Are you still taking drugs?'

'One a day. But there are no side effects according to the doctor. The force will send you my file, I'm sure.'

She lifted a beige file from beside her computer. 'It already has.'

'Then there was no need to ask. You already knew.'

'But I didn't know how you were going to answer, Detective Inspector, did I?'

'No, but I did.'

She licked her lips before continuing. 'You know the job is only temporary?'

'Three months is what I was told.'

'Do you know what the job entails?'

'I'm sure you'll tell me.'

'A coroner's officer is an advocate for the dead to safeguard the living.'

'A pretty broad job description.'

She sighed. 'It is, and that's the official job one from the Chief Coroner's Office.'

'Sounds like management-speak. The police force is full of it these days.'

'Consultants?'

He nodded. 'Crawling out of the woodwork. One lot comes in and recommends a reorganization. Two years later, another lot recommends the exact opposite. I often wonder if they're operating together to create work for each other.'

She made a moue with her lips. 'Not so different from the Coroner's Service, but in reality our job hasn't changed since just after the Norman Conquest in 1066. We were created then as servants of the crown, hence coroners, to separate the investigation of death from the legal process of judgment. Not a lot has changed since then.'

'A long time...'

'The law is always reluctant to change. It's one of the strengths, and the weaknesses. There are just under one hundred people like me in England and Wales, and our jurisdiction is limited to determining who the deceased was and how, when and where they came by their death. When the death is suspected to have been either sudden or from unknown cause, the coroner decides whether to hold a post-mortem examination and, if necessary, an inquest.'

'It's a wide remit.'

'And seems to be getting wider all the time. We have a boss, he's part-time but don't ask me why, appointed after the 2009 Coroners and Justice Act.'

'Just after I started in the force.'

For the first time, Ridpath saw a change in Mrs Challinor. She looked down and then began to rearrange the files on her desk nervously. 'The Act was passed in response to murders by Harold Shipman.'

'The doctor who killed over 300 pensioners? Was Hyde part of your district?'

She shook her head. 'It was South Manchester, but the truth is I wouldn't have spotted the deaths either. If a doctor certifies death, as Shipman did, we are unlikely to investigate.'

'Even now?'

She nodded again. 'The Smith Commission reported on the Shipman murders and offered a whole raft of measures to prevent them happening again. But, of course, the government of the day ignored the recommendations.'

'Why?'

She flicked away a long curly strand of grey hair which had fallen across her eyes. Ridpath noticed her fingers: long, graceful and beautifully manicured.

'A reluctance to change. Cost. Stupidity. Or a combination of all three,' she finally answered. Her jaw set and her voice became forceful, emphatic. 'But I am determined nothing like that will ever happen again. We will investigate all suspicious deaths, and discover the truth to the best of our ability, Ridpath. Is that clear? Your colleague, Jim Howells, never understood what his role was. Thought this job was a cushy number. Well not when I'm in charge, understand?'

He nodded. 'What do you expect me to do?'

'Your absolute best. Nothing else is good enough.' She passed across a blue file. 'The exact details of your role are in here. Your job is to carry out investigations on the coroner's behalf. A coroner's investigation may involve a simple review, or it may involve a complete examination of the circumstances behind a death.' She paused for a moment to look at him. 'It also includes investigating every death that happens in police custody. Would you have a problem investigating your own colleagues?'

He thought for a moment. *Would he have a problem?* He shrugged his shoulders and decided to answer truthfully. 'I don't know.'

She continued to stare at him. 'At least you're honest,' she finally said. And then her voice changed pitch and she lightened the mood. 'I'm not without a few powers to help in any investigation though. A coroner's court is a court of law, and accordingly the coroner may subpoena witnesses, arrest offenders, administer oaths and sequester juries during inquests.' She reached over and tapped the file she had given him. 'You're basically going to do anything and everything I ask of you.' The green eyes stared at him through the darkened lenses. 'Do you understand?'

He shrugged his shoulders. 'I understand.'

'You were CID?'

Ridpath nodded.

'The difference between the Coroner's Office and the police is stark, Detective Inspector. We don't chase convictions, we don't chase criminals, we don't chase promotions. We simply represent the families and we look for the truth. Who died? When did they die? How did they die? Who was responsible? Is that clear, Detective?'

'Crystal.'

'As soon as we can, we'll get you on an officer's course.'

'Even though I'm only staying three months?'

'I don't care about the time, Detective, I care about your effectiveness. You will go on the course. In the meantime, though, we have ongoing investigations that need to be progressed.' She opened a drawer and pulled out a pink file. 'This will be your first case.'

She passed across the file.

'We have been instructed by the high court to reopen an inquest into the death of Alice Seagram. The exhumation of her body will be performed at 6:30 a.m. tomorrow morning. I'd like you to be there.'

'Alice Seagram?' The name stirred something in the far recesses of his brain.

'One of the victims of James Dalbey. He has convinced the family he had nothing to do with her death, and that somebody else was responsible.'

'I saw the news reports. An unknown man. They've been asking for the case to be reopened for years.'

'There were so many flaws in the original post-mortem, it was only a matter of time before the high court agreed.'

'You know I was involved in this case?'

'So I was told.'

Ridpath wondered who she had been talking to. 'It doesn't disqualify me?'

'Not in my eyes. The undertaker, Mr Ronson, will perform the exhumation tomorrow morning. You will be the representative of the Coroner's Office. There is a detailed list of your duties during the exhumation in the file.'

'My first day I'm going to be digging up a dead person?'

'Think of it as a perk of the job.'

Chapter Seven

'How'd it go? 'His wife was taking off her coat in the hallway, shouting through to the living room.

He was reading the blue file given to him by Margaret Challinor. She was right. A coroner's officer did everything and anything: from informing families about the death of loved ones to attending crime scenes, investigating cases to chasing down witnesses, visiting mortuaries to liaising with doctors. The job was a glorified social worker cum private investigator cum general dogsbody.

She appeared in the doorway, her straight black Chinese hair still damp from the rain. 'Didn't you hear me? How'd it go?'

He looked up from the blue file. 'Charlie Whitworth and John Gorman are looking out for me, but the deputy chief has "reservations".' He formed his fingers into sarcastic quote marks.

'What does that mean?'

'It means they want me to be the coroner's officer for three months.'

'What does one of them do?'

He held up the blue file. 'I'm just finding out. But it should be a less stressful job, with regular hours. An easier life.'

'You're not getting a desk job at headquarters? The least they owe you is a desk job.'

Ridpath shook his head. 'I asked for one but there are none available. The cutbacks...' He looked away from her and back to his job description, hoping she would forgive him for the fib.

She sat down on the couch opposite. 'You didn't ask, did you? You asked to go back to work as a detective.'

How did Polly always know when he was lying? She would have made a great copper.

'Tom, you promised me.' She reached out to touch his hand. 'Your health, it—'

He shrugged the hand off his arm. 'The doctors said I was fit to work. I've been prodded and poked like the last butty in the chip shop for the last nine months, Poll. I've been running and working out for the last three. Feel that.' He flexed his biceps, 'Strongest I've ever been.' His voice softened. 'I've got to get back to work. Can't stand doing nothing anymore.'

'Can't stand being around me, you mean?'

'It's not about you. I can't stand being treated like a child.'

'I'm just worried about you. The doctor said if you get a cold or flu, it could be dangerous.'

'He also said I was fit for work.'

She raised her voice. 'Fit to go back to work. Not fit to run around Manchester chasing bloody nutters.'

A silence like a shroud of fog settled between them. Outside the window, there was the soft patter of rain on the cobblestones of the patio he had laid last week. Inside, the clock on the mantelpiece ticked loudly. Upstairs, the dull thud of his daughter's music shook the ceiling.

Ridpath finally broke the silence. 'I went into Eve's bedroom this evening. She's got pictures of half-naked Chinese men on her walls.'

'They're not pictures of half-naked men. They're pictures of half-naked boys. Korean boys.'

He looked at her, as if to say give me a break.

'It's BTS, the latest Korean boy band. The craze is going around all the schools at the moment. Half my class wants to go to Korea. The other half haven't got a clue where it is. At least it helps me teach geography.'

'I don't like it. She's only ten, for God's sake.'

'She's ten going on twenty-three. Girls grow up quicker these days.'

'I still don't like it.'

'Well, if you want her to take them down, you can ask her yourself. I'm not going anywhere near that minefield.' She stood up. 'Fancy a cup of tea?'

He put down the file. 'Nah, I'm going to walk the dog.'

'We don't have a dog.'

'He's going to get walked anyway.'

She leant over and kissed him on the cheek. 'Quiz night at the Horse and Jockey?'

He nodded.

'I thought you'd had enough of coming second?'

'Those bloody students can't win every week. Anyway we've got a new team member, appeared on *University Challenge* a few years back.'

'So you and your mates have brought in a ringer?'

'Not a ringer. A buzzer. Could beat them tonight.'

'Can you can drop in the office on your way back from the pub, get some milk?'

He looked around for his coat. 'I still don't like those posters.'

'Well, if you want to start World War Three…' She left the rest of the sentence unfinished.

'What is it with girls today?'

'Oh, Mr "Girls should know their place and it's behind the sink" is showing his face, is he?'

'It's not that. She's only ten. They're supposed to be into Barbie and stuff.'

'You're treading on thin ice…'

He opened the door. 'I'd better tread on it on the way to the pub. And it's the naked men I worry about…'

'Naked boys, actually.' There followed a long sigh. 'If you want, I'll have a chat with her and see if she can't find some different posters.'

'Thanks.'

'And wrap up before you go out. Wear the wool fleece with your coat over the top. And don't forget to wear a scarf, the thick blue one...'

He made a face at her.

There was another long silence between them. This time it was Polly who broke it. 'I don't want to lose you, Ridpath. Eve doesn't want to lose you. I don't know what I'd do if...'

He reached over and held her tight. 'I know, Poll, I know.'

Chapter Eight

The cemetery was on a spur overlooking the flood plain of the river Mersey. Morning mist hovered over the water, sneaking like a thief into every tiny nook and cranny. The sun was just trying to peer over the horizon, its weak rays lightening the dark skies. The bare whispers of a north-east wind hustled over the ground, creeping between the gravestones and rustling the branches of a row of lime trees.

Ridpath pulled his thick coat over the woollen fleece. The teal-blue scarf around his neck was nearly choking him, but he had promised Polly he'd wear it.

The doctors had warned him to be wary of catching cold or flu. If he did, he would be whisked off back into the isolation unit of Christie's. Bloody doctors and their bloody fears. There was no way they were getting him inside the hospital again. Not in a million years.

He would have loved to smoke a fag right now. The tarry aroma of tobacco in the early morning air was like the first cough of spring, but he had promised Polly he would cut down. Not eliminate, just cut down.

God, she was good at getting him to make promises. Almost as good as he was at breaking them.

The undertaker, Albert Ronson, had already erected blue plastic sheets on three sides of the grave, leaving the side hidden from the main road open.

The message on the headstone was simple:

> Alice Seagram, 1990–2008.
> Taken from us far too early.

In front of the headstone, a bunch of flowers bought from Tesco wilted in the early morning gloom.

'I didn't inter this client.' The undertaker spoke out of the side of his mouth, not looking at Ridpath, whispering so as not to wake the dead.

The undertaker was almost a cliché of his profession: tall, dressed in black and with a sallow complexion which hadn't seen sunlight since the Dark Ages. 'Only one customer in the grave, so it should be a simple exhumation.'

The voice was monotone, without any sort of inflection or stress. Funereal was the adjective to describe him, Ridpath decided.

'The last time, I had three caskets on top and two cremation urns. Delicate job... delicate job.' He blew on the ends of his sallow fingers in a futile attempt to warm them up in the cold morning air. Ridpath kept his hands in his pockets.

The gravediggers had already started to remove the grass that grew over the plot, putting the sods on top of a tarpaulin on one side. 'Won't use a mechanical digger on this customer.' Albert looked over his shoulder. 'Treat her with respect just in case the family comes down to watch.'

'Do families normally come?'

'Some do. Some don't,' said Albert enigmatically.

A car, its headlights cutting through the early morning mist, was parking at the side of the road.

'It's him, checking up as usual.'

A large, rotund man approached them wearing one of those dark-blue duvet jackets that made him look like a miniature version of the Michelin Man. 'Morning, Albert,' he nodded at the undertaker. 'You must be the new coroner's officer. I'm Health and Safety.'

He held out his hand. 'Morning. Inspector Tom Ridpath, on temporary secondment to the coroner from Manchester Police.'

'Lovely morning for it.' He stared at the gravediggers and tut-tutted. 'Albert, you know they should be wearing their masks before they start digging. See to it, will you?'

Albert glanced across at him mournfully, sneering with all the panache of a Professor Snape, before moving off to talk to the transgressing gravediggers.

'Always tries to cut corners, does Albert.' The man stomped his feet on the cold ground. 'Been working long with the coroner?'

'First day.'

The man made a moue, his tiny eyes being swallowed up by the large red cheeks. He leant in closer. 'Got a reputation, has Mrs Challinor.' He leant in even closer until Ridpath could smell his breath. 'Man-eater,' he whispered. 'But you didn't hear it from me.'

The spades of the gravediggers cut through the damp earth with a rhythmic ease, breath puffing out of their mouths like aged steam trains as they carefully laid each clod of turf on the tarpaulin, under the watchful eyes of the undertaker and Mr Health and Safety.

'And watch out for Carol Oates. Ambitious, that one is. Not happy just being area coroner, is she?'

'I don't know, is she?'

The man stopped smiling for a moment, wondering whether he was being made fun of. Ridpath kept his face still and unmoving.

'She is. Wants to be head coroner, that one does, but Mrs Challinor is sitting in the hot seat.'

'You seem to know a lot about what's going on.'

'Health and Safety, mate. I keeps my ears and eyes and nose close to the ground.'

An image of a jowly bloodhound with the man's face leapt into Ridpath's head as another car arrived at the side of the road.

'Looks like the family has finally come.'

But only one man exited the car. Ridpath recognized the thin, tall, slightly bowed shape.

'Morning, Charlie, what are you doing here?'

Charlie Whitworth stroked his moustache. 'Wouldn't miss your first day on the job, would I, Ridpath? And anyway, this is about that bastard Dalbey. Me and John Gorman were the ones who put him away.'

Mr Health and Safety leant into their conversation with his hand held out. 'Rob Campbell, Health and Safety.'

Charlie Whitworth ignored the hand and continued speaking to Ridpath. 'Alice Seagram was his fourth victim. You caught him with the fifth, remember?'

How could he forget? The day he had chased after James Dalbey, catching him in the lock-up next to the allotments. The police arriving. Looking up and seeing the girl – Freda Scott was her name. Naked and shackled to a blood-spattered wall at the rear of the building. Covering her with his jacket as she shivered in his arms. Her words: 'Save me… save me… save me,' repeated again and again and again.

'No, no, no… Albert, they need to be wearing their masks. They can't take them off to breathe.' Mr Health and Safety marched off to the graveside.

'Dalbey's trying to wriggle out of it. Prove his conviction was dodgy to get a pardon.'

'He was a vicious bastard, Charlie.'

'Aye, but we nicked him.'

The gravediggers had put their masks back on and returned to digging.

'How did yesterday go?'

'Mrs Challinor doesn't have much time for Jim Howells.'

'Who would? But let us know what's going on there, Ridpath. Wouldn't like it to get away from us.'

Ridpath turned to face his boss for the first time. 'Second time you've asked me. I'm no nark, Charlie.'

'Never said you were, but—'

The sound of the tip of a spade hitting wood.

'Looks like we've hit the mother lode,' Campbell shouted back towards them. 'And she's in good condition, too, from the sound of it.'

The gravediggers quickly removed the remaining earth covering the casket and jumped out of the grave. The undertaker took his own time putting on a white Tyvek suit, finally pulling on a pair of bright-pink plastic gloves given to him by Mr Health and Safety. He lowered himself into the grave, carefully placing his boots on either side of the coffin.

'Apparently I have to observe this part,' Ridpath said, moving to the graveside.

The undertaker was bent double, carefully scraping the last remnants of soil off the tarnished brass nameplate on the lid of the coffin. 'I can read the name. It's Alice Seagram.'

Ridpath remembered the words from the file he was supposed to say at this time. 'Please remove the coffin, Mr Ronson.' He then stepped back to allow the gravediggers to move the trestle, with its lifting ropes, over the grave.

The undertaker removed himself from the grave with an athleticism which surprised Ridpath.

'Fancy breakfast? There's a good greasy spoon next to the flower shop,' said Charlie Whitworth, now standing beside him.

'I'll hang on here till the undertaker's put the coffin in his van, and the thing is on its way to the pathologist.'

'Following the rules to the letter, are we?'

Ridpath ignored him. The gravediggers, with the help of Ronson, were manoeuvring the ropes under the coffin so it could be lifted out of the grave. One of the gravediggers tugged on a rope attached to a pulley and the click of a ratchet echoed through the air.

The sun was fully up now, the mist being burned off by its rays. Off to the left, a blackbird was proclaiming his dominance of this graveyard from the top of an ancient yew tree.

Mr Health and Safety was encouraging the gravedigger. 'Up a bit, slowly, that's it, she's coming up.'

The gravedigger was ignoring him, just going about his work with a singular concentration.

The ropes were taut and the dark, earth-stained wood of the coffin slowly rose into view. Ridpath expected a strong smell, perhaps of a rotting corpse, but there was nothing. Just the scent of the earth: a rich, black, fertile aroma.

They held the coffin above the grave as one of Ronson's assistants brought out the gurney from the back of the van. He locked the two sets of wheels and trundled it across the grass, positioning it next to the grave.

Mr Health and Safety's voice rang out again, loud enough to wake the dead. 'Swing it round, gentlemen. Watch the straps.'

The gravediggers, with Ronson on one side, ignored him again, carefully moving the coffin from above the grave to the gurney. As they did so, Health and Safety decided they weren't moving quickly enough and pushed the side of the coffin with his gloved hand. The edge caught on the side of the gurney, before wobbling for a moment and then settling down.

'That was close,' he said. 'Nearly fell off the straps.'

As he finished speaking, one of the straps snapped and the end of the coffin slipped down, crashing to the soft earth.

The two gravediggers and Ronson jumped backwards as the coffin landed on the ground with a loud thud. The lid popped open and slowly slid off to one side.

The undertaker recovered his composure quickly, leaning over to peer into the coffin. Then he stood upright and, in the loudest voice he had used in years, said, 'Inspector, I think you should come and look at this.'

Ridpath stepped forward, walking around the gravedigger to stand beside the undertaker.

The man's long arm, still with the incongruous bright-pink plastic glove covering his hand, pointed downwards. 'The coffin… it's empty.'

Chapter Nine

James Dalbey rearranged the pens on his desk so they were at exact right angles to the pale-yellow plaster walls of the cell, and checked his books were still in alphabetical order as the first rays of dawn wheedled their way through the barred window above his head.

His final act that morning had been to say three Hail Mary's and five Our Fathers in front of the wooden cross hanging on the wall, crossing himself quickly seven times.

The bed had been neatly made already, and the toilet bowl scrubbed and cleaned. It still leaked slightly from the cistern, a drip, drip, drip into the pan every minute of every day like a liquid metronome. He had asked for it to be repaired countless times, but so far nothing had happened.

He would keep asking.

He always kept asking.

He had been assigned to this cell away from the others in the High Security Unit because nobody else would share a cell with him for more than a week. Their complaints were numerous:

'He's crazy, that one. Up in the middle of the night, pacing up and down like a fuckin' robot, shaking his head and muttering to himself.'

Or:

'He's always fuckin' cleanin'. All day long, does me fuckin' head in.'

Or:

'I hit him a couple of times, just to knock some sense in him, but he didn't stop. Carried on folding up my stuff and arranging it. Well, it's not on, is it? You don't touch another con's stuff.'

Eventually, they had given up and given him a cell on his own. He hadn't planned it this way but he was glad it had happened. He didn't want to be with anybody. They all smelt, the other cons. That peculiar sour prison smell of sweat and cabbage and stale sperm.

He didn't like the smell; it reminded him of home too much.

He opened the diary on his desk and wrote down his to-do list for the day. There were just three things on it:

1. Write to the Seagram family.

2. Research the Criminal Law and Justice Act.

3. Research the Coroners Act 2009.

From the first day he arrived in Belmarsh, he had badgered the deputy governor with the persistence of a woodpecker searching for a beetle hidden in the bark of a tree:

Please sir, can I work in the library?

Please sir, can I work in the library?

Please sir, can I work in the library?

Please sir, can I work in the library?

Eventually, the man had allowed him to spend three hours each day cataloguing the books. With a mind like his, the job took less than 30 minutes. The rest of the time he could do his research. And when the new deputy governor came, he was allowed to take the books back to his cell.

The man believed a prisoner should use his time in jail to improve his mind.

He was going to use his time in jail to prove his innocence.

For a short time in 2014, the idiot minister, Grayling, had prevented prisoners like him from receiving new books, saying: 'We believe offenders need to behave well and engage in their own rehabilitation if they are to earn privileges and incentives.'

What a smug tosser.

Luckily, the governor had simply ignored the edict, arguing he would have a riot on his hands if prisoners were deprived of the means of self-education.

Too right. He would have been the first on the barricades if they had shut the library. It was his only source of freedom, his only chance to escape.

'Focus, James.'

On the floor above, he heard somebody moving. The jail was beginning to stir and the other prisoners were waking up.

What had the judge intoned that day?

'James Dalbey, you have been found guilty of the heinous murder of one woman and the unlawful incarceration of another. You will be taken from this court and detained at Her Majesty's pleasure for a period of 30 years.'

Pompous old prick. What did Her Majesty care for him? And why did it give her pleasure that an innocent man was going to spend time in jail?

Then the judge waved his hand like he was swatting away a fly. 'Take him down, Sergeant.'

The copper standing next to him had gently touched his arm, turning him to go down into the cells beneath the court. From the gallery, a woman had shouted: 'It's too short. Hang him. Hang the bastard for what he did.'

He had wanted to turn back and tell her he was innocent, somebody else had killed Alice, proclaim the truth from where he stood in the dock, with its irregular handrail. He had asked the sergeant to fix the handrail but he had been ignored. Now, it was too late; the handrail would never be fixed.

'Focus, James,' he said out loud again.

The noises were getting louder along the wing. Shouts from the rapist in cell 223. Laughter from the murderer in 246. The sound of farting from the flatulent con next door. Doors sliding open, metal against metal, as the screws changed shift, whispering to each other. The creaking of the building as the cold bricks were warmed up in the early morning sun of April.

It was the one thing he missed: the sound of silence. What most people don't realize is you can survive the mind–numbing routine. You can stand the acrid smells. You can even withstand the aching ugliness of the four green walls. But it was the lack of silence that got to him. The constant noise of prison. Even in the dead of night, when he lay in his bunk unable to sleep, there was still noise somewhere.

He missed the sound of silence.

'Focus, James.'

James Dalbey picked up his blue pen with the 0.18 nib he had exchanged for his allowance of cigarettes, pulled a sheet of clean, white paper from the diary and wrote the first words:

Dear Mrs Seagram…

Chapter Ten

The lid had slipped off, forming a sharp diagonal across the top half of the coffin. The hazy morning light had crept inside to highlight an empty ivory satin pillow, sitting on a darker, yellower fabric.

Ridpath could see nothing.

He sniffed the morning air, expecting to smell the aroma of decayed flesh.

Again, nothing but the scent of freshly turned earth.

Had the body slipped down to the bottom of the coffin? Had it somehow moved when it was being buried?

Should he wait for forensics? Or take a look inside? If he called a team out to a false alarm, he would get a right bollocking for wasting time and resources.

Then he remembered he was now a coroner's officer, not a detective any more. Could he call for a forensics team or would he have to ask Charlie to do it?

He made a decision. 'Give me a pair of gloves.'

Mr Health and Safety reached inside his bag and produced another pair of bright-pink latex gloves, still in their wrapper. 'It's the only colour we've got in the stores,' he said, shrugging his large shoulders.

Ridpath took them and rolled them onto his hands. He leant further forward, trying to peer deeper into the coffin.

Nothing but blackness. Still no smell though. Would the body have decomposed by now, reduced itself to an elemental mass of fat and tissue? Or would it have simply dried on the skeleton?

He didn't know.

Tentatively, he reached out and touched the coffin lid with one pink-gloved finger.

The lid stayed where it was.

'I don't think you should do that,' said Mr Health and Safety, 'You're not wearing a suit. Breaks all the rules.'

Ridpath ignored him.

This time he pushed a little harder, using two fingers. The lid moved a little, wood scraping against wood as the light revealed more of the inside.

He peered into the dark interior. What was that? Something grey and mottled.

A sound to his left. He glanced back towards Charlie Whitworth, who winked at him, popping a sweet in his mouth.

Ridpath placed his fingers on the side of the coffin lid.

'I wouldn't do that if I were you,' said Mr Health and Safety stepping backwards. The gravediggers and the sallow undertaker were both staring at him. Charlie Whitworth shrugged his shoulders as if to say 'nothing to do with me'. Even the blackbird had stopped singing from its perch in the yew tree.

They were all waiting for him to act. Perhaps he would be the first coroner's officer to last exactly one hour in the job before he was fired. The shortest secondment ever in the history of Manchester Police. That would go down well with the deputy chief.

Sod it – in for a penny, in for a pound. He pushed the coffin lid harder. Again the wood of the lid scraped against the base, before finally sliding off to rest against the tarpaulin.

'What the fuck?' said Charlie eloquently.

Inside the coffin, three mottled-grey breeze blocks with an abstract palm leaf design lay resting on the stained ivory satin lining.

Dead breeze blocks.

Very dead breeze blocks.

'What are we going to tell the family?' said the undertaker in his monotone.

'I'm going to need a forensics team, Charlie.'

The DCI was bending down, staring into the empty coffin. Ridpath repeated his request.

'What am I going to tell them? We opened a coffin and there was nothing inside?'

'Tell them what you want, Charlie.' Ridpath reached into his jacket and held out his phone. 'Or you could tell the coroner.'

The chief inspector ran his fingers through his thinning hair, scratching the bald patch on his crown. 'And what am I going to say to the super? John Gorman is already twisting my ear about wasting resources.'

'We need the coffin and the earth from the grave examined.'

'Examined for what, Ridpath?'

'The Scene of Crime Officer will tell us that when he gets here.'

'So we have a crime scene, do we? What's the crime?'

Ridpath looked into the empty coffin, with the three breeze blocks resting comfortably against the ivory satin lining. 'Let's try theft for starters. After that, we'll see where it takes us.'

Chapter Eleven

Lesley sat opposite the girl on a 1970s chair she'd found abandoned in the workshop upstairs. It was already 5.30 and he was late.

The girl was weeping softly, her body and soul crushed by the night she had spent alone in this wretched place. Lesley had given her water when she returned. Not too much – just enough to keep her alive. But no food. He didn't like them to have food in case they made a mess later.

He always thought ahead.

She examined the girl in front of her.

With her clothes removed, the body was exactly as he specified: thin to the point of emaciation with the greasy hair and sores around her mouth of a drug user. Lesley could already see her teeth were starting to go, a side effect of the chemicals used in the manufacture of crack, the girl's drug of choice.

She checked her watch again: 5.40.

He'd told Lesley to wait until he arrived, to do nothing until he arrived. She always obeyed him; she always would.

The girl was chained to the brick wall, her wrists fastened by manacles and held slightly above her head. She had been here since the previous day. Lesley had brought her back, manacled her to the wall and injected a large dose of lorazepam into her left arm.

It would be enough to keep her quiet while Lesley went home to rest. The girl would wake up thirsty, hungry and disorientated, but no matter. They were in no rush to experiment with this one.

The building was an abandoned workshop on the edge of Stockfield, just off the A6 to Buxton. They used to make hydraulic pit head props here in the sixties and seventies, but Thatcher's crushing of the coal industry had signalled the death of the mines in places like Poynton. They weren't 'economically viable' anymore, so workshops like this and thousands of others had slowly gone out of business. The owner, who was still alive somewhere in the bottom of a whisky glass, had tried to make a go of it, but he had finally given up, retiring to his detached house in Woodhead with the decanter attached to his right hand.

'You've done well, Lesley.' He was pleased with her when she told him about the workshop over the phone. His words sent a shiver racing through her body. 'You won't be punished this time.'

She was happy she wasn't going to be punished. She knew she deserved it; he told her she deserved it, but not this time. She had done well.

'Meet me there at five o'clock tomorrow,' he ordered.

But she couldn't. She had to prepare her mother's tea. Her mother always ate at the same time every evening. Five o'clock. So she could watch Noel Edmonds and *Deal or no Deal*, imagining herself as one of the contestants, choosing a suitcase number based on her infallible system. So far she had won six million pounds, thanks to Noel. At least that's what her mother said.

'I don't think I can do it.' Her voice was tentative, hoping he would agree.

'Meet me in there at five o'clock, not a second later,' he insisted.

What was she going to do? Then it came to her. Give her mother sandwiches and tea early. Surely her mother wouldn't be angry.

'I'll be there,' she answered him.

'Good. For a moment, I thought you deserved punishment, Lesley. You know how much I hate to punish you.'

'I know. I'll be good, just wait and see the girl in the workshop. She'll be perfect.'

There was silence on the other end of the phone. She hoped she had appeased him, deflected him from his anger at her reluctance to obey.

Eventually, the answer came. 'We'll see.'

The dial tone echoed in her ear as she held the phone. 'We'll see.' Was that good or bad?

At 4.30 she went into the living room to check on her mother. The TV was flickering in the corner with the sound turned down low but the subtitles switched on. Some woman was showing a couple a dreary house in suburbia.

It would take her 15 minutes to drive to the workshop. She had to start preparing now. He was particular about her clothes and make-up.

Her mother looked up for a moment from her word-search puzzle. 'What do you want, Lesley?'

'Nothing, Mother.'

'Then why are you bothering me?'

'I'm sorry, Mother.'

'You have become extremely thoughtless recently, Lesley, going out far too much,'

Lesley laughed nervously. 'Just meeting friends.'

'You don't have any friends.'

Oh but she did, and she knew nothing about him. 'I'll make your tea now.'

But she didn't go straight into the kitchen. First she went upstairs, changing from her uniform into the purple twinset and pearls he liked so much, giving herself a quick spray of Chanel No. 5. Not too much, though. He didn't like it to be strong: it made him sneeze, and if he sneezed he would punish her. She left her face bare otherwise. She would have preferred to have a touch of lipstick and blusher but he liked her face to be bare. More natural, he called it.

After checking herself in the mirror to see she was perfect, she ran downstairs into the kitchen to make a cheese sandwich.

Mother liked cheese sandwiches, but not too much butter and not too much cheese. The kettle had already boiled so she added two PG teabags to the pot – Mother never drank anything else – and poured the hot water in.

She assembled the plate of sandwiches, cut into triangles, on a tray and added a pot of tea, a jug of milk and two cubes of sugar on the saucer. Then she walked into the living room, placing the tray on the side table next to her mother's right hand.

'Is it time for Noel already?'

'Not quite, Mother. I thought we would have tea a little earlier tonight.'

Her mother's face screwed up into a paroxysm of pain. 'I don't want my tea a little earlier. I want it with Noel.' She pointed to the television with a crooked finger. 'Does that look like Noel to you?'

Lesley glanced across at the box in the corner. On it, the couple were being shown around a different house by a jolly plump lady with a plummy voice.

'I thought we would have it a little early tonight.'

'I don't want it early.'

The travelling clock beneath its glass dome on the mantel-piece said 4.40. If she drove quickly she could still make it.

'Let's be different today, have our tea early.'

Her mother scowled. 'I don't want to be different.' With her crooked hand she pushed the sandwiches off the tray to land on the beige carpet.

Lesley rushed over to pick them up, placing them back on the plate.

'I'll make some fresh.' She began to pour the tea, placing the milk in the bottom of the cup first just like her mother expected. 'At least drink your tea. I'll bring your food when Noel starts.'

Her mother sulked but accepted the cup and saucer, slowly sipping the tea through wrinkled lips with their smear of scarlet lipstick.

Four forty-five.

The sleeping tablets were taking effect. Already her mother's head was beginning to nod forward to her chest, and the book of search puzzles had slipped onto the floor.

She took the cup from her mother's liver-spotted hands and placed it back on the tray. The old witch wouldn't have anything to eat tonight, but she would never know.

Lesley would make it up to her tomorrow, and buy her favourite Battenberg cake from the grocer's as a special treat.

A groan from the girl brought her back to the workshop with its brick walls speckled with blood. She could see the arms were already white as the blood had drained out of them. A pasty white like uncooked dough. Should she release one of the hands? Let the blood flow back into it?

But he had told her to wait.

She always obeyed him.

The girl was groaning loudly now, shaking her arms, twisting her head left and right, struggling against her restraints. Should she give her another injection? Perhaps the girl would injure herself before they started.

He wouldn't like that. He didn't like them to be damaged before they started.

She heard a noise behind her as the trapdoor swung open.

He was here. He was finally here.

She sat at attention, still looking straight at the girl as she had been told. She sensed his presence behind her, feeling the slight movement in the chair as the tips of his fingers brushed the back. Then he was standing beside her.

'You have done well, Lesley. She's perfect.'

He was happy. She knew she could look at him now. She turned her head and stared up into the black face. A halo had formed around his head. His eyes stared beatifically down on her, shining out against the black satin of the mask.

'This one deserves something special, I think, don't you?' He held up the Black & Decker drill for her to see. 'Do you want to go first this time?'

Chapter Twelve

Ridpath spent the rest of the morning at the cemetery.

Charlie finally called in a forensics team after ringing John Gorman to get his approval. The guv'nor had hummed and hawed before finally saying yes, the clinching argument being the reminder of their fraught relationship with the coroner.

They sent him Protheroe, one of the better pathologists, as well as Sarah Castle to help with logistics. She didn't look too pleased at being taken off the woman with the swan tattoo case, but they were short of staff and everybody had to double up these days.

As soon as she turned up, Charlie Whitworth introduced him. 'This is Tom Ridpath, the coroner's officer.'

'You were at the briefing – ex–CID aren't you?' she said as she shook his hand.

Ridpath immediately bristled. 'Still CID. It's Detective Inspector Ridpath.'

She reddened again. She seemed to spend most of her time these days blushing. 'Sorry, sir.'

'No worries, I'm just on temporary secondment to the coroner.'

Charlie Whitworth coughed. 'Well, I'll be off. You'll be in good hands with Sarah.'

Ridpath looked around as the forensics team began to set up their tent to cover the open grave and the bare coffin. 'Who's running this investigation? Somebody has to be the SIO?'

Charlie Whitworth stroked his straggly moustache. 'It looks like you are, Ridpath. DS Castle will stay here until the forensics have finished, then I need her back on the job.'

'I'm running it?'

DCI Charlie Whitworth shielded his eyes with his hand and stared off into the distance, looking around the whole of the cemetery and across to the Mersey. 'I don't see any other Ridpaths around here, so it must be you. We haven't got anybody else, and you were still CID the last time I looked. I'll cover it with the district commander, so don't cock it up.' He nodded once and strode quickly over to his car.

Sarah Castle went straight to work, blocking off the scene with tape, creating a perimeter around the exhumation. People were beginning to arrive in the cemetery to lay flowers at the graves of their loved ones. The detective sergeant was polite but firm with them, not allowing anyone near the crime scene.

Once the area had been cordoned off, Protheroe and his team went to work.

'You touched the coffin lid?'

Ridpath nodded.

'Bloody idiot. Didn't they teach you anything on the coroner's officer course?'

'I haven't been on the course.'

Protheroe stared at him through his thick glasses, finally taking them off to get a better look. 'Don't I know you? Weren't you CID?'

This was becoming tedious. 'We worked on the tram case together.' A bunch of kids had thrown bricks through the windscreen of a moving tram and then ran away. Unfortunately, they had given the driver a heart attack. Protheroe had lifted a print off one of the bricks and they found it belonged to an eleven-year-old boy, Martin Shuttleworth. Not one of the cases Ridpath had enjoyed working on.

'I remember you. Detective Sergeant Ridley, isn't it?

Protheroe was famous throughout the force for never remembering names or faces. He had once asked the chief constable who he was and why he was cluttering up his crime scene.

'Actually, the name is Ridpath. Detective Inspector Ridpath.'

'Well then, Detective Inspector Ridley, you should have known better than to contaminate a scene. Did you wear gloves?'

Ridpath showed his pink-gloved hands.

'Good.' He turned to one of his team. 'Steve, can you bag these gloves for me? And while you're at it, better take his shoes too. You don't know where Ridley's been.'

'Will do,' was the curt answer.

'But I don't have anything else to wear.'

Protheroe stared at his feet. 'Size 9, I would say. You can borrow a pair of wellies from the van. Give them back, mind. Wellies don't grow on trees.'

Ridpath felt the technician lift and bag his hand.

'What about the chief inspector – did he go anywhere near the coffin?'

Ridpath thought for a moment. 'No, he stayed away. Didn't come anywhere near.'

'Smart man. No wonder he's a chief inspector. Now where's my coffin?'

Protheroe trudged towards the open grave, leaving Ridpath to be molested by the white-suited technician.

'Do you really need to take my shoes?'

'If the boss says we do, we do.'

His brand-new brogues were placed in a brown paper bag, numbered and identified. Ridpath was issued with a receipt and a pair of purple wellies, size 9. 'I know, I know, bring them back.'

'Actually, you can keep these. I wore them on a case up on Saddleworth Moor. They're starting to leak.'

'Thanks for that.' Ridpath stood up and squelched down towards the gravediggers' hut. He'd only gone three steps when

Mr Health and Safety sidled up to him. 'I'm going to have to file a report, you know. I did warn you not to open the coffin lid. And you weren't wearing a suit. A grave offence, that is. I'll put it all down in my report.'

'Send me a copy, won't you?'

'Don't worry. Mrs Challinor will get one too.'

'Lucky for her.' Ridpath noticed the technician placing his bagged shoes and gloves in the white SOC van. He waved to them. 'You need to take this man's shoes too.'

The technician ran across. 'You stood near the grave, did you?' A Welsh accent. Ridpath could almost hear the word 'boyo' at the end of the sentence.

'Not for long, I was—'

'Better give me your shoes then.'

'But I—'

'And he touched the coffin.'

'Did he? Well, I'll have to take the gloves too. Don't want to miss anything. Old Protheroe's a stickler for the rules at a crime scene.'

Ridpath turned away and squelched down the path to the gravediggers' hut, a smile creeping across his face.

He knocked on the door and walked straight in without waiting for a response. The two gravediggers were sitting around a rickety wooden table in their stockinged feet, drinking mugs of tea. The undertaker and his assistant were standing with their arms crossed, not saying anything.

'I see they've already been here.'

'Aye, took us boots. Can't work with no boots.' The elder gravedigger spoke through his thick moustache. It was as if the words were filtered through the ginger and white hair.

He looked at the undertaker's feet. They were shod in highly polished black patent leather, with no decoration.

'I always carry a spare pair, just in case. Can't bury a customer in dirty shoes.'

'Can't have the corpse complaining, can we?' said Ridpath.

Albert Ronson sniffed. 'It's a customer, not a corpse,' he said drily.

'Well, I need to take your statements,' said Ridpath.

The undertaker stared at him. 'But you were there with us, you saw everything we did.'

'It doesn't matter, still have to do it.'

'When?'

'Now is as good a time as any, while it's still fresh.'

The undertaker looked at his watch. 'I have an embalming at twelve.'

'Is that before or after lunch?'

The undertaker's mouth remained pursed, as if he had been sucking a particularly sour lemon. 'During, actually,' he finally answered.

Ridpath's eyes screwed up, trying to understand.

The undertaker helped him. 'Tuna sandwiches, no lettuce, plenty of mayo. I find the flavour goes well with the smell of embalming fluid.'

There was no answer to that. 'I'll interview you two first then.'

He took the undertaker and his assistant aside and ensured they described the morning's events in their own words, writing it down in his neat capital letters. The undertaker read it through and signed it at the bottom.

'I'll get it typed up and you can come in to sign your statement properly.'

'Is that necessary?'

'Look, if you are called to give evidence at least you will have this to fall back on.'

'I suppose you're right. Is there going to be an inquest?'

Ridpath shrugged his shoulders, 'Who knows? It's for the coroner to decide.'

'I'd forgotten about Mrs Challinor. She's not going to be too happy about this.'

Ridpath had forgotten about Mrs Challinor too. 'Thanks, we're finished now. I'll call you when it's ready.' He held up the witness statement.

The undertaker and his assistant said goodbye to the two gravediggers and placed their top hats on their heads, adopting a look of funereal calm, before leaving the hut.

'Our turn now?' the elder gravedigger asked.

Ridpath held up his hand. 'Give me a sec.'

He stepped outside and watched the undertaker climb into his van without taking off his hat. He took his mobile phone from his jacket and rang the Coroner's Office.

'Jenny Oldfield speaking.'

'I need to speak to Mrs Challinor.'

'I'm afraid she's in court at the moment. Can I take a message?'

At least she sounded efficient. 'It's Tom Ridpath—'

'The new officer?' she interrupted.

'Correct—'

Before he had time to speak, she was already talking. 'I'm so looking forward to meeting you, Carol said you came in yesterday but I missed you, what a shame. She was soooooo complimentary. It's going to be great working with a real police officer.'

He got the impression the office manager was a woman in her mid-forties, but this voice sounded like that of a young girl. An extremely naïve young girl. What could he say? 'Thanks. Could you ask Mrs Challinor to call me back on the mobile as soon as she can? There's a problem…'

'Doesn't sound good. Will do. She'll be out as soon as she's finished the Lorry inquest.'

'Bye, Jenny.' He switched off the phone before she could say anything else.

The gravediggers were waiting for him in the hut with fresh mugs of tea in their hands. They didn't offer him one. 'Right, let's get started. You are?' He pointed to the elder gravedigger.

'Ned Thomas. And this here's my son, Jasper.'

A father and son grave digging team? It's one way to keep jobs in the family. 'How long have you been working in the cemetery?'

The father answered for both of them. 'Bin here 42 years myself. Jasper here's done 10.'

'Eleven, dad,' the younger man answered laconically before taking a long swallow of tea.

'So you must have dug her grave in 2008?'

The father took a long draught from his pint-sized, tannin-stained mug. 'Probably.' Both father and son were men of few words but gallons of tea.

'Well, did you or didn't you?'

'Probably we did. But maybe we didn't.'

Ridpath waited for him to explain, but he didn't, just taking gulps of tea. Finally, he gave in and asked. 'Could you explain?'

The younger man answered. 'Well, back in 2008, there was another gravedigger, Alf Basset. He dug graves too.'

Well, he would – he was a gravedigger, thought Ridpath.

Before he could ask the next question, the younger man continued. 'But his rheumatism was giving him gyp by then so it was probably us. Couldn't do much digging by then, could Alf. Retired in 2009, he did.'

'No, 2008,' said the father.

The son counted slowly on his fingers. 'Aye, you're probably right, Dad. Our Daniel is ten now and he wasn't born when Alf retired.'

'That's what I said: 2008.' The father took another long slurp of tea from his bottomless mug.

'Probably us what dug it,' the son finally said.

'Good, I'm glad we've got it sorted.' Ridpath realized it was useless asking them the next question, but he had to try. 'Do you remember digging the grave?'

'No,' said the father.

'No,' echoed the son.

'You didn't think long.'

'Listen, son, I've dug over 2,000 graves in my career. After the first one, they're all pretty much the same. Only the weather changes.'

Silence, followed by two long slurps of tea.

Ridpath was about to finish the interview with his speech about typing up the statement and getting them to sign it, when the elder man spoke again.

'I will say one thing though.'

Ridpath waited. And waited. 'What's that?' he finally asked.

'Wellllll…' – the word was dragged out – 'that grave ain't been dug since.'

'What do you mean?'

'That grave ain't been disturbed since last time it were dug.'

Ridpath tried to get his head around what the man was saying. It was the son who helped him out.

'The grave ain't been dug since we dug it in 2008.'

Ridpath thought for a moment. 'How do you know?'

The elder man harrumphed. 'After digging over 2,000 graves, I knows about soil and digging. That grave ain't been touched since the day it was first dug.'

'So you're saying the coffin went into the ground like we found it today?'

The elder gravedigger nodded once, taking a slurp of tea.

'It was empty when it went into the ground?'

'Oh, it weren't empty. It had three breeze blocks in it.'

Father and son nodded to each other, both slurping their tea.

Chapter Thirteen

After two hours the forensics team had bagged and marked all the clothes, sampled the soil on the coffin and in the grave, and taken enough photographs to fill up a Grattan's catalogue. Protheroe had swabbed the inside of the coffin and then used a square of clear plastic tape to go over every inch of the ivory satin lining.

The lid was replaced and the coffin placed carefully on a gurney, before being moved to the forensics transit van.

Ridpath had been watching all this with DS Castle. As soon as the coffin was safely on the gurney, Protheroe began to peel off his gloves and walk towards them. 'That's me done. We'll do more tape work back at the lab – conditions will be better there. You can close up the grave, DS Castle, but leave the sheeting around it until you've finished. From experience, there are always a few ghouls who come hunting at crime scenes for "exhibits".'

'OK, I'll get the gravediggers.'

'There's a problem there,' said Ridpath. 'He's taken their boots.'

'Not to worry, lay a tarpaulin over it and they can close it tomorrow. Make sure it's surrounded by a cordon though,' said Protheroe.

'Why did you use the clear plastic tape inside the coffin?' asked Castle.

'Are you going to tell her, Ridley, or shall I?'

'It's Ridpath. Detective Inspector Ridpath.'

'Of course it is. Well, do you know?'

Ridpath thought for a moment, working out the answer. 'We're looking for a missing body—'

'That's right. I was using the tape to check if it hadn't fallen down the gaps in the lining.'

'Let me finish…'

Protheroe held his hands up.

'According to the gravediggers, the grave hadn't been disturbed since the coffin was buried. So the question is…' He scratched his head, trying to stimulate his copper's brain – a way of thinking that had become ossified in the last nine months. 'The question is, whether the body had ever been in the coffin in the first place.'

'Correct, Inspector. If it had ever been there Locard's exchange principle would come into play.'

'Every contact leaves a trace,' interjected DS Castle. They both looked at her. 'Hello, I did a forensics course at uni.'

'Oh God, not another one…'

Sarah Castle stared at him.

If looks could kill, he'd be in the electric chair. Ridpath liked her already.

'Anyway, I couldn't see anything but it doesn't mean something wasn't there. Hence the tape.'

'But what about the swabs?' Ridpath asked.

'He was looking for traces of blood.'

It was Ridpath's turn to stare at her.

'The clear squares of tape are used to look for skin samples or oils that may have come off the body if it had touched the satin inside the coffin. The cotton buds had luminol sprayed on them. The chemical reacts with blood. If any was inside the coffin, the ends of the buds would have gone purple. Was the bloody uni course worth it?'

Protheroe nodded. 'Ten out of ten, Sergeant.' He turned to Ridpath. 'You can come to the lab tomorrow afternoon. I should have the results by then. Or I can just send them across to you?'

'No, I'll swing by. Around 4.30 OK?'

'Should be done by then. It's pretty straightforward, not brain surgery.'

'Can I come too?'

They both looked at her.

She blushed again. 'I just want to learn more...'

'Will Charlie mind?'

'I don't think so. Anyway, until the name of the victim is found, there isn't any family to liaise with.'

'I'll see you there at 4.30.' He turned and began walking back to his car. Then he stopped. 'There's one thing you can do for me though.'

'What's that?'

'Those breeze blocks, can you check where they were made?'

'Sure, should be easy. Common or garden breeze blocks.'

Something flashed across his mind: an image, a memory he didn't have time to process. And then it was gone, like a whisper on the wind. 'Just check them out, will you?

Chapter Fourteen

It was close to lunchtime before he managed to get back to the Coroner's Office, grabbing a quick salmon and cream cheese sandwich on the way. The doctors had told him to eat more fish, so salmon sandwiches had become his standby, even though he hated them.

He felt like he had been back at work for years as he pushed open the door. The aches and pains from standing around a cold cemetery were beginning to get to him. Perhaps the nine months off work had taken more out of him than he thought.

The reception desk was empty again. Would he ever meet the elusive Jenny Oldfield or was she on permanent lunch break? He walked though into the main office. And then it struck him: where was he supposed to sit? Nobody had actually told him if he had a desk, a computer, what the password was or even how to log on. He supposed it was the elusive Jenny Oldfield's job.

Four empty desks stared back at him. Which one was his? He tried to bring all his detective skills to bear on the problem but all four looked occupied and used.

'Yours is over there.'

He turned round to find Margaret Challinor towering over him, coffee in hand. At least, it felt like she was much taller than him but that couldn't be − he was nearly six feet tall. Then he looked down at her legs; she was wearing four-inch heels.

'Thanks. I presume I can get all the office passwords from Jenny?'

'She'll be back after lunch. I heard about this morning.'

'Oh?'

'A little bird called Rob Campbell from Health and Safety rang me.'

She brushed past him and he smelt the faint but pleasant presence of a perfume. He couldn't quite catch the aroma – Chanel No. 5, was it?

'You'd better come in.'

He followed her into her office. The oak desk was as neat as yesterday, with files to the left and right in orderly piles. A computer monitor on her left. A pristine blotter and an array of pens next to a pile of unopened letters.

She sat down behind it, putting the paper cup of coffee on a coaster next to her. 'Tell me what happened.'

'To cut a long story short, we opened the coffin and it was empty.'

'No family there?'

'Not that I saw. A few people were visiting graves, but none of Alice Seagram's family.'

'Good. I'm stuck in court all afternoon so you're going to have to break the news to them. You've received the latest family liaison guidance, Tom?'

He nodded. 'Actually, I prefer to be called Ridpath. I always felt Tom was such a namby-pamby name.'

'Given by your mother?'

'How did you know?'

'It has a female touch about it. A woman who wants to keep her son a boy rather than help him become a man.'

He was uncomfortable with the accuracy of her insight. Had she done the same to her children? He felt it was too early to ask her directly; instead he returned to the problem they both faced. 'You want me to go alone?'

She thought for a moment, her eyes closing slightly behind the thick lenses of her glasses. 'I'll get Carol to go with you. A female presence in times like these always helps.'

'You seem calm about this.'

'The missing body?'

He nodded again.

'Inside, I'm seething. A fairly straightforward procedure of exhumation will now turn into a major investigation. Plus, once the newspapers get hold of this, all hell will break loose.'

'I've started the investigation already.' He looked down at his lap. 'Charlie Whitworth asked me to handle it.'

Her left eyebrow rose half an inch, almost touching a lock of grey hair hanging down across her forehead. 'You should have called me first.'

'I did. Left a message with Jenny.' Ridpath omitted to mention he had already accepted the job from his DCI.

Margaret Challinor leant forward and rifled through a neat pile of slips on her desk. 'So you did.'

'I interviewed the witnesses and John Gorman provided a forensics team to look at the coffin. They'll report back tomorrow.'

'Who's paying for it?'

'He is. For now.'

She tapped her fingers on the desk. 'Good. Discover anything?'

'Not a lot. The gravediggers were pretty certain the ground hadn't been disturbed since the body was placed in the plot in 2008.'

'So we're not looking for a Charlie Chaplin copycat then?'

Ridpath understood the reference to the infamous theft and attempt to ransom the comedian's body in 1977. 'Doesn't look like it.'

More tapping of fingers on the blotter. 'So it means we need to discover if the body was ever in the coffin in the first place.'

Ridpath was impressed with how quickly she had got to the nub of the issue. 'Exactly. The lab will let us know tomorrow.'

'Looking for traces of DNA, hair or epithelial cells.'

'You know your forensics. We drop flakes of skin all the time. If the body had been in the coffin, there would be traces.'

Margaret Challinor pressed the intercom on her desk. 'Carol, can you come to my office, please?'

'Will do.'

She looked back at him. 'I'll postpone the inquest pending your investigation. I can give you some time but not a lot; the high court is breathing down my neck and that particular judge has a bad case of halitosis.'

'How long?'

'About a week, not longer.'

Ridpath took the opportunity to raise an issue. 'I think the Health and Safety man at the exhumation this morning is going to write a report…'

'Campbell? Don't worry about him, he's a twat. Just covering his rather expansive arse.'

Ridpath found himself slightly shocked at her language. Of course he was used to it, having worked on the streets of Manchester, but enunciated in such beautifully pronounced vowels it still shocked him. Had he become a prude in his old age?

Carol Oates appeared in the doorway. She was dressed in black, as yesterday, but it was a neater, more austere look. Her blonde hair was still pinned up in a chignon.

'I need you to go with Ridpath to see the Seagram family this afternoon.'

'I have the Sinclair suicide to depose at four o'clock.'

'Oh, shit, I forgot.'

'I can do it alone,' said Ridpath.

'Are you sure?'

He nodded.

'Carol, give him the file on the family. Be careful with them – they have managed the press well.'

'Manipulated the press well,' said Carol from the doorway.

'No cock-ups, Ridpath. I'm relying on you.'

Chapter Fifteen

He killed this girl with a garrotte.

They had played with her for two hours before he lost patience. Using the drill on her knees, the bit digging deep into her kneecaps, recording the screams through an ancient tape machine he had picked up for five pounds at a car boot sale.

'Ian Brady and Myra Hindley used to listen to their victims on Sunday afternoons. They played the tapes after she had cooked him a roast dinner. His favourite was pork with lots of crackling and applesauce. Afterwards they made love,' he said as the girl whimpered on the ground beneath him, her left hand smashed by a hammer.

'I'd like to do that.'

'Do what?'

'Listen to the tapes.'

He touched her under her chin, his fingers soft and gentle. She knew she had pleased him this time.

'But we are not like those two criminals; we perform experiments. It's your turn', he announced.

The girl on the ground tried to speak, spitting blood through her broken lips.

He knelt in closer to her mouth. 'What's that? What are you saying?'

'No… no more… no more.' The words came out in a rough, broken voice. Her hair – long, dark and bedraggled with sweat – hung down over her face. Spots of blood dripped onto the ground, mixing with the sweat and spit to pool on the stained concrete.

He leant in closer. 'I can't hear you. You want more?'

The girl shook her head violently, spraying blood and sweat onto his trousers. He reached into his pocket, producing a clean handkerchief and wiping the spots carefully from the fabric.

'This tart wants us to experiment more on her, Lesley. This one is a woman after my own heart.'

She picked up the ball-peen hammer from the table. It was new, bought that morning from B&Q on the outskirts of Liverpool. As he'd instructed, she chose a time when the cashiers were busy, added lots of other items to her basket, turned away from the cameras covering the till and made sure she paid in cash.

She advanced on the girl, staring down at the body beneath her.

He smiled, encouraging her to go ahead.

The first time with the prostitute she picked up in Moss Side, she had just watched while he did all the work. He had used a scalpel to slice off the woman's lips and then her ears, finally removing the scalp and peeling back the hair from the skull like one would peel off a pair of plastic gloves.

When he had finished and the girl was dead, he had said, 'I've always wanted to scalp somebody since I watched the Indians do it on TV when I was a child.' Then a look of disgust came over his face as he stared down at the body lying on the sticky carpet. 'This one is too ugly, Lesley – we won't let the police find this one. She will be disposed of where she will never be found.'

With the second girl, the one with the swan tattoo on her arm, she had been reluctant to begin at first, but he encouraged her. 'Feel the joy of causing pain,' he whispered in her ear. 'It's just another experiment. A frog in human skin.'

She could feel his breath on her skin and the soft plastic touching her ear. Was it only a fortnight ago? It seemed an age and half a lifetime away.

After a little hesitation and a few whispered words of encouragement, she had finally hit the girl.

Then again.

Then again, harder.

Again and again and again. Feeling the hammer crunch into the side of her head with every blow.

Finally, he had caught her arm and pulled her to him, whispering 'Did you enjoy the pain?' into her ear.

Their third plaything now lay at their feet. This time, she didn't need to be encouraged. She stood over the girl on the floor, seeing her as a mass of dyed hair attached to a thin body. The girl was panting, her back wracked with sobs, her shoulders tense and stressed, resting on her elbows cradling her broken index finger.

The cockiness was gone now. The swagger of the cigarette and the demand for money vanished like the posturing bully she was, replaced by a quivering, blubbering mass.

She chose her point carefully, bringing the round end of the ball of the hammer down on the middle of the girl's radius. She didn't swing too hard this time, letting the weight of the hammer do the work, just as he had shown her. There was the impact of the hammer against her skin, followed by the dull thud as the radius cracked into pieces.

A wail of surprise and pain erupted from the girl's mouth.

She could see the fillings inside. Cheap National Health work – metal amalgam fillings stark against the ivory of the teeth. She should have gone to a better dentist.

The girl held her limp right arm with her left arm, bringing it across her chest, still screaming in pain.

He walked across to check the reel to reel recorder. The tapes were revolving slowly, the illuminated dials flickering crazily with each one of the girl's screams.

She brought the hammer down again. This time against the girl's left kneecap. This time the crack was much louder as the girl howled, rolled onto her back and screamed into the empty rafters of the workshop.

He smiled at her.

He smiled at her.

She lifted the hammer again, ready to bring it down on the other kneecap, but he grabbed her hand. 'Enough. Let's finish this.'

He knelt down behind the girl's head and lifted her body into a sitting position. Then he gently placed the garrotte around her neck, pulling the wire tighter and tighter.

The wire cut into her skin, the sharp edge producing a thin line of blood around the neck. The fingers of the girl's left hand were reaching it, her legs jerking crazily, her mouth no longer screaming, just gasping for the last remnant of life.

He pulled tighter and tighter, the only effort on his face a slight tightening of the jaw and mouth.

She looked into his eyes and he smiled at her.

God, she loved this man.

Chapter Sixteen

The Seagram house wasn't what he expected. It was a detached new build, created out of old stone rather than brick and located in the streets close to the centre of Didsbury, one of Manchester's more expensive neighbourhoods.

He had called them earlier. Or rather Margaret Challinor had called them, with him listening in on speaker phone. The woman's voice on the other end was pure Manchester, with the nasal whine made familiar by the Gallaghers.

He had read through the file. Their daughter had been kidnapped by the Beast on 4 March 2008, just over ten years ago. The body had been found four days later, dumped by the side of a stream in Withington, not far from Didsbury. She had been strangled and tortured and was just 16 years old.

He rang the bell.

The door was opened by a woman in a housecoat. Her hair was grey and piled on top of her head in an old-fashioned beehive, like something escaped from the 1960s.

'I'm Tom Ridpath, the coroner's officer.'

She opened the door wider, 'You'd better come in.'

Having read the file, he didn't tell her he was a police officer. This family had just spent the last ten years criticizing the police for the investigation into the murder of their daughter. This time, it was better to take cover behind the anonymity of the Coroner's Office.

He followed her into a comfortably, and expensively, furnished living room. A man, presumably Mr Seagram, sat in an armchair, reading the *Daily Mail*. When he walked in the man didn't acknowledge him, just folded up the newspaper and placed it beside him.

'Can I get you some tea, Mr Ridpath?'

'That would be lovely, thanks.'

He sat down on the settee and bustled about pulling out the files from his folder and arranging his notepad on his knee.

The man just watched him all the time, not saying a word.

Ridpath looked around the room. Everywhere photographs of a young girl stared out from mantelpieces and shelves and ledges. Smiling directly into the camera; playing with two friends; one in semi-profile, taken for some school event, dressed in uniform; a candid shot, at age 11 or so, beside the beach, her feet kicking up the seawater towards the camera.

The girl may have been dead for ten years, but in this room, she still lived on.

Only one photo was different. A young boy on his own, not smiling, just staring straight into the camera, determination etched into the tightness of the jaw.

The woman returned with a tray, complete with tea and biscuits. She poured Ridpath a cup and handed it to him, giving one to her husband but taking nothing for herself.

She spoke first, just after Ridpath had taken his first mouthful of tea. 'I suppose you're here about the exhumation this morning?'

He nodded, placing the tea down on the side table next to him. 'You didn't send anybody to observe?'

'My son is at work and I couldn't face it,' she answered. 'I want to remember my daughter like this' – she pointed to the pictures all over the room – 'not how she was after...' Her voice trailed off.

The man opposite still said nothing, just watching and breathing heavily.

'Your son?'

'David, he works for Granada, the TV station. He's been the one pressing for the review of the case...'

That explains the management of the press, thought Ridpath.

'He doesn't believe my daughter was murdered by James Dalbey.' The woman looked down at her small, fragile hands clasped in her lap. 'It's been such a long time…' she whispered.

Ridpath took a deep breath; this was going to be difficult. 'I'm afraid I have some distressing news.'

The woman reached over to touch her husband. 'What is it?'

He licked his lips. How could he tell somebody their daughter's body was missing? He looked around the room again, finally focusing on a picture of a young, happy 16-year-old, long blonde hair and beautiful smile, staring into the camera with openness and innocence.

He took another breath. 'I'm afraid I have some bad news to tell you. This morning at six o'clock we opened your daughter's grave, removing the coffin from it. On opening the coffin in the presence of an undertaker, a senior police officer and a council representative, we found it was empty. I am sorry.'

'What?' The question was almost whispered.

Ridpath swallowed. 'We found the coffin was empty. Your daughter's body wasn't inside.'

The woman's face went pale. She searched for her husband's hand, finally clutching at it like one would seize a lifebelt when drowning. 'Can't be. There was the funeral, the priest, carrying her into the church…'

'I'm afraid it's true, Mrs Seagram. I was there when the casket was opened. There was nothing inside.'

The man's voice when it spoke for the first time was full of malice. 'This is more incompetence from the police. We wanted our daughter to be exhumed to prove the police got it totally wrong. They arrested an innocent man for her murder. James Dalbey couldn't have killed her.'

'I understand how you feel at a time like this, Mr Seagram—'

'You understand nothing, sonny. My daughter was murdered, her body thrown out on the street with the rubbish.

80

The police didn't look for the man who did it. They simply pinned it on an innocent man. And now you're telling me they've lost her body too.'

Ridpath took another breath. 'The police didn't lose the body, Mr Seagram – it was stolen by somebody. And I'm going to find out who did it.'

'Stolen?' The wife whispered, 'Who would steal my daughter's body?'

Chapter Seventeen

As he walked down the path to the gate, Ridpath could hear the sound of a raised voice from the living room. Mrs Seagram was shouting a stream of abuse, followed by the crash of something breaking against a wall.

Ridpath rushed back to the door, ready to break it down, but something made him stop for a moment. Inside he could hear the sound of sobbing and a voice speaking – a softer, gentler voice, that of Mr Seagram. 'It's all right, love, it will be all right.'

He listened a few seconds more before walking away, unwilling to intrude on their private grief, desperately reaching for the cigarettes in his inside pocket.

The interview hadn't gone well.

'You're gonna find out who stole her body, are you?' Mr Seagram had shouted. 'Why don't you find out who stole her life?'

The wife had reached for his arm again, grasping it just above the wrist where a faded tattoo was covered in hair. An army tattoo or one from the navy?

'I need some details of the funeral arrangements in 2008.' He deliberately spoke to Mrs Seagram. 'Who was the funeral director?'

'We hired Mr O'Shaughnessy because he'd done such a lovely job with my sister when she died of the cancer.'

At the mention of the dreaded word, Ridpath looked down at his pad and wrote the words 'O'Shaughnessy' followed by 'CANCER' in block capitals, underlined. 'Do you have an address for the funeral director?'

'I've got it somewhere. She walked over to a drawer in the sideboard and pulled out a Catholic mass card, edged in black. 'Here it is', she said, passing it to him.

'Do you mind if I keep this?' The address of the director was on the back. On the front, a picture of Alice Seagram was smiling out at him. Beneath the picture in black type:

> A requiem mass for the soul of Alice Seagram will be said at St Ann's Church, Chester Road, on 21 March 2008, followed by burial at Stretford Cemetery.

'We have plenty more. She was a popular girl, was Alice.'

'Thank you. Now, I'm sorry, but I have to ask you to go through the details with me again.'

'Details?'

He would have to be clearer with his words. 'Of your daughter's disappearance and her funeral.'

Mr Seagram spoke quietly. 'We've told this so many times.'

'I'm sorry, I just need to hear it in your own words.'

They both looked at each other. Mrs Seagram finally spoke. 'It was 4 March. Alice had gone out with her friends to a party. We lived in Stretford then, not far from the Quadrant.'

Ridpath nodded. He knew the area well, close to Old Trafford and the cricket ground.

'She left the party early. She was never a great party girl, much preferred to bury her nose in a book. Anyway, that's the last anybody saw of her. We went to the police the following day, but they did nothing. Thought she was just another runaway. But I told them she wasn't like that. They didn't want to listen. Then she was found in Withington on 8 March.'

'Which one of you identified the body?'

'I did,' said Mr Seagram, 'but they wouldn't let me see her face.'

'Why not?'

'Said she wasn't fit to be seen. My beautiful daughter, not "fit to be seen".' His voice rose and then he took two deep breaths, regaining control. 'Her face was covered by a plastic sheet when I saw her in the mortuary.'

'Then how did you know...' Ridpath never finished his sentence.

'She lost a toe on her left foot when she was child. They let me see the left foot.'

For a moment, Ridpath thought about this own daughter. What would he do if he had to identify her body in some cold, sterile mortuary? Even worse, what if she had to identify his body? The thought sent a tsunami of fear down his spine.

Mustn't think like that.

Must keep focused.

'So you appointed an undertaker to take care of the burial?'

Mrs Seagram answered. 'My daughter's body was released back to us after the pathologist had finished with her on March 18th. She was buried on the 21st.'

'And you arranged the funeral with Mr O'Shaughnessy?'

'Of course we bloody did. Who else was going to do it?'

'I'm sorry, Mr Seagram. I'm just trying to make the details of the funeral clear in my own mind.'

'Our son arranged it,' Mrs Seagram whispered.

'I'm sorry, I didn't hear what you said.'

She swallowed and spoke louder. 'We were too distraught. He handled everything. I don't know what we would have done without David.'

'Do you have his number? I may need to ask him a few questions.'

She passed him her mobile phone with her son's name displayed on the screen. 'He always answers this one.'

Ridpath closed his notepad and put his pen back inside his jacket pocket. 'I think I have enough for the moment, Mr and Mrs Seagram.' He stood up. 'If you need anything please contact me at the Coroner's Office. I'm afraid I don't have a card to give you yet — I've just started.'

'So now they're sending us boys barely out of their pants,' sneered Mr Seagram.

Ridpath stared at him. 'I'm a detective inspector in the Manchester Police with ten years' experience.'

The man stared back. 'So let me get this right. They've sent another copper to investigate the disappearance of my daughter's body, ten years after one of his mates botched the investigation?' He didn't wait for an answer. 'You couldn't make it up if you tried.'

'I will not cover anything up, Mr Seagram, I give you my word.'

The only answer was a loud snort from the man.

'I think I'd better show you out, Mr Ridpath.' The woman touched his arm.

'Thank you for your time. I will keep you informed of any progress.'

As Ridpath opened the door to leave the room, he turned back. 'One last question: how can you be so sure James Dalbey didn't murder your daughter?'

It was Mrs Seagram who answered. 'Because we were with him at the time he was supposed to have committed the—' She stopped speaking, unable to say the words.

Her husband continued speaking. 'He was with us in our house when they said he did it. That clear enough for you?'

She led him out into the hallway and opened the door. Just before he left, she leant in closer, whispering. 'You will find her, Mr Ridpath. You will find my daughter, won't you? Her soul, it can't be lost.'

Then she closed the door.

Chapter Eighteen

After a short drive back to Stockfield, Ridpath parked in front of the Coroner's Office, feeding the parking machine with pound coins before going in. At least the council was making money off him.

It was close to eight o'clock and the April sun had already set. Lights burned brightly through the windows of the Victorian building despite the late hour.

Jenny Oldfield wasn't on reception again so he walked straight through. Margaret Challinor was in her office.

'How did it go?' she asked.

'As well as could be expected when you're telling an old couple the body of their daughter has gone missing from its grave.'

'That bad, huh?'

He sat down in front of her desk. 'They don't believe James Dalbey killed their daughter.'

'They have good reason not to.'

'What do you mean? I caught the man, in the lock-up, his fifth victim manacled to the wall.' He then told her the story of his first day on the job, the chase and his fight with Dalbey. 'It was sheer luck. If he hadn't hit Sergeant Mungovan during a routine traffic stop, we wouldn't have caught him.'

'So you're convinced of his guilt?'

'One hundred and ten per cent.'

'The high court is less sure.'

'I don't understand.'

She sighed and sat back in her chair. 'The evidence against Dalbey for the murder of Alice Seagram was badly handled.'

'He was guilty. They found the DNA of at least five women in the lock-up.'

'But they could only identify one of the victims, Alice Seagram. They never found the bodies of the others. So he was only charged with one count of murder and one count of false imprisonment.'

'The woman I found?'

'She was added to the charge sheet but no others were brought against him.'

Ridpath thought for a moment. 'Why are the Seagrams saying he was with them when their daughter was killed?'

'Because the initial post-mortem stated she died between 4 p.m. and 8 p.m. on 7 March.'

'Initial post-mortem?'

'Two were performed in this case, by the same pathologist, Harold Lardner.'

'That's not so common, is it?'

'It gets worse. The second post-mortem extended the time of death considerably, extending it until midnight on 7 March.'

'I remember now. The judge and jury were shocked at the cold-bloodedness of Dalbey. Going from the family home to torturing and murdering their daughter that same night.'

She brushed a long strand of grey hair behind her ear. 'He was painted as an evil, vicious man by the prosecuting barrister. The defence, on the other hand, was less accomplished at protecting him.'

'But most murders are committed by friends, husbands, lovers or acquaintances of the victim. It's the first place police look.'

'So when you caught Dalbey in the garage and they discovered he knew Alice Seagram and, even worse, he ate a meal with the family on the night she disappeared, they thought they had caught the Beast.'

'But they had. I caught him.'

'The problem was, they had a post-mortem report giving a time of death when he was still in the victim's house.'

Ridpath sighed. 'Times of death are notoriously difficult to pinpoint precisely.'

'Hence a second autopsy. By widening the possible time of death, Dalbey comes into the frame for the murder.'

'Shouldn't they have used a different pathologist?'

She shrugged her elegant shoulders. 'Apparently none was available.'

'So you think the police put pressure on Harold Lardner?'

'I think nothing, Ridpath, and neither must you. Our job is to find out the truth, not chase a conviction. How did Alice Seagram die? When did she die? Did the pathologist act correctly at all times?'

'But by asking those questions, you bring into doubt the police investigation.'

'That's what we've been asked to do by the high court and it's a job *we* will perform to the best of our ability, despite our personal views. Understand?'

The heavy emphasis on the 'we' made it perfectly clear what his answer ought to be.

She sat forward. He was suddenly aware of the energy in the woman and her immense drive. He wouldn't like to get in her way when she wanted something to happen.

'It seems to me we have two jobs. The first, as ordered by the high court, is to reinvestigate the circumstances of the death of Alice Seagram. I've already opened an inquest and postponed it until 7 April. We were to have performed another post-mortem but...' She didn't finish her sentence.

'After ten years, a new post-mortem wouldn't give you any information on time of death.'

'It would have allowed us to check on the work of Harold Lardner, plus, with the scientific advances in testing, we may have been able to find trace elements of DNA which would prove, or disprove, the involvement of James Dalbey in her murder.'

'It would have been a long shot.'

'But it had to be done. And now, with no body, we have nothing. It won't stop us proceeding though. I'll check the details of the post-mortem. In this case, of the two post-mortems. Were the findings evidentially-based? Was the pathologist correct in his conclusions? What was the evidence pointing to James Dalbey as the killer?'

Ridpath raised an eyebrow. 'As a coroner, you are competent to do that?'

'No, I will ask an outside pathologist to examine the reports. But after the Shipman case, I felt it was no longer enough for me to have a law degree to do my job. I added a forensic science degree to my list of qualifications. As a coroner I felt it was my duty to know more about the latest advances.'

His opinion of her had risen another notch.

'If you are so concerned about the original investigation, why don't we get Professional Standards Department involved?'

'And have Manchester Police handling the inquiry into their own investigation? Not likely. As a coroner, I have a wide range of leeway on how I proceed.'

'The police won't like it.'

'Is that speaking as a police officer or as a coroner's officer, Ridpath?'

'Both.'

She frowned. 'The chief constable may appeal to my boss, the chief coroner, but I think I can handle it. And by the time he does, we should have completed our investigations.'

Ridpath frowned. He was desperate for a cigarette. He should have had one before coming in. 'You said I had two jobs?'

'The second is pretty obvious, isn't it? Find the missing body.' A smile like that of a tiger who has just seen a goat tied to a tree crossed her perfectly lip-glossed mouth.

'How long do I have?'

'Until the inquest on the 7th.' She checked the calendar. 'About a week, before the proverbial shit hits the fan.'

'Not long.'

'So what are your next steps?'

'Interview the undertaker first, Mr O'Shaughnessy, and then meet with Tony Seagram. According to the family, he was the one who organized the funeral.'

'Be careful there. Not a pleasant man. After the interviews?'

Ridpath thought for a moment. 'Depends what happens. I'll definitely check the mortuary records. The body will have been placed in there until it was released to the family. There must be a trail of paper. Either the body was placed in the coffin and then removed, or it never found its way into the coffin.'

'There's one other thing you should do.'

'What's that?'

'Read the original police file on the Dalbey case.'

'Have you already requested it from the chief constable?'

'I have… but he's dragging his feet.' She looked straight at him. 'Could you get the file?'

'Might be difficult.'

'But you know somebody who could do it?'

He thought for a moment. The keen, blushing face of DS Sarah Castle popped into his head. She could get the file easily, especially as she was supposed to be checking the MO of her recent case against that of James Dalbey. 'I do know someone,' he finally answered, 'but as the coroner looking into one of the murders, they must eventually send it to you.'

Again the smile of the tiger. This time with its teeth buried in the neck of the goat. 'I will get it… eventually, but I would then be reading what the chief constable wanted me to see…'

He finished her sentence: '…rather than what you want to find out.'

'And what they remove from the file will be far more interesting than what they leave in.'

Ridpath sat back in his chair. 'You are a devious woman, Mrs Challinor.'

'Unfortunately, thanks to years of experience working with your colleagues.' She tucked her hair behind her ear. 'You know, my father, a barrister of the old school, always used to tell me a good police force was one that caught more criminals than they employed.'

'A cynical attitude, Mrs Challinor.'

'Oh, he was a cynical old bastard, a man who'd seen far too much and forgotten far too little. He wasn't far wrong though.'

Ridpath stared at her. If his bosses ever found out he was talking like this, he would be looking after the toilets in Cheetham Hill nick for the rest of his career.

And then another thought struck him. Why was she telling him all this?

Chapter Nineteen

When Ridpath finally arrived home, the house was in darkness. He found Polly sitting alone in the living room, television off.

'Where's Eve?'

'Asleep. It's a school night.' The answer was monotone.

'Why are you sitting in the dark?' He switched on the light. In the bright yellow glare, he saw her flinch and turn away from him. 'Turn it off.'

'What's wrong?'

She turned back towards him. He could see her eyes were red. 'You promised this wasn't going to happen again.'

He stood there, transfixed.

'It's nearly ten o'clock. No phone call. Nothing.'

'I was in meetings,' he answered weakly.

'Meetings? You were supposed to be home at six. A less stressful job, you said. Regular hours, you said. An easier life, you said. IT'S THE FIRST BLOODY DAY!'

'You're upset...'

'No shit, Sherlock.'

'Look, it's a difficult case...'

'I thought you were a coroner's officer, not in the CID.'

'They still have cases. It'll get easier when I learn the ropes. I promise.'

'I can't take much more of this, Ridpath. You've just had nine months off work. You were diagnosed with myeloma, for Christ's sake. You have to take it easy until your body builds up strength again.'

He knelt down in front of her and wrapped her in his arms, feeling her resist for a few seconds before finally succumbing and melting into his body. 'You know what it's like for the first few days. Getting up to speed, learning the ropes, working on new cases. It's only to be expected.' He pulled back and looked into her wet eyes. 'At least I'm not running around Manchester chasing after nutters like I used to.'

She laughed. 'I remember the time you came home with two black eyes, like a bloody panda.'

He laughed too at the memory. 'Tiny Tim was his name. Six foot six of steroid-grown muscle, off his head on special K. Took four of us to hold him down. Bob Trenton broke his knuckles on Tiny's nose.' Ridpath smiled at the memory. 'Wrote a lovely apology letter to each of us, did Tiny.' A pause. 'I'm sorry, love. I'll try to sort it out. Promise.'

He pulled her back to him, feeling the warmth of her body.

She pushed herself away. 'You've been smoking too, I can smell it.'

'Just one or two.'

'The doctor said you can't smoke.'

'Actually, he said "You should try to give up smoking." I'm trying. It's not easy.'

She stood up, pushing him away. 'You're an unfeeling selfish shit, Tom Ridpath… who couldn't give a toss about his wife or child, only caring about the next case or the next collar. You make me sick.'

She pushed him away again and stormed out of the room. He listened as her feet stomped up the stairs and waited for the ritual slam of the bedroom door.

It didn't happen.

Even when she was pissed off with him, she would never wake Eve up.

She had a point though. It was pretty stupid still smoking his Marlboro Reds, having just recovered from cancer. Not the smartest move, Ridpath.

He went over to the drinks cabinet and poured himself a single shot of Laphroaig, changing it into a treble as he poured. He sipped the pale, straw-coloured liquid, tasting the smoke and the peat and the sea spray off Islay, followed by a honeyed bitterness as it slipped warmly down his throat.

Inevitably, his mind drifted back to the case. Had John Gorman put pressure on the pathologist? Had the police case been rigged against James Dalbey?

He drifted back to the time in the garage lock-up. Saw the whitewashed brick walls covered in rust-coloured bloodstains. The girl hanging from the manacles on the wall, her beaten face and body a mass of bruises and blood. And his hands, sticking to the floor as he touched it, seeing the red globules smeared on his fingers

The place was a charnel house. James Dalbey had the key.

He had to be guilty.

Didn't he?

Chapter Twenty

The following morning, Ridpath was up with the larks, making a breakfast of honey nut crunch for an uncommunicative, sleepy, tousle-haired daughter and tea and toast for his wife, delivered in bed.

'You're still on the naughty step,' she said, chewing on the toast.

'I'll try and take it easier, but you know what it's like on a case. You get wrapped up in the whole momentum of it.'

'I don't get wrapped up in anything except worry for you. I don't think you know when to stop.'

'I'll take it easier, promise.'

'We'll see.' He got up to leave her bedside. 'And don't forget, Eve has her school concert tomorrow night. She wants you to be there.'

'Is Eve the silent girl sitting in our kitchen eating cereal?'

'That's her. She's not a morning person.'

'Or an afternoon or evening person by the look of it.'

'She just takes a while to get started.'

'Maybe I should put antifreeze instead of milk on her cereal?'

'Tried that. Doesn't work.' She glanced at the bedroom clock. 'Oh shit, is that the time?'

Ten minutes later, Ridpath finally managed to usher both wife and daughter out of the house and into the car for school. His daughter managed a mumbled 'Goodbye, Dad' before parking herself in the rear seat and staring zombie-eyed out of the window.

A quick kiss and a farewell of 'Don't forget to wrap up well' from his wife and she was off in a cloud of fumes from the exhaust pipe of the car. He would have to take it into the garage when he had time.

The morning was one of those clear, eggshell-blue spring days with the leaves just forming on the trees and enough bite in the air to freshen the cheeks and the tips of the ears.

A beautiful day to spend looking for a missing body.

He drove out to Stockfield along the clogged mess of the M60, roadworks slowing the traffic to a crawl, but at least it was still moving. Like a snail on sleeping tablets, but still moving.

The parking machines took the last of his change and he strode past the empty reception desk into the coroner's office. He could see Margaret Challinor was already behind her desk. Didn't the woman ever go home? But there was still no sight of the elusive office manager. Did she exist or was she merely a figment of the collective imagination?

He sat down at his designated desk and went to turn on the computer, seeing a note on the screen. 'Will give you a password when I see you.'

'Should be sometime around 2025 the rate we're going,' he said out aloud.

'Actually it will be around 9.26 according to the clock.'

He turned round to see the person behind the voice. She was roundish and short, as if somebody had pressed down on her head and she had expanded sideways, wearing an extremely short dress exposing an expanse of white thigh and dimpled knees.

'You must be the elusive Jenny Oldfield.'

'One and the same. But I prefer to think of myself as the *exclusive* Jenny Oldfield.'

Her make-up was thick, as if laid on by a brickie on his day off, highlighted by bright-purple eye shadow and matching lips. Ridpath stuck out his hand. 'Pleased to meet you, Jenny.'

She looked him up and down. 'So you're Tom Ridpath? Carol didn't say how handsome you were.'

He blushed, not answering. There wasn't a lot he could say.

She handed him a tiny square of paper. 'The password. The council suggests you eat the paper after you've memorized it. I always add a spot of salt and pepper to aid the digestion.'

He looked down at the machine-printed and sealed paper.

'I was just joking about eating it. But you dispose of it safely somewhere. Mrs Challinor is a stickler for security.'

He nodded.

'Don't say much, do you? I like that in a man. Now let me take you through the logging-on procedures and then I'll show you where everything is kept.'

She spent the next half-hour giving him a tour of the office, before finally leaving him alone at ten with a cheery 'If you need anything just shout.' With a wave of her beringed, dimpled fingers she was gone, leaving behind a vast emptiness where she had once stood.

Time to get to work.

He googled all the local undertakers, finding O'Shaughnessy listed in bold type as 'a purveyor of services to the bereaved since 1968'. He rang the number and a young voice with a strong Irish accent answered.

'O'Shaughnessy's.'

'Could I speak to Mr O'Shaughnessy, please?'

'I'm afraid he's not available. Perhaps I could help?' The voice was fresh and sparkling, the exact opposite of Albert Ronson.

'I would like to speak to Mr O'Shaughnessy himself.'

'I'm afraid he's not here, but if it's bereavement services you're looking for, I'm your man.'

'It's Mr O'Shaughnessy I'm looking for.'

'I'm sorry – as I said, he's not in the office. My name is Padraig Daly, perhaps I could help?'

'I'm ringing from the Coroner's Office, Mr Daly. We'd like to speak to Mr O'Shaughnessy about a funeral he organized in 2008.'

'I'm afraid that would be a wee bit difficult, as Mr O'Shaughnessy availed himself of our services five years ago.'

'You mean he's dead?'

'We prefer to use the word deceased, Mr...?'

'Ridpath, Detective Inspector Ridpath.'

'Unfortunately, Mr O'Shaughnessy passed away after a tragic accident.'

Chapter Twenty-One

The undertaker's was situated in an imposing detached building set back from the road in the suburb of Northenden, not far from where the Seagrams lived in Didsbury, but a quite different kind of area.

Northenden was on the other side of the Mersey; streets of Victorian terraces huddled around an ancient church dating from Norman times. It retained its unique character sandwiched between the middle-class enclave of Didsbury and Europe's biggest council estate in Wythenshawe. So far it had escaped the creeping gentrification of Manchester: old-fashioned chippies sat next to tiled pubs, fruit and vegetable merchants ranged alongside local butchers. No Starbucks, no wine merchants and definitely no artisan bakers. The only corner of modernity was an art deco cinema converted into a Jehovah's Witness temple.

Ridpath parked beneath a sign saying 'O'Shaughnessy. Funeral Directors.' Immediately, the image of Cecil B. DeMille in an undertaker's frock coat flashed through his mind, shouting, 'I want more tears. Gif me more tears.'

Padraig Daly was waiting for him in the reception area, standing next to a huge spray of flowers. On closer inspection, Ridpath realized they were plastic.

The man was dressed in an argyle jumper, tartan trousers and a pair of Nikes, as if he had just come from the golf course. He led Ridpath through to an elegantly decorated conference room, complete with flat-screen TV on the wall and a fake walnut centre table.

'How can I help you, Mr Ridpath?' he asked as soon as they had both sat down.

'You said Mr O'Shaughnessy had passed away.'

'That's correct. Five years ago. A sad story.'

Ridpath raised an eyebrow and kept silent, waiting for Mr Daly to continue.

'An accident. A tragic accident, but we all have to go sometime, Mr Ridpath. The only thing is we don't know when. God's funniest joke on us all. Ah, but it keeps the wife in handbags and myself on the links, so I'm not a man to complain.'

The conversation was making Ridpath feel uncomfortable. After his brush with his own mortality, it was the last thing he wanted to hear about. Time to bring the conversation back onto safer ground.

'You said he had an accident?'

'A fire at the bungalow. Apparently, he fell asleep on the couch with a cigarette in his hand. In his retirement he liked a wee dram, I heard. Don't we all? Body was burnt to a cinder, unrecognizable. Not a nice way to go.'

Ridpath looked around him. The O'Shaughnessy name was everywhere: on coasters, etched into the side of water glasses, displayed in a brass plaque on the wall.

'We kept the name when we bought the business in 2009. My dad wasn't an egotistical man, and Mr O'Shaughnessy had built up a good following, particularly amongst the Irish in south Manchester. It made sense to continue as it was.'

'Under new management but with an old name?'

'Exactly. As my dad always says, "There's a good living in dying." We're never going to be short of customers and it's not going out of fashion. It's a recession-proof business. And between you and me, you're not going to skimp on a bob or two when you're laying a relative to rest.' He laughed to himself. 'We don't have to do one of the "two for one" offers or "buy one, get one free" you'll see down the local supermarket. High turnover, high profit margins, with an endless stream of customers. We did the analysis and it seemed to be the perfect investment business.'

'You weren't an undertaker all your life?'

He laughed. 'Not at all. My dad and I ran a chain of shoe stores. We bought the business off Mr O'Shaughnessy in 2009 and he stayed on for a year to show us the ropes before retiring.'

'Why do you think he retired?'

Daly shrugged his shoulders. 'I don't know. He wasn't an old man – just 55, I think. Maybe he was sick of death and dying? He'd been in the business as a man and boy and never married. The classic old-school undertaker.' Daly pulled his fleshy bottom lip forward between his fingertips. 'A meticulous man. His accounts were correct to the last penny when we examined them. We couldn't believe our good fortune. The business was a steal at what we paid for it. And, with the changes we made to the operation to reduce costs, it's been a little gold mine ever since.'

Ridpath picked up a hint of something. 'You said he was a meticulous man?'

'The accounts were the best we'd ever seen. Too good to be true, almost. Plus he kept a detailed record of every funeral he ever organized.'

Bingo. There it was. 'Could I see those records?'

'I don't see why not. Each year he opened a new book. The diaries of death, we call them. We don't do it any more, though. Which year would you like to see? It starts in 1981.'

'Show me 2008, please.'

'Give me a sec, I'll dig them out for you. My dad wanted to throw them out last year, but I hung on to them. Gives the place an authenticity – a heritage, if you like. I was going to display them in the lobby, but it didn't fit in with the brand image we wanted to portray. Would you like a guided tour? We've modernized all the operations and brought in the latest embalming machines from Porti-Boy. You know, magnetic driven pumps, precision valves and switches, digital read-outs.

The latest gear basically, allowing the embalmer to match their style to the needs of the customer.'

'I think I'll pass. Thank you.'

Ridpath could see Mr Daly was disappointed in his lack of interest in the latest technology. The undertaker left the conference room, shouting loudly for a Miss Hargreaves.

Ridpath was left on his own. All this talk of death was unnerving him. He didn't want to think about these sorts of places. One day somebody would have to do it all for him. Until then, the less he knew about the process, the better.

He remembered when he was told he had cancer. For a few months, pains in his back and chest had been bothering him. Even worse, they kept moving around as if something was inside his body, poking here and there. He'd visited the GP a few times but nothing had been diagnosed. He thought it was just stress from the job: the antisocial hours, eating badly, running all over Manchester chasing cons. He even tried a course of acupuncture at some quack Polly's mother recommended.

'He very good, trained in China.'

After two weeks of being stuck with more needles than a pin cushion he felt no better.

At the time he was in the middle of a major investigation, his first time in charge since his promotion. He had been feeling tired and achy for a month with a cough that just wouldn't go away despite drinking gallons of Boots' magic mixture. He thought he was just a little run-down from the pressure of being in charge. He so wanted to prove himself to John Gorman and Charlie Whitworth, repay their faith in him.

Finally, Polly had threatened him with divorce if he didn't go to see a specialist. Of course, because he had a cough, they sent him to a thoracic consultant. He went, reluctantly, patiently explaining how busy he was at the moment and could he have some antibiotics to kill the cough. The consultant, a woman, had listened quietly, asking simple questions.

'How long have you had the cough?'

'About four weeks?'

'Any other aches and pains?'

He told her of his tiredness and general fatigue, and of the ache in his bones, like he had forgotten something.

'Sore throat?'

'A little, but I have been speaking a lot recently.' He showed her his Strepsils.

'Any weight loss?'

He looked at the waistband of his trousers. It had been loose recently, but he thought it was because he had been eating so irregularly. The bastards who had been importing the crack were constantly on the move, changing houses every other day. He had to keep up with them.

She had finally put her pen down. 'I'm booking you in for an MRI scan tomorrow.'

'So quick?'

'No time to waste, Mr Ridpath.'

Of course, the MRI picked up the damage to his bones straight away.

The consultant was firm. 'I'll give you a course of antibiotics, Mr Ridpath, to help clear up the cough, but I think you should go to see another specialist to look into the underlying causes of your tiredness and weight loss, and to examine these results.' She pointed to the MRI scan.

'It's just the job. I'll be fine once this case is in the bag.'

'I would advise you to see a specialist at Christie's.'

The name of the famous hospital immediately hit home. 'You think I have cancer?'

The doctor looked straight at him. 'I'm not sure, Mr Ridpath, but I think we need to check out the symptoms, don't you? If it is a cancer and it is malignant, it would be much better if we catch it early.'

He hated the 'we'.

We didn't have cancer, *he* did.

'I'd like to think about it.'

'My advice is to check it out. I think we can get you an appointment with a specialist in a week.'

He stood up. 'Maybe, after the case is completed.' He held out his hand. 'Thank you, doctor.'

The pain struck that evening. He was just debriefing the team. They were going in mob-handed the following morning to raid one of the premises of the gang. With a bit of luck, they would get the money and the drugs and the whole bloody lot of them. He was just going through the operational directions when he felt a stabbing pain shoot up through his chest. He stopped talking and sat down immediately.

Harry Makepeace was by his side. 'You OK, boss?'

He nodded his head and tried to carry on speaking, but the pain intensified, coming in waves. He asked Harry to take over and finish for him, while he sat on a chair holding his side.

'You're not looking great, boss – white as the National Front.'

'I'll be all right, Harry. Just need a good night's sleep. See you here at six tomorrow?'

'You sure, boss?'

'Of course I'm bloody sure,' he snapped, instantly regretting his show of temper. 'See you tomorrow morning, Harry.'

Of course he had gone home and not said a word to Polly, holding the pain inside. But sleep was difficult, lying horizontal only making it worse. Eventually he found the only comfortable position was sitting upright in bed, the pillows supporting his back.

'What's wrong?' ask Polly sleepily.

'Nothing, go back to sleep.'

'What's wrong?'

'Nothing. Just an ache. It's nothing.'

She was instantly awake, propping herself up on her elbow. 'I know something's wrong. Tell me.'

It was time to own up. 'I went to the doctor. They've booked me in to see a specialist at Christie's.'

She sat up. 'Christie's, oh God, no.'

He raised his arms painfully to quieten her. 'Don't worry, Poll, it's just the doctor covering her arse. You know, they book everyone in to see specialists these days.'

'What did she say, Thomas Ridpath?'

There it was, his full name in all its Victorian splendour. Under her forensic questioning he was forced to tell her everything: the pains, the coughing, the aches, the sudden chills and the immense sense of weariness suffusing his body.

'Right, you're calling in sick tomorrow.'

'But, the case, we're so close—'

'The case can bloody wait. There'll always be another case, Manchester's never going to be short of chuffin' criminals: they breed them on every street. But Eve isn't going to be short of a dad, nor me of a husband. I'm going to ring the doctor tomorrow and get you an appointment as quick as we can.'

She was as good as her word. The consultant confirmed the diagnosis of myeloma and his body was soon being emptied of blood by a nurse who didn't look like a vampire but who certainly enjoyed her profession.

'Just another vial, Mr Ridpath. Can't have too much blood for our tests.'

Oh yes, you can, he thought, but kept his mouth shut.

Daly interrupted his memories by bustling in through the door carrying a simple black book under his arm. On the cover, '2008' was embossed in gold against the black leather. 'Now which month would you be wanting?'

Daly flicked open the book. Each separate page contained a date, time of funeral, name of the deceased, name of the chief mourners, time and place of the service, time and place of the burial, number of mourners, number of cars, make and model of the casket, and finally the instructions for the burial. Next to some of the names were symbols in bright red ink: a downward arrow, an upward arrow and a Maltese cross. They must be some arcane undertakers' code, he thought.

Ridpath glanced across at a few of the instructions for burial:

> The deceased to be dressed in a floral yellow dress with a picture of the grandchildren next to her.

> The deceased to be buried with a book of common prayer.

> The deceased to have an open coffin in the church. Canon Birch to deliver the memorial words beside the grave.

These were the wishes of the dying to be carried out by the living.

During his illness, just after he'd started chemo when he felt like death warmed up, Ridpath had left the same kind of instructions: his favourite Bowie song, 'Starman', to be played as his body entered the church. Then, a non-requiem mass with the lesson read by his wife. Even though he was not a religious man, he had chosen John 14:27 as a message to her: 'Peace I leave with you; my peace I give you. I do not give to you as the world gives. Do not let your hearts be troubled and do not be afraid.'

As he left the church in his coffin, Ewan MacColl's 'The Joy of Living' to be played through the speakers. Shame he wouldn't be able to hear the Salford Scot's voice.

It had been one of the darkest days in his whole life. The day he planned his own funeral.

'What date would you like?' asked Padraig Daly.

The undertaker's voice dragged him back to the present. Ridpath tried to remember what Mrs Seagram had told him. 'March 21st, I think. The deceased was called Alice Seagram.' He was even talking like them now.

Daly flicked though the pristine pages of the book. January, February, March – so many deaths, so many burials.

18 March: one burial, one downward arrow.

19 March: two burials.

20 March: one burial, one upward arrow.

23 March: three burials, one with a downward arrow.

24 March: one burial.

25 March: one burial.

Daly flicked back through the pages. 'It doesn't look like there were any interments on that day. Are you sure you have the right date?'

Ridpath checked through his notes. March 21st, Alice Seagram buried at Stretford Cemetery. O'Shaughnessy, undertaker. 'It's the right date.'

Daly flicked through the pages again, more slowly this time, checking each individual page and continuing on until the end of the month. 'Nothing, I'm afraid. Are you sure O'Shaughnessy was the funeral director?'

'Can I take a look at the book?'

Daly handed it over.

Ridpath went through each individual entry. Nothing for an Alice Seagram.

He was about to close the book when his finger caught on a torn edge in the gutter of the entry for 20 March. He picked it up and opened it as wide as he could, holding it up to his nose so he could look down the crease between the pages.

There it was. The faintest suggestion of an edge hidden in the binding. He found the opposite page on 10 May and checked it out. The page had been cut with something sharp – a scalpel perhaps.

Two days were missing.

March 21st and 22nd.

One of them just happened to be the day Alice Seagram was buried.

Chapter Twenty-Two

Sarah Castle took a long swig from the coffee on her table and immediately wished she hadn't. It was bitter, cold and tasted like somebody had pissed in it.

Perhaps somebody had pissed in it.

She looked over her shoulder. None of the other officers was looking at her and none sniggering like schoolboys behind their hands.

She exhaled and let her shoulders relax. You're getting paranoid. Sarah, the bastards are starting to get to you.

It was only to be expected. She was one of the fast-track people: detective sergeant in only four years, slated for promotion to inspector three years from now after time spent at the police training school in Hendon. All she had to do was keep her nose clean and she would enjoy a rise like a rocket on bonfire night.

It helped having the deputy chief take an interest in you personally. Totally professional, of course, but she couldn't help notice him staring at her open blouse in the interview. Stupid tosser. Five minutes online would have told him she wasn't interested in men. Or dogs.

The investigation still hadn't discovered the name of the victim. It should have been easy with such a distinctive tattoo, but last year there were 100,000 incidents of missing women in England. And those were only the cases reported. There must be countless others where a disappearance went unreported; when there were no living relatives, people no longer talking to each other, no close friends or simply nobody who actually cared.

All around her the other detectives had been chasing up leads, out on the streets knocking on doors or following up with other forces. She had just one job to do: call Belmarsh HSU and ask after James Dalbey. But she'd been putting it off since she returned from the graveyard.

She had spent the morning there, closing up the grave of Alice Seagram after the forensics team had finished. By the time she had arrived, the gravediggers, who dressed and talked like some throwbacks to the English Civil War, had already begun.

'You should have waited for me to get here.'

The older one stopped shovelling the earth back into the grave for a moment, resting his foot with its new boot on the spade. 'Got a double to do before noon. Mother and daughter killed in a car crash. Don't know what the world's coming to. Cemetery will be full soon at this rate.'

He resumed digging. The younger gravedigger had never stopped, shovelling earth with all the regularity of a human metronome. Within half an hour they were finished. The only evidence of an opened grave was the mound of fresh black earth.

The undertakers' men came later to pull down the blue tarpaulins and take them away.

When they had finished, she stood next to the grave. She wasn't at all religious but it felt right to have a moment of silence. In the quiet, she heard a blackbird singing from the yew tree. Was it the same one as yesterday?

Probably. Even in this place of death, life carried on. A shudder went down her spine. She didn't like graveyards. Too many dead people.

One last check of the site and she left to return to the station, only the blackbird calling her to stay.

After a quick lunch at her desk – cheese and tomato sandwich on white bread – she started her breeze block research for Ridpath.

Despite all the modern advances in police detection, she still used Google when she wanted to find stuff. With police resources so stretched, she might get an answer to a query in five days if she was lucky. With Google she had her answer in 0.18456333 seconds recurring.

A bit slow today.

She stared at the image on her screen. It looked exactly like the three breeze blocks they found in the coffin. Or casket. Or whatever they called them these days. The breeze blocks had a name, Cloverleaf, a design popular in the sixties and early seventies, but hardly manufactured any more. Who would have used them in 2008? Were they freshly made? Or were they left over from some building site? They might have a maker's mark on them. She would ask the forensics team to take a look when she went to the lab this afternoon with Ridpath.

Time for a break. She wandered over to Harry Makepeace's corner and sat on his desk. 'Something's been bothering me, Harry.'

'There's a cream for it from Boots.'

Makepeace was being his usual droll self. 'You know I was working with Tom Ridpath over at Stretford Cemetery?'

'What about it?' he said without looking up from his computer.

'Well, what's his story?'

Makepeace looked over his shoulder twice. 'Ridpath? He was one of the guv'nor's blue-eyed boys...' he whispered.

'Was?' She found herself leaning closer to him as he spoke.

'Blotted his copy book last year during an investigation. Collapsed, didn't he? The guv'nor put it about it was cancer, but I know better.' He touched the side of his nose. 'Reckon it was a nervous breakdown. Couldn't handle the stress of being a DI, could he? Gorman had somehow wangled it to give him time off on sick leave for nine months.'

Ridpath didn't look like someone who would buckle under pressure – exactly the opposite. From what she saw yesterday, he loved it, thrived on it even more than she did. Some people crumble; she was one of those who sucked it up and asked for more. Tom Ridpath seemed exactly the same type.

She caught Makepeace looking down her blouse as he spoke to her. She sat up straight. 'Thanks, Harry, but cancer is not one of those things you use as an excuse.'

He shrugged his shoulders. 'Whatever. Still think Ridpath's not up to the job. That's why they've put him out to grass as a coroner's officer.'

She got up from the DI's desk and wandered back to her own. Makepeace was an idiot. Everybody knew around the station.

She checked the clock on the wall. Like everything in headquarters it was running five minutes late. She couldn't put it off any more.

'Come on, get it over and done with. Procrastination is your middle name, Sarah,' she said out loud, geeing herself up.

'I thought it was Emily?'

This was from Alan Butcher on the computer opposite. Smart-arse.

She ignored him.

Time to ring Belmarsh. The phone was answered after three rings by an operator and she was transferred to a deputy governor.

'HMP Belmarsh, Reynolds speaking.'

She coughed once to clear her throat. 'Hello, Mr Reynolds, this is DS Sarah Castle from Greater Manchester Police. I just wonder if you could tell me about James Dal—'

'Who are you?' he interrupted.

'DS Sarah Castle from Greater Manchester Police and I'd like to find out about James Dalbey.'

'How do I know that?'

'I'm sorry?'

'How do I know you are DS Sarah Castle? You could be anybody.'

She had a right one here. A jobsworth. 'I'm ringing from Greater Manchester Police HQ.'

'Perhaps you are, I don't know.' Then there was a pause at the other end. 'Listen, DS Castle, I don't want to mess you about, but since the high court decision to exhume Dalbey's victim, I get 20 phone calls a day pretending to be from police officers or probation officers or his solicitors, and this morning I had a call from his wife, even though I know he's never been married.'

'Point taken. Why don't you call me back, going through our switchboard? That way you can verify my identity.'

'Number?'

This man had all the grace of an elephant and, for a moment, she wondered if his arse was as big.

'Number,' he repeated.

She gave it to him, put down the phone and waited. And waited. And waited.

Just as she was about to call him back, the phone on her desk rang.

'It seems you are who you say you are, DS Castle.' No apology. No 'I'm sorry for doubting your word'. No nothing. The image of an elephant sitting behind a desk at HMP Belmarsh came into her mind again.

'I'm a busy man, how can I help you?'

She straightened up, trying to banish the image from her mind. 'I'm enquiring about James Dalbey?'

'You've already said that.'

This man was a pain. 'And you haven't answered me yet,' she said sharply.

There was a pause on the other end of the line. 'Prisoner Dalbey is working in the library as usual. He is a quiet, self-reliant prisoner who gives us no trouble.'

'You have seen him yourself?'

'Of course not. But that's where he always is at this time of the day.'

'Thank you, Mr Reynolds – that's all I wanted to know.'

'Stupid question, if you ask me. A waste of my time.'

'Just following orders.'

The voice much softer now, almost world-weary. 'I understand.'

At last, sympathy for a fellow jobsworth. 'Thank you for your time, Mr Reynolds.'

She put the phone down before he could reply, quickly scribbled a note for the boss and left it on his door

She grabbed her jacket and scarf, swallowing the last of her cold coffee. With a bit of luck and no traffic she should be able to get to the lab with plenty of time to spare.

Oh, the joys of being a copper, running on adrenalin and caffeine, while trying to make the world a better place for Joe Public. She recognized she was an idealist but she didn't care. It was why she'd joined up in the first place from university. All her mates thought she was crazy, but she wanted to make a difference and she wasn't going to do that by being some product manager for Procter & Gamble.

'You look like you're going out.'

It was that fuckwit, Makepeace. 'I am.'

'Where to?'

Why was he so nosy all of a sudden? 'Just out. Got something to do for the guv'nor.'

She stepped around his slow-moving body.

'When you coming back?

She waved goodbye without looking over her shoulder. She wasn't going to tell Makepeace where she was going, not in a million years.

Chapter Twenty-Three

He was sitting at a table, staring at his mobile phone. 'You've got five minutes,' said Tony Seagram without looking up.

They were meeting in a Costa Coffee at the bottom of the Media City block. Ridpath had rushed over because it was the only time Tony Seagram was available.

This area was the centre of media operations in the north: a barren windswept desert of concrete and glass towers on the site of the demolished Salford Docks. The place was as bland and characterless as the people in the new buildings. As if to underline the shoddy nature of the place, even the shopping mall nearby, where he had parked, specialized in outlet stores.

Ridpath pulled out a chair and sat down.

Tony Seagram continued to stare at his phone.

'My name is Tom Ridpath, and I'm—'

'I know who you are, you told me on the phone. What I want to know is what you are doing to find the body of my sister.'

Ridpath coughed. 'Yesterday morning, we—'

He looked up at Ridpath for the first time, blue eyes staring from beneath hooded lids. 'I know all about yesterday morning. What I want to know is what you are doing about it today.' The voice became angrier, with a stress on the last word.

Ridpath licked his lips. This was going to be more difficult than he expected. 'If you let me finish, Mr Seagram, I was about to explain we are presently looking for the whereabouts of your sister's body and we are following up various lines of inquiry.'

'In other words, you haven't got a clue.'

Ridpath decided to ignore the jibe. 'I need your help, Mr Seagram. What do you remember of the day of your sister's funeral?'

'Not a lot.'

'Why?'

'I didn't go.'

'But I was told you organized it...'

'I did, but at the last minute I couldn't face the crying faces and the sadness and the hypocrisy. All those idiots mouthing their platitudes over someone who nobody knew.' He sat up and pointed his finger. 'Only I knew my sister. Only me. Not those hangers-on. You know what we call them? Media junkies. The women with their handkerchiefs pressed to their faces, tears running down their cheeks, waiting for a press photographer to spot them and take a photo. It's a circus. Just a fucking circus.'

'But don't you work in the same business?'

'I work in real journalism. Investigative journalism. How dare you compare me to the ambulance chasers of the *Sun* and the *Daily Mail* and all the rest of the tabloids. You saw the reports after the Manchester bombing: reporters pretending to be bereavement nurses, tins of biscuits given to hospital staff with two thousand quid inside asking for information. Scum, the lot of them.'

'I can't defend their actions—'

'And you lot tipping them off. You know the first pictures of James Dalbey were from inside the police station? Some copper had taken a picture of the Beast of Manchester and sold it to the *Sun*. Never mind that he was innocent.'

'He was guilty, Mr Seagram. He was found with a key to a lock-up where a young woman was manacled to a wall.'

'It was a set-up. James wouldn't hurt a butterfly. He was a gentle soul.' For the first time, a trace of humanity appeared on Tony Seagram's face.

'How can you be so sure?'

He jabbed himself in his chest. 'Because I introduced him to my family and my sister. He loved my sister, and would never harm a hair on her head.'

'It still doesn't change the evidence. He was found with the key to the lock-up. Your sister's DNA was all over his clothes, a hammer with her DNA on it was found in the van he was driving and the blood of at least four other victims was found at the lock-up.'

'Look, evidence can be faked. James was with us when my sister died.'

'Not according to the second post-mortem.'

'The one the police arranged when the timings from the first didn't fit their theory? And what happened to the bodies of the other women The Beast was supposed to have murdered?'

'They were never found. We conducted extensive searches but Dalbey never told us.'

A pause as Tony Seagram stared directly at Ridpath. 'What rank are you, Mr Coroner's Officer?'

Ridpath was taken aback by the sudden change in direction of the conversation. 'Detective Inspector,' he said quietly.

'In the Greater Manchester force?'

Ridpath nodded.

Tony Seagram pushed back his chair. 'Time's up, Detective Inspector Ridpath. Five minutes are gone.' He leant forward on the table, his face just a foot from Ridpath's. 'Let me tell you this. I'm not giving up until James Dalbey is out of jail and somebody from Manchester Police is sitting in his cell. Do I make myself clear, Detective Inspector? And I've got a great narrative. Brother of victim wants killer released. Imagine the power of that tabloid headline.'

'It seems, Mr Seagram, that although you hate the press, you're not above using it to achieve your goals.'

'I don't hate the press. I hate the police.'

And with that parting message, he turned and left the cafe.

'Join the queue,' said Ridpath to his departing back.

Chapter Twenty-Four

She was waiting for Ridpath in the lobby when he arrived carrying two paper cups of coffee.

'I got you a latte – hope it's what you drink.'

She took the coffee. 'You're a lifesaver.'

'I needed it. Just had a meeting with Tony Seagram. Spent ten minutes fighting with myself over whether to have a cigarette. The cigarette nearly won. Decided a latte might be the lesser of two evils. Although having tasted it, I'm not so sure.'

'Giving up fags is one of the hardest things to do.'

'You used to smoke?'

She shook her head. 'Never got the taste for them. Had one when I was 15 in the school bike sheds and was as sick as a dog. Never touched them again.'

'Lucky you. Satan's coffin nails.'

'Talking of coffins… Protheroe will call us up in a minute. He's just getting his ducks in a row.'

As if hearing his name, Protheroe appeared in front of them. 'You can come through now.' He beckoned with his index finger as if they were guilty children who had been caught stealing apples.

They walked through a quiet and expensively decorated office. Workstations with the latest computers, chairs that actually worked and a carpet free of coffee stains.

This was one of those companies newly set up by private investors to profit from the outsourcing of police services. Never mind the loss of expertise and experience of an internal forensics lab as well as the benefit of quality control. In the new orthodoxy, even the investigation of murder should be governed by market forces.

Beyond the office, they were shown into a spacious, well-lit lab. This was the other side of the coin. In the expectation of large profits, the labs were kitted out with the latest equipment; each time it was used another bill went to Her Majesty's Government.

The coffin stood in an isolation area behind a glass wall.

'Right, let's get started, shall we? Do you want the top line or the full bells and whistles?'

'Top line will be enough.'

'Thought so – the science bits can be a bit overwhelming even for those who have done a course in forensics for a couple of weeks at university.' He looked archly at DS Castle over the top of his tortoiseshell glasses. 'The top line is: no fingerprints on the inside of the coffin. No fingerprints on the breeze blocks. No presence of any epithelial cells on the lining or the pillow of the coffin. No presence of blood anywhere. No trace of any hair or any DNA. And the soil on your brogues? Manchester's finest, great for the roses.'

'So what you're telling us is… you found nothing?'

'Exactly.'

Sarah Castle coughed before she spoke. 'The body was never in the coffin?'

'Exactly. This coffin is as pristine as the day it was made.'

'Nothing at all?'

'Nada. Zilch. Not a sausage. Bugger all, if you'll excuse my French.'

'Any maker's mark on the breeze blocks?'

'None that I could see. Common or garden building materials.'

'So what happened to the body?'

'That's for you to find out, detectives. I'm not in a position to speculate, nor am I paid to do so.' He held up a thick index finger. 'I will tell you one thing though. Alice Seagram's body never lay in this coffin.'

Chapter Twenty-Five

Ridpath had succumbed to the lure of the cigarette. As he lit his first Marlboro of the day and inhaled, he felt the smoke surge down into his lungs. Acrid, bitter smoke tinged with shame and regret.

He immediately stubbed it out against the side of a white plastic planter and threw it into the damp soil where it lay next to a dirty crisp packet and thousands of other beige tips.

'What are we going to do next?'

Sarah Castle was standing next to him. He noticed the 'we' in the question. 'Buggered if I know.'

There was silence between them. Not the comfortable silence of old friends but the uncomfortable knowledge that neither of them knew what to say.

He made conversation. 'How's the investigation going?'

'Investigation?'

'Into the murder of the girl with the swan tattoo?'

She stared at him. 'I forgot you were at the briefing. Not good. Still haven't discovered her identity. The post-mortem is tomorrow.'

'They're slow.'

'Backed up, according to the pathologist. The boss is pulling his hair out.'

'He didn't have much to begin with.'

'He's got less now.'

'Where are you parked?'

'Down the road on the right.'

'Same place as me.'

They began walking down the main road to their cars. Traffic hurried past. At a pub opposite, young drinkers, some no older than 15, were spilling out of the doors to enjoy the late evening sunlight.

It was Sarah who spoke first. 'I followed up on the breeze blocks. They're a pattern called Cloverleaf. Not manufactured any more, popular in the sixties and seventies, retro according to Google.'

'Could we track them down?'

'Impossible, I think. They're available on eBay and other sites. But whoever put them in the coffin may have just found them lying around, left over from some building or stored away somewhere. As Protheroe said, common or garden back then, just a lot rarer now.'

Something flashed into his mind again for a split second. What was it? He tried to force it to come back but it wouldn't.

Sarah Castle interrupted his thoughts. 'I could check eBay if you want? See if anybody bought a job lot back in 2008?'

'Do it, but it's a long shot. As you say, whoever placed them in the coffin could just have had them hanging around. It looks like he cleaned them before using them anyway.'

Silence again. They walked on.

Ridpath wanted to light another cigarette, just so he would have something to do with his hands as he thought about the problem. But he didn't; one bout of guilt and shame was enough for today. 'Let's think this through. We have a missing body: Alice Seagram. Protheroe was clear it had never been inside the coffin. Either the undertaker removed it or it never got to him in the first place.'

'But why have a funeral then? If the body had never reached him, surely he would have informed the family and the mortuary? It doesn't make sense.'

'Somebody put those breeze blocks inside to imitate the weight of Alice Seagram. Somebody wanted the pall-bearers to think there was a body inside.'

'Who?'

'That's the million-dollar question.'

'After the post-mortem, the body would have been stitched back together and placed in the mortuary. When it was released for burial, the undertaker's men would have taken it to a laying-out parlour and prepared it according to the family's wishes. You know, washed, dressed in her favourite clothes, made as presentable as possible, and then sealed into the coffin for eternity.'

'Sounds like you know all about it.'

She thrust her hands into the jacket pockets. 'I've buried my mum and dad in the last year. Sick of funerals.'

Ridpath was tempted to ask about the details but stopped himself in case he heard the dreaded word: cancer. He changed the subject quickly. 'Let's come at this from a different angle. Why?'

She frowned. 'Why what?'

'Why was the body stolen? Why would anybody want to steal a murder victim's body? And what happened to the bodies of the other victims of the Beast?'

Again, silence as they walked on.

'It doesn't make any sense,' she finally said.

'Unless… somebody was trying to stop us doing what we're doing now.'

'I don't understand.'

'The only reason we've discovered the body of Alice Seagram is missing is because the high court ordered the inquest to be reopened…'

'So?'

He held up his hand. 'And the only reason they reopened the case was problems with the evidence against James Dalbey.'

'And because the family has been pushing for the case to be reopened,' she interjected.

Could they be involved? From his meeting with the mother and father he doubted it. But Tony Seagram was a different kettle of arrogance. 'Could you check on the son for me?'

'I suppose so. What do you want to know?'

'Everything. Who he is. What he does. His background. The works.'

'What are you going to do?'

'I need to go back to the beginning on this case. Interview the pathologist, Harold Lardner, see what he remembers. I'll check out the mortuary. Perhaps they'll know who the attendant was back in 2008 or, if I'm really lucky, he's still working there.' He took a deep breath. 'I also have a favour I need to ask you.'

'Go on,' she said doubtfully.

'I need to see the files for the original police investigation.'

'Just ask Charlie Whitworth. I'm sure he'll release them to you.'

'And there's the problem. I don't want Charlie to know I have them.'

'Why?'

He liked the bluntness of this woman. 'Because the coroner wants to see them.'

'Get her to ask through the usual channels.'

'She's done that already.'

She was silent for a moment. 'Ah,' she said pointedly, 'she wants to see all the files, not just the ones Charlie wants her to see.' A beat. 'What's in it for me?'

He did like this woman. 'The eternal gratitude of the coroner.'

'I'll survive without it.'

He thought again. 'The knowledge it would help the coroner discover the truth.'

'Laudable, but not motivating enough.'

'Having me check out your theory that the MO of the latest murder and those of James Dalbey were similar.' He could see her eyes flashing back to her moment of humiliation in the squad room. She began to blush again.

'I'll think about it,' she finally said.

They walked past a newsagent's. Outside on a stand, a hand-written poster for the *Manchester Evening News* in big bold, black letters loudly proclaimed:

WHERE IS MY SISTER'S BODY?
ASKS BROTHER OF ALICE SEAGRAM

'It looks like the shit has hit the fan,' said Ridpath, reaching for his phone.

Chapter Twenty-Six

James Dalbey lay back on his bed, arms folded under his head. Around him the rest of the prison was winding down after a long day of doing nothing.

There were the usual prison noises: the creaking of the building as it cooled down at the end of the day; a prisoner in a nearby cell weeping quietly, hoping nobody would hear him; two other cons on the landing above having sex; a prisoner officer's slow tread down the corridor as he completed his evening rounds.

The usual sounds of the animals in the human zoo.

He had just finished saying his Hail Mary's and Our Fathers in front of the crucifix. Father Keaveney would be giving mass on Sunday. He liked the priest: a gentle man with the patience of a saint and the aroma of whisky on his breath.

Surely it wouldn't be long now. They would have to let him go soon.

The radio announcer had reported the disappearance of the girl's body with an edge of incredulity in his voice, followed by a report hinting strongly at a series of damning mistakes by Manchester Police.

How long would it be before they joined up the dots? How long before they worked out the man in black was responsible, not James Dalbey? How long before they realized that without a body, they couldn't keep him here much longer?

He had checked the law books in the library that morning. Funny – the best-stocked part of the prison library was the law section. But despite the place being full of cons, hardly anybody used it except him.

The books had told him what he needed to know. For assaulting the police, he would be up for a six stretch at most. And as he'd already served nine, he should be able to get out straight away.

Today was a good day.

They could charge him with the murders of the other girls, but it wasn't likely. After ten years, any new witnesses would be difficult to find. And if they had damning evidence, they would have charged him in 2008.

Besides, he knew something they didn't.

He was innocent.

There was no way he would have hurt Alice. He loved her – maybe too much, but he loved her. She was the only one who spoke to him kindly. The only one who helped him with his reading on Sundays. The only one he allowed to touch his hand.

That's what the police didn't understand.

He would never have harmed her, not in a million years.

But he had to get out of here. All he had to do now was keep up the pressure. He would call Tony Seagram tomorrow. Get him to demand he be released. The newspapers would be all over the story like a pack of wolves. What better story than the brother of a murder victim calling for the release of her accused killer?

A front page, without a doubt.

One thing he'd learnt about British newspapers was if you gave them the story and the angle, they would print it verbatim, without checking any of the facts. They were the laziest journalists in the world. After all, when you worked for a Beaverbrook or a Murdoch what did truth have to do with anything? The angle was the story, not the facts.

He smiled again, turning it into a loud laugh, which fed on itself. What a joke this world was. Inhabited by a bunch of idiots intent on scrambling to the top, one over the other. Didn't they realize the game was rigged from the start?

He screamed with laughter.

A bang on the wall from the con next door. 'Shut the fuck up in there. I'm trying to sleep.'

He placed his hand over his mouth, stifling his laughter.

Today was a good day.

Tomorrow would be even better.

Chapter Twenty-Seven

Two hundred miles further north, Ridpath was also lying in bed staring at the ceiling. But in his case, the only noises he could hear were the gentle snores of his wife beside him.

After seeing the *Manchester Evening News* headline, he had called Margaret Challinor. 'I presume you've seen the papers?'

She sighed on the end of the phone. 'Tony Seagram pushing his own agenda again.'

'His parents must have told him and he went straight to the newspapers.'

'Let's hope it won't be picked up by the nationals or TV. If it is, the chief coroner will be sticking his rather long nose in from London. It's the last thing I need.'

As soon as he got home, he'd switched on BBC News.

'Hi, Dad, how was your day?'

'Give me a second, Eve, I just need to check something.' He turned the sound up.

His daughter mimed a face and mouth with her hand. 'Hi there, Eve, how was your day? Fine thanks, we're doing a science project at school,' she answered herself, letting one hand speak to the other. 'Do you know the man over there? I think he's a Mr Ridpath, our dad, but I'm not sure.'

He turned the TV off. 'Sorry, sweetie, how was the science project?'

'Pretty easy, except I don't like touching the frogs.'

'Have you tried kissing them?'

'Yeeugh, no!'

'You mean you haven't checked if one of them isn't a prince who's been turned into a frog by a wicked teacher like your mother?'

'Not these frogs, Dad. Mr Stevens grew them from tadpoles. There's as much chance of any of them being a prince as you playing for Manchester United.'

'Didn't I ever tell you about the day I had a trial?'

He hadn't told her or anybody. He'd turned up at the training ground one afternoon with all his kit after being spotted by some scout while playing for his school. He was excited and nervous. This was his big chance to mix with the stars like Beckham and Scholes and Sparky Hughes.

He was met by a man sweeping leaves on the front driveway. The training ground looked deserted.

'Trials?' The man stopped sweeping and scratched his head, 'Ain't no trials today, lad. That were yesterday. Made a right mess, they did too.'

He had gone home and locked himself in the bathroom, crying as silently as he could. Of course, his mum noticed but she didn't say a word. She didn't want him to go in the first place, just like she didn't want him to go into the police.

In the last nine months, he found he had been thinking about the past a lot, trying to make sense of it all. Trying to understand how his mum had managed after his father had died. Cancer had taken him at the age of thirty-nine, when Ridpath was just five years old. Perhaps the Ridpaths were fated to die young.

'Dad, what's up with you? You've got that dreamy look about you again. Can we have risotto tonight?'

'Risotto? Sure. Can you check with your mum?'

His wife was in the bath, something she often did after a day at the school – to wash away the smell of chalk dust, she joked.

'I'm sure it will be OK.'

He stood up. 'Can you help chop the mushrooms and grate the Parmesan?' In their house, he did most of the cooking; his wife could just about boil an egg on a good day. Actually cooking a meal was far beyond her. So they spilt responsibilities. He cooked; she cleaned up after him.

It worked for both of them: she had the clean kitchen she loved, he ate food that was palatable.

He and Eve worked together well as a kitchen brigade. Within no time, the table was set, risotto was oozing across their plates, white wine was poured into glasses, with orange juice for Eve, and Polly had come down smelling as fresh as an English country garden.

'Looks delicious,' she said, sitting down at the table.

'Eve made it.'

'Don't fib, Dad, I helped grate the Parmesan.'

'And chop the mushrooms.'

'So, a joint effort. I'll help by finishing my plate,' his wife said.

And then Ridpath's mobile rang.

At first he ignored it, desperately pretending it wasn't ringing as he raised his glass in a toast with Polly.

It stopped ringing, only to start again five seconds later.

'Oh, for God's sake, answer it. You know you want to.'

He picked it up; it was Mrs Challinor.

'Turn on your television. Channel 4.'

He walked through to the living room and searched for the remote before finding the right channel. A presenter was standing in front of Alice Seagram's grave, the freshly turned earth dark against the grey of the gravestone. Ridpath turned up the sound.

'...Sources tell us the exhumation occurred in the early hours of yesterday morning. The grave was opened and the coffin removed, but no body was found inside the coffin.'

The camera panned right to reveal the elderly gravedigger standing nervously next to the presenter.

'I have here with me Mr Ned Thomas, the gravedigger who opened the grave. What did you see, Mr Thomas?'

'Nothing.'

The presenter looked flustered. 'You did open the grave yesterday morning?'

'Aye, that was me and my son, Jasper.'

'So what happened?'

'Well, we opened her up like, and took the coffin out, but she were empty.'

'The coffin was empty?'

'That's right. Just a couple of breeze blocks in it. Never seen the like before and I've been digging here for 40 years, man and boy.'

'Thank you, Mr Thomas. This is Stuart James for *Channel 4 News* in Manchester.'

He stared at the television. The shit really had hit the fan.

For the rest of the evening, Polly had tried to chat with him, before finally going to bed. He had joined her after two large glasses of Laphroaig. Now here he was, staring up at the ceiling, thinking about the job, unable to sleep.

Why had a coffin filled with breeze blocks been buried in Alice Seagram's grave?

What had happened to her body?

Who had stolen it?

Was there any link to James Dalbey and the murders of the Beast of Manchester?

Why had they never found the bodies of his other victims?

The questions swirled round and round in his mind, tumbling and twisting like rubbish caught in a whirlpool.

The last question repeated itself again and again as he finally fell asleep.

Would he ever make sense of it all?

Chapter Twenty-Eight

Lesley had gone over her instructions in her head three times. As usual he had been precise.

Drive to Northenden; turn right down Mill Lane; continue to the end of the road as it bends round to the right; park in the car park of an abandoned pub.

She had followed his instructions to the letter. She was now sitting in the car park in front of the Mersey. On her left a row of Victorian houses was quiet, just one light showing in an upstairs window.

In front of her, the Mersey flowed noisily over a weir, the water cascading and frothing. Over the river stood a metal pedestrian bridge painted bright green.

Check the car park.

Empty. No other cars here. Why would other cars park here at this time of night?

If all clear, open boot and remove body.

She stepped out of her white BMW. The night was overcast, with a fresh breeze ruffling the row of trees along the river. From the left, the haunting hoot of an owl. Behind her, in amongst the Victorian terraces, a baby crying plaintively for its milk. All around her the low drone of constant traffic on the M60, echoing off the buildings. Looming over her like a giant black ogre, the dark, boarded-up windows of the abandoned pub.

Her senses were so alive.

This is what he had told her to enjoy. The hyper-awareness of the world, as if each sense, from smell to taste, to hearing, touch and sound were amplified and reinforced.

She was in control.

She knew everything.

She felt everything.

The metal of the boot lid was icy to her touch. It squeaked as it opened, rocked for a moment on its hinges and then stilled itself.

Lesley looked around. The light in the upstairs window was off now. The far bank of the Mersey, where the golf course was, was dark and deserted, waiting for the thwack of club against ball at first light. In front of her the river rushed past, racing down to Liverpool and the sea.

Take the body out of the boot. Check your surroundings once more. Then walk up the steps to the pedestrian bridge.

The body was wrapped in a moth-eaten blanket. It didn't look like a body, just a lump beneath the grey wool. A dark stain had appeared at one end where her head should be. Was that her blood? She reached out and touched the stain with her fingertips.

Damp.

She smelt her fingertips and then touched them to her tongue.

Metallic. Rusty. An aftertaste she couldn't describe, like someone's soul in liquid form.

She knew what she wanted to do with the next one now. Would he mind if she took the lead? Suggested something new to assuage the boredom? She would see what sort of mood he was in before she broached it. She didn't want to be punished, not again.

She hefted the body across her shoulder as she did when she was moving her patients from their beds, dead or alive. The girl was lighter than normal. The crack had done its work on her fragile body.

There would be no more crack for this young girl. No more fumbled encounters in steamy cars. No more standing on the mean streets.

No more pain.

Lesley took one last look around the car park – eyes, ears and pores open for anything new, anything different.

All clear.

She strode the three yards up the steps onto the wooden boards of the bridge.

Take her to the middle of the bridge, where the river is deepest, and throw her over the left-hand side towards the weir. Keep hold of the blanket. The police will find her eventually, but not until the water, and the weir, has removed any forensic evidence.

She strode to the centre of the bridge, feeling her footsteps reverberate under the wooden boards, stopping in the centre on the left-hand side.

The river was dark and deep flowing, with the fresh scent of decay in the air. It had rained heavily last night, the water pouring down from the Pennines into the waiting banks of the Mersey.

On her right a sharp scream of death. The owl had swooped down, catching an unwary field mouse in its talons. She could see the black outline of the bird as it flew back to the roost to devour its feast.

Nature red in tooth and claw.

She positioned the body on the metal parapet, checking it was going to fall into the deepest part of the river. She watched as it slowly tumbled into the dark waters, landing with a splash.

The noise was so loud somebody must have heard. She glanced left and right. Her body tensed, waiting for the shout: 'Oi, you, what you doin' there?'

But no sound came. Just the river flowing down to the sea beneath her feet.

The body won't sink, but it will float down over the edge of the weir, buffeted by the current until it finally comes to a halt. It may get caught up on a sandbank or in some reeds, but it doesn't matter where as long as they find the body. Remember, we want them to find it. Fold up the blanket and place it back in the boot of the car. Drive home, and park in the garage.

Everything so precise, so ordered. She knew exactly what to do.

She began to roll up the blanket but, as she did, a gust of wind raced down the valley, tugging it from her hands. For a moment, it hung in the air like a giant bat before floating away from her into the dark.

What should she do? She thought about clambering down the banks and wading into the river to get it. She stared out into the dark water. Where had it gone?

She had no instructions for this. What should she do?

She looked over the metal parapet. No sign of the body or the blanket. Just the white caps of the water as it struck the metal stanchions of the bridge.

If she didn't tell him, he would never know. She had another blanket exactly the same – she could just cut herself and stain it. He will never know it's not the right one.

That was it. That's what she would do.

She rushed down from the bridge into her car, putting it into gear and racing away from the bridge.

He mustn't find out she had failed him.

He must never know.

Chapter Twenty-Nine

The following morning, Ridpath went to the station at nine o'clock. This time it felt like coming home. The sergeant on the front desk recognized him and he was buzzed straight through without waiting.

The office was as busy as ever, every desk occupied in readiness for the meeting. He had picked up a text from Charlie Whitworth when he awoke telling him to come in.

He strode over to the Bubble and knocked on the door.

'Morning, Ridpath. I see it's all gone tits up for you.'

His detective chief inspector held up a copy of the *Daily Mail*. In a spread on page four and five was the bold headline: 'What Happened to Alice Seagram?' with a picture of the gravestone, the newly turned earth now greyer than in previous shots. Standing in front of the grave was a grieving man, captioned as Alice's brother, Tony Seagram. He scanned the article. They'd interviewed the family and the gravediggers, plus there was a whole sidebar with Mr Health and Safety covering his not inconsiderable arse.

'The coroner is giving a press conference at 2 p.m. today to present an update. She's visiting the family this morning to reassure them.'

'You not going?'

Ridpath shook his head. 'She wants me to keep investigating. Find out what happened.'

'Lucky you. We've got enough problems identifying a body from a day ago never mind one that vanished ten years ago.' He picked up a sheaf of folders from his desk. 'Come on, you're invited to the update on the murder of the swan tattoo girl. In the interests of co-operation with the Coroner's Office, of course,' he finished archly.

Ridpath followed him through the office to the incident room. Most of the detectives were already assembled and waiting, a few hurrying into the room as they saw the boss had arrived.

The room had changed. Pictures of the dead woman were pasted on the walls, including close-ups of her neck, the tattoo on her arm and wider shots of the scene beside the canal. The same faces were here from last time. He looked across at Sarah Castle. She looked away without acknowledging him.

Charlie Whitworth strode right to the front. 'Right, you lot. John Gorman's been on the blower. He wants this cleared up ASAP. No pissing about, understand? Luckily, thanks to young Tom Ridpath over there, all the attention from our friends in the press is focused on his missing body. Thanks for that, Ridpath.'

All the detectives turned to look at him. He pretended to be making a note in his notepad.

'So we've got a window of opportunity to crack this case in the next couple of days without having to deal with a rabid pack of would-be novelists queering our pitch. Let's make good use of it. Harry, anything from the local toms?'

'Besides the clap?' said somebody from the back.

A buzz of laughter went around the room.

'Aye, Harry would know – wouldn't you, Harry?'

Harry didn't answer, looking down at his notes. 'Nothing from the locals. Apparently, this girl was new. They remembered seeing a young one with a swan tattoo on her arm, but you know how protective they are of their patches.'

'Worse than coppers?' asked the same voice from the back.

'Much worse,' said Harry. 'They had a few words with her and moved her on to the end of the street. None of the pimps or drug dealers were looking after her, so she was fair game for the hyenas.'

'Any name?' asked Charlie Whitworth.

Harry checked his notes. 'One of the toms thought she was called Christine, another said Angie. One thought she was called Harry.'

Another rumble of laughter.

Charlie Whitworth raised his arms. 'Let me remind you a young woman has been murdered here. It's not a joke.'

The room instantly went quiet.

Charlie Whitworth stared out across the room. 'Continue, Harry,' he muttered.

'Not much left.' His voice perked up. 'One of the toms did say she thought the girl was Scottish from her accent. Definitely not local.'

'Get on to Police Scotland, check out their National Resources unit and send them the pictures of the tattoo.'

'Will do, boss.'

'And how about the CCTV?'

'There was a camera on the marina building overlooking the parking area and part of the path, but guess what?'

'It's not working.'

'Got it in one, boss. As the owner said, it was more for show.'

'Anything else?'

'We've taken footage from the Chester Road cameras going towards Sale and to central Manchester. Where she was found is just 60 yards from the main road, but perhaps 10,000 cars an hour use the road. Until we have a tighter time frame...' He left the rest of the sentence unsaid.

'I'm meeting the pathologist at 10.30. We should have a time frame for you once I see his report. Dave, how was the house-to-house?'

'Not great, boss. All the houses face away from the canal and there's not many of them. The people who live in them saw nothing, heard nothing and spoke even less. We visited all the local workshops and warehouses, but they were as much use as a gallon of whisky at a teetotallers' convention. I asked a couple of the plod to hang around and approach any walkers, anglers or anybody on the path, but got nothing. If I wanted to choose a spot to dump a body, this is the place I'd choose.'

'What about the dog walker who found her?'

'Checked him out. Works the late shift at Tescos, married, two kids. No record except a bit of shoplifting as a kid. A United season ticket holder.'

'Poor bastard,' said a voice from the back.

'Did you get anything out of him?'

'Not a lot. He was walking the dog as he always does when he gets home from the night shift, before making the kids' breakfast. His normal route is down by the canal, because he doesn't have to pick up the dog's shit there. The dog went racing off into the undergrowth at the side of the fence separating the canal from the backs of the houses along Haig Road. The dog started barking and he thought maybe one of the anglers had thrown away a fish or summat. Anyway, he saw the body, said he didn't touch it and immediately rang 999.'

'OK, thanks. Keep the local plod down there for a couple more days. I want them interviewing anglers, runners, cyclists, dog walkers, anybody and everybody who uses the tow path. Got it?'

'Got it, boss.'

He looked around the room. 'Chrissy, where's Chrissy?'

A tiny woman put up her hand.

'Anything on HOLMES or PNC?'

'Not a lot. Seems to be a dearth of serial killers or kidnappings at the moment. Swansea may have a case, but they haven't classified it at the moment. Newcastle is the same. But it's not surprising, after Manchester last year and then London, most resources have gone into anti-terrorism. Intelligence on common or garden crimes like murder has taken a back seat. When that's coupled with 21,000 fewer coppers on the beat, not to mention the cuts in Police Community Officers and support services, well, I'm not surprised we—'

'We all know about the cuts, Chrissy,' DCI Whitworth interrupted the woman forcefully, 'but moaning about them here isn't going to help us track down our murderer. Let's stay focused on what we can do, shall we?'

'Yes, boss.'

'Get on to Swansea and Newcastle. I want the files on their cases on my desk this afternoon.'

'I'm on it.'

'And pull anything you have on serial killers in England in the last ten years.'

'All of them?'

'All of them. And check if anybody on the sex offenders' register has been released recently. Screw it, check if anybody has been released who committed any sort of assault against women. Period.'

'Could be a lot of files, boss.'

'We've got the people to check them. Just do it.'

He looked around the room once more. Most of the detectives avoided his gaze, concentrating on something in their notebooks.

'What about foreigners? Any reports of Eastern Europeans on the game in Manchester?'

'I'm still looking into it, boss,' answered Chrissy. 'There were some reports of girls from Bulgaria working the airport hotels.'

'Follow it up, and quickly.'

He let out a long sigh of exasperation. 'Right, so we've got nothing. Close to 20 officers on this and I have to go back to John Gorman and tell him we have bugger all? Do you lot want to put me forward for early retirement right now? Or would you prefer me to wear my balls around my neck when he hands them to me?'

Silence from the team, everybody finding something interesting to look at in their notebooks, on the floor or on the ceiling.

'I want you lot to shake things up. Fred, bring a few toms in with their pimps and charge them.'

'What with, boss?'

'I don't know – breathing will do for starters. I want them to know we will shut down the whole bloody street unless we get some answers. No more pussyfooting around. Rattle a few cages and see if anything falls out, Fred. Now is not the time for softly-softly.'

'Right, boss – cages being rattled,' Fred said, with a certain amount of enjoyment.

Harry put his hand up. 'You going to get the press involved?'

Charlie Whitworth thought for a moment. 'Not yet. If we do a press conference asking for information, all the bloody nutters will come out of the woodwork and we'll be flooded with useless leads. Let's play our cards close to our chest. The rest of you, shake the trees. Ask around, see if anybody's heard anything. Even if it's the slightest whisper. Somebody must know something, somewhere.' He paused for a beat. 'Well, what are you waiting for?'

The room became active. Detectives stood up and talked with their counterparts, others rushed towards the door. Others went to check with Chrissy.

A smile came over Charlie Whitworth's face and he raised his arms. 'Hang on, hang on. We've forgotten one thing, one important thing.'

Everybody stopped what they were doing and the room went silent.

Charlie turned to Sarah. 'DS Castle.'

'Yes, sir.'

'You had a theory the murders were somehow linked to James Dalbey. You were going to check on the Beast for us?' He let his eyes wander over the detectives, sharing the joke with them.

'I was, sir… and I did.'

The smile became a leer now. 'Well?'

Sarah Castle's face became bright red. 'He's still in Belmarsh, sir.'

'Safe and secure, is he? Did you check where he was when the body was found?'

She went even redder. 'I did, sir.'

'And?'

'According to the deputy governor, he was either in the library or in his cell.'

He turned to the rest of the detectives, wide-eyed with fake joy. 'Well, lads, we should thank DS Castle for her work. We now have one less suspect. Only 18 million other men to go.'

The room erupted into laughter. Sarah Castle looked across at the picture of the tattoo, staring at it, avoiding all the other detectives.

Then for a split second, she looked back at him. And, with hardly a movement of her head, she nodded.

An almost imperceptible movement, which nobody else would have seen, but Ridpath knew its meaning.

Charlie Whitworth picked up his files and hustled out of the room. Ridpath took the opportunity to stop him for a second. 'I hear you're off to the mortuary for the post-mortem. All right if I tag along?'

'You got nothing better to do than watch a young woman being cut up?'

'It'll help with my report to the coroner. She needs to open an inquest into the girl's death.'

The DCI shrugged his shoulders. 'It's your funeral. Or hers. We're leaving in five.' He then bustled past him, back to the Bubble.

Ridpath took one last look at Sarah Castle before he followed Charlie Whitworth. She was staring at the picture of the murder scene, her eyes fixed on the battered face of the murdered girl.

Chapter Thirty

The mortuary where the post-mortem was to take place was located in the middle of the Manchester Royal Infirmary complex just off Oxford Road. The building was relatively new, constructed from the ubiquitous red brick of all government buildings of the 1990s.

As soon as he stepped in and started walking down corridors to the post-mortem room, Ridpath noticed it. An acrid chemical smell crept into his nostrils and constricted his throat. Not the antiseptic smell of a hospital, but something harsher, more acerbic.

Charlie was waiting for him outside the room. 'You're an observer – you don't say nothing in there. Understand?'

Ridpath nodded.

They both moved back to the wall as a gurney with a green body bag lying on it was pushed past them by a bald porter.

'We come into the world crying and screaming and we go out of it silent and alone, wrapped in a green plastic bag.' Charlie stared at the gurney as it was pushed away from them down the corridor. As if embarrassed at being caught speaking his thoughts out loud, he pushed Ridpath ahead of him through the door into the room. 'Let's get a move on. I hate this place.'

The door led out onto a viewing gallery above the post-mortem area. Below them a gleaming stainless steel table with a sink at one end was placed in the middle of the floor. To its right, a steel tray held a variety of instruments: circular saws, bone saws, knives and scalpels. Another tray on the left had a reddish-brown liver on it. Ridpath could see the lumps of creamy fat covering its surface. A drainage tube led from the tray down to a container. Inside was a dark, viscous substance.

An assistant, a young woman, from her shape beneath the mask and white post-mortem protective clothing, was handing the pathologist a saw.

On the table, the body of a young woman lay, her chest opened from her neck to her vagina, the two flaps of skin folded back to reveal her ribs and intestines. The back of her head had been completely smashed in. It was almost as if Ridpath was looking at half a head. On the right arm, the tattoo of a swan was clearly visible.

'Good morning, gentlemen. I wondered when you would arrive. As you can see I started without you.'

The voice whispered from a speaker mounted on the wall. It had a slightly detached tone as if this was just another day and another dead body.

Charlie Whitworth leant into a microphone. 'Good morning, Dr Lardner, anything so far?'

'Not so far, Charlie. Who's that with you?'

'Detective Inspector Ridpath, Doctor.'

'I've seen you before, haven't I?'

Ridpath blushed. He was hoping the pathologist wouldn't remember him. 'I'm now on temporary secondment to the Coroner's Office. I'd like to have a chat after you've finished, if that's possible.'

'Say hello to Margaret for me. I'm due to start a drowning at 2 p.m., so we can chat before then.'

Charlie Whitworth leant forward to the microphone again. 'Could we crack on, Doctor?'

'Of course, Charlie. I see you're as patient as ever. I've just removed the liver.' He pointed to the red fatty mass in the tray. 'Not the healthiest I've ever seen. Our Jane Doe didn't treat her body well in the time it was on earth. I would estimate she's between 26 to 28 years old, 5 feet 6 inches tall, weighing 99 pounds. Despite her relatively thin appearance, she has a fairly high body fat percentage, indicating unhealthy eating habits. No distinguishing marks except the tattoo of a swan on her arm. The tattoo has been professionally drawn and does show some artistic merit. Probably the easiest way to identify her, Chief Inspector.'

'We're working on it.'

'There was no evidence of sexual activity in the hours before her death—'

'You don't think she was a sex worker?'

A slight irritation entered the pathologist's voice. 'I didn't say that, Charlie. I said there was no evidence of sexual activity. No sperm or lubricants in either her mouth, vagina or anus.'

'That's a strange one. A tom who doesn't have sex.'

'She could have showered that morning. Or...'

'Or?' asked Charlie.

'The killer could have cleaned her body before it was placed beside the canal. I've taken swabs of her skin and asked the lab to test for cleansing agents such as soap.'

'He was removing all traces of himself on her, wasn't he, Doctor?'

'It would seem that way, Charlie. We have an extremely clean killer.'

Charlie didn't say a word, just stared at the woman's body.

The pathologist coughed. 'Shall I continue?'

'Yes,' was the single-word answer.

Dr Lardner pointed to grey flesh in another tray. 'From the condition of her lungs, she was a smoker: tar deposits are quite evident even to the naked eye. But tobacco wasn't the only drug she used. From the condition of her teeth and the severe acne around her mouth, I believe she was a crack cocaine user. Toxicology will confirm my belief, and the presence of any other drugs in her system. But I've seen this type before and I'm pretty certain crack cocaine was her drug of choice.'

'No track marks?'

'No evidence of needle marks in the usual places on her arms or feet. It doesn't mean she wasn't using heroin, only that I can't find needle marks. Again, toxicology will come back with the answers.'

'Any epithelials beneath her nails?'

'As with her body, her fingernails have been scraped clean.'

'This killer knows how we work, Doctor.'

'It would appear so, Charlie.'

For the first time the doctor looked away from the body and up at them, then quickly returned his gaze to the body. 'No wedding ring or signs she has ever worn one. The middle finger was broken before death, perhaps in the initial struggle with the killer.'

'Not after death when the body was dumped?'

'From the bruising and presence of broken capillaries beneath the surface of the skin, I would say definitely before death. Fingerprints were taken at the crime scene. Is she on the database, Charlie?'

'No, she hasn't been arrested in the UK. We're checking abroad.'

'I have a feeling she's from the UK.'

'Why do you say that, Doctor?'

'Her teeth. Despite half of them being smashed in, I can still see the presence of multiple fillings. The dentists of the NHS have a particular fondness for them which most other countries seem to lack. This woman has at least seven fillings in her molars and canine teeth. Not the work of the most skilled dentist.'

'Could we find her identity through her dental records?' Ridpath asked, receiving a stern look from Charlie Whitworth.

'You could, but it would be like looking for a single tooth in a denture factory. Possible but time-consuming. And while we are dealing with her head, it is not the prettiest sight. The back of it has been attacked repeatedly with a blunt instrument...'

'A hammer?' asked Charlie.

'I don't know at the moment. It's a possibility, but it could have been anything hard enough to produce this damage.

A metal bar, a heavy wrench or even a police truncheon; I'll know more once we do some lab tests.'

Charlie checked his watch. 'Let's move on, Doctor. Time of death?'

'The perennial question, Charlie. Any time between 2 p.m. on Tuesday afternoon and 8 a.m. on Wednesday morning.'

'Can't we narrow it down a little, Doctor?'

'No, we can't, Charlie. That's the time I'm reporting.'

Another silence from Charlie.

The pathologist continued speaking. 'Despite everything, the injuries were not the cause of her death.'

'How did she die, Doctor?' asked Ridpath.

'She was strangled, manually, with a thin metal wire.' He held up a short length of thin steel cord like a cheese-cutter. 'This was still embedded in her throat.'

Chapter Thirty-One

Ridpath settled into a seat in Harold Lardner's tiny office. The pathologist had discarded his lab coat and was dressed in a light-blue shirt, matching tie and dark trousers. The salt-and-pepper hair was brushed back off his head and gelled. Outside the post-mortem theatre he didn't look half as threatening or as powerful. Indeed, to Ridpath, he looked positively benign, like a slightly overweight bank manager.

Perhaps it was the theatre of the mortuary with its acrid smells, pristine white surfaces, bright spotlights and stainless steel surfaces, all worshipping the way of death. It was like being in some church with the pathologist the high priest, like the Egyptian priests with their pharaohs. Giving the dead eternal life through science.

Charlie Whitworth had already gone back to headquarters.

'Are you sure you won't have anything to eat, Mr Ridpath?' The pathologist was picking at a limp salad.

Ridpath shook his head as he watched the man shovel food into his mouth.

'How can I help you?'

'It's the about the Alice Seagram case...'

The pathologist's head tilted to one side. 'I remember you. Didn't they call you Vomit Man?'

Ridpath scratched his head. 'You know about that?'

'Very little escapes me, Detective Inspector. Part of the job.'

Ridpath was transported back to his first autopsy in 2009. A child. It had to be a child. Four years old, found after the mother had called 999 saying he wasn't breathing. The plod who'd answered the call found the child was dead when they got there. They also found bruising to the upper arms and torso. The mother said she'd tried to revive her baby, but the sergeant was unconvinced. The coroner ordered a post-mortem performed by Lardner. Ridpath was required to attend. There was something about this man – this alien in his strange costume, calmly talking into a microphone while he cut into the breast bone of a four-year-old with a circular saw – that got to Ridpath. He'd rushed out of the autopsy suite and vomited straight into a rubbish bin.

He had witnessed many autopsies since then, but the nickname had stuck.

Vomit Man.

Now even Lardner remembered. He was tempted to explain but thought better of it. This was a man who cut up dead bodies every day of his life. He was unlikely to understand.

Lardner looked at his watch. 'I have two other clients to look into before five this evening, Detective Inspector. I would appreciate it if you would ask your questions as speedily as you can.'

'Of course, Dr Lardner. I'm investigating the disappearance of the body of Alice Seagram. I believe you were the pathologist for the post-mortem?'

'I was.'

'The case was reopened recently because the high court found problems with your attribution of time of death.'

'That was one of the reasons for reopening the case as far as I understood it. But there were others. The chain of evidence from the Crime Scene Manager was unreliable, plus the killer had managed to get the family on his side, unlikely though it sounds.'

Ridpath decided to plough on. Lardner watched him impassively. Behind his head in the bookcase, copies of the *Journal of Forensic Pathology*, *Scientific American*, *Forensic Magazine* and *Academic Forensic Pathology* were neatly shelved by date and month of publication. 'Can you tell me about the first post-mortem?'

'It was ten years ago.'

'Whatever you remember.'

'The client was brought in; it wasn't a particularly busy period so we prepped her immediately. She had been hit once with a hammer, stabbed repeatedly – 34 times if my memory serves me – then her throat was slit. Afterwards, her body was doused in sulphuric acid. We found a ball-peen hammer which matched the indentation on her skull and, of course, the DNA on the handle matched James Dalbey.'

'Wasn't there a problem with the attribution of the time of death?'

Lardner breathed out heavily; he had obviously explained this a thousand times before. 'Time of death is notoriously difficult to decide. It depends on body temperature, the victim's state of health, where she had been kept, et cetera, et cetera. I performed the first autopsy quickly and called the time of death as between 4 p.m. and 8 p.m. on 7 March. When the police asked me to look again at my findings, I decided the timing was too narrow because of the unusual warmth of the evening.' He looked down at his hands stretched out against the white paper of his desk blotter and bit his bottom lip. 'The post mortem wasn't my best. I rushed it.'

'Why was that?'

Another long sigh. Ridpath could see the doctor's eyes dancing from side to side as if he were weighing up what he was to say next.

'It was a difficult time for me. My wife was dying of breast cancer. A beautiful, giving woman, taken far too early in life. I was rushing from Christie's back to the Royal Infirmary to Christie's again. I made mistakes I shouldn't have.' Then he stared at Ridpath, eyes narrowing slightly. 'But you know all about that, don't you, Detective Inspector?'

Ridpath sat there like an escaping prisoner caught in a searchlight. 'Who told you?'

'I think Chief Inspector Whitworth may have mentioned it.'

'So everyone knows about my medical history. I thought it was supposed to be confidential.'

'I trained as a doctor before specializing in pathology. Perhaps he thought I would understand.'

For a second Ridpath was thrown, then he decided to press on. 'It's not about me—'

'I can see I've upset you, let's pretend I never mentioned it.'

Ridpath ignored the words. Concentrate on the interview. 'So you altered your time of death attribution?'

'Yes.'

'By doing so, Dalbey became the main suspect.'

'He was always the main suspect. He was discovered with the keys to the lock-up where a woman was imprisoned. Wasn't it you who arrested him?'

Whitworth had been talking. When? Not today; he had been with them both all the time.

The doctor looked at his watch again.

Ridpath realized he had just one more question to ask. 'Could I see the notes from the post mortem?'

'Of course, it's on file somewhere. I'll get my secretary to send it over to you.'

'The transcript as well as the written notes, please.'

'Of course.'

Ridpath stood up and held out his hand. 'Thank you for giving me your time, Doctor.'

Lardner stood up as well. 'I hope you find the missing body.'

'I hope so too. I'm just going down to the mortuary to interview the attendants.'

The doctor scratched his head. 'I don't think there are many left from 2008. Nobody likes spending time with dead people.'

Chapter Thirty-Two

Eleanor Norris can just sod off – I'm not doing it any more. He felt his feet pounding into Ford Lane, jarring his knees. It's just not on. How many other people have to work Saturdays? This was his third weekend in a row spoilt because she wanted to impress the team from London with her proactive approach to the account.

Bollocks.

He ran past the allotments, smelling the aroma of freshly turned earth. A group of men were looking after their patches, preparing the ground for planting the summer veg. One old fool was leaning on a spade, wearing a soft hat that had last seen the inside of a washing machine sometime in 1943.

The red-faced tosser waved at him. He increased his pace, ignoring the old man.

How was he ever going to get his miles up for the Manch-ester Marathon if he had to work every bloody weekend? It's not like the work for the account was urgent or anything.

Up over Simon's Bridge, glancing down at the dark waters of the Mersey as it flowed beneath his feet.

He turned right, following the bend of the river as it came back on itself. Legs feeling good. Arms pumping nicely, slight pain in the right shoulder but he could ignore it. Breathing easy.

God, he loved running. He knew this route so well he could run it in his sleep. He liked the different textures of road, grass, gravel and cinder beneath his feet on this circuit. His mind drifted off as he ran; it always did. It was almost as if his body took the route, while his mind soared free.

He followed the river as it wound between the golf courses – a water trap to end all water traps. He wondered how many balls ended up in Liverpool because some fat fart from Didsbury was so hopeless at golf he shanked his drives into the Mersey.

He ran under the M60. Above, the cars raced to God knows where. So much rushing here and there, too little time to smell the roses. Story of his life, especially since the Witch had taken over. Well he wasn't going to stand for it any longer. Martin Sharples didn't need the money or the hassle – she could stuff her stupid job up her not inconsiderable jacksie.

His anger was driving him forward now, his feet racing over Ford Lane and up the hill to the ancient church. Probably been sat there for years, that church. Perched on its outcrop of rock, watching the comings and goings on the river for donkey's years, while the city grew up around it and the quiet village of Northenden was swallowed by the whale that was Manchester.

Left down Boat Lane and straight across the car park at the bottom. Not far now, legs feeling great, body relaxed. Another 10k in the bag and the marathon only six weeks away. He wanted to beat his best time this year: 3 hours 30 was the goal. Should be able to do it with a bit of luck.

Up over the green bridge, feet echoing on the wooden boards as he crossed the river again to turn left past the weir.

He'd beat his time if she let him. For a moment, the image of her face close to his, his fist going back and smashing into the red-painted lips, and then again into the retroussé nose. And again. And again.

His eyes caught something in the water next to the sandbank below the weir.

What was that?

A dark, sodden lump. Clothes? More rubbish?

He slowed down, allowing his eyes to focus. The lump began to form into a recognizable shape. An arm. A leg bent at a crazy angle. Long hair flowing in the water.

The body bobbed up and down in time with the current from the weir.

A body?

What was a body doing here?

Should he call 999? He looked all around him.

Nobody.

Off in the distance, two middle-aged men were playing a round of golf, just putting on the green. In front of him, the river flowed on ceaselessly to the sea as it had always done.

Martin Sharples was running on the spot.

Should he ring 999?

But if he did, he would be late back to the office after lunch. The witch would be on his case, complaining like a banshee.

Sod it, somebody else can report it.

He looked up. Movement at a window in the flats next to the river. His eyes met those of a young woman carrying a baby over her right shoulder. She came out onto the balcony and shouted something at him.

Silly tart. Sod it, she can report the body, not him.

He pulled his hood down over his eyes and started to run towards Palatine Road, moving as quickly as he could. Got to get away from here. The woman was dead anyway; what did it matter if she lay in the water for another ten minutes?

His work was important. That artwork for the Persil account had to be ready this afternoon.

Behind him the woman lay with her hands on the sandbank and her legs sticking out into the water as if she were trying to crawl out of the river to safety.

She had already been dead for 18 hours.

Chapter Thirty-Three

The senior mortuary attendant was a big, beefy man with a handshake like a vice. His face had the healthy sheen of a man who loved the Manchester diet: fish and chips, meat pies and plates of curry washed down by five pints of cask ale. A roll of fat peeped out above the purple turtleneck sweater beneath his lab coat.

'So you're the new coroner's officer? My name's Brown – Don Brown. The pathologist said you wanted to talk about Alice Seagram?'

'You've heard about the case?'

The big man shrugged. 'It was on the news. Let's go through to the bereavement centre.'

'Won't someone be in there?'

'Not now. It's not visiting time.'

Ridpath shook his head. 'You have a visiting time? I thought this was a mortuary?'

He pushed open a door. 'You'd be surprised the number of families who want to see their relatives lying in a white box.'

'Checking they are really dead?'

'Probably.'

Ridpath was led into a room off to the left which looked as though it had been designed by a colour-blind decorator. Various garish shades of pink, purple and green assaulted his eyes. A few out-of-date magazines lay scattered on a table. In the corner, a child's play area was an incongruous addition.

'We've had kids as young as five here, brought by the parents to say goodbye to grandma.' He shrugged again, 'Can't say anything though. Just keep schtum, that's my job.'

Ridpath looked around the bereavement room. What were they thinking?

'This was supposed to be "restful" according to the woman who designed it. Me, I come in here when I want to get away from the white walls downstairs.'

They sat facing each other on two of the most uncomfortable armchairs known to man.

'I'm looking into the disappearance of the body of Alice Seagram—' began Ridpath.

'Don't ask me where she's gone. None of my clients get up and walk out of here.'

Ridpath counted to three in his head. 'Were you working here in 2008?'

'No, didn't start till 2010. Not many people last long in the mortuary. We've got high turnover. It's the pay, you see. And some people don't like working with the dead. Me, I don't mind them, they don't give me no trouble. Not like the visitors.'

'Is there anybody who was working here in 2008?'

'Nah – as I said, we've got high turnover.'

Ridpath made a note in his book to contact HR and see if he could get the address of anybody who was here. He looked back up at Don Brown. 'Now, could you take me through the procedure in a mortuary?'

'Hasn't changed for donkey's years.'

This was like pulling teeth. 'Just take me through it, will you?'

The man nodded his head slowly. 'We have about 3,000 clients a year from the hospital, Manchester Royal, and the surrounding area.'

'Do you take clients from the pathologist?'

'Of course – likes cutting them up, does that one. He puts them back together, but not so as a relative can see them.'

'So after the pathologist has finished his post-mortem, they come down here?'

'Not on their own – somebody brings them down.'

Ridpath counted to three again 'And after that?'

'They stay here until you give me a form to release them back to the relative.'

'I give you a form?'

'Or someone like you. The coroner's officer has to decide when a body can be returned to a family for burial.'

'So you receive the form, what do you do?'

'Nothing. Welllll… to tell you the truth, I file it.'

1… 2… 3. 'And afterwards?'

'I usually get a call from the family's undertaker to arrange a time for pickup. The undertaker or one of his oppos comes down and signs a form to take the body away.'

'A lot of forms.'

'You wouldn't believe it, mate. I can't scratch my arse without signing a form in triplicate.'

'So where do you keep these forms?'

'In the book.'

'Can I take a look at the form for Alice Seagram?'

'It'll be in the 2008 file. You'll have to come round the back with me.'

They walked out of the bereavement room and through a pair of double doors into the back area of the mortuary. Along the green painted walls a row of gurneys sat with khaki body bags resting on each one.

'We're a bit backed up at the moment. There's a new heart surgeon.'

Ridpath made a mental note never to have heart surgery at Manchester Royal Infirmary.

'But don't worry, we'll have them all resting comfortably in the meat lockers by this afternoon.'

They turned a corner and entered a room with the words 'Mortuary Manager' stencilled on the glass. 'He's away at the moment on a course for bereavement counselling. I did it last year. Teaches you empathy, it does. Some people can't handle death. Me, I think it's just a part of life, you know what I mean?'

He opened a cabinet and searched through the files. 'Here it is.'

'Your system seems to be efficient.'

'Aye, it's all filed under the year. Pretty easy.'

He brought a large file out. 'Here we go. There were 2,894 clients in 2008. It's filed by entry date. When was the client admitted to the mortuary?'

'Around 8 or 9 March, I think, and released to the family on 18 March.'

He flicked through the file and stopped. He went backwards and forwards a few times before saying: 'Strange, no Alice Seagram here. Are you sure you have the right dates?'

'Positive.'

He went to the end of the file. 'We put the orphans here. He flicked through six forms, clipped together. 'No Alice Seagram. Weird, it must be here somewhere. Perhaps it's under a different date?' He flicked through the rest of the book. 'Still can't see it. But not to worry...'

'Why?'

'Well, we only have the copy. You'll have the original, won't you?'

'At the coroner's office?'

'Where else?'

More documents missing. Something was really starting to stink about this case. Ridpath glanced up at a clock on the wall.

'Shit. Shit. Shit.'

It was 1 p.m. already. He was supposed to be in a press conference at 2 p.m. with Margaret Challinor. He stuck out his hand. 'Listen, I have to rush off. Can you do me a favour? Can you keep looking for the form in case it's been misfiled?'

Don nodded his head. 'I don't understand it. Mr Herbert is a stickler for filing. Checks it at the end of every day. By 6 p.m. we have to be up to date, or else.'

Ridpath was already at the door. 'Give me a call if you find anything.'

And then he was gone, rushing down the corridor, hoping and praying the Oxford Road traffic was going to treat him kindly.

Chapter Thirty-Four

The press conference had already started in the coroner's court when Ridpath finally arrived. Oxford Road hadn't been kind; neither had Rusholme and the A34, while Wellington Road had been positively cruel.

Mrs Challinor raised her eyebrows slightly as he pushed his way in and sat down, stopping her speech for a second before continuing.

'Yesterday morning, at 6.10 a.m., my officers carried out the exhumation of the grave of Alice Seagram in accordance with a high court writ dated 4 April 2018.' She stopped for a moment to allow the journalists seated in front of her to catch up.

On her left sat Carol Oates, dressed once again in a different version of her black outfit and with her blond hair pinned up in an even more elegant chignon. Jenny Oldfield was taking notes on a computer, tapping away on the machine, finishing almost at the same time as Mrs Challinor stopped speaking. Her outfit was a loud baby pink, matching her eyes.

The coroner adjusted her spectacles and continued speaking. 'On disinterring the casket, it was found that Alice Seagram's body was not inside. The East Manchester Coroner's Court and its officers are presently conducting an investigation into the disappearance of the body and will report back when its investigations are complete. The inquest into the autopsy finding on Miss Seagram has been postponed until then. I thank you for your time, ladies and gentlemen.'

She stood up to leave. Before she could get away, one of the journalists shouted out a question. 'How did you know the casket was empty?'

Mrs Challinor was poised in her reply. 'It is standard operating procedure to check the condition of the body before removal to the lab. Next question.'

'What are your next steps, Coroner?'

'As I explained, the coroner's officer, Thomas Ridpath, will carry out an investigation. When we are happy we have discovered enough evidence to point to a conclusion, we will hold an inquest hearing, calling witnesses.'

'Will the family be involved, Mrs Challinor?'

'We always put the wishes of the family at the centre of everything we do. The coroner's officer visited them yesterday and I went to see Mr and Mrs Seagram this morning. They will be kept up to date on the investigation. Just a reminder for the press, the Coroner's Office has only two goals in any inquiry: the first is to represent the interests of the family and the second is to discover the truth. These have, and always will be, our guiding principles.'

The journalist who had asked the first question raised her hand. 'Will you be inquiring into the conviction of James Dalbey for the murder of Alice Seagram?'

'That is not within the purview of my office. The high court has asked us to reopen an inquiry into events surrounding the post-mortem of Alice Seagram, not to apportion guilt. That is the role of the police and the courts. Now, if you'll excuse me, I'm sure you'll understand we have a lot of work to do at the moment.'

'What's happened to Alice Seagram's body?'

'We will let you know as soon as we have completed our investigations. Thank you for your time, ladies and gentlemen.'

She stood up and walked out of the court, followed by Carol Oates, leaving behind a buzz of journalists questioning each other to work out what had just been said.

Ridpath quietly left the court and made his way back to the office. Margaret Challinor was waiting for him with Carol Oates.

'You were late.'

'I'm sorry, Mrs Challinor, one of the interviews ran over.'

'Anything I can tell the family?'

Ridpath went through the pathologist's answers and those of the mortuary attendant.

'The release form was missing?'

'The attendant couldn't explain it. He said we would have the original.'

'Jenny...' Margaret Challinor shouted out her open door.

The office manager appeared in seconds.

'Can you dig out the file on the Alice Seagram case from 2008?'

She produced a manila folder from behind her back. 'I thought you might be asking for it.'

Margaret Challinor opened the file, sharing the contents with Ridpath. 'See, we opened an inquest on 10 March after the body had been discovered, postponing it pending the result of police inquiries.' She turned over another page. 'Here is a note from Jim Howells's predecessor, coroner's officer, Anthony Chettle.' She pointed to a dated and signed handwritten minute. 'He called John Gorman asking if the body could be released to the family. Gorman answered in the affirmative.'

'Chettle kept good notes.'

'He was a stickler for correct procedure. A good man and an even better officer.'

'Where is he now?'

'Retired to Cheshire, I think. Near the Cloud in Congleton. Used to love walking around there.'

'Not a bad life."

'Why do you ask?'

'I might want to interview him. Get a handle on the time-line.'

Carol Oates leant in. 'There's another note on the next page in Anthony's hand.'

Mrs Challinor stared at it, deciphering the hand writing. 'John Gorman called him back an hour later asking him to hold off on speaking to the family. They were going to have another autopsy.'

'This was to check the time of death. The pathologist had originally put the time of death at between 4 p.m. and 8 p.m. on 7 March. By now, James Dalbey was in custody but he had an alibi for that time,' explained Ridpath.

'So they ordered another autopsy to change the time of death to when Dalbey was available to commit the crime.' Carol Oates shook her head. 'Is this for real?'

'Time of death is notoriously difficult to assess, Carol, let's not jump to conclusions.' She located Anthony Chettle's address in the file and passed it to Ridpath.

'I'll go and see him when I have a second. Perhaps he'll remember something that's not in his notes.'

'Perhaps,' muttered the coroner, quietly turning the page. 'Here's the release form signed by Anthony two days later. No note on it this time. The police obviously felt it was time to return the body to the family.'

'Well they would, wouldn't they?' Carol Oates said. 'They'd got the result they wanted from the pathologist and their man James Dalbey had been charged with Alice Seagram's murder. A murder he couldn't have committed based on the findings of the first post-mortem. How convenient.'

Chapter Thirty-Five

The news came through as they were absorbing the results of the post-mortem. Sarah Castle had just received another bollocking from Charlie Whitworth and wasn't in the best of moods.

It was Harry Makepeace who ran into the ops room. 'Boss, there's been another body discovered out in Northenden, on the river. A naked woman with her head smashed in.'

Charlie Whitworth grabbed his jacket from the back of the chair. 'Let's get out there. You lot carry on working on this. Sarah, you're with me.'

She grabbed her notebook and followed him down the corridor to the rear of the building where the cars were parked. Harry got in the driver's seat of the unmarked car and immediately switched on the siren.

'Turn the bloody thing off, Harry. I can't hear myself think.'

The whooping noise stopped instantly.

He got in the front seat and Sarah in the back.

'Who's in charge?'

'A Sergeant Harris from Northenden.'

'Get on the blower to him, Sarah. Tell him we're on our way and to keep everyone away till we get there. Then get on to the SOC team and have them there ASAP.'

Harry was pulling out of the station and racing down Oldham Road, reaching into his jacket pocket with his right hand. 'It's the last number, Sarah.' He tossed the mobile to her.

She didn't know what she had done to deserve this but she was happy anyway. At least she was away from the office and off the bloody computer.

She dialled the sergeant at the scene of the crime. He answered immediately, telling her in detail what he had already done.

She took the phone away from her ear to report to Charlie Whitworth. 'The body's on a sandbank in the middle of the Mersey, boss. The sergeant has cordoned off a perimeter on both sides of the river. Apparently SOC are already on their way.'

'Ring them anyway to check.'

'Will do.'

The car raced down the M60 in the outside lane, coming off at the airport exit and turning left after the Brittania hotel.

'Mill Lane's on the right, Charlie,' said Harry.

'Know the area well, do you?'

'Grew up in Wythenshawe.'

'Lucky you. Any of your schoolmates out of prison yet?'

Harry Makepeace didn't answer.

'The SOC team will be here in ten minutes, boss. The crime scene manager is called Diane Fenton.'

'Good, we'll have a shufti before it's covered in people wearing white plastic suits and blue gloves.'

Harry swung the car right into Mill Lane, forcing the oncoming traffic to stop. The car hit the cobbled street and immediately began to judder.

'One day we'll get a car with suspension that hasn't been repaired by a butcher.'

'Fat chance, boss.'

'Where are they?'

'There's a car park down the end next to a derelict pub, the Tatton. Spent many a happy night in there, I did, when I were courting.'

'Didn't know they had pubs in the Middle Ages, Harry.'

As they neared the pub car park, they saw a uniform guarding the entrance. Charlie Whitworth rolled down his window and flashed his warrant card. 'Where are they?'

'Over the bridge and to the left past the weir.'

'Don't let anybody in here.'

They pulled in and ran up the steps of a green bridge. Sarah was behind her two colleagues as they ran over the bridge, hearing their heavy footfalls on the wooden planks, followed by her much lighter tread.

She could see activity to her left, on the footpath next to the river beyond a weir. A crowd of onlookers had already gathered, kept back by some police tape and a couple of beleaguered constables.

They ran down towards the crowd.

'Harry, call the local nick and get some help down here right now. I want this scene as tight as a duck's arse.'

A sergeant was helping to push the crowd back along the path. Half of the people were carrying golf clubs.

'Sergeant Harris. DCI Charlie Whitworth.'

'You finally got here.'

'What have we got?'

'A woman on the sandbank.' He pointed back towards the river. Sarah followed his arm. A dark object was floating next to a dank muddy shoal. In her mind it gradually formed into the shape of a body: blond hair, arms, a torso, all bobbing in the grey waters of the river.

'Jesus!' It was Harry Makepeace who spoke. 'How are we going to get there?'

'I want all these people moved back at least 60 yards, Sergeant. And make sure the paths are blocked around the pub, the bridge and this part of the river.'

'Yes, sir.'

'Sarah, tell the SOC team they can set up a situation area next to the pub.'

She got on the phone. 'They're already there, sir. Just suiting up.'

He turned to the sergeant. 'Who called it in?'

'A woman from the flats over there.'

'Go and see her, Sarah. I want all the details while it's still fresh.'

She watched as the boss walked to the bank of the river, staring at the body floating just fifteen yards away. She could make out the head and shoulders of the body much clearer now. One side of the face looked like it was collapsed in on itself, an empty eye socket staring sightlessly out into the river.

'Please let it not be him', she heard her boss whispering to himself, before he turned back to her. 'Haven't you gone yet?'

Chapter Thirty-Six

'You're not a great fan of the police, are you, Carol?' Ridpath thought it was time to confront this woman.

'Not really, no. Too slow, too thick and too willing to charge the innocent for crimes they didn't commit.'

'That's rubbish and you know it. If you knew the evidential hoops we have to jump through simply to get the Crown Prosecution Service to consider a case, you wouldn't speak such tripe.'

'"We?" I thought you worked as a coroner's officer now?'

'We're all on the same side, aren't we?'

Margaret Challinor was looking at both of them with an air of amusement.

'Are we? Our job is to find out the truth, not to rush to convict.' Carol Oates's carefully manicured hair was beginning to unravel slightly as her voice rose.

'We don't rush to convict. We look at the evidence and let it lead us to a conclusion.'

'Rubbish. You bring all the prejudices and preconceptions of a bunch of macho white males into every investigation. All blacks are thieves. All Muslims are terrorists. All women are gagging for it. It forms the basis for every investigation. You don't want to hear the truth.'

Ridpath could feel himself getting angry. 'That's a bloody prejudiced statement, if ever I heard one. The truth? We don't seek the truth because it doesn't matter in a court of law. We seek evidence, it's all that counts. The truth always lies. Only evidence is clear. Pure, unadulterated evidence.'

Margaret Challinor held her hands up. 'Shall we agree to disagree?'

Ridpath reluctantly nodded, followed curtly by Carol Oates.

'We must stay focused on the case in hand. Ridpath, what's your next step?'

He thought for a moment. 'I'd like to interview James Dalbey.'

Margaret Challinor's eyebrow rose slightly. 'Why?'

'It seems to me the one person at the centre of this case is him. Unless we understand why he attacked those women, we're never going to get far. Plus, the documentation at the undertakers and in the morgue is missing. Why?'

'He was locked up well before those documents went missing,' said Carol.

'Exactly. Why? If he was charged and imprisoned, why remove the documents about one of his victims?'

'And why steal her body?' asked Mrs Challinor.

'None of it makes sense. But in order to start putting this jigsaw together, I have to understand the key piece: James Dalbey.'

'When do you want to go?'

'As soon as I can. Tomorrow if possible.'

'I'll call the prison and make the arrangements for tomorrow afternoon.'

There was a gentle tap on the door and Jenny entered. 'I think you should see this.' She held up a copy of the late edition of the *Manchester Evening News*: the headline read 'CORONER ADMITS MISTAKES'.

'Oh shit,' said Mrs Challinor, raising her eyes to the ceiling.

Ridpath couldn't help but notice a tiny smile crossing Carol Oates's face as she pushed back a stray hair that had come loose from her chignon.

Chapter Thirty-Seven

Sarah Castle was making her way up the stairs to the third-floor flat when her phone rang. She knew exactly who it would be.

'Did you get it for me?' asked Ridpath.

'Listen, I don't feel good about this—'

'Did you get it?'

She stopped on the landing just below the woman's floor. 'It's on a thumb drive. Not as much as I expected though for a major investigation.'

'You got all the files?'

She was getting annoyed with his questions. She was the one doing him a favour, for God's sake. 'All of them.'

'Good.'

'Another woman has been murdered.'

'What?'

'I'm just going to interview the woman who called it in.'

'Shit.'

'Exactly. Charlie Whitworth's at the scene with the SOC team.'

'I need to get the thumb drive tonight.'

'I'm going to be here till late.'

'I'll come to you. I need to check out the crime scene for the coroner anyway.'

'I've got to go.'

She cut him off before he could reply. She was already regretting downloading the files for him, but what the hell. What was done was done.

She climbed the last few steps to the fire door, pulling it open. The woman's flat was on the left, number 23. She knocked on the door and it was immediately answered by a female constable. Why did women always get the liaison jobs while the men did the bloody investigating?

'How is she?'

'Fine, trying to put her kiddie down for a nap.'

'You go for a break, I'll interview her.'

The constable stepped out of the way to allow her to enter. A woman was standing in the living room, holding a baby to her breast and rocking left to right. The woman stared at her and raised a finger to her lips.

Sarah Castle stood still, watching the baby's eyes flutter briefly before closing.

The woman stopped rocking and started walking towards the crib. As soon as she did a wail far louder than any police siren erupted from the tiny body. The woman began rocking again, singing a plaintive, out-of-tune lullaby.

Sarah Castle stood there waiting.

Finally, the baby settled down again and closed its bright-blue eyes. The woman kept on rocking for ten more seconds before walking over to a cot in the corner and placing the baby gently down on the mattress, covering her over with a pink blanket.

'I've been trying to get her to nap for the last hour. There's too much going on,' she whispered, tiptoeing away.

The woman was young: late twenties, Sarah guessed. Her hair was blond and lank and she had the careworn look of all young mothers faced with a 24-hour vigil over a young baby whose husband was never around to help.

'Do you want a cuppa?' She pointed to the kitchen.

Sarah nodded yes. 'My name is Detective Sergeant Sarah Castle—'

The woman placed her finger on her lips again. 'Can you keep your voice down? She's a light sleeper.'

'Sure', Sarah whispered. 'I'm here to ask you about what you saw.'

The woman placed a mug of tea in front of Sarah and pushed the bowl of sugar towards her. 'You don't know how much I look forward to this. Sad, isn't it? A cup of tea is the highlight of my day.'

'About the body you saw...' Sarah took out her notepad and wrote the time and date at the top of the page.

The woman put her mug of tea down on the table. 'It was the man who made me look.'

'What man?'

'The one who was standing on the riverbank. I was hanging up her onesies to dry. She spends her life shitting on them and it doesn't half smell. What is it about babies' poo? I mean they only drink bloody milk, don't they?'

Sarah shrugged her shoulders.

'You don't have kids, do you? I mean you're too normal. Haven't you noticed new mums all have this air of distraction, as if they know they've forgotten to do something but they just can't remember what it was?' She took another large mouthful of tea.

'You were telling me about the man?'

'I was, wasn't I? He was standing on the riverbank, staring at something. I was standing at the window trying to get her to sleep. He was there for at least a minute. I wondered what he was looking at so I went out onto the balcony.' She took another gulp of tea. 'He was staring at something on the sandbank. I looked across and it seemed to be just a lump of something that had drifted down over the weir.'

'What did you see?'

'I looked closer and it wasn't a bundle of clothes at all, but a woman floating there, her arms outstretched and resting on the sandbank. So I shouted at him...'

'What did you shout?'

'I think it was "Oi, you" or something like that. He looked up at me like he was scared or something, then he took a quick look at the body and took off.'

'Which way did he run?'

'Towards town.'

'And what did he look like?'

'Medium size, sharp featured, with a goatee. Quite lithe and athletic, if you know what I mean – not muscular, like my husband Ian used to be. And he was bald too.'

'Ian?'

'No, the man who ran away. He was bald. Ian just thinks he's bald.'

Sarah wrote the description down in her notebook. 'And what was he wearing?'

'All black. A black hoodie – Adidas, I think – a black T-shirt and black leggings.'

'Anything else?'

'Yeah, he looked scared when I shouted, like a kid who'd been caught doing something naughty.'

The baby gave a quick sniffle, turning over in its cot. The woman froze, not saying a word. When the baby was quiet again, she patted her chest and drank again from the mug.

'Would you recognize him?'

'Ian? Probably.'

'No, the man?'

The woman thought, before nodding. 'It wasn't a face I'd forget.'

'Good, I'll get someone to come round and show you some of our photofits.'

For the first time the woman became animated. 'You mean like one of the police artist impressions you used to see on *Crimewatch*?'

'Exactly, but it uses photographs, not drawings, and it's done on a computer.'

'Isn't everything these days? Except this…' She grabbed her right breast and lifted it up. 'Ian used to call them Pinky and Perky. After the baby, he renamed them Flopsy and Dropsy. Did I tell you I was married to a right bastard?'

Sarah stood up. 'Here's my card, Mrs…?'

'Prendergast. Cecilia Prendergast.'

'If you think of anything else, Cecilia, just give me a call. I'll arrange for the photofit people to come to you.'

As she finished speaking, the baby erupted into a pained fit of screaming on the scale of A flat.

Mrs Prendergast rushed from her chair into the living room, picking up the baby and lifting up her shirt to allow it to suckle.

Sarah waved goodbye, but received no response from the woman who was gently rocking the quietened baby in her arms, staring down at its peaceful face.

Thank God I don't have any children, she thought. Not likely to either.

Chapter Thirty-Eight

When Sarah went back to the riverbank, Charlie Whitworth and the other detectives had moved over to Mill Lane, and the outer cordon around the scene had been widened.

'The crime scene manager thinks the body was thrown from the bridge,' Harry Makepeace told her.

Sarah could see two white-suited figures silhouetted against the green bridge.

'We also think the killer probably parked next to the pub before dumping the body.'

The car park was empty of vehicles now, with two more of the SOC team searching the ground for clues.

'The river current presented a bugger of a challenge for the SOC team. The sandbank was unstable so nobody could stand on it. They had to borrow a boat from a nearby rowing club.' He made quotation marks with his fingers as he said the word 'borrowed'. 'The crime scene photographer even had to balance on it as he took his pictures of the body and the area.'

'Not an easy place to manage.'

Harry shook his head. 'At least the divers are here now and have moved the body to the shore.' He pointed to a place on the near side of the riverbank where a compact white tent had been set up by the SOC team.

Next to it, a team of divers was combing the banks, searching for debris. One held up a child's rusted tricycle like he had found pirate treasure. Another was pulling a long piece of grey fabric from the reeds next to the weir.

Harry Makepeace nodded towards the DCI. 'I'd stay away from him for a while. He's got a touch of the Alex Fergusons.'

'Full hairdryer?'

'Maximum power.'

Charlie Whitworth strode towards them. 'Sarah, you get suited up. Harry, you check the cordons on the paths beside the river are properly manned – we've extended them 200 yards either way.'

'Yes, boss,' said Harry, moving away quickly.

'You took your bloody time.'

'The woman had a baby. It was a difficult interview.'

'Well?'

Sarah relayed the woman's statement.

'Get on to the photofit guys. I want a composite of the man ASAP.'

'Already done, sir. They'll be here tomorrow morning.'

'Not good enough – I want them here today. If they give you shit, tell them John Gorman's given this priority.'

'Yes, boss.'

After she made the call, they were finally given permission by the crime scene manager to enter the tent. They suited up in the white Tyvek onesies, hairnets and blue latex gloves, pulled aside the flap and entered.

The pathologist was already leaning over the body.

'It's a murder, isn't it, not a jumper?' were Charlie Whitworth's opening words.

'Good afternoon, Charlie, it's pleasant to see you too on this bright April afternoon in Northenden.'

'Don't piss me about, Harold. Is this a murder?'

The pathologist sighed loudly. 'Looks like it from a preliminary examination. See, the wire of the garrotte is still around the neck. The face has been smashed in. It could have happened if the body had crashed into the weir but I don't think so. There's blood in the bruising, suggesting she was still alive when these marks were made. We'll know more when the post-mortem has been completed.' He pointed down to the legs. 'See the kneecaps. It looks like somebody has been drilling holes. Was she tortured?'

Sarah stared at the legs, fascinated. The white skin was puckering and covered in dirt, but around the knees she could see four distinct holes surrounded by red bruising.

Another technician was kneeling down at the side of the body, carefully bagging the right hand.

'How long has she been dead?'

'I haven't a clue.'

'Come on, Harold, you can do better.'

The pathologist turned his head away from the body. 'I can't and I won't. After all the James Dalbey rubbish recently, I'm not sticking my neck out for anybody. I've had the coroner's officer give me the third degree this afternoon.'

'Don't worry about Ridpath, I'll handle him.'

'Still can't give you anything. Look, you know time of death is notoriously difficult to estimate for bodies in water. The body temperature doesn't follow the usual pattern of losing 1.5 degrees for every hour after death.'

'Give me something to work with, Harold.'

The pathologist let out a long sigh. 'More than an hour, less than three days. Until we get back to the lab, there'll be nothing better I'm afraid.'

'Any ID on her?'

The technician shook his head. 'I didn't find nuffink on her,' he said laconically in a London accent.

'Another Jane Doe. John Gorman won't be pleased.'

The technician had finished bagging the right hand and now moved on to the left. He stopped for a moment and tapped the pathologist's shoulder, pointing to the hand.

The pathologist examined it. 'Interesting. The index and middle finger of the left hand have been broken at the knuckle.'

'What's that supposed to mean?'

'It means it's interesting, Charlie. From the redness of the bruising the hand was broken before death.'

'Does this confirm she was tortured?'

The pathologist shrugged his shoulders, saying nothing.

The technician lifted the lifeless arm. The pale white bloodless hand hung limply down. The nails were a dirty, dingy white and the fingertips had puckered and wrinkled. Then he wrapped the hand in a numbered evidence bag, sealing it with a tie from his pouch.

'Finished, Terry?' asked the pathologist.

The laconic technician nodded.

'Help me to move her.'

They both knelt either side of her with their hands on her shoulders. A whispered '1, 2, 3' and the girl was placed on her bag.

Sarah Castle stared into the woman's lifeless eyes. The face was flecked with mud from the sandbank, with more oozing out from both nostrils. The left side of her face was smashed in by repeated blows, breaking the occipital bone and the cheek and jawbones. The left eye socket was empty – a dark hollow where an eye once rested.

But it was the mouth that horrified Sarah. It was pulled back in a rictus scream, gums exposed and tongue stuck out, revealing smashed teeth.

The smile of death.

The pathologist sat back on his haunches and stared at the body. 'I have some bad news for you, Detective Chief Inspector.'

'What's that?'

'I think the MO is similar to the girl with the swan tattoo.'

'Shit,' said Charlie Whitworth.

'And worse, he's escalating. The damage to this body is more severe.'

'You think he's going to strike again?'

Harold Lardner just nodded once. 'I think he will.'

Sarah Castle stared at the body of the young girl.
She didn't say a word.

Chapter Thirty-Nine

Ridpath hadn't told his wife about his trip down south yet. He would save that dubious pleasure for later. He parked the car next to the SOC van at the top of Mill Lane and walked down towards the crime scene.

The technicians were already setting up lights; it was obviously going to be one of those long nights. Others were taking pictures, moving equipment or simply waiting for instructions. All were dressed in the SOC uniform of white plastic and blue gloves looking like a posse of Teletubbies.

Charlie Whitworth and Sarah Castle were standing to one side, also dressed in white, with Harry Makepeace beside them in his street clothes.

'Look what the cat's dragged in.' It was Harry Makepeace being his usual cheery self.

'How's it going?'

Charlie Whitworth shook his head. 'Not good. Another body displaying some but not all of the trademarks of our previous killing. Body was in the water so I'm not expecting a lot from forensics. Victim unknown again. No ID, no tattoos. You here on business or pleasure?'

'A bit of both. Pleasure at seeing Harry here finally doing an honest day's work and business for the coroner with you.'

'Oh aye?'

'She'd like to see the police notes from the investigation into James Dalbey.'

'Jesus, Ridpath, I'm in the middle of a major investigation and you're hassling me about somebody we put away ten years ago? Tell her to go through official channels.'

'She has already.'

'John Gorman said yes?'

'He had to. It was an official request.'

'OK, come down tomorrow afternoon for them.'

'I can't, I'm away tomorrow. Can I get them now?'

'What's the rush?' His eyes narrowed for a moment. 'Where are you going tomorrow?'

In for a penny, in for a pound, thought Ridpath. He was going to find out sooner or later, best get it over with now. 'I'm off to see James Dalbey.'

'That bastard! You're going to see that bastard?' Charlie Whitworth exploded, causing all the SOCOs nearby to turn and look at him. 'Well, good luck. I hope he remembers you. The man who actually caught him.'

'We'll see. So can I have them now?'

'John Gorman agreed?'

'So I've been told.'

Whitworth sighed. 'OK, OK. Sarah, would you mind going back to the station and digging out the files on James Dalbey for our colleague, the coroner's officer?'

'I'd much prefer to stay here, boss.'

'You've done all you can. Go back and set up the incident room with the pictures of the girl and the photofit of the man the witness saw when they've finished creating it.'

'OK, boss.'

'I'll give you a lift, Sarah,' said Ridpath

They walked back towards his car.

She glanced across at him. 'You're a manipulative sod, aren't you?'

'He would have given me them anyway... eventually.'

She eyed him suspiciously. 'Has John Gorman agreed?'

'He will do by tomorrow.'

'He's going to kill you when he finds out.'

He smiled, looking back at the Mersey. 'I'll cross that bridge when I come to it.'

'You're a bastard, you know?'

'Have you got the thumb drive?'

'I'm not sure I should give it to you now.'

'DCI Charlie Whitworth has given his permission.'

'Because you lied to him.'

'He doesn't know that.'

They stopped beside his car. 'I need the notes, Sarah. I'm interviewing Dalbey tomorrow and I need to get up to speed on the investigation before I see him. What have the police to hide anyway? The investigation was well-documented and the courts found him guilty.'

Sarah Castle reached into her jacket and handed him a thumb drive in the shape of a Swiss army knife. 'They're all here, everything I could find.'

'You're a star, Sarah.'

'And you, Ridpath, are a prize shit. The least you can do is give me a lift back to HQ.'

Chapter Forty

Ridpath edged along the row of seats mumbling his apologies as people lifted their legs out of the way. Of course, his wife had chosen the middle seats.

On stage a young boy was playing Beethoven's 'Für Elise', hitting just one bum note in three. The piece actually sounded like something by the Clash.

'I'd thought you'd forgotten,' she leant in and whispered in his ear as he settled himself.

'How could you, Polly? Of course I remembered – it's Eve's big night.'

The truth was, he had forgotten. After driving Sarah back to the station he'd rushed home, intent on printing out the files so he could read them on the train. But when he arrived, the house was in darkness, with no sign of his wife and child.

On the mantelpiece above the fire was a short note in block capitals: 'AT THE SCHOOL. CONCERT NIGHT.'

'Shit. Shit. Treble shit.'

He'd driven like Lewis Hamilton to the school, parking on a double-yellow line outside.

'So you didn't see my note on the mantelpiece?'

Oh, Polly, he thought – you forget I've been trained in the subtle art of interrogation. 'What note?' he asked coyly.

'The one you didn't see, on the mantelpiece which isn't there.'

'That note?'

She nodded.

'Didn't see it.'

The boy finished with a rousing arpeggio. It was the first time Ridpath had ever heard 'Für Elise' ending in an arpeggio, but it seemed to work. The crowd applauded politely.

'She's up next.'

'What's she doing?'

'One of Hamlet's soliloquies.'

'Isn't that a bit advanced for her age?'

'She's an overachiever, like her mum.'

Ridpath nodded his head. 'OK. You know, the only thing I could recite at her age was the Manchester United football team: Macari, Hughes, Giggs...'

'Shush, she's on.'

On stage his ten-year-old daughter was picked out by a single spotlight. She was wearing a pair of purple tights and a pink T-shirt several sizes too big for her.

'She's got my T-shirt.'

'She liked the colour, felt it conveyed the anguish of Hamlet's tortured mind.'

'It's my favourite T-shirt...'

His daughter began to speak the famous lines, giving them a melancholy he hadn't heard in her voice before. It was as if she were Hamlet asking herself about the meaning of her life:

To be, or not to be: that is the question:
Whether 'tis nobler in the mind to suffer
The slings and arrows of outrageous fortune,

It was strange to hear these words delivered in the tones of a girl whose voice was not yet mature, but he felt that for the first time he understood their meaning. English lit. had never been his passion at school. Nothing had been his passion. After his father's death, his mother had pushed him, always pushed him to do better, not to let his father down.

But he couldn't remember his father. His face was clouding in the mists of the past: there but unreachable, untouchable.

Vague and unformed. He wished he could remember more but he couldn't, no matter how hard he tried. The memories he did have were of his mother's words, of her paying for tutors to help him pass maths. God, was he hopeless at maths. And her delight when he got into university.

It was as if all her hopes and dreams for life were vested in him and his sister, with none left over for herself.

Thus conscience does make cowards of us all;
And thus the native hue of resolution
Is sicklied o'er with the pale cast of thought,
And enterprises of great pith and moment
With this regard their currents turn awry,
And lose the name of action. – Soft you now!
The fair Ophelia! Nymph, in thy orisons
Be all my sins remember'd.

She finished and there was silence. Then the clapping began. Eve was at the front of the stage now, taking a bow, his pink T-shirt bowing with her.

He looked across at his wife; a single tear had dropped onto her cheek. Not a teacher's tear on seeing a pupil do well, but a mother's tear of pride.

Now was probably not a good time to tell her he would be away down south tomorrow, visiting a serial killer in a maximum security prison.

Was there ever a good time for that sort of news?

Chapter Forty-One

At the police station, Sarah set about creating a new information wall in the incident room. She pasted up pictures of the victim, adding the photofit image when it arrived.

For her, the photofit was worse than useless: a picture of a bald man wearing a hoodie. It looked like half the scallies in Manchester and all of them in Salford. If they published it in the papers, they would be getting thousands of phone calls, none of them useful.

Back at her desk, she logged on to her computer and checked out Tony Seagram as she had promised Ridpath.

There was nothing recent on the files. He seemed to be squeaky clean, worked for Granada in their special reporting team. Had produced and written a couple of hard-hitting documentaries, one of which was sharply critical of the lack of police action against financial crimes. Not married and with no current girlfriend, he lived in the middle of the Northern Quarter. There were no outstanding warrants, not even a speeding ticket.

The man seemed to be a paragon of virtue.

'Too good to be true,' she said aloud.

'You're looking at my Facebook profile,' said Alan from the desk opposite.

'Not a cat in hell's chance. Your profile would be too bad to be believed.'

'You know me too well, Detective Sergeant Castle.'

She returned to her computer screen, deciding to go further back.

Bingo.

She called up an arrest sheet for August 2007. Seagram was charged with assaulting a woman, an ex-girlfriend, punching her twice during an argument. She checked the rest of the file. Apparently the case never went to court as the woman dropped all charges. Had Seagram put pressure on her? Or was she so frightened of him she couldn't face him in court?

Was this significant? She didn't know, but she was sure Ridpath would love to hear about it.

For the next 15 minutes she checked out Tony Seagram, but the incident in 2007 seemed to be his only arrest. She sent the charge sheet to the printer so she could give it to Ridpath later, even though after that business with the case files, he wasn't in her good books.

She tidied up her inbox, logged in her hours and her movements, before finally checking her mail for the fourth time to see if there was anything from Charlie Whitworth.

Nothing.

The files from the 2008 investigation were sitting on her computer desktop. Glancing over her shoulder to make sure nobody was watching, she opened the first one and began reading. It was a transcript of an interview with James Dalbey on 10 March. It must have been the first interview after he was arrested and brought back to the station. The time was 6.30. They must have let him stew for five hours to unnerve him.

DCI GORMAN: This is Detective Chief Inspector John Gorman.
DI WHITWORTH: And this is Detective Inspector Charles Whitworth.

It was strange reading Charlie say his proper name, almost as if it was a different person. This was obviously before the police had rewarded their successful conclusion of the Dalbey case with promotion. What was the Peter principle? You get promoted to your level of incompetence – that was it. The lectures from her student days drifted back into her memory.

She carried on reading.

DCI GORMAN. The time is 6.30 and this interview is being conducted in Room 3 at Greater Manchester Police headquarters. I have a Mr James Dalbey sitting opposite me. Please confirm your name and date of birth.

DALBEY: What?

DCI GORMAN: Say your name and date of birth.

DALBEY: James Dalbey. 20 June 1963.

Whoever had transcribed the tapes was writing down everything. They must have been new to the job.

DCI GORMAN: Mr Dalbey, I have to remind you that you do not have to say anything, but it may harm your defence if you do not mention when questioned something which you later rely on in court. Anything you do say may be given in evidence. Do you understand? Please answer for the tape.

DALBEY: (mumbling)

DCI GORMAN: Please speak clearly.

DALBEY: (unclear)

DCI GORMAN: For the record, Mr Dalbey has nodded his head.

DCI GORMAN: James Dalbey, you have been charged with assaulting a police officer in the course of his duties. In legal terms, this is deemed aggravated assault and I have to warn you this offence carries a jail sentence of up to one year and a £50,000 fine.

DALBEY: I didn't mean to do it. He was close to me and I don't like it when people get too close to me.

DCI GORMAN: Sergeant Mungovan says you punched him, forcing him to fall backwards after he had stopped your van for a broken rear light. Sergeant Mungovan is now receiving treatment in hospital for a broken collarbone.

DALBEY: I didn't mean to push him.

The interview carried on like this for another page, getting the details of the traffic stop. He had admitted pushing the police sergeant so he was screwed. She jumped ahead; Charlie Whitworth had started speaking for the first time.

DI WHITWORTH: Now, James. I can call you James, can I? Would you like some tea? Something else to drink? No? OK, well, I have something else to ask you. Take your time when you answer, but it is extremely important to tell us the truth. You know what the truth is, don't you?

DALBEY: It's telling it how it is.

Sarah smiled. They were double-teaming Dalbey. Gorman, the plain-speaking copper and Whitworth the friend who just wants to know the truth. Charlie Whitworth was playing the good cop; he must have hated that job.

DI WHITWORTH: Telling it how it is. Exactly. Now, James, can you tell us what you were doing between 4 and 8 p.m. on the night of 4 March?

DALBEY: I... I'm not sure.

DI WHITWORTH: Come on, James, you can remember. It was the night a girl was kidnapped.

DALBEY: I remember that night. It was sad. I loved Alice.

DI WHITWORTH: You knew her?

DALBEY: Yes, from church. She was in my Sunday school class.

DI WHITWORTH: So you're telling us you knew Alice Seagram?

DCI GORMAN: Tell us what you were doing, Dalbey. Did you murder Alice?

DALBEY: No... no... no... no... no... (tapping noises on the table)

DCI GORMAN: You killed Alice, didn't you?

DALBEY: No... no... no... not me.

DCI GORMAN: You had the keys to the lock-up, where we found the other girl alive, Freda Scott.

DALBEY: He told me to go there, I didn't know.

DCI GORMAN: You kidnapped Freda too, didn't you? Admit it. We found you in the lock-up.

DALBEY: No... no... no... not me.

DI WHITWORTH: Tell us the truth, James. Did you take Alice to the lock-up too?

DALBEY: I can't remember... can't remember (tapping noises louder now).

DCI GORMAN: And the evening of 7 March, where were you between the hours of 4 and 8 p.m.?

DALBEY: (Tapping noises cease) At her house, where I went for my tea. We had sausage and chips and beans... my favourite.

DCI GORMAN: You were in her house that evening?

DALBEY: Yes. It's a Friday. I always go to their house on Fridays for my tea.

(END OF INTERVIEW)

Whitworth and Gorman had closed the interview pretty quickly after this piece of information. They must have gone to check with the family. Suddenly their prime suspect was not a prime suspect any more. He had an alibi.

Sarah read this part of the interview again. It was something Dalbey had said. 'He told me to go there.' What did that mean? Who had told Dalbey to go there?

She glanced around the office. A few of the support staff were working but most of the detectives were down at the riverside with Whitworth. Nobody was looking at her. She inserted a thumb drive and copied the files. She would finish the rest of her reading at home.

Something wasn't right about this case; there were too many inconsistencies and too many mistakes.

And then it struck her with the force of baseball bat. If James Dalbey was innocent, it would mean the real killer was still out there on the streets of Manchester.

He had been free for the last ten years.

Chapter Forty-Two

'You made a mistake, Lesley.'

She was kneeling down in front of him, head bowed. He had drawn himself up to his full height, making himself tall, looming over her.

'Errors are costly. They have consequences.'

'I understand.' She could feel the girls' blood sticking to her knees. Black dank blood that seemed to flow up from the carpet, clinging to her legs.

They were in the workshop. She had received an urgent message from him telling her to come. But she already knew why.

The blanket.

He knew everything about the police investigation.

Everything.

Nothing escaped him. She couldn't escape him now.

'You should have told me.'

'Yes.'

'Why didn't you tell me?'

'I was frightened.'

'Because you made a mistake?'

She nodded.

She felt his hand gently touch her forehead.

'We all make mistakes, Lesley,' he said softly. 'It's what makes us human.'

'I'm sorry. It won't happen again.'

'I know it won't happen again.'

He moved to one side to pick up the soldering iron from the top of the wooden table. 'Mistakes will not be tolerated, Lesley, you know my rules.'

'No.'

'You don't know my rules?'

'No… I mean, yes…' she stammered. 'I mean, I know mistakes will not be tolerated.'

She saw the red-hot end of the soldering iron approach her face and hover in front of her nose, before moving slowly towards her eyes. She could see the bright red tip, a thrill of smoke drifting lazily off it.

She closed her eyes.

She could feel the heat from the end of the iron. She could smell the arid aroma of molten metal. She could hear the tingle of electricity through the wires.

'Would you like me to take your right eye out, Lesley? Would that be the correct punishment?'

She could feel the heat through her eyelids.

Must say the right thing. Must say the right thing.

'It won't happen again, I promise,' she blurted out.

'But you haven't answered the question. Is losing an eye the correct punishment?'

The burning end of the soldering iron moved closer. For a second, she opened her eyes, seeing the red-hot tip burning brightly. 'It's the correct punishment. I made a mistake, I deserve to be punished.'

She closed her eyes tightly.

The heat of the soldering iron was moving closer, closer. She could feel it burning through her eyelids, searing into her eye.

'I still have use for you. I still have use for your eyes.'

The heat moved away.

She opened her eyes. She could still see. He had spared her. A bright wave of emotion rushed through her body. A combination of fear, exaltation and sheer relief.

'Roll up your sleeve and hold out your arm.'

She did as she was told.

Instantly, he stabbed the red-hot soldering iron into the soft crook of her elbow. The happiness of a second ago was replaced with a searing jolt of pain like 1,000 volts of electricity coursing through her body.

Then it stopped, to be replaced by nothing.

A vast emptiness.

Then the pain kicked in again. Burning, caustic pain. She could smell her skin frying, sizzling under the heat of the soldering iron.

'There will be no more mistakes, Lesley. Is that clear?'

The pain eased and she cradled her right arm in her left.

'No more mistakes.'

There would be no more errors. She would follow his instructions to the last letter, whatever the consequences.

He was the master and she the slave.

No more mistakes.

'It's time to go further, Lesley.'

'I understand.' She knew this was the right response. 'When?'

'When I tell you. But this time we must choose somebody who matters. These women...' – she could hear the sneer in his voice – 'these fallen women are beneath us, beneath our talents. We must find somebody more... difficult.'

'Whatever you say, sir.'

Chapter Forty-Three

Sarah parked her car outside her house. She lived in Sale, a quiet suburb in Trafford, only 15 minutes' drive from the station at that time of night. In the rush hour though it was a different story, taking more than 45 minutes on a good day.

The front garden was small, a postage stamp, but at least it had a few roses brought from home by her mum. Sarah occasionally watered them, but by and large they looked after themselves.

A bit like herself really.

She opened the front door and listened to the house.

All quiet.

It was a time she enjoyed – coming back to an empty house. Most people would have hated it, but for her it was a magic time. A time when, after she closed the door, she was in her own world, answering to nobody.

Her last girlfriend, Tina, she had kicked out a year ago. One of those women who had been doted on throughout their lives and expected exactly the same treatment from their girlfriends. Sod that for a game of soldiers. The request for breakfast in bed was met with a cold saucepan of baked beans being poured over her head. 'Your breakfast is served, madam.'

Tina moved out half an hour later. Sarah had seen her at Sainsbury's once since then, grocery shopping with a new girlfriend. There were no regrets; she hoped the new woman enjoyed her dual role as lover/maid.

She switched on the light. The kitchen was spotless, as it always was. An empty draining board. Clean breakfast table. Sparkling chrome fixtures.

Wine or cocoa?

She chose the latter, placing a saucepan of milk on the stove and getting the tin of Bournville out of the cupboard. She fetched her laptop from the living room as the milk warmed up, booting it up as she walked back.

Three spoonsful of cocoa in the milk, she then whisked it until a froth began to form and the milk to foam. A big mug from the rack and she was set.

The laptop had finally booted up and she inserted the thumb drive in the port, moving the files onto her desktop.

Where should she start?

She opened up the report of the post-mortem on Alice Seagram.

The usual pro forma appeared on her screen.

One blow to the back of the head from a round, blunt instrument. She remembered later tests had matched the impact of the blow to the ball-peen hammer found in Dalbey's van. That and a DNA match with Alice's blood had clinched the case.

The rest of the autopsy was unsettling reading. Bruising to the legs and thighs. Sexual molestation with a blunt object, possibly the shaft of the hammer. Fingers broken on left hand. Swabs taken of fingernails. No evidence of strangulation. Eyeballs without any petechiae. Multiple stab wounds and the throat slit with a sharp knife. Finally, the body had been doused in sulphuric acid.

'Why douse the body in acid?' she asked herself. 'To remove all DNA traces on the skin,' she answered herself out loud. 'But then, why leave a hammer with DNA on it?'

Sarah went back to the line 'fingers broken'. What had the pathologist said at today's crime scene? She tried to remember his exact words. 'The index and middle finger of the left hand have been broken at the knuckle.'

Was that the link?

She opened up the medical report on Freda Scott, and quickly scanned it. The woman found alive in the lock-up had her left index finger broken too.

Why had nobody mentioned anything? Why hadn't it been flagged up as part of the MO?

Strange.

She looked at the clock on the wall: 2.30. Somehow the cocoa had become cold. She thought about reheating it in the saucepan and carrying on with her reading of the files, but decided not to. Tomorrow was going to be a long day; she'd better get some sleep.

She washed the saucepan and cup, leaving them to drain by the side of the sink. She would put them away tomorrow morning before she went to work.

As she climbed up the stairs to her bedroom, one thought kept rattling around her brain.

Was James Dalbey innocent?

Chapter Forty-Four

The next morning Ridpath was on the 6.15 train from Manchester Piccadilly to Euston, from where he would take the underground to Plumstead.

He settled into his seat, removed the printouts from the files Sarah had given him and began to read.

The documents seemed well written and comprehensive, as if John Gorman had realized somebody might be reading them later. The interviews with James Dalbey were documented in exhaustive detail up until the point he had stopped speaking. In the margins were handwritten notes checking out Dalbey's story, all of which were initialled 'CW'.

Had Gorman asked Charlie to check everything? It certainly looked like it.

Next to a sentence from Dalbey talking about a man who had booked the van for him, Charlie had written:

> Checked 12/03/08. Van hired over the phone by a man from Prospect Limited on 7 March. Picked up by Dalbey in person morning of 10 March. Mileage records show it was driven 20.8 miles. Distance from hire firm to Chorlton 7.4 miles.

And later on, when the man was mentioned again:

> SOC team performed a complete forensic examination of the lock-up garage. No other DNA was discovered except for that of Dalbey and the five

victims. Bodies of three of the victims still missing.
Have questioned Dalbey but he claims to know
nothing.

Outside the window of the train, the English countryside
rushed past, a blur of green marked occasionally by some ugly
buildings or industrial development. Every ten minutes another
new business park seemed to come into view, as if they were
growing like a rash across the landscape.

He returned to the documents, examining the pathologist's
report. It seemed fairly standard: detailing the injuries suffered
by Alice Seagram. Attached was a hand-written note from the
pathologist, Dr Lardner:

> After a reappraisal of the evidence, and taking into
> account the unusually warm weather conditions
> for the time of year, I have decided to broaden the
> possible time of death to midnight on 7 March. An
> exact time of death is impossible to ascertain at this
> moment until new evidence comes to light.

It was signed by Dr Lardner and dated 11 March, the day
after James Dalbey had been arrested and interviewed. Had John
Gorman put pressure on the pathologist to change his report?
Then he remembered he hadn't taken his Revlimid. 'Shit. Shit.
Shit.' Polly usually reminded him, but he had been in such a
rush he had forgotten. She always joked, 'One a day to keep
the doctor away.' But there was always a hint of sadness in her
voice as she said it.

He took the pack out of his bag. Such a little pill to save his
life. He flashed back to the day his treatment had started.

He was put on an experimental treatment of a combination
of Revlimid, cyclophosphamide, and dexamethasone called
RCD by the consultant, all of which were taken by mouth in
28-day cycles. The cyclophosphamide was the chemotherapy,

while the 'D' element was a steroid. Some days he had to take over 32 tablets.

He had four cycles and then went on to stem-cell collection, high-dose melphalan and stem-cell transplantation. More days visiting the hospitals, more injections and long hours sitting with a vein in his right arm and another in his left, connected by tubing to a machine that took stem cells out of his blood and then returned the blood back to his body.

It felt like something from a 1930s Frankenstein movie with him as the recreated monster.

Then came the killer time when they gave him high doses of melphalan to kill off the cancer cells and reintroduced his own stem cells. Four weeks in total isolation at Christie's, unable to touch or hold Polly and Eve. A bastard of a time, not knowing if the treatment would work.

He couldn't face that again.

Not again.

The train went through a long, dark tunnel. Classic timing, he thought, a bit like my life back then.

He sat there in the dark, his eyes closed, reliving those moments alone in his bed at night listening to the sounds of the hospital around him.

Never again.

Chapter Forty-Five

The meeting was starting in two minutes. This time, Sarah had no role; Charlie Whitworth would chair it from the beginning.

She took her seat next to Harry Makepeace. He looked tired; obviously he'd been at the crime scene all night, watching the SOCOs collect evidence under powerful arc lights. She was also tired, having woken up early to finish reading the files before she went to work. There were a couple of things she didn't understand from the first and second autopsies on Alice Seagram, not least the consistent pattern of broken fingers nobody seemed interested in questioning.

She'd call Ridpath after this meeting and tell him about the fingers and about Tony Seagram's conviction for assault.

She looked around the room; the usual suspects were there, but no Charlie Whitworth yet. The photos of the crime scene she had put up last night stood out against the white of the wall: a wide shot of the river and the sandbank with something resting on it; a medium shot of the area with the lump more clearly visible; and a close-up of what was obviously a human body face down in the water, arms and upper torso on the sand and the rest of the body in the water. Finally, a close-up of the face of a woman, hair wet and skin flecked with dirt.

A pretty face.

A tired face.

A dead face.

Next to it was the photofit of the man seen leaving the scene by Mrs Prendergast, with a blown-up description. To her, he still looked like half of the hoodies she arrested in her days on the beat. A shoplifter, maybe, but a murderer?

The back of the room suddenly stiffened; people no longer slouched against the wall, notebooks came out. Somebody was weaving their way through the detectives.

John Gorman entered, followed by Charlie Whitworth.

A small man carrying that sense of presence of all small men. Salt-and-pepper hair scraped back from the forehead, neatly combed into place either side of tiny, feminine ears. A blue jacket slightly too large for him and shiny black shoes. Were they patent leather?

He positioned himself at the front of the room with Charlie by his side, scratching his nose as the detectives went silent. She noticed an elaborate yellow ring on his left hand. A citrine? Not the sort of jewellery one would expect to find on a superintendent of police.

'Good morning.' Instantly the room went silent. 'I asked DCI Whitworth if I could say a few words this morning.' He paused, scratching this nose once again. 'Last night, we discovered the body of a woman in the Mersey at Northenden. What I'm about to tell you must not leave this room.' He looked around at the detectives to make sure they had understood his words. 'The preliminary findings of the pathologist suggest a link between this killing and that of the unknown victim with the swan tattoo found beside the Bridgewater Canal in Stretford and another possible victim, a Miss Irene Hungerford, a sex worker from Newcastle who had been working in Moss Side.'

Sarah sat up straighter. Another victim? This was news to her. When had another victim been discovered?

'We are treating this case as one of multiple murder. It is the most important investigation in the unit at this time. Let me repeat. It is the most important investigation. Drop everything else. All available resources will be devoted to catching this man before he kills again.' He paused, scratching his nose once more. 'To this end, I have asked Jonathan Holburt, a consultant profiler, to give us the benefit of his vast experience in dealing with crimes of this type.' He pointed to a man at the back of the room.

Harry Makepeace whistled softly. 'Three thousand quid a day for this guy. They must want our perp badly,' he said out of the corner of his mouth. Sarah pretended she hadn't heard.

John Gorman carried on. 'He will present his preliminary findings during this meeting. I will now leave you in the capable hands of DCI Whitworth. We need this man stopped, ladies and gentlemen, and we need him stopped quickly. I am expecting you to do it. That's all.' One last look round the room and he sat down at the front.

'You all heard the Chief Super. This is our most important investigation. Drop everything else. Understand?'

Whitworth received a series of nods and 'OK's from the assembled detectives.

'Harry's going to fill you in on last night.'

The detective next to Sarah stood up and consulted his notes before speaking. 'A woman's body was spotted in the river Mersey at 2.25 yesterday afternoon by a woman, Mrs Eileen Prendergast who lives in one of the flats overlooking the river. The area was cordoned off at 2.42 by the first attending officer, Sergeant Harris of Northenden. The boss, I and DS Castle arrived at 3.20. The SOC team arrived at 3.30. The Underwater Police Search unit arrived at 5 p.m. and the body was moved to a SOC tent at 5.50. A preliminary search of the river was carried out by divers until dark. The search resumed at 6.30 this morning.' He stopped for a moment and checked his notes.

'A search of the riverbanks revealed the body of the woman was probably dropped from a nearby bridge and floated down from there across a weir before lodging itself on the sandbank. A forensics team are examining the bridge and the car park next to it for evidence, but it is likely the scene was compromised by first responders.'

A detective put his hand up.

'Go on, Chris.'

'Was the body weighted down?'

'Not that we know of, but we'll have to wait for forensics.'

'How long had the body been in the water?'

'We're waiting on the answer from the pathologist.'

'When did she die?'

'We're waiting on that too. Look guys, and...' – Harry was about to say 'girls' but decided against it, '– ladies. You know how it is. We'll get those results out as soon as we have them. Two interesting matters to note.' He pointed at the photofit picture. 'This man was spotted by Mrs Prendergast at the scene. Did he carry the body and throw it off the bridge? We need to find him as quickly as possible.'

He shuffled across to a new picture. One she hadn't put up: a grey blanket with a dark stain in the centre, still visible despite being immersed in the water. 'The second matter is that this was found in the Mersey, caught on a dumped pram.' He pointed to a picture of the blanket. 'To my tired eyes, this stain looks like blood. But we can only confirm this when the forensics team reports back.'

Charlie Whitworth stepped forward. 'Right. Let's hear from our consultant profiler. Jonathan, can you give us the benefit of your experience?'

Harry Makepeace sat down next to Sarah. 'Watch him tell us stuff we already know...' he said bluntly.

Holburt walked through the assembled detectives and took Charlie Whitworth's place at the front. 'Thanks for having me here today. It's a great honour to be working with the Greater Manchester Police once again.'

'The honour's all ours. Three thousand quid's worth,' Harry Makepeace said under his breath, but loud enough for Sarah to hear.

'Let me get right into it. Those who know me, know I'm a profiler who uses forensic behavioural analysis. It's a method I've developed myself which has proven successful in the past.

I'll produce a full report for you guys before the end of today, but here's my top line.' Jonathan Holburt looked down at the floor, and then began speaking. 'We're dealing with a practised and proficient killer. The offender is male, over 40 years old, same race as the victims. He has normal to above-average intelligence. He acts alone and will have the rep for being a loner wherever he works. He is probably self-employed and using his own vehicle.' He paused for a moment, tugging at the sleeve of his jacket to pull it down over his expensive watch. 'The murders are planned and rehearsed, organized to the nth degree. He probably brings his own tools, buying them in a series of DIY outlets to avoid being noticed. He is scared of women and lashes out at them to hide his fears. Was he abused as a child? So far he has left no DNA evidence, suggesting he is aware of police investigative procedure. But since the popularity of the programme *CSI* it's not unusual. Interestingly, all the bodies so far have been found close to water. Is this significant for him? Is water a source of terror for him? Or of joy?'

'No, it's just an easy place to dump bodies...' said Harry under his breath.

Jonathan Holburt pretended he didn't hear. 'Be careful with this one, gentlemen... and lady,' he said, looking at Sarah. 'He will kill again. Even worse, his killing will escalate, perhaps expanding like the Yorkshire Ripper away from sex workers to include the general female population. This man will not stop until he is caught.'

A silence descended on the room. Charlie Whitworth stepped forward. 'Thank you, Jonathan, that was extremely illuminating.'

'...not,' said Harry once again.

'Fred has some interesting information from rattling the cages of our local sex workers.'

Sarah noticed how Charlie's language had changed in the presence of his boss and the consultant.

Fred stood up and opened his notebook. 'Still no name for the tom with the swan tattoo, but two things of interest came up. First, another girl went missing about two weeks ago, an Irene Hungerford from Newcastle. One of the pimps said she had come down from Newcastle to work for him. Did a couple of days on the streets then buggered off. He thought she had just done a runner. But last week the sister rang him from Geordieland asking where she was. Could be nothing, but it's the first time I've seen a pimp worried about a girl'.

'OK, put a question mark on the board with the name Irene Hungerford. Fred, get a description and a picture from the sister. We'll check the morgues and missing persons. Let's play it safe on this one, John Gorman thinks this could be another victim.' Charlie nodded in his direction of his boss.

'Second,' Fred continued, 'one of the toms identified a picture of the girl with the swan tattoo. Said she was definitely from Glasgow. They talked one night after sharing some crack. She can't remember much else though, other than she was new to Manchester.'

Fred sat down and closed his notebook.

'Good work. Chrissy, any luck with missing persons?'

'Nothing, boss. Glasgow were supposed to get back to me but I haven't heard anything yet.'

'I'll follow up with Police Scotland – I know the super from a course we attended at Hendon. I'll give him a bell, but you keep hassling.'

Chrissy nodded.

'CCTV?'

Dave shook his head.

Fred stuck his hand up. 'Sorry, one other thing. One of the pimps noticed a white BMW hanging around the streets, driving up and down but not asking for business.'

'Check it out, Dave, but he probably just wants one as his pimpmobile and that's why he noticed it.'

He held his hands out wide like the Pope in the middle of a mass. 'Come on, guys, somebody must know who this bloody woman is?'

Sarah put up her hand. 'Have we thought about releasing the swan tattoo girl's picture to the media?'

Charlie Whitworth rolled his eyes extravagantly. 'Of course we've thought about releasing the picture. I was going to do it this morning, but with the latest killing it would be like a red rag to a bull to the vultures of the press. We'd have half the world's hyenas on the steps of the station waiting to pounce.'

Sarah shook her head, trying to work out the number of animals in the last sentence. 'Why don't we release the photofit of the man beside the river, boss? It's pretty generic but we could just say we're looking for this man to help with our inquiries. Nothing about the case at all.'

Charlie Whitworth thought for a moment. 'Not a bad idea. Make it happen, Sarah. And a reminder: any of you lot thinking of earning a little bit on the side from the rat pack, think again. You'll be out of the Major Incident Team quicker than a Blackpool donkey gets off the beach. Get it?'

A chorus of 'Yes, boss.'

Charlie Whitworth let out a long sigh. 'Listen, we have the name of one missing sex worker but no body. And for the other two victims, we have the bodies but no names. It's not good enough. This man will kill again. We need to make sure we catch him before he does. Understood?'

'Yes, boss,' from the assembled detectives.

'Luke, you're on house-to-house in Northenden. Dave you're at the crime scene. Make sure the CSM has everything she wants.'

'Yes, boss.'

'Harry, you're on the toms again.' A few laughs from the team. 'Ask if anybody is missing, but don't let on we've found another body. Not yet.'

'They'll start to think he's a regular,' said a voice from the back.

'Somebody tell his missus he's been spending time with working girls. Stuff him up good and proper.'

Charlie Whitworth raised his hands. 'I'm on the post-mortem this afternoon. Any questions?'

Sarah saw the opportunity and raised her hand. 'Can I join you there?'

'Ghoul girl,' came the same voice from the back.

Whitworth thought for a moment. 'If the identity of our Mersey victim is not discovered by this afternoon, join me, DS Castle.'

'Thank you, sir.'

Inwardly, Sarah was smiling. Now she could ask the pathologist about the broken fingers. Why hadn't they made more of this?

Chapter Forty-Six

To get inside the main prison Ridpath had already negotiated seven gated doors, produced his police ID six times and had his fingerprints scanned.

On arrival at the High Security Unit – a windowless grey concrete building opposite the main prison's recently built five-a-side football pitch – the security checks began again.

Surrounded by CCTV cameras in a carpeted reception area – the only carpet in the block – he removed his shoes and belt and put all his belongings through an X-ray machine. He walked through a metal detector and was given a body search – the lining of his jeans, the soles of his feet and inside his mouth were all checked.

'As a copper, you're just getting a light check,' said the tattooed prison guard.

'I'd hate to see what you do to the inmates.'

'They get moved every couple of weeks and the whole cell is strip-searched. We've got good security at Belmarsh,' he said proudly. 'Have to, mate – got some real bad 'uns in here.'

At the end of the reception area he saw a red iron gate. He strode up to it and stood outside. He was conscious of the camera above the gate zooming in to stare directly at his face. Some unknown guard hidden in a control centre far away was studying his face and comparing it with security footage when he entered the prison and with the picture on his police ID.

Finally, after a minute, the gate was buzzed open. Once through, he was faced with four more gates.

The guard had followed him. 'Each one of these gates leads to a different wing of the HSU. And no two in the unit can be opened at the same time. Security, innit?'

'Is it meant to keep people in? Or to keep others out?'

'Both, mate. We don't have no bother at Belmarsh. Been open nearly 30 years and nobody's ever got out unless we let them out.'

He was shown into a spacious office, behind which sat a tall man with a military bearing and a grey goatee.

'Paul Reynolds. Pleased to meet you.'

The hand was out and Ridpath shook it. His hand felt like it had been squeezed in a vice. 'Tom Ridpath, on temporary assignment to the Coroner's Office.'

'Take a seat.' The deputy governor opened a file in front of him. 'You're here to meet James Dalbey, I believe?'

'Correct. The coroner has reopened the case of one of his victims, Alice Seagram.'

'Dalbey is an interesting character.'

'Why?'

'He makes a change from the usual murderers, rapists and recidivists.' He opened the file in front of him. 'His psychological assessment is particularly fascinating — a cocktail of OCD, adult ADHD, narcissism and possibly Asperger's, but the psychiatrist wasn't sure. And on top of it all, there's a diagnosis of early onset schizophrenia when he was 12.'

'He's been a problem for you?'

'On the contrary, Mr Ridpath, James Dalbey has been a model prisoner.' He leant forward, interlocking his fingers in front of him. 'You have to understand, the main problem in any prison is boredom. People are locked up for long periods with nothing to do. The mind can play awful tricks on anybody when it's got time to work its worst. Dalbey doesn't have that problem. He spends 24 hours a day trying to prove his innocence of the murder of Alice Seagram.'

'There were other killings, but he was never charged.'

The deputy governor sat back. 'Interesting, he never talks about those – just Alice Seagram.'

'Do you think he's innocent?'

Paul Reynolds threw his hands up. 'I don't think anything, Mr Ridpath. My job is to ensure the safety of all the prisoners here while they remain in our custody. Innocence. Guilt. For me, they are just words that have no meaning inside HMP Belmarsh.' He closed the file in front of him. 'You know, the cons have a saying, you only do two days in prison: the day you go in and the day you leave. We make sure the time between those two days is as quiet, peaceful and safe as is humanly possible.'

'Funny to think of prison as a safe place.'

'That's what it was always meant to be. A prison is a place where society is free from its inmates and the inmates are free from their exterior problems.'

'Is James Dalbey free?'

A long sigh. 'He's free as long as he's obsessed with getting out of here, Mr Ridpath. My fear is what happens when that is denied.'

'Or even achieved?'

The deputy governor placed the file away in a drawer. 'Dalbey will be ready for you now. The officer will take you to a meeting room.' He stood up and opened the door. Outside in the corridor, a portly officer, also with a grey goatee, was waiting.

'A word of warning, Mr Ridpath. James Dalbey will test you. He tests everybody – it's one of his obsessions.'

Chapter Forty-Seven

A wave of excitement washed over Sarah. She felt her face reddening. They were standing in the gallery looking down on Harold Lardner and his assistant as they began the autopsy.

She knew it was strange but she loved this part of the job. She loved the smell of the formaldehyde. The glitter of the steel instruments in the spotlights. The cleanliness of the pathology suite.

As a student, one of her roommates was studying to be a doctor. She had joined him once for one of his anatomy courses. He had dared her one day and she had taken him up on his challenge. All she had to do was don a white coat, borrow one of his clipboards and tag along with him.

She remembered watching the large man being cut up on the table, layers of creamy fat tinged with blood on the stomach. The professor, an elegant man wearing a bow tie, enunciated in beautiful tones the name of each part of the body as he cut it away and removed it, laying each organ on the table beside him.

One of the medical students fainted when the heart was removed. But she had stared, transfixed.

The voice of the pathologist cut through her memories. 'The time is 12.06 on 2 April. My name is Harold Lardner and I am performing the autopsy of a woman found in the Mersey yesterday. The client is a white female, aged approximately 20. A preliminary examination of the body reveals no tattoos or distinguishing marks, other than a childhood vaccination scar on the upper right arm.' He examined the body minutely. 'No other scars or injury marks. No track marks, suggesting this woman wasn't an intravenous drug user. The client has a below-average body weight for her height and size.' A check of the hands and the feet, removing the bags first 'Bitten fingernails, but manicured and polished toenails – a strange combination. The detritus beneath the fingernails has already been removed for examination in case there should be any epithelials from scratching or fighting her assailant.' He stepped back two yards from the steel table, looking at the body as a whole. 'The body exhibits the puckering of the skin common from being immersed in water. Impossible to estimate the length of time she had been lying in the water. It would have been longer than eight hours, though, from the amount of puckering.'

Charlie Whitworth pressed the button on the console in front of him. 'Any idea of time of death?'

The pathologist looked up at the gallery, his eyes sandwiched between the surgical mask and the Tyvek cap. 'I know you're in a hurry, Charlie, and patience isn't your strong suit, but give me a chance – I've only just started the examination.' The voice was querulous, annoyed, so unlike the one he used when speaking into the microphone.

Charlie Whitworth thought about responding, but then changed his mind, releasing the intercom button.

The pathologist resumed his examination of the body. 'There seem to be three small bite-sized marks on the outside of the left thigh.' He leant in closer. 'Too small for human bites, I would think, and the teeth are the wrong shape and size. I would guess *Rattus rattus* decided to have a spot of breakfast on the woman's body.'

Charlie Whitworth spoke again. 'What does that mean, Mr Lardner?'

'It means, Detective Chief Inspector, the rats of the Manchester rivers, probably our friend the brown rat, had a little nibble at our client. It also suggests she wasn't in the river too long, or there would be far more bites. We'll check the bites against our database and confirm later. But I'm pretty certain it's Mr Rat.' He leant forward to examine the body more closely. 'But that's interesting…'

Charlie Whitworth couldn't stop himself. He pressed the button and asked, 'What?'

'The index and middle finger of the left hand have been broken. There is swelling to the knuckle on the left compared to the right hand. See?' He held both hands side by side. The assistant took a close-up photograph.

Sarah touched the intercom button before Charlie Whitworth could intervene. 'You think this finger was broken by the killer, Mr Lardner?'

'I don't know. It could have been. Or it may have been broken by the body striking an object in the river, for example when it went over the weir.'

'Any way of knowing?'

'Knowing whether it was *pre-* or *post-mortem*?'

'Yes.'

'Of course, I'll examine the hand for subcutaneous bleeding. If the finger was broken before death the finger will have a red hemorrhagic appearance.' He continued to examine the right hand. 'There does seem to be red bruising around the wrist and fingers. We'll have to check the tissue under a microscope but my opinion is the fracture was caused before death.'

Charlie Whitworth was staring at her. She continued anyway. 'Did the Jane Doe two days ago, the woman with the swan tattoo, have a similar break on her hand?'

The pathologist stopped for a moment. 'If memory serves me, she did. To the little finger.'

Charlie Whitworth interrupted their conversation. 'Where are you going with this, Sarah?'

She held her hand up. 'One last question. Mr Lardner, do you remember your examination of the victim of the Beast of Manchester? Weren't Alice Seagram's fingers broken too?'

'Jesus Christ, Sarah, you're not still on about this. Dalbey is in prison, for God's sake.'

'It was ten years ago, Detective...?' The pathologist's voice boomed from the loudspeaker.

'DS Sarah Castle,' she answered.

'Well, DS Castle, I think you are correct, but once I've finished here, I'll check my notes to be sure.'

'Give it a rest, DS Castle.' Charlie shoved Sarah's hand away from the intercom button. 'Please carry on with the autopsy, Dr Lardner.'

'Righto, moving along to examine her injuries. The right knee has four holes in it, probably caused by a drill. I'll experiment to find the exact size of the bit for you later. These drill holes were made while the victim was still alive as shown by the...'

But Sarah wasn't listening. There was a link between the two series of killings ten years apart, and she had just proved it.

Now she only had to convince her boss, who was, at present, staring at her with a look of sheer disdain.

Chapter Forty-Eight

James Dalbey was sitting upright and alert behind a low table. Ridpath tried to remember the man when he had last seen him – eyes full of fear, strands of hair falling across the dirty floor, covering up his face as Ridpath raised his arm to bring his fist down on his temple.

The man who sat in front of him had hardly changed. The Bobby Charlton comb-over was still there, although neater and shorter now. The glasses were the same heavy black frames. The skin was just as white and untouched by the sun. A few more wrinkles around the eyes betrayed the passage of time maybe. The clothes had changed, obviously, into the prison uniform of a light-blue shirt and grey trousers. But other than that, it was like being taken back ten years.

He walked over and pulled out a chair. Dalbey watched him all the time, not saying a word. Ridpath noticed a plastic water cup stood right in the centre of the desk on his side. Had Dalbey placed it there?

The eyes stayed on him, unblinking.

Ridpath remembered his interview training. If a suspect looks down or to the side, he's usually trying to be evasive, has something to hide. A suspect who looks straight at you is trying to be part of the process. He's opening himself up.

'My name is Tom Ridpath, I'm the coroner's officer for East Manchester—'

'I recognize you.' The words were slow and precisely articulated like a man who had not spoken for a long time. 'You gave evidence at my trial. You were the policeman who arrested me.'

Ridpath moved the cup from the centre of the table, Dalbey's eyes following his hands all the time. 'That was me,' Ridpath admitted, 'a younger version.'

'You've changed a lot, Mr Ridpath. You've been ill.'

How did he know? Had somebody told him about the cancer? The deputy governor, maybe? Tony Seagram?'

'You think I've been ill?'

The eyes, slightly magnified though the heavy glasses, stayed on him. 'I know you've been ill. You're going to ask me how I can be sure. And I am going to answer that in prison people become ill all the time. One of the highest natural death rates occurs in prisons, Mr Ridpath, did you know?'

'I didn't know.'

'Cancer, mainly.' He leant forward across the table. 'I don't want to die in prison. I'm an innocent man. Innocent men shouldn't die in prison.'

'This isn't about me, James. Can I call you James?' Ridpath struggled to retain control.

'Oh, but it is about you. And me. And truth. And justice. All those things and more.' His eyes remained on him.

'You know why I'm here?'

James Dalbey nodded. 'God sent you.'

Had he heard correctly? Before he could ask another question, Dalbey continued speaking.

'God heard my prayers to the high court and he sent you. The prayers were blocked before, but now God listens to me.'

Was this man mad? Or was he just pretending? Using the Myra Hindley tactic of having found God to try to escape his sentence? 'I'm afraid God hasn't spoken to me.'

'God spoke to the judge and to them.'

This was becoming tedious. This man wore his armour of God like Joseph wore a Technicolor dream coat. 'You are aware the high court ordered her body to be exhumed?'

'Yes.'

'And there was no body in the coffin?'

'Yes.'

The man had become monosyllabic. He needed to get him talking. 'What do you think happened?'

'He took her.'

'Who took her?'

'The man who murdered her.'

'It wasn't you?'

'No, I'm innocent.'

Ridpath opened the police file in front of him. Time to use shock tactics. 'Alice Seagram died from being beaten about the head with a ball-peen hammer, stabbed multiple times and then having her throat slit from ear to ear. After her death, she was possibly raped with the same hammer and then her body—'

James Dalbey covered his ears with his hands. 'It wasn't me. He did it. He did it.'

Ridpath checked the psychiatric assessment at the time. A diagnosis of paranoid schizophrenia. But if this man was certifiably insane, why wasn't this used as a defence?

With a speed which Ridpath found uncomfortable, James Dalbey removed his hands from his ears and returned to his calm state.

The detective tried a different tack. 'Can you tell what you remember of the day I arrested you?'

James Dalbey's eyes flickered upwards and to the right as he thought back.

'Just try to remember what happened.'

His eyes fluttered closed but Dalbey remained motionless, hands clasped in front of him. 'He told me to go to a garage off Claridge Road...'

'Who told you?'

'The man. He knew everything about me, was helping me to get better. Said I had to go to a garage to become better. One of my tasks for the day.'

'What was his name?'

The eyes bulged behind the closed lids. 'He never told me his name, said it wasn't important.'

'So he told you to go to the garage?'

'I was driving the van—'

'Was it your van?'

'No, he gave it to me.'

Ridpath checked the police notes. The van had been hired over the phone the day before. Cash paid.

'What happened then?'

'I heard this loud noise behind me. At first I thought it was an ambulance but then I realized it was the police. I got scared.'

Ridpath glanced at the file. 'You'd been in trouble with the police before?'

'Bad men, policemen. They lied.'

The file stated Dalbey had a conviction for resisting arrest two years earlier. Sentenced to probation. 'So what did you do next?'

'I tried to get to the garage. He said I would be safe in the garage.'

Ridpath flashed back to the day ten years ago, his police car chasing the white van, lights flashing, siren blaring. 'But you stopped.'

'He told me to stop.'

'But you were the only one who was in the van.'

'No, before I drove the van. He said if the police came, to drive quickly for three minutes and then to stop.'

Ridpath's mouth was dry. He looked down at the plastic cup at the side of the table, considering whether to drink, but decided it was too risky. 'What happened then?'

His eyes opened. 'You know what happened. You were there.'

'I want to hear it from you.'

A slow nod. The eyes closed again. 'I stopped the van. I saw a large copper walk towards the rear and bend over to check the brake light.'

Ridpath could see Dalbey was in the moment; he was back in that day ten years ago. His foot was tapping on the floor as if he were walking down the road towards Sergeant Mungovan.

'The policeman stood up and pushed me away, said I was too close. I was just trying to explain about the light. The man had smashed it.'

'Why?'

'I don't know why. He never told me why he did anything.'

'So the police sergeant pushed you…?'

'I don't like anybody touching me, so I pushed him back and he fell over, banging his shoulder against the wheel.'

That was when Ridpath had looked up, seeing this man towering over his sergeant. What had he been doing in the car? Checking the vehicle registration, that was it. The voice coming from control. 'Proceed with caution, over. Driver of Ford Transit FB05 TBY wanted for questioning regarding abduction of prostitute from Moss Side…'

Ridpath checked the police files. There was an anonymous tip-off that the van was involved in the abduction of a prostitute. Anonymous tip-off? But according to Dalbey the van was only given to him that morning. It had been hired late on the previous night.

'…And then I ran. You see, he told me to run to the garage if I was stopped. Whatever I did, get to the garage.'

'I chased after you.'

'You kept shouting for me to stop but I had to get to the garage.'

'How did you know where it was?'

'He showed me that morning. He said "You must run here. Understand?" I understood.'

'So you ran there even though you knew I was chasing you?'

'I ran as fast as I could but you caught up with me. I didn't know which key to use, see. I'd never been inside the garage before.'

Ridpath remembered standing on the mound; Dalbey was searching through the keys looking for the right one.

'You attacked me as I opened the door.'

'I didn't attack you. I arrested you.'

'You jumped on me, I tried to defend myself. I don't like it when people touch me.'

The dark garage. His arms over his head. Ridpath with his fist raised, bringing it down hard against the man's temple. 'You know what was inside the garage?'

'The girl against the wall. Blood. Dirt and decay. Disorder. I don't like things to be untidy or dirty.'

'You were taken to the station?'

'They said I could never leave. I would have to stay there forever.'

'Who said?'

'The policeman with the moustache. He said I'd done a bad thing and I was never going to leave the police station until I signed.'

Ridpath remembered his return to the station. The other police officers lining up to pat him on the back and offer their congratulations. Charlie Whitworth and John Gorman taking him aside to tell him how pleased they were with his conduct and how, in the future, they would look after him. 'You've got a bright career ahead of you, Tom, mark my words. We'll look after you. Me and Charlie here. We always take care of people.' Followed by a little knowing laugh. One of the happiest days of his life.

He dragged himself back to the interview. 'So you signed the confession?'

He nodded quickly. 'Told them about the man but they didn't want to listen.'

Ridpath checked the files. There was a note in Charlie's handwriting. 'Suspect talks of "another man". No corroboration. Psychiatric evaluation?'

'Even when I signed it, they wouldn't let me leave. They lied to me so I refused to talk to anybody. I don't like people lying.'

'You never said another word?'

'No.'

'Not to the psychiatrist?'

'Especially not to him. Sticky man, his palms were sweaty.'

The notes contained a full psychiatric evaluation. 'Patient cooperative and talkative.'

'You didn't speak to the psychiatrist?'

'Not a word.'

Ridpath was about to point out the discrepancy in the files, but he decided not to bother. He was sick of this man, this place, the smells, the noises and the ticking of the clock on the wall. 'I think we've done enough for today, Mr Dalbey.'

A hand came out across the table and seized his wrist. 'You do believe I'm innocent, don't you?'

Ridpath stared down at the hand holding his wrist. Slowly, Dalbey released his grip.

'It doesn't matter if I believe you, Mr Dalbey. The evidence is all that counts.'

'But it isn't for a coroner, is it? According to the Coroners and Justice Act 2009, the coroner's job is simply to find out the truth.'

'You seem to know the law well.'

'I've had a long time to study it.'

Ridpath got up and packed his files into his battered briefcase. 'Thank you for your time, Mr Dalbey.' He put out his hand.

Dalbey just stared at it without moving.

Ridpath turned and banged on the door to be let out. A guard immediately opened it up.

Just as he was about to leave the room, Dalbey spoke again. 'You'll never find her, you know.'

'Find who?'

'The body of Alice Seagram. That's who you're looking for, isn't it?'

Ridpath stopped. 'Do you know where she is, Mr Dalbey?'

Again, the violent shake of the head. 'But he does. He took her away.'

Chapter Forty-Nine

'What the hell do you think you were doing in there?'

They hadn't gone two steps outside the mortuary before Charlie Whitworth was in her face. The autopsy had lasted two more hours with Mr Lardner performing his usual Y-section, examining the vital organs of the deceased in minute detail. All they had discovered was that she hadn't drowned – there was no water in the lungs – and she hadn't been sexually active on the day of her death. The death itself was confirmed as manual strangulation by garrotte after a beating with a blunt instrument around the head. Time of death was any time in the 24 hours preceding the discovery of the body.

'My job, sir – just asking questions.'

'My job, sir.' Charlie mimicked. 'I'll tell you what your job is, Detective Sergeant. When we are in an autopsy, your job is to take notes and keep your mouth shut. Is that clear?'

'But I was just pointing out the similarities between the two murders so far and those of the Beast of Manchester back in 2008.'

'We caught the Beast – his name was James Dalbey. Where is he now, Castle?'

Sarah noticed the absence of both a rank and a Christian name. 'In Belmarsh Prison.'

'And you know this how?'

'Because I rang the prison, sir. They said he was in his cell.'

'So how can he be committing murders in bloody Manchester?'

'With all due respect, sir, it seems to me—'

'With all due respect, Detective Sergeant, you need to concentrate on the investigation we have at the moment, not dig into matters already dead and buried.'

'Not in the case of Alice Seagram. Her body has gone missing.'

Charlie Whitworth rolled his eyes and let out a long sigh. 'You're beginning to piss me off, Detective Sergeant, trying my patience. The murders of the Beast of Manchester were solved in 2008. End of. We put him away. His name was James Dalbey. End of.'

'Could it be a copycat killer?'

Charlie ran his fingers through his non-existent hair. 'Not according to the bloody expensive profiler we've just hired. According to him, the killer is a first-timer who is developing his methods as he goes along.'

'But surely, sir—'

Charlie held up his hands. His voice was firm and commanding. 'I'll say this once and once only. We are looking for a new killer. He has committed at least two heinous crimes, maybe more. Your job is to help me catch him before he commits a third. You job isn't to chase some wildcat theory from the pages of some trashy women's magazine.'

Sarah remained silent.

'Do you understand, DS Castle?'

'Yes... sir,' she added reluctantly.

His voice dropped a register.

'Listen, Sarah, I'm all for coppers having a bit of initiative, but when it starts getting in the way of an active investigation, then it has to stop. Let's hear no more of your bullshit theories. Old-fashioned police work is going to solve this crime. Chasing and squeezing the evidence until it gives us the man we need. Clear? Now let's go and get a sandwich. Autopsies always make me so hungry. Maybe it's seeing all the meat on display.'

Chapter Fifty

Outside the prison, Ridpath immediately lit a cigarette, trying to replace the smells of incarceration with the bitter taste of tar. He exhaled a long draught of smoke into the sky, hoping Polly would forgive the transgression just this once, but he needed nicotine right now.

The Uber would arrive soon to take him back to the station.

He had a problem. Even though he had arrested Dalbey, found him with the keys to the garage where a woman was manacled to a wall. Even though a hammer with the blood of Alice Seagram was found in the back of the van. Even though Dalbey had been found guilty by a jury of his peers. Despite all this, Ridpath thought he was innocent.

He didn't know why. Call it copper's gut. A feeling something was wrong somewhere.

The files on the case looked open and shut. All procedure had been followed to the letter, even to getting a psychiatric assessment of Dalbey, but still the nagging doubt remained in Ridpath's mind that something wasn't right.

The Uber pulled up in a squeal of brakes. He looked back at the stark grey prison walls. Imagine spending time inside there – a living death. A bit like having a cancer – not just inside you, but surrounding you as well.

He had another appointment with Dr Morris tomorrow. Just a check-up, but he hated them. More blood taken by the nurse who couldn't find a vein if it was as wide as the Mersey. 'Just an armful this time, Mr Ridpath.' She always told the same joke, channelling Tony Hancock.

He shouldn't complain but he always felt like a guinea pig. There were always a couple of students hanging on the professor's every word, being tested about his illness while he lay there watching them watching him. One of them even had the temerity to start poking him in the stomach as if he had an ulcer. He was tempted to shout: 'I've got cancer, not a tummy bug – and warm your bloody hands next time.'

The Uber driver waited patiently for him to finish his cigarette; he must have picked up a lot of cons outside these gates.

He wasn't looking forward to his next visit to the hospital. At the back of his mind was the big fear. He sensed it every morning from Polly before he left to visit the doctor.

'Have you got everything?'

'Of course.'

'What time's the appointment?'

'At 10.30, but I won't get to see him until 11.30 – he's always running late. It's why they call us patients.'

Polly didn't smile, simply saying, 'He's busy.'

A quick peck on the cheek and he'd leave the house, knowing she was watching him through the window, waiting for him to get in the car and drive away, wondering if he would be coming back that evening.

Because the big fear in his mind was that the doctor would tell him he was no longer in remission and the cancer had returned.

He finished his cigarette, stamping the butt down with his shoe where it joined a whole factory of other butts. This must be the place where all the prisoners had their first fags of freedom.

He would have a lot of thinking to do on the train back to sunny Manchester; too much thinking.

He opened the car door and got in.

'You just got out?'

Ridpath glanced over his shoulder at the prison receding quickly into the distance. 'You could say that.'

'Funny, you don't look like you've been inside long.'

'Why?'

'You look too healthy. Most of the ex-cons I pick up look like they're going to die tomorrow. Not a healthy place, prison. What did you get?'

Ridpath was staring out of the window, distractedly. 'What?'

'What did you get?'

'Life,' he finally answered.

Chapter Fifty-One

Sarah called Ridpath's mobile. The number rang for a minute then went into voicemail. She left a message. 'Hi, I need to talk to you urgently. I think I've found something on Tony Scagram and on the murders. Call me back as soon as you get this. Oh, it's Sarah, by the way... DS Castle,' she finally added.

It was 8 p.m. and the incident room was still buzzing. Harry Makepeace had just come back with a confirmed ID on the girl found in the Mersey.

'She was a sex worker, right enough. Name of Debbie Ashworth from Knowsley, near Liverpool. One of the other toms recognized her as a new girl. Had only been on the streets for a week.'

'Well done, Harry. Get on to Merseyside Police and see if they've got anything on her. She's probably got form for soliciting. Also get an address for the family. Sarah, you're the family liaison officer: contact them tomorrow morning when we have the address. You'll have to drive across to Liverpool.'

'Will do, boss.'

After this, a local businesswoman, Mrs Norris, came forward saying she thought the photofit picture in the *Manchester Evening News* reminded her of one of her employees, Martin Sharples. She had his address, so Charlie Whitworth, Harry Makepeace and Norman Dean had gone charging off to knock on his door.

Before he left, Charlie had asked Sarah to check all the witness statements compiled from the house-to-house, looking for anomalies and inconsistencies. She and he both knew it was make-work: something to keep her busy and away from the investigation itself. A little punishment for speaking up this afternoon.

She had completed it anyway, placing the finished files on his desk, having added two suggestions for follow-up interviews. The family address still hadn't come in from Liverpool; the Scousers were always a bit slow.

She looked at the clock. Already 10.30.

She thought about ringing Tom Ridpath again or perhaps going round to his place. She needed to talk to someone about the broken fingers and about Tony Seagram. But then she remembered he had a wife and child. Perhaps they wouldn't be too pleased to see a bedraggled copper knocking on their door, wanting to discuss a case until the small hours.

It could wait till tomorrow. Nothing was urgent anyway. The murders had happened ten years ago, they weren't going anywhere.

She signed off on the log sheet for her overtime and then packed up her stuff; two packets of Polos and a half-eaten cheese and tomato sandwich.

After his reaction at the mortuary, she'd have to make it up to Charlie somehow, get back into his good books. Otherwise, she could find herself doing traffic for the rest of her life. The thought of spending her days stuck in a dark room staring at televisions showing the M6, the M61 and M62 gave her a headache.

Anything but that.

She took one last glance into the incident room. It was empty at the moment. The pictures on the walls were a stark reminder of the case they had to solve. A new picture stared out at her: the smiling face of a pretty woman, haloed by a frizz of curly hair. This must be the woman from Newcastle who went missing in Moss Side. What had happened to the body?

She knew she was on to something. She just had to get more evidence, prove there was a link to the murders in 2008. And, if Charlie Whitworth still wouldn't listen, take it to John Gorman.

A risky strategy, for sure. She would be either a hero or a zero.

Either way, she would do what was right and damn the bloody consequences.

Chapter Fifty-Two

Lesley watched in her rearview mirror and saw her coming out of the station and walking across the car park. This was the woman she wanted. The description fitted her to a tee: wearing a red jacket, carrying a black shoulder bag, shoulders slightly hunched and blonde hair tied up in a ponytail.

The woman looked tired, her body moving slowly, without energy.

Good, it would make it easier for her.

He had said it was time to take it up a notch, to test themselves against the angry hornets' nest this would provoke.

No more working girls.

No more misfits and strays from the streets.

No more junkies.

At first she was scared, worried she wouldn't be able to pull it off. But then she saw the beauty, the audacity of the plan, and it thrilled her. They had to change who they were targeting, otherwise nobody would know what they had done. There had been very little in the papers about their earlier victims.

No major reports.

No concerned citizens.

No letters from 'Angry of Hale'.

'It was because they were nothings. Meat for the use of men. The papers don't care about them. Nobody cares about them. We have to do something they will notice.'

Now was the time to change, take it to the next level. She had been merely practising before, perfecting her craft, he said.

This was the real test, the acid test. The way to really make them sit up and take notice.

And what better way than to take one of their own?

At last, she could prove herself to him.

At last, she could win his trust.

At last, she could win his love.

The death of this copper would be an act of love. Not everybody would see it that way, but he would – and he was all that mattered.

She watched as Sarah Castle climbed slowly into her Audi. The lights went on and she began to pull out of the car park. The woman followed her, keeping back 100 yards as he had advised.

He had already told her where the woman would be going. All she had to do was be patient and make sure she wasn't spotted.

They drove down Chester Road, through the ghost town that used to be the centre of Stretford. It amused her that 2,000 years ago, Roman centurions had marched this way, off to kill the Brigantes. Now here she was, off to kill a copper.

The more the world changes, the more it stays the same.

Past the turn off to the canal where she had dumped one of the other bodies. The girl who had screamed as she had smashed the hammer into the side of her face.

She had enjoyed the screams. It reminded her of the time her mother forced her to watch her drown the kittens in the bath when she was seven; the kittens screaming as they tried to scramble up the white enamelled sides. Her mother catching hold of them and pushing them under the water until they no longer struggled.

They had killed five kittens that day.

She had killed three women so far.

It was easier than killing kittens.

The policewoman turned left in Sale. It was clear she was going home. She lived alone, so the house would be empty, but it didn't matter.

Nothing mattered.

The car pulled up outside a house on the left. The police-woman reached into the back and got her bag. As he'd instructed, she pulled up alongside, winding down her window.

The policewoman was standing beside her car, locking the door.

'Excuse me,' she asked, 'could you tell me the way to Market Street in Altrincham?' She held up the road map. 'I think I took a wrong turning somewhere.'

Play the foolish woman, he'd said, channel Marilyn Monroe and her dumb blonde act. Remember this woman's a copper; she wants to help people, it's in her DNA.

'Sorry, I didn't hear. Where did you say you were going?'

'Market Street in Altrincham.'

'Oh, you're miles away,' Sarah Castle said, smiling. 'Don't you have satnav?'

She saw the copper's eyes checking the back seat to see if there were other passengers and then the visible relaxation as she saw the car was empty, with only a middle-aged woman driving.

'It's bust – I've been meaning to get it fixed for ages. You know me, leave everything till the last minute. Could you show me on the map?'

He'd told her to switch on the cabin light and hold the map on her steering wheel, force her to lean in the window, to look. The copper would be relaxed: outside her own home, a lone woman needing help, nothing to fear.

She raised the map slightly. 'Where exactly am I?'

The policewoman put her bag on her shoulder and leant forward, resting her arms on the open windowsill.

Just a little further.

'You're not far from Sale town hall. Let me see the map.'

Leaning in closer.

She could smell her perfume now. Still faint traces – she must have re-spritzed earlier – but mixed with sweat and tiredness.

The policewoman's head was leaning in through the window, looking at the map, finding her position with her finger. Leaning in a little further to catch the light. A trail of faint blonde hair on her neck.

She brought the syringe up and jammed it into the area just below the ear, depressing the plunger.

'You have 30 seconds', he'd told her, '30 seconds before the drug takes effect. Control her, don't let her go.'

The policewoman slapped her neck with her left hand, feeling the hard plastic of the syringe sticking out. 'What the hell?'

Lesley took hold of the ponytail and smashed the copper's head against the metal edge of the door.

Once.

Twice.

Three times.

She could feel the copper struggling to escape her grip on the hair.

Four times.

She felt the ponytail become heavier as the copper's legs gave way, slumping against the door.

Move quickly, he had told her.

She let go of the ponytail and tried to open the door, feeling the woman's body weight against it. Don't panic, he had said. If she is leaning against the door, exit via the passenger door.

She did as she was told, wriggling out of the driver's seat, opening the passenger door and taking a quick glance up and down the road.

Still empty.

On the other side of the road, a light went on in an upstairs bedroom.

She froze.

A woman in shadow came to the window and began drawing the curtains, stopping for a couple of seconds before continuing. Lesley stayed where she was, ducking down behind the car.

The woman finished closing her drapes and she could see her shadow vanishing from the light.

She ran round to the driver's side, grabbing the inert body of the copper under the arms and dragging her to the rear of the car.

'Remember how strong you are,' he had told her.

She lifted the copper's body onto the edge of the back seat and rolled it in, pushing in a leg that was sticking out. She closed the back doors quietly and went back to the driver's seat.

'Don't forget to check if she's dropped anything.'

She looked where Sarah had fallen. Her bag had opened, spilling out her wallet, some pens and what looked like a half-eaten sandwich. She shoved all the stuff back in the bag and jumped into the driver's seat.

She had just 30 minutes to get to the workshop before the effects of the sedative began to wear off.

'Drive slowly and carefully. The last thing you want is a speeding ticket or to come to the notice of any nosy coppers.'

This time she would follow his instructions to the letter.

No mistakes.

No foul-ups.

No errors.

The copper was going to die.

As she drove away, she didn't notice the curtain twitch open for a second before closing once more.

Chapter Fifty-Three

The train was pulling into Piccadilly station in Manchester when his voicemail pinged again and again and again. The Wi-Fi had been so abysmal, Ridpath had given up trying for a signal. He had also given up looking for a seat, eventually finding a corner on the floor next to one of the toilets.

It was a very tired and extremely grumpy Ridpath who finally disembarked, vowing to never take Virgin again.

As he walked along the platform to the exit, he checked his voicemails. The first was from Polly.

'Hey you, the man who pretends to be my husband. You forgot to tell me what time you were getting home. I made you a nice dinner, but it's burnt now. Tough shit. If I'm asleep when you get in, don't wake me. And don't forget you have a check-up at Christie's tomorrow at 2.30. Goodnight...' A long pause. 'I miss you, you bastard.'

He smiled. The clock said ten minutes past eleven. He would catch the tram home and, with a bit of luck, would be back before midnight. She would be awake, waiting up for him.

He went to the second voicemail. 'Hi, Ridpath, Margaret Challinor here. Can you be in at 8.30? We have our weekly progress meeting tomorrow, and you need to be there. Plus you can fill me in on your meeting with James Dalbey. Hope you had a good trip.'

Not much sleep, but he'd manage. He hoped he could get away in time for the hospital appointment. He hated going there – nothing to do with the Christie's staff, they were wonderful – it was just the awful sense of anticipation as Dr Morris studied his notes and looked at him over the top of his half-moon glasses. What was he going to say?

Never mind. It had to be done.

The third message was from Sarah Castle. 'Hi, I need to talk to you urgently. I think I've found something on Tony Seagram and on the murders. Call me back as soon as you get this. Oh, it's Sarah, by the way... DS Castle.'

What had she found that was so important? He descended the escalator and waited at the stop. He boarded the tram and, as it pulled away, called Sarah's number.

It immediately went to voicemail.

Strange. She didn't strike him as a person who would ask him to ring back and not answer her phone. Nor was she somebody who went to bed at 10 p.m. with a cup of cocoa.

He tried again, and again it went to voicemail. This time he left a message. 'Hi, Sarah, it's Ridpath. Got your call. What have you found? Will call back tomorrow morning. Have a good night.'

He switched off his phone and stared out of the window at a neon-lit Manchester rushing past. A city changed immensely in the last 20 years, since the IRA bomb that had devastated the centre in 1996. Some people thought it was the best thing that had ever happened; Ridpath wasn't so sure. In gaining so many high-rise yuppie apartments had the city lost its soul?

He remembered the Northern Soul nights with his mates Fast John, Deadly Dave and Paralytic Pete, wearing their wide trews and carving out areas of the dance floor to flash their moves as the girls looked on.

Northern Soul was dying in the late 1990s when he became obsessed with it, but perhaps that was the attraction. Being part of a group of people who knew every song, the story of every singer and the sadness behind every move. He'd been to the Haçienda, but the fake E-driven lovey-doveyness of the scene was not for him. He preferred the energy, sweat and madness of a decent night out with real music, not some moronic synthesizer monotone, twiddled by a fat, balding, overpaid DJ.

He dragged his mind back from something he loved to something he hated. He couldn't avoid it any longer.

What was he going to do about James Dalbey?

On the train back, he had examined every detail of his story. There was something disquieting about it. And then he realized what it was.

The story was plausible.

Was he just another dupe of an incredibly clever and manipulative psychopath?

He went through all the details in his mind again. He didn't think so. There were just too many problems with the evidence, the police investigation and the autopsies of the victim. When added together with Dalbey's explanation of why he had the keys to the lock-up, it all came together into one inescapable conclusion.

James Dalbey was innocent.

Shit. Shit. Shit.

He ran his fingers through his hair. God, he was tired. He would have to tell Mrs Challinor tomorrow. And even worse, he would have to tell Charlie Whitworth.

More importantly, if Dalbey was innocent, then who was the Beast of Manchester? And why had he stopped killing after Dalbey was arrested?

And then an idea struck him that drained his face of blood.

Had the Beast stopped killing?

Chapter Fifty-Four

They were all gathered in the badly furnished meeting room of the Coroner's Office. Ridpath had arrived early to avoid the morning rush hour and had nipped out to Starbucks for a takeaway latte. At least that's what they called it. He could only taste milk with a slight flavouring of something – sawdust came to mind, but it could hardly be described as coffee. Never mind, at least it was warm and comforting.

While waiting for the coffee to be made by the people Starbucks jokingly referred to as 'baristas', Ridpath had called Sarah Castle, reaching her voicemail once more.

'Hi, it's DS Sarah Castle, you know the drill.'

Strange, he thought; why ring someone and then not answer your phone? 'Hi, Sarah, it's Ridpath again, call me back when you get this. I'm stuck in a meeting but I'll take your call. What was it you wanted to tell me?'

The others looked at him as he bustled in. Margaret Challinor was at the head of the table, with Carol Oates on her right; Jenny was on her left with a man he had never seen before, dressed in a black suit and conservative tie.

Ridpath sat in the only seat available, at the bottom of the table. There was obviously a rigid pecking order in this office, as if he hadn't worked that out already.

'Good, you finally made it. We're all here now – let's begin, shall we?' She gave the half-smile, half-patronizing smirk beloved of meeting chairs everywhere.

'Ridpath, have you met David Smail? He's a senior coroner from Derbyshire helping with the workload.' It turned out it was quite common for coroners to work part-time across a number of jurisdictions and to be paid a daily rate for doing so, even when they were full-time coroners in other districts. It was a strange system. He could only imagine the kerfuffle if, as a detective, he presented a bill for work done to help Lancashire Police.

'If you'll open the printout of the Excel spreadsheet Jenny has prepared, you'll see it's a busy time: 144 active cases, 27 adjourned inquests, 86 unusual deaths, 24 accidents and 7 possible suicides. You'll be pleased to hear we won't be going through them all. As coroner's officer, you would normally be involved in all of them, Ridpath, but, as you're new, Jenny has spared you until after your course. When is that, Jenny?'

'I've booked one for the end of April, in Leeds. I hope that's OK?' Jenny's purple eyelids glistened under the bright lights. These women were already beginning to order his life.

Margaret Challinor didn't wait for him to answer. 'Carol, the inquest into the death by drowning of Mr Azhar Ali is on Tuesday? All in order?'

Carol was wearing a different black suit. Ridpath imagined her wardrobe at home. Twelve black suits, all in different cuts and materials. Her definition of rebelliousness would be to wear a cream blouse instead of white one.

'All done, Margaret. Witnesses confirmed, should be fairly straightforward.'

'And the family?'

'The situation has been explained to them through an interpreter.'

'Good. Make sure we have an interpreter in the court, Jenny. What do they speak, Urdu or Hindi?'

'Actually, it's Punjabi,' said Carol.

Margaret Challinor smiled. 'Of course it is. Make sure we have an interpreter in court, Jenny. Use Mrs Singh – she speaks all three languages, doesn't she?'

'And Gujarati, but not Tamil. We have to get Mrs Pereira for Tamil.'

'Good, moving along, the fire at Molton's Brewery. David, where are we?'

And so it went on. A catalogue of accidents, possible suicides, murders, unexplained deaths and one death in custody – a 17-year-old boy who died of an asthma attack.

Then Mrs Challinor finally reached him. 'Now, Ridpath, our most vexing problem at the moment. Where are we with Alice Seagram?'

He decided to be candid. 'As you know, the body was not in the coffin when it was opened—'

'Are you likely to find it after ten years?' Carol Oates interrupted.

'You never know. It—'

'But the chances of it being discovered are minimal, even if we had Sherlock Holmes on the case.'

This was an obvious attack on him, but why? The answer came in her next question.

'Weren't you the coroner ten years ago, Margaret?'

'I was, Carol – thank you for reminding me. I have already spoken to the chief coroner. He is not happy with our handling of such a high-profile case. The minister has been asking questions, plus the local MP has jumped on bandwagon talking about "incompetence" and implying corruption.'

Carol Oates produced that morning's *Guardian* from her bag, opening it to page six. 'I think he's getting his information from here.'

There was a picture of a well-dressed man Ridpath recognized as Tony Seagram. Beside him was a large headline: 'DID MY SISTER DIE IN VAIN?' with a smaller subhead: 'Did the Police Fudge the Post-mortem Report?'

'Surely this is a police problem,' said David.

'It would be, except the high court has asked us to reopen the inquest.' She paused for a beat. 'The high court also rang me yesterday. They want to know about the progress of our investigations.'

'But without a body, there can be no progress…' said David.

'Exactly, and without progress his honour, Lord Malahide, who ordered the reopening of the inquest, is going to look a fool.'

'No judge likes to look a fool,' said David, stating the obvious.

She looked down the table at Ridpath. 'Unless we resolve it soon, we're going to have a Ministry of Justice investigator here causing us even more strife. How was your meeting with James Dalbey yesterday?'

Ridpath closed his eyes and pinched the top of his nose. 'I think…' he said slowly, 'I think James Dalbey is innocent.'

'What?' said Carol, losing her icy cool for the first time.

'You heard me. I don't think he killed Alice Seagram.'

There was silence in the room. Finally Margaret Challinor spoke. 'What are you going to do now?'

'I want to go and see my predecessor, Anthony Chettle. I need to understand what was happening in 2008.'

'You don't have much time left, Ridpath.'

'I know.'

A smile crossed Carol Oates's face.

'Unless I go and see him today, we are never going to get any closer to solving this.'

'Or finding the body,' said Margaret Challinor.

'And the inquest opens on Monday,' added Carol Oates.

Ridpath hung his head and ran his fingers through his rapidly thinning hair. He only had three days left to work it all out.

What if he failed?

Chapter Fifty-Five

Her head was resting against something soft and damp. It smelt of iron and rust and shit. Her body trembled; she was cold and thirsty, very thirsty.

What happened? Where was she?

Her head hurt. A thick, solid pounding on the right-hand side of her brain, spreading downwards towards the tight neck muscles.

She licked her chapped lips, trying to find a drop of saliva in her dry mouth. A groan came out involuntarily from her throat. She shivered again.

Feeling cold, very cold.

She was lying on the floor, wearing only her shirt and trousers.

Where was her jacket? It only cost 60 quid from Next but she liked that jacket. Made her look tall and slim. Where was it?

She shivered again. More importantly, where was she?

Think, Sarah – what happened?

She remembered driving home, locking her car and then a woman… a woman asking for directions.

What happened next?

Hard as she thought, the only thing that surfaced in her mind was a big black hole of emptiness.

Must get up, drink water.

She tried to use her arms to push herself up from the sticky floor but they were too heavy, far too heavy.

Open your eyes.

They were stuck together. Had she not removed her mascara last night? Did she go to bed with her make-up on? She didn't remember being drunk.

She forced her eyes open. Everything was blurred, unreal, hazy. She closed them again.

Concentrate, Sarah. Focus.

She opened her eyes again. The dark sticky floor slowly came into view, stretching off into the distance. Next to her eyes, a sharp piece of something white lying on the floor. What was it?

She let her eyes take in the rest of the room without moving her head. It was large and not well lit, dissolving into dark shadows. One light picked out an aluminium table to her right.

She moved her head slightly to see more, but a sharp pain slashed into her brain.

OK, OK, take it slowly.

She closed her eyes again and concentrated on breathing.

In. Out.

In. Out.

In. Out.

She tried to move her arms but they were too heavy. Why were they so heavy?

Breathe again.

She opened her eyes and pushed down on the floor with her arms, raising her body a few inches off the ground.

'Hello there, DS Castle. I wondered when you were going to join us.'

'Water… water.'

'Thirst is one of the unfortunate side effects of the drug you were given.'

Sarah squinted into the darkness behind the light. A woman's voice. Where was she?

From her right, footsteps changing pitch and tone as they went across a concrete floor and onto something softer. A rim

245

of plastic being placed against her lips. Cold, wet liquid flowing into her mouth and throat.

'Not too much, DS Castle – save some for later.'

She knows my name. How does she know my name? She pushed herself up to a sitting position. Her arms were still heavy. She looked down and saw a large iron manacle attached to her right wrist. A chain led from the manacle to an iron ring on the wall.

She reached over with her left hand to remove the manacle, but it only moved two inches before jerking to a stop. Her left arm was manacled too.

'You're probably wondering where you are.'

She was standing next to something, adjusting it, looking across to a box on her right.

'Good, that's better,' she said to herself. 'You don't mind if I film you, do you? He likes to watch. And you are going to provide such good viewing.'

'Where... where...?'

'Where are you?'

'The location is not important. The situation is. You will have worked out through that drug-addled brain of yours that you are manacled to a wall.'

'How... how did...?' Sarah was trying to formulate the words but they wouldn't come out. Why wouldn't they come out?

'How did you get here?'

Sarah nodded.

'Not really important, but by car, if it helps.' The woman moved in front of the light, becoming a dark silhouette. 'I see from your face it doesn't.'

'Police... will look for ...me.' Finally, she managed to get the words out.

'Probably, but not yet. Anyway, that's all been taken care of. He doesn't make mistakes.'

Sarah's eyes were getting heavy again. She shook her head, trying to stay awake.

'Oh, I forgot to tell you. I put a little more tranquillizer in the water. You should be feeling sleepy again, but don't worry, you won't be out long.'

Sarah's head nodded forward towards her chest.

Tired, so tired.

She forced her eyes open one last time, focusing on the floor in front of her. As she drifted off into opioid dreams, she realized the white object flecked with red in front of her was bone.

Human bone.

Chapter Fifty-Six

After the meeting had finished, he tried Sarah's phone. Again it went straight to voicemail. Why didn't she ring him back? Yesterday, everything was so urgent and now it seemed like it didn't matter. Didn't she want to know about James Dalbey?

He decided he would stop by at the Major Incident Team office before he went down to Congleton to see Anthony Chettle. It would mean driving into Manchester and out again, but what the hell, he needed to talk to someone about his meeting with Dalbey. And Sarah was the only person who shared his misgivings about the 2008 investigation.

He got in the car and started the engine, making his way towards town. First though, he would have to ring Christie's hospital.

'I'm afraid I'll have to cancel my appointment this afternoon.'

'Name?'

'Thomas Ridpath.'

'Yes, Mr Ridpath, you're down to meet Mr Morris at 2.30.'

'I'd like to reschedule, if I may?' Why were English people always so deferential when talking to bureaucrats? He would never use sentences like 'if I may?' in normal conversation. Years of being serfs and servants, he supposed. 'Something has come up at work' he added by way of explanation.

'Hmm.' He had never heard so much disapproval expressed in one sound. It was followed by the clicking of a keyboard. 'I have another appointment at, let me see, 3.30 p.m. on 5 May.'

Whispered words in the background. The voice suddenly animated down the end of the phone. 'You're in luck, we've just had a cancellation for tomorrow at 9 a.m. Can you make it?'

Ridpath thought for a moment, gallons of blood flowing out of his veins into a vast frothy vat crossed his mind.

'Hello?'

'Yes, book me in.'

'Good, don't be late. Thank you for calling Christie's.' The cheery sign-off was in contrast to the stern warning. He could understand though. Organizing patient appointments must be like herding cats, only twice as difficult, especially with people like him, desperate not to visit a hospital ever again.

A barrier appeared in front of the car. He was pulled out of his memories by the face of a security guard at the driver's side window. How did he get here? It was like the car had driven itself. He would have to concentrate more on what he was doing. Perhaps the drug had side effects. He would have to ask the doctor tomorrow.

If he went.

He flashed his ID to the guard and was let through the gate, parking neatly behind Charlie Whitworth's Vauxhall. He ran up the steps. The same sergeant was on the front desk.

'It's you again. You'll be living here soon.'

A quick 'I hope so,' and he was buzzed through.

Sarah's desk was empty. All her files were neatly stacked and the computer was switched off.

Harry Makepeace was walking past.

'Where's Sarah?' he asked.

Harry glanced back at the empty desk and shrugged his shoulders. 'Dunno, why don't you ask her?'

'If she was answering her phone, I would.'

'The prodigal son returns. How was the Beast?' Charlie Whitworth shouted from his open doorway.

Ridpath strode past Sarah's empty desk. 'Fine, boss. James Dalbey is still in Belmarsh and still saying he's innocent.'

'Don't they all? I need a word.' Charlie pointed to his office.

They both went in and sat down. Charlie cradled his hands in front of his face. 'John Gorman's not happy...'

What had Ridpath done now?

'...That woman, Margaret Challinor, requesting the case files, and now she seems to have broadened her inquiry.'

Ridpath frowned, 'Broadened her inquiry?'

'She's looking into the whole case against the Beast, not just the post-mortem on Alice Seagram.'

'Inevitable, boss, once the body went missing.'

The DCI's fist came crashing down on the table. 'You were supposed to keep us informed. Instead, you're traipsing off to interview probably the worst serial killer who ever walked the streets of Manchester.'

'That's unfair, boss.'

'That's unfair, boss,' Whitworth mimicked him. 'I'll tell you what's unfair, Ridpath. When the deputy chief constable decides you're still unfit for duty and John Gorman doesn't say a word to defend you. That's unfair. When you're looking for a new job and John Gorman won't give you a character reference. That's unfair. When a copper doesn't stand up for his mates. That's unfair. Really unfair.'

'Charlie, I—'

'Don't "Charlie" me. We want to know every move she makes from now on. If she farts, we want to hear about it. Understood?'

'But—'

'If you want our support, earn it. Clear?' The DCI's eyes narrowed. 'Why are you here anyway?'

Ridpath thought about making something up, but decided against it. Now was not the time to tell porkies to Charlie, but the complete truth was out of the question. 'I came to see Sarah – she's not answering her phone.'

'And why should you two be ringing each other?'

'She said she would check up on the breeze blocks found in the coffin.'

Charlie Whitworth laughed. 'Getting her to do your work, were you?'

'She was helping out. But she's not at her desk, nor is she answering her phone.'

'Probably at home taking a sickie. Time of the month and all that. Harry!' he shouted, Makepeace's head appeared around the door almost immediately.

'Yes, boss.'

'Where's DS Castle?'

'Search me, boss.'

'She's part of your team, Harry, you're supposed to know.'

'I'll send someone round to her place. She's probably taking a sickie.'

'You do that. And Harry, give her a bollocking while you're at it. She keeps her phone on no matter how sick she is. Understood?'

'Yes, boss.'

Harry ran back into the office.

Charlie Whitworth stood up. 'Remember, we want to know everything.'

It was time for Ridpath to get out of there and go and see the former coroner's officer, Anthony Chettle.

'Of course, Charlie, you'll know everything from now on.' It was the only way he was going to get out of the office alive.

Chapter Fifty-Seven

It was a relief to get out of the station and head down to Congleton on the A34. He found himself gripping the steering wheel tightly. The meeting with Charlie Whitworth had done nothing for his stress levels. He was now becoming the meat in the bloody sandwich caught between Charlie Whitworth and Margaret Challinor.

A knackered, chewed and bloody piece of meat.

To make matters worse, he now believed an innocent man had spent the last ten years in jail for a crime he didn't commit. And the body of one of his supposed victims had gone missing.

What the bloody hell was he supposed to do?

He put on Bowie in the car stereo and let himself relax to the beat of 'The Jean Genie', remembering his youth waving his arms to the music of the Thin White Duke. When everybody else was listening to the dreary music of the Smiths, Stone Roses or the Mondays, he had discovered early Bowie. Like Northern Soul, it was music out of its time, but for him, it was the only sound that made sense of his feelings.

As he drove down the A34, negotiating an obstacle course of roundabouts, roadworks, slow-moving lorries and congenital idiots who had somehow been given a driving licence, he considered his position.

Charlie Whitworth and John Gorman were not enemies he could bear to have if he still wanted to survive in the police. They controlled his future as a detective. Any chances of promotion or career development were down to them and their recommendations. In cop shows, you often saw people moving forces, but it rarely happened. Usually, a copper stayed with one force for life. Piss off somebody above you in the pecking order and they would remember.

For the rest of your career.

What did he owe to Margaret Challinor?

Nothing.

She was merely his temporary employer while he was seconded to the Coroner's Office. A job, as she said, lasting three months at most, while she found somebody with medical experience.

Mick Ronson's guitar solo and Mickey Woodmansey's drumming increased in tempo. Ridpath increased the volume. 'The Jean Genie' filled the car as he sang along with Bowie, receiving stares from other motorists.

Sod them.

He knew one thing. He was never going to report on her to his bosses. The honest side of him, the man he knew was still there, deep down beneath the bluster and the mateship, was never going to be a stoolie. He wasn't a Harry Makepeace, so scared of losing his job he would do anything and everything to butter up his boss.

He would never become a spy for them against Margaret Challinor, however they threatened, cajoled or bribed him.

The situation had to be managed. He didn't know how yet, but manage it he would.

He was a detective, not a grass.

Chapter Fifty-Eight

PC Deborah Howard had lucked out again. Her sergeant had received an instruction from the MIT to go and check up on one of their detectives who wasn't answering her phone.

'You're shitting me, Dave. You want me to go round and wake up some poor bloody detective who's probably slept in after a long night, simply because she's not answering her phone?'

'That's the length of it, aye.'

'Don't I have better things to do? Like catch criminals? Or look into the set of burglaries on Cromwell Road? Or even check out the parks to see if any of the youngsters are smoking dope?'

Her sergeant scratched his nose. 'Aye, you probably do. But as everybody else is out and you're the only one still in the station, it looks like it's you.'

'Can't Jim Stannish handle it?'

'Jim's got a domestic over on Washway Road. And you may have forgotten, PC Howard, but I arrange what people do and don't do in this nick, not a probationary police constable.'

The reminder of her status shut Deborah up for a moment. 'Can't I just finish this report on the burglaries?'

'No, the MIT want her checked out now. Here's her name and address. It's only 15 minutes away. You'll be back before your tea goes cold.'

Deborah stared at the fresh cup of tea she had just brewed sitting next to her computer.

He picked it up off her table. 'On second thoughts, I'll look after this for you.' He began drinking it. 'Not a bad drop – you make a fine cuppa. You got any sugar?'

She handed him a sachet she had taken from McDonald's.

'Now, off you pop. You can make some fresh when you come back.'

Deborah stood up, putting on her police overcoat. 'It's bloody freezing out there.'

Her sergeant checked his phone. 'Actually, it's a balmy eight degrees with a wind chill of two degrees.'

'Another Manchester spring?'

'Aye, and don't forget to put your sunscreen on before you go out.'

'Ha bloody ha!' She went out the back door and climbed into the squad car. Her oppo, Harris, was on sick leave today. 'Everybody's bloody sick today, including me,' she said to no one in particular as she turned the key in the ignition, hearing the starter motor fight against the cold, before eventually turning over.

She drove to the address, hoping the heater would warm the car before she got there. But it wasn't working. She turned it off after sitting in a blast of cold air for two minutes.

She double-parked the car, nipping out to knock on the door. The house was tiny but well kept: newly painted door, fresh blinds and the garden neat and tidy with roses growing in pots.

She knocked again.

No answer.

She didn't know why but the place felt empty. She'd probably already left for work. Those bloody idiots in the MIT wouldn't know their arse from their elbow. They even lost their own bloody coppers now. Lord save us if they have to investigate anything.

A tired woman in a housecoat with her hair in curlers stepped out from a door across the street. 'Are you the police?' she shouted.

Deborah was tempted to answer, 'No, I always go around wearing a stab vest and driving a blue and yellow checked car with "Police" written down the side.' Instead, she adopted her dealing-with-the-public face. 'Yes, madam, just looking for Detective Sergeant…' she checked the name on the piece of paper, 'DS Castle.'

'Well, she's not here. Are you coming because I rang this morning?'

Deborah Carr scratched her head. She walked over to the woman, 'You called this morning?'

'I thought about ringing for a long time, then went to bed, but it kept nagging at me and I couldn't sleep, so I got up early and rang you lot.'

'Sorry, who did you ring?'

'The sergeant at the police station. He came round to the community centre six months ago and gave us a lovely talk – called "Policing in the Community", it was. Well, I laughed, we called it "Policing in the Community Centre". Our little joke, you know.'

'Sorry, you've lost me. Can we start again? Your name is…?'

'Norah Finch. Mrs Norah Finch.'

'Right, Mrs Finch, you called us this morning?'

The woman folded her arms across her ample chest. 'I did, spoke to the sergeant myself. It was around 5 a.m.'

Deborah Carr closed her eyes. Start again. 'Why did you call us?'

'Well, I was just about to go to bed last night at 11.30 when I heard Sarah's car pull up into its usual place.'

'Sarah?'

'The policewoman who lives at number 23.'

'DS Castle?'

'Yes, Sarah. Anyway, I saw her park her car then another car pulled up next to it.'

'Another car?'

'A BMW 320 diesel, white.'

'You know your cars.'

'Used to work in a second-hand dealership, didn't I? Bunch of shysters. You know one team—'

'So the BMW pulled up,' interrupted PC Howard, 'And then what happened?'

'Well I watched them talking for a few seconds then Sarah leant into the car. It looked like they were kissing.'

'Who was kissing?'

'Sarah and the woman in the car.'

'There was a woman in the car?'

'I was pretty certain it was a woman, because the light went on, and she had long hair.' The woman leant closer. 'Sarah is that way inclined, you know. Not that I care myself. Nothing to do with me what the lesbians get up to in the privacy of their own homes, is it?'

'But they were kissing on the street?'

'I thought they were kissing but then the woman in the car started banging Sarah's head on the side of the car door. Quite hard it was too. And you could hear the bumps against the metal.'

Deborah Carr took out her notebook. 'What happened next?'

'The woman in the car got out of the passenger side. I could see quite clearly she was a woman now. She went round to the driver's side and moved Sarah to the back seat.'

'Let me get this right. Sarah... I mean, DS Castle was unconscious?'

'It looked like it to me.'

'So you rang the police?'

As if on cue, a squad car appeared around the corner and parked up behind Deborah.

'That's right. This morning. I thought about it all night, I wasn't certain you see, it was dark and everything. Sometimes, you don't want to interfere if it's an argument between friends do you?'

'Which one is Sarah's car?'

'The blue Audi over there.'

Deborah strode over to the Audi, ignoring the arrival of the two coppers in the squad car.

She knelt down in the middle of the road. A set of car keys was next to the driver-side door, just behind the front tyre.

Strange. Had DS Castle dropped them?

She stood up, took two steps back and checked the road. There, just two feet away, was a tiny pool of dark liquid. She knelt down and stared at it. And there were more splashes dappling the grey road surface. She knew exactly what they were, having witnessed the same or similar in Manchester city centre after the pubs closed and the fights began.

Blood.

She got on the radio back to the station. 'Sarge, you know you sent me round to check up on DS Castle?'

'Right. Knock her up, did you?'

'No. I think we've got a problem, boss. A big problem.'

Chapter Fifty-Nine

The Cloud turned out to be a sharp-edged lump of rock sticking out almost vertically from the Cheshire Plain, just three miles south of Congleton. Ridpath parked in the village of Timbersbrook, next to one of the decommissioned red phone boxes that had been turned into a library. Inside were a few books and a note saying, 'Please leave a book and take one for yourself.'

It was one of those lovely village notices harking back to a bygone age when people didn't lock their doors and kids played out on the street. Perhaps in this village they still did. He would check in the boot to see if Eve or Polly had left a book there and add it to the village's little library.

He strode across to Chettle's house, one of a row of four classic cottages. Forget-me-nots, daffodils and hyacinths were in flower in the garden. Somebody obviously had a lot of time on their hands.

He knocked on the door.

It was immediately opened by a tall, broad-shouldered, military-looking man – grey-haired and distinguished, like an ageing Hollywood actor still desperate for leading man parts.

'Anthony Chettle?'

'Himself. You must be Tom Ridpath. Margaret told me about you. How's the cancer?'

Did everybody on earth know his medical history? 'In remission, it's why I'm back on the job.'

'You may as well come in. The wife's at the vets in Congleton. She's having her nails clipped. The dog not the wife. Fancy a cup of tea?'

'Perfect.'

As Chettle made the tea, Ridpath made small talk. 'Looks like a lovely place to live, this village.'

'It is. Peace and quiet and a walk every day with the dog up the Cloud. Used to be a working village this, but not anymore. Only old people left here now and retirees, like me and the missus. How do you like your tea?'

Ridpath was wandering around the living room, looking at the photos of a man and his wife, both dressed up to the nines, a medal pinned to the man's chest. 'Milk, no sugar, please,' he finally answered.

'That's me and the missus at the Palace receiving the CBE in 2008 for services rendered to Coroner's Court.'

'You must have been proud.'

'Me? Couldn't give a toss, but the missus loved it; she'd only ever been to London once before.'

He sat down on the couch, placing the tray with two mugs on the coffee table. 'Now you didn't come all the way from Manchester to talk about my bloody CBE.'

Ridpath sat next to him. 'No. Do you remember the Beast of Manchester case?'

'Who could forget?'

'The High Court has ordered us to reopen an inquest into the death of Alice Seagram.'

Chettle nodded. 'And you've lost the body.'

'Can you tell me about it?'

'Not much to tell. Like you I was on secondment to the Coroner's Office from Manchester Police. For me, the job lasted 20 years and I loved it. Hated being a copper and loved being a coroner's officer. You see, in the Coroner's Office we weren't after chasing convictions; our job was to help bereaved families. I liked that. We wanted to understand what happened, not convict somebody.'

'You worked with Margaret Challinor?'

He stared off into the distance. 'Great woman, Margaret – believes in what's she's doing. She was devastated by the Harold Shipman case.'

'Why?'

'Because the doctor had killed over 300 people in Tameside and nobody knew, least of all the Coroner's Office. We only get involved if the cause of death is suspicious. So Shipman killed his victims and then signed the death notice himself as the doctor. The cause of death was always natural: heart attacks, old age, pneumonia and so on. No need for the coroner to get involved. It was only when Shipman became greedy that he was caught by one of the relatives. Tried to create a fake will, leaving all the money to himself. For a clever man, he was incredibly stupid.'

He topped up his tea from the pot. The tea now had the colour of terracotta.

'Margaret wanted to retire when Shipman was found guilty, but they wouldn't let her.'

'Retire?'

'She felt guilty even though it wasn't her district. Probably why she works so hard now. Can't let another Shipman happen again, even though the government made a balls up of the reform of the coronial system with the 2009 Act. Didn't want to spend money on it to make it really effective. That's when I retired.'

'You'd had enough?'

'For me, it was never going to change, but Margaret was determined to fight within the system to make it better. I just got fed up of banging my head against a brick wall.'

'Was the case against the Beast of Manchester a catalyst?'

'Not really. Looked open and shut to me. He was caught in a lock-up with one of the victims, wasn't he? John Gorman and Charlie Whitworth may have put pressure on the pathologist, but...'

'Harold Lardner?'

'He was a good pathologist, the best we had. They all made mistakes though, did the pathologists. They're only human after all.'

'This was when Alice Seagram's body was released and not released?'

'Luckily I hadn't called the family when Charlie rang me back telling me there was going to be another autopsy. He said Lardner had asked him if he could do it again.'

'Lardner asked? He never told me.'

'That's what Charlie said. But you never know with Charlie. The truth is extremely flexible with our Mr Whitworth.'

'O'Shaughnessy was the undertaker?'

'He was. He did a lot of the funerals. A meticulous man, but always looking to bend the rules. His own death was suspicious too...'

'I thought he died in a fire?'

'So did everybody, but I heard whispers he'd been seen on the Costa del Sol living it up. Nothing concrete, mind, just rumours.'

Ridpath made a mental note to check up on the death of the funeral director. The coroner must have opened an inquest if the death was accidental. For now, though, he had to concentrate on Alice Seagram.

'You arranged for the body to be picked up?'

'Not really. After the pathologist had performed the second autopsy, I informed the family of Alice Seagram she could be collected for burial. I think it was the brother Tony Seagram who arranged everything.'

'I've met him. Not a pleasant man.'

'No, he wasn't back then either. It was almost as if he was looking to blame everybody except the man who had committed the murder.'

'He still is.'

'You know I went to the funeral?'

'Whose funeral?'

'Alice Seagram's. I've got the album here.' He walked over to the cupboard loaded with china and opened a drawer. 'Kept an album of all the cuttings for the cases that interested me. Most of it is Shipman, of course – the bastard still lives on in here.' He tapped the top of the scrapbook as he lifted it out of the drawer.

He sat down again and flicked through the album. Ridpath could indeed see page after page on the Shipman case. Finally, he stopped.

'Here it is. The paper is dated 22 March but the funeral took place the day before.'

Ridpath leant in to read the faded cutting from the *Manchester Evening News*. 'Funeral takes place of Beast Victim' stated the headline in heavy type.

Beneath was a grainy photograph of a coffin being carried by pall-bearers in a graveyard, behind them a long procession of mourners led by the Seagrams.

Ridpath leant in closer.

'Who's that on the left?'

'O'Shaughnessy, the undertaker.'

'And beside him?'

'I dunno, one of his assistants, I suppose.'

Ridpath recognized the man in the picture immediately. Why hadn't he said he worked for O'Shaughnessy?

Chapter Sixty

'Chrissy, I want all the Highways CCTV at 11.30 last night from this area to be checked. We're looking for a white BMW 320.' Charlie Whitworth was on the phone to the MIT's support officer back at headquarters.

'Any reg number, boss?'

'Not at the moment, but you'll be able to find it on the CCTV. We need it yesterday.'

The chief inspector switched the phone off and turned back to face the team. They were outside Sarah Castle's house. Her car was surrounded by a phalanx of SOCOs all dressed in their Tyvek white suits and blue gloves. The road had been cordoned off 100 yards in either direction, with policemen from the local nick forming a barrier in front of the kids and housewives, all stretching their necks like giraffes to see what was going on.

In the middle of the road, another group of SOCOs were collecting samples and photographing the blood pool and the blood splatters.

'Charlie, what do you think we've got? A domestic or something more serious?' Dave Hardy stood in front of his DCI.

'Dunno, but I feel in my water it's not a domestic. According to her friends, Sarah didn't have a girlfriend and wasn't in a relationship at the moment. It could have been someone she met on Tinder but I doubt it. The witness says it was a violent attack but over quickly. It's the car that's worrying me, Dave.'

'The BMW?'

'One of the pimps reported a similar car was in the area when the girl with the swan tattoo went missing. Get on the blower to Chrissy again and get her to also check the CCTV around the canal on the night before the body was found.' He ran his hand through his thinning hair. 'No, scratch that, you go and check it, Dave. I want Chrissy to stay focused.'

'I'm on it, boss.'

The pathologist, Protheroe, was also lurking nearby.

'You got anything yet?'

'Nothing from the car so far except fingerprints which match those of Sarah Castle.'

'I could have told you that.'

'But you couldn't have told me the blood on the street is Type A, which just happens to be DS Castle's blood type. We can match the DNA with hers if we find a hair from a brush or something on her clothes. But to do that, we have to get in there.' He pointed to the house opposite.

'For once, I can give you an answer, Protheroe.'

The pathologist's eyebrow rose to touch the Tyvek of the white hairnet.

'The car key ring. There are some extra keys on it. I'll bet you a bottle of scotch one of them fits the front door.'

'Gambling is the work of the devil, DCI Whitworth, but I will try your suggestion nonetheless.'

Harry hovered next to Charlie.

'Anything more from Mrs Finch?'

'Not a lot, boss. Her timings are accurate though. Sarah was attacked at 11.30 p.m. The attack lasted less than a minute and the white BMW drove off towards Sale town hall.'

'Great, well done.' He stroked his moustache and said softly, 'Get a bloody move on, Chrissy.'

'What's that, boss?'

'Nothing, nothing. Make sure the plod keeps those people back – this is a crime scene.'

'Yes, boss.'

Charlie Whitworth looked down at the ground. One of their own was missing and he was going to pull out all the stops to make sure she was found.

Behind his back, his fingers were crossed.

Chapter Sixty-One

She woke with a pain lashing through her right hand.

'Sorry, been a while since I did this.'

The woman was attaching something to her right hand. Again, a shot of pain up her arm.

'There. Finally done.'

The woman stepped back to admire her handiwork. Sarah tried to reach out to grab her, to stop her, but her movements were slow and ungainly. It was as if she no longer controlled her body.

'The drugs will begin to wear off soon. He's said you are not to receive any more. He wants to enjoy the pain in your eyes.'

The woman's words began to penetrate the fog in her mind. 'Pain in my eyes?' What the hell is she talking about?

Slowly Sarah was taking in her surroundings. The woman had strolled to a box on a stand and was adjusting it. Was she being filmed? Was somebody watching her?

A spotlight to the left shone directly into her eyes, putting everything behind it into shadow. All she could see was the woman, the camera and the desk to the left with a monitor sitting on it.

She was on the monitor: her blonde hair hanging bedraggled over her face, her white shirt dirty with blood and sweat, her arms hanging from manacles attached to a brick wall. She was sitting on the floor, her legs tucked under her.

'Is that better?'

The woman wasn't talking to her but to somebody else not in the room.

'A bit closer?'

Sarah could see her picture on the monitor becoming larger as the woman zoomed in, until her face filled the frame.

A haggard, worn face – the face of a criminal. That wasn't her. It couldn't be her.

'Too close?'

The framing zoomed out until just her body filled the frame.

'Perfect? Thank you. I've attached the drip to her hand.'

Sarah turned her head slowly to her left. Her arms were stretched out, slightly higher than her head, like Jesus on the cross. The chain had been shortened on the manacle so she could only move a couple of inches. Attached to her hand a thin tube snaked upwards to a saline drip.

She remembered the time when she had broken her leg wakeboarding at 18. Trying to do a bigger jump and realizing as soon as she landed something was wrong. The trip in the ambulance was shocking, each bump in the road causing a searing stab of pain to shoot up her right leg. The doctor in A&E, young and inexperienced, telling her it was just a sprain until the X-rays came back showing a fracture. The operation: going under the anaesthetic, waking up in the middle of it to hear the doctors talking about her, and then afterwards, in bed, the drip with its wonderful supply of morphine and saline attached to her left hand.

Just like now.

Except now she was lying on the sticky floor of some warehouse with a madwoman filming her.

Sarah shook her left arm. It moved just three inches, the tube leading into the saline drip not moving at all.

'She's a feisty one, this one.'

The woman wasn't talking to her, but seemed to be listening to an earpiece, tilting her head slightly, her mouth open as she listened to the words.

She reached over and flicked a switch on the monitor. Instantly the room was flooded with the sound of a man's voice.

'Good morning, Sarah. I hope you slept well. Lorazepam usually gives you a quiet night.'

The voice was soothing, emollient. Did she recognize it? Had she heard it before?

'You have probably noticed the drip Lesley has attached to your hand. The saline should help to rehydrate you. Unfortunately, thirst is one of the side effects of your sedation. A shame, but it can't be helped.'

Sarah tried to speak but her mouth was dry; nothing but a croak emerged from her lips.

'Give it time to work, Sarah. Don't be so impatient.'

Sarah tried to speak again. 'Let... me... go.'

'What was that? You want to leave? But we're only just getting started. You wouldn't want to miss the fun, would you? Unfortunately I can't be there, but Lesley has thoughtfully rigged up the camera so I can watch everything that transpires. If you look over to your left, you will also see a reel-to-reel tape recorder. We wouldn't want to miss any of your screams, would we?'

Sarah tried to stretch her legs out from under her body. Immediately, she felt a rope tighten around her throat. She tucked her legs back to where they were before and the pain around her neck stopped.

'I think you've just discovered one of Lesley's little inventions. You created it when you were a psychiatric nurse, didn't you, Lesley?'

'The rope binding the legs is looped around the neck. The patients soon learnt that in trying to kick me, they would only strangle themselves.'

'Totally illegal, of course. But we won't bother ourselves with legal niceties at the moment.'

Sarah was panting, her breath coming in short, sharp gasps. Sweat dripped from her face onto the sticky carpet beneath her body. The white piece of bone had been removed. 'What do you want from me?'

'That's better, Sarah. See, Lesley, I told you Sarah would be better when the drugs wore off. What do we want from you? A little experiment, that's all. If you look above the saline drip, you will see another bottle feeding into it. This bottle contains formalin, a 37 per cent solution of formaldehyde. You may know it better as embalming fluid. Undertakers use it to preserve bodies to prevent decomposition. Now, most undertakers inject at least 11.3 litres of the fluid into the cadaver's arterial system and body cavity to slow decay for burial ceremonies.'

He stopped talking for a moment and Sarah heard a rasping sound, like a file being scraped against metal. The voice continued.

'However, we are not going to be so lavish with our precious formula. The Americans think just 38 millilitres of formalin is enough to kill somebody. Lesley thinks 35 millilitres will be enough. I, however, think you are quite a strong young woman and have opted for the round figure of 40.'

Another pause. Did he have a problem breathing or was he just taking his time, drawing out the agony?

'Already one millilitre should now be circulating around your system. The amusement for us will be watching how you die. Will it be from convulsions? Or vomiting? Will you go mad first? Or will respiratory failure gradually make you unable to breathe?'

The voice laughed. A sound like that of a man watching a hanging and delighting in the legs kicking beneath the trapdoor.

'Our little experiment is to see how long it takes a person – in this case you, Sarah – to be embalmed alive.'

Chapter Sixty-Two

He had driven like a madman down the A34, running the gauntlet of roundabouts, slow drivers and roadworks. He no longer had a flashing red light or siren to clear his way so he had to rely on his driving skills.

Inevitably, as he entered Manchester, he was slowed down by traffic. Luckily most of it was heading the other way: commuters heading home to the comfort of the suburbs from their work in the concrete jungle.

He parked in front the mortuary on a double yellow line. Bugger it, this was far too important. He ran up the steps and through the entrance. A receptionist tried to stop him as he barged through the door into the working area at the back. He brushed her aside, pulling out his expired warrant card and shouting, 'Police.'

He ran down a long green corridor, turned the corner and there he was, wheeling a gurney with a bright-green body bag placed carelessly across it.

Don Brown took one look at him and started to run, shoving the gurney across the corridor. Ridpath pushed it to one side and chased after him.

Brown glanced back over his shoulder and turned left past the chapel of rest.

Ridpath chased after him, narrowly missing a middle-aged woman coming out from saying her prayers.

Luckily, Brown was fat and out of shape – a diet of cigarettes, alcohol and salt and vinegar crisps not the best training for running away from a copper who was determined to speak to him.

He tried though, diving through rear double doors and jumping down steps where two men were having a quiet fag.

Ridpath jumped past them too, shouting 'Stop, stop,' as he did so.

Neither man moved, carrying on smoking their cigarettes as if nothing had happened.

Ridpath ran past a children's nursery. Where else but Manchester would you find a mortuary next to a children's nursery? Those just starting their lives and those who had already finished theirs in close proximity.

He turned another corner. Brown was just fifteen yards ahead now and slowing fast.

'Give it up, Brown,' Ridpath shouted.

The man glanced over his shoulder, eyes flaring wildly, but kept on running. Two other men in white coats looked across to see what was happening, but neither moved to stop Brown. Just another day in the life of Manchester Royal Infirmary.

They were both on the Boulevard now, the road that dribbled through the hospital buildings. Brown was just four yards ahead, then three.

He turned a corner just as Ridpath drove his shoulder into the man's back, sending him sprawling along the pavement. Ridpath fell with him, landing on top of the fat man, placing his knee in the centre of the man's back and dragging his arms round to be handcuffed.

Ridpath reached for his cuffs. Nothing there.

Keeping hold of the man's arm and twisting it up behind his back, he dragged him upright.

'You're nicked, Brown.'

'Me, I ain't done nothing.' Blood dripped from the man's forehead where it had scraped along the ground.

'Stealing a body is an offence.'

'I didn't steal nothing – it was O'Shaughnessy. It was him, I swear it.'

Ridpath eased his grip on the man's arm, letting it drop to his waist. He could always twist it upwards again if Brown gave him trouble.

'You're going to tell me everything, understand?'

Brown nodded, hesitantly. 'It wasn't me, it was O'Shaughnessy.'

Chapter Sixty-Three

'Boss, we've got a hit on the BMW.'

Dave Hardy passed his mobile phone to Charlie Whitworth.

'It's Chrissy. We picked up the white BMW going down Chester Road and turning right onto the ring road. The number is WF16 TUW. Kept to the main roads after it came off at Cheadle, but then we lost it. The roadworks have taken out all the cameras.'

'Great work. Check the vehicle registration and get me an address straight away.' DCI Whitworth started walking towards his car with his ear still glued to the phone, followed by a phalanx of detectives.

'Already done, boss. The car's registered to a Lesley Taylor at 83 Tarporth Road in Poynton.'

'We're on our way, Chrissy. Keep following the car on CCTV, find out where it went last night.'

'We're on it, boss. We've keyed in the number to ANPR and we're following it through the system. I'll let Dave know – he's looking for it around the marina on the night before the woman with the swan tattoo was murdered.'

'Chrissy, you're a marvel.'

'One last thing, boss. It looks like the witness was correct. We've blown up a picture of the driver and it's a woman.'

'Jesus. Well done. Put the picture on the system for me.'

Charlie Whitworth switched off the phone and jumped into the front of the car. 'Tarporth Road in Poynton, Alan. Use all the bells and whistles.'

Immediately the lights on the police car began to flash and the siren whooped. The car accelerated away, followed by two other cars packed with detectives.

Charlie Whitworth was on the phone straight away to his guv'nor.

'John, we got a lead on the kidnapped officer, DS Sarah Castle. Could be tied into the murders of the toms. What? OK, I'll make sure we're as clean as my old mum's knickers. Can you get the chopper onto it plus a firearms team? We don't know what we're going to face. The address is Tarporth Road, Poynton.'

The cars raced through the streets of Manchester, sirens echoing off the buildings. Ahead of them, cars pulled to one side as if scared by the noise, letting them pass. Alan, a trained police driver, slowed at red lights before accelerating through as soon as he knew it was safe. Past Princess Parkway, along the Airport Eastern Corridor and through the 1930s suburbs – all neat gardens, well-trimmed hedges and blossoming cherry trees.

Above, Charlie Whitworth saw the chopper hovering at 1,000 feet. 'Get a move on, Alan, we haven't got all bloody day.'

The car surged forward as the driver stomped on the accelerator, leaping through the traffic-slowing roundabouts in the centre of Poynton, the car's tyres screeching as it took a sharp right into Tarporth Road.

'It's up there on the left. Switch off the siren.'

The noise ceased instantly and silence returned again to the car.

'Stop here.' Charlie Whitworth slammed his hand down on the dashboard and Alan jammed on the brakes. The police Vauxhall fishtailed to a stop, the other cars stopping behind it with a loud squeal of brakes.

Sixty yards ahead was the target house. A single-storey brick bungalow built with all the lack of style of the 1960s: a tiny garden in front, a Victorian shop-style bay window, and an attached garage almost as big as the house.

It was the blandness of suburbia personified. It didn't look like the home of a serial killer. But then again, what did?

The whirling blades of the helicopter were loud as it hovered directly above their car.

'Are we going in, boss?'

Charlie looked at the front of the house. There was no BMW parked in front, but it could have been locked away in the garage. Where would they keep Sarah? In the garage too? But surely the neighbours would have heard noises.

'What's the ETA of the firearms team?'

Alan asked the question on the police radio. 'Twenty minutes, boss.'

Shit, they couldn't wait that long. 'Let's go in. Dave and his team around the back. You, me and Harry's team at the front. Come on.'

Charlie opened the door, signalled to Dave where he should go and placed the other team in front of the house. He strode calmly up to the front door, his heart beating loudly in his chest.

'You want me to kick the door in, boss?' asked Alan.

Charlie shook his head. Standing to one side, he pressed the doorbell.

No answer.

He rapped on the frosted glass.

Still no answer.

'Kick it in.'

Alan took a leap at the door, hitting the latch with his boot. It burst open with a splintering of wood. Charlie charged in, followed by the other detectives. In front of them was a kitchen.

Empty.

A door to the right. Charlie rushed in.

An old lady was sitting in an armchair watching the television, a word search book on her lap. Slowly, she looked at them through rheumy eyes.

'Where's Lesley Taylor?'

The voice snapped back at them. 'Who are you? And what are you doing in my house? I'll call the police.'

'We are the police, madam. Where's Lesley Taylor?'

'I haven't seen her since last night when she made my cocoa. And there was no tea and toast for breakfast this morning and I had to get my lunch. If you see my ungrateful daughter, tell her I'm angry, extremely angry.'

Chapter Sixty-Four

A shiver ran the length of her body. Why was she so cold?

She pulled her left hand down against the manacle. Blood ran off her wrist, down the length of her arm, before dripping off her elbow onto the sodden carpet.

She was cold again.

And tired.

So tired.

She looked up. Another large drop of formalin had splashed into the saline above her head. She imagined the chemical surging around her body, seeking out her heart, lungs and brain. Its poison contaminating every cell.

She screamed once again, struggling against the chains holding her arms tight to the wall.

'I've already told you, the more you struggle the faster your heart will beat. When your heart pumps more blood around your body, the formalin will circulate through your system, killing you even quicker.' The woman's voice was cold, clinical, heartless. She walked over to the camera and made another adjustment to the framing.

Sarah screamed again. Long and loud.

Somebody had to be able to hear her. Somebody had to come. They must have realized she was missing by now, mustn't they? Sarah imagined the MIT office – all of them sitting behind their computers, typing away. Did they know she was kidnapped?

She had rung Ridpath, leaving a message. He would ring her back, looking to know what she had found. He would ring back, wouldn't he?

A surge of pain shot through her stomach and she vomited up yesterday's cheese and tomato sandwich. Another surge of pain and her body jerked wildly, hanging by her arms from the chains.

'I did tell you screaming would only increase the progress of the formalin, didn't I?'

Sarah vomited again, her throat convulsing as the hot acid and bile from her stomach shot out of her mouth.

She breathed through her nose, desperately trying to suck air into her lungs, avoiding the vomit-stained lips.

Through her half-closed eyes, she watched as the woman strode to the saline drip and stared at it.

'Twenty-three millilitres. It won't be long now.'

Chapter Sixty-Five

Ridpath escorted Don Brown back to the bereavement centre. The man was quieter now, subdued; all fight had left him.

'Sit down here. You're going to tell me everything you know about Alice Seagram.' Ridpath passed over a handkerchief.

Don Brown dabbed the blood off his forehead.

Time to use the softly-softly approach. 'You want a cup of tea?'

Don Brown nodded meekly.

Ridpath walked over to the machine in the corner and put in two pound coins, returning with something that looked and smelt vaguely like washing-up water, but at least it was hot and sweet.

Brown took the plastic cup with a mumbled thanks.

Ridpath sat next to him taking out his notebook. 'Tell me what happened to the body of Alice Seagram.'

'What do you want to know?'

'Everything.'

Ridpath waited, pen poised over the notebook, as Brown took a sip of the warm tea.

'I worked for O'Shaughnessy for five years. He weren't a bad boss – paid well, on time and, unlike others, shared the tips from the family after the funeral. After three years, he took me aside and asked if I wanted to earn a few extra bob. Well, I was pretty broke at the time. All the nags had three legs, if you know what I mean?'

'You had a gambling problem?' Ridpath said softly.

'That's a nice way of putting it. I owed money to some unsavoury Maltese who were threatening to break my legs.' He took another sip of tea, grimacing slightly as it slipped down his throat. 'Anyway, I jumped at the chance. And true to his word, O'Shaughnessy was generous with the bonuses.'

'What did you have to do for them?'

Another sip of tea. 'O'Shaughnessy had two scams going on. The first involved the coffins and the men at the crematoria. You know, they don't fire the furnaces every day so they have to store the coffins and the deceased in the crematorium until they're ready to set them alight.'

'So when the coffin vanishes behind the curtain, it doesn't go straight into the furnace?'

'In most cases, no. Anyway, O'Shaughnessy had the bright idea of simply reclaiming some of the coffins and reselling them to another family.' Another sip of tea. 'You know, some of these oak coffins cost up to three thousand quid. O'Shaughnessy was sharing the money with the men at the crematoria.'

'So he was basically reselling the same coffin over and over again, making three thousand quid each time he did it?' Ridpath made a note in his diary and then stopped. 'But what did he do with the bodies?'

'That's where I came in. My job was to drive round to the crematoria and collect the coffin and the corpse before they were cremated. Now, we had two different places to take the corpses. The first was here. O'Shaughnessy had these forms where he showed the person had donated their body to medical science.'

'So you used to bring them here to be operated on by medical students?'

'Right. The anatomy classes are always short of bodies. O'Shaughnessy filled a gap in the market.'

'That was good of him.'

'But Alice Seagram was different.'

'In what way?'

'O'Shaughnessy was scared somebody would recognize her – you know, one of the medical students. So he told me to take the body to a place near Preston.'

Ridpath frowned. 'Why there?'

'It's a place where you lot do your work.'

'I don't understand.'

'It's where your mob, the police, the pathologists, the forensics people, do their work.'

'I still don't understand.'

'It's where the animal farm is. Where they use pigs and cows to work out rates of decay, effects of heat and cold, larvae and insect activity, all that stuff.'

'Sounds horrible.' Ridpath scratched his nose. 'But what's all this got to do with Alice Seagram?'

'That's what I'm coming to.' He took a last sip of the tea, staring into the bottom of the plastic cup. 'You see, we only ever did the coffin switch on cremations – couldn't do it if the body was being buried, could we?'

'Impossible, the family would see.'

'But O'Shaughnessy came to me the evening before the burial. Told me not to put the body in the coffin but to add a few breeze blocks instead. So I asked him was he sure? And he said, "I've been told to do it."'

'Are you sure those were his words?'

'I remember them like yesterday.'

'So what did you do?'

'As I was told. I cleaned the breeze blocks, felt I should treat them with some respect seeing as how they were replacing the body, and placed them in the empty coffin.'

Ridpath's eyes widened. That's where he had seen the breeze blocks before. The wall in front of O'Shaughnessy's building. He was getting slow in his old age. Either that or the drugs he was taking did have side effects. He would ask Dr Morris tomorrow. He concentrated on the man in front of him who was staring into the bottom of his plastic cup.

'What did you do with the body?'

'I took it to the cold store and left it there, covered in a sheet.'

'The following day, the funeral went ahead?'

Brown nodded. 'It was a bit weird seeing the family crying over a few breeze blocks.'

Ridpath had to keep this man focused. The next question was key. He had to get him to confirm his account. 'What happened to the body after that?'

'O'Shaughnessy told me to drive it to a place near Preston. So I went off in the van the day after the funeral.'

'March 22nd.'

'Probably, if that was the day after the funeral. When I got there, I realized it was the animal farm where they do forensic testing.'

'What did you do?'

'I delivered the body to the place and drove back. O'Shaughnessy was never the same. He sold up to those bastards, the Dalys, a year later...'

'And you lost your job, and came to work here?'

Brown laughed ruefully. 'Seems like my whole life I've been surrounded by dead people. I prefer them to the living. They don't give you no problems.'

Ridpath closed his notebook. 'You know I have to arrest you?'

Brown nodded.

'Donald Brown, I am charging you under section 11 of the Theft Act 1968 that you knowingly stole a dead body, removing it from a place open to the public. Anything you say may be taken down and used in evidence against you. But if you wish to remain silent...'

Ridpath crossed his fingers. He didn't have a clue which section of which law Don Brown had broken, but theft was a nice catch-all charge for the moment.

Chapter Sixty-Six

They had just finished questioning the old woman when Charlie Whitworth's phone rang.

'Boss, Chrissy here. We've traced the BMW using ANPR. It was last seen just off the A6 on Middlewood Road, not far from you.'

'How long ago, Chrissy?'

There was a pause before the answer came. 'At 11.30 a.m. But nothing has come up since then indicating recent movement.'

Charlie Whitworth took the phone away from his ear for a moment. 'Dave, get the chopper to check out Middlewood Road, look for a white BMW.'

'One more thing, boss. Norman's finished looking at the CCTV footage from the area around the canal. The same white BMW comes up at midnight on the evening before the body was found.'

'Bingo. We got her.'

Dave was off the phone. 'Boss, the chopper says there's a white car parked outside a workshop, close to the old brick-works.'

'Address?'

'Number 343 Middlewood Road. It looks disused, in the middle of a clearing in the woods.'

'Who owns it?'

Dave got on the phone to Chrissy. 'It's registered to a man named Lawrence Frinton. He doesn't come up when she enters his name in the system, boss. Seems to be clean as a whistle.'

Charlie Whitworth was already on his feet. 'Well done. Get a team to check him out. We're going to the workshop.'

Dave Hardy and Harry Makepeace were just a step behind their boss as he turned and pointed at the old woman.

'Harry, get on to the local nick and get somebody over to sit with her. Make sure they seal off the area around the house and have a forensics team in here.'

'Yes, boss.'

They ran across to the waiting police car.

Alan was already at the wheel, entering the address into the satnav. 'Ten minutes, boss.'

'What are you waiting for? Get a bloody move on.'

Chapter Sixty-Seven

'Thirty-six millilitres.' Lesley stared at the bottle of formalin. 'Far more than I expected.'

'I told you she was a strong woman.'

She put her fingers on the pulse below the ear. 'Still alive too. The pulse is weak but still there.'

Sarah's head was lolling forward, resting on her chest, her blonde hair matted with sweat, her shirt stained with vomit. Her arms were hanging loosely in the manacles, not being tugged or pulled at any more. Blood still dripped gently down her arm onto the carpet.

Lesley wiped her fingers on her lab coat. She had seen worse in some of the psychiatric wards she had worked on: patients pulling out their own fingernails with their teeth. Others smashing their heads repeatedly against a brick wall. Still more calmly chewing on their own lips.

But those wounds had all been self-inflicted. She had never experimented on a living subject before. The thought sent a shiver of pleasure down her spine.

She had done it now.

Before she started, she had expected to be frightened, nervous, but when it came to the point when it had to be done, she hadn't hesitated at all. Instead, a wonderful calm had taken over her body, a scientific calm. It was just another experiment, that was all.

She checked where the manacles were fastened to the wall. The ring had held, but only just. Lesley could see flakes of dust where the woman had worked at the concrete holding the ring in place. She was strong, there was no doubt. Lesley would have to find a different, more secure way to fasten the manacles to the wall for the next one.

Would there be a next one?

She hoped so, but the decision had to be taken by him. She was simply there to do his bidding.

The detective mumbled something through her cracked lips.

'She's still alive – 37 millilitres now.'

'I estimate she'll go over 40 before the body and the organs shut down. You can dispose of her tonight as we agreed, Lesley. Follow my instructions to the letter.'

'Yes, sir.'

Lesley took one last close look at her experiment before returning to the camera. He wanted a close-up on the face when the moment of death happened, to see exactly what occurred.

Would there be a momentary flicker of recognition in her eyes as she died? Or would her heart simply stop beating? Would he be able to pinpoint the exact moment of death? Or would it be gradual, a transition from a living, breathing human being to an empty sack of skin and bones. And what about the soul? Would he be able to see when the soul left the body?

Lesley believed that people had souls. Her mother had told her they did, and she was always right.

The experiment would be over soon and they would find out. The detective didn't have long to live. She had completed her time in this world. Her allotted number of days were done and dusted.

Ashes to ashes.

Dust to dust.

It wouldn't be long now.

Chapter Sixty-Eight

The cars accelerated through the open gate and along the potholed driveway, sliding to a stop in front of the workshop door.

Charlie jumped out of the car and hesitated. Should he charge straight in or wait? Above him the helicopter circled, its camera staring straight down at the police cars below.

Off to the left, the white BMW was parked in full view, as if the kidnappers were confident the police would never find them.

'The chopper says no sign of movement, Charlie,' said Dave. 'Plus the ETA of the armed response squad is three minutes.'

He told one group to cover the back of the workshop and waited for them to get into position. 'We're going straight in. Dave and Harry, you're with me. Alan, you stay here and guide the armed team when they finally get here.'

'Shouldn't we wait for them, boss?'

Charlie shook his head. 'We've got to move now. Sarah's in there and the bastards may have heard us arrive. Can't wait any longer.'

He checked his watch.

'It's time. Be careful.'

They ran towards the ramshackle building, keeping their eyes open for movement.

In front of the workshop, a loading bay with a metal shutter was next to a cramped wooden door. Charlie checked the metal shutter; sealed with a large, rusted padlock, it hadn't been opened in years. He ran to the wooden door and pressed himself up against the outside wall. It was at times like this he wished they were all routinely armed, instead of having to wait for a team to arrive from Sedgeley Park.

What the hell. Time to go in.

He counted down: 3... 2... 1.

Harry rushed forward and shoulder-charged the door. It exploded under the impact, flying open, the rotten wood around the lock splintering into shards.

Charlie rushed in first, followed by the others, one by one.

Empty.

Totally empty.

The workshop was twenty yards long with brick walls and a high vaulted ceiling. In one corner an ancient press or grinding machine sat forlorn and uncared for, covered in black dust and rust. Along the walls brown shelves held a variety of cans, canisters and grey bottles. The floor was covered in a thin layer of brown dust.

The first one to speak was Dave Hardy. 'They're not here, boss.'

'They must be here, the car's parked outside. Search the place.'

Chapter Sixty-Nine

Above her head, Lesley heard the door smashing open.

'They're here,' she said to the monitor.

'You know what to do. Follow my instructions exactly.'

He had warned her a moment like this would arrive one day. The police would track either her or him down. That's why everything had to be kept in her mother's house; nothing could be traced back to him.

She listened for a movement above.

Nothing.

Perhaps they wouldn't find her down here? Perhaps they would go away, leaving her alone? Perhaps they wouldn't find the entrance?

But he had given her the orders. They must be carried out. First, check the girl: 42, nearly 43 millilitres. She was done for, nothing could save her now. She placed her fingers on the woman's carotid artery. Still a pulse, weaker than before. She wouldn't last long.

Second, disconnect the monitor and the camera. Her last connection to him.

Should she say something? Tell him how much she loved him? Let him know how much she cared? But the link was already broken from his end. He would be removing any evidence of her ever having existed on his laptop. He told her he would do it if they were ever faced with the possibility of discovery.

The process had already started. She couldn't stop it now. Shame, she would have liked to say goodbye. To hear his voice one last time.

Lesley disconnected the monitor and turned off the reel-to-reel recorder. She had enjoyed listening to the tapes with him. There was a terrible beauty in the sound of pain. A beauty transcending all others.

He understood.

And now so did she.

The camera's motor was still turning over. She walked over to it and turned it off. He had told her to erase the footage of their experiment. But she couldn't bring herself to do it. If she did, the world would never know the beauty of what they had done.

She opened the drawer in the desk. Everything was in its place inside. The preparations had been made according to his instructions on the first day they had visited the workshop together.

It seemed such a long time ago.

She took the hypodermic needle out of the box, removing its plastic sheath. The bottle of morphine was standing next to it.

Above her head, the sound of running feet, followed by stomping on the wooden door leading down into the basement.

They had found her.

She took one last look at Sarah Castle hanging off the manacles against the white brick wall. Their prisoner wasn't moving now; it was about time she died.

Still.

Lifeless.

Over 46 millilitres of formalin had entered her body. A strong woman, like he had said.

But she was a strong woman too.

She plunged the hypodermic through the seal covering the morphine.

Chapter Seventy

The armed response team arrived in a crescendo of sirens, klaxons and squealing brakes, before jumping out of their cars, Heckler & Koch automatic rifles pressed to their shoulders.

'Get some bolt cutters on that lock.'

Dave ran off to the car, coming back immediately to attack the rusted lock. Within seconds it was cut open and the shutters rolled up.

Light flooded into the workshop. Charlie could see more clearly now. Cobwebs trailed across the corners of the broken windows. Dust covered everything. On the floor, the body of a dead, desiccated bird lay untouched and unloved.

It was empty.

'Check it out,' Charlie ordered.

The rest of the team rushed in, opening the doors to the back and checking the rear of the workshop.

'I think there's something here.' It was Harry, shouting from the left.

Charlie ran to where he was standing.

Harry kicked the floor. A hollow echo came from inside.

'Get it open.'

Two coppers knelt down, trying to get their fingers under the lip of the trapdoor and prise it open.

'Shut from the inside, boss.'

'We've got an axe in the back of the van,' said one of the armed response team, a sergeant.

'What are you waiting for? A pat on the back? Get the bloody thing.'

The sergeant ran off, returning 30 seconds later with the axe. 'Give it to me.'

Charlie swung the axe down into the wood, splintering the trapdoor.

Again and again, it swung down, chopping into the wood. Gradually a hole formed. Charlie could see steps leading down into a basement.

He attacked the trapdoor with renewed energy, joined by a constable from the armed response team with another axe, slashing down into the wood, the sharp point of the axe biting deeper with every stroke.

'Hang on.' Charlie's hand stopped the constable in mid-strike. He knelt down, stuck in his hand through the hole and felt for a bolt, sliding it across.

He looked at the sergeant in charge of the armed team. The man raised his Heckler & Koch rifle and nodded his head.

Charlie levered his fingers under the edge of the trapdoor and threw it open.

The sergeant launched himself down the steps, rifle swinging left to right. He was followed by two other officers.

Charlie watched as they turned a sharp bend and went out of sight, only their black shadows betraying their presence.

Finally, a shout of 'All clear' from down below.

Charlie rushed down the steps. The basement beneath the workshop was slightly smaller than the room above. The brick walls were freshly painted in a white lime wash.

Charlie pushed his way past the armed officers. A woman with long dark hair lay on the floor in the centre of basement, a hypodermic needle sticking out of her left arm.

Charlie looked past the woman to the white brick wall. Sarah Castle was manacled there, her body slumped to one side, a saline drip leading into the back of her hand.

'Jesus Christ,' he said quietly.

A soft moan came from her mouth.

'Get an ambulance, immediately,' Charlie shouted, rushing over to her unconscious body. 'She's still alive.'

Chapter Seventy-One

Before Charlie Whitworth could help Sarah Castle, another shout came from Dave Hardy.

'Boss, look at this.'

He pointed to a computer on a table to one side. On the black screen, a time was counting down.

2.15.

2.14.

2.13.

'Shit.' Charlie looked around him. The armed response team were guarding the entrance; his own officers searching in the back of the basement; Harry Makepeace cradling Sarah Castle's head.

2.06.

2.05.

2:04.

'Everybody out, except Harry.'

'But boss—' whined Dave Hardy.

'Out now, all of you. That's an order.'

The team looked up from their search, uncertain what to do.

Charlie shouted louder. 'OUT. ALL OF YOU.'

The armed response team ran up the stairs out of the basement, followed by the rest of Charlie's team. Only Dave Hardy and Harry Makepeace remained behind.

'Charlie, I think—'

'Get out now, Dave. Get that ambulance.'

The detective chief inspector looked down at Harry Make-peace who was tugging at the manacles holding Sarah's arms to the wall. 'She's not coming free, boss,' he shouted over his shoulder.

Dave Hardy hesitated for a moment.

'Get the ambulance ready for when we come out, Dave,' said Charlie.

The detective sergeant glanced back at Harry Makepeace tugging at the wall.

'That's an order, Dave.'

He hesitated for a moment and then ran for the stairs.

1.44.

1.43.

1.42.

'Take that bloody drip out of her hand,' ordered Charlie as he moved towards the prone body of Sarah Castle lying unconscious on the floor, her manacled arms stretched up and behind her.

Harry Makepeace ripped the saline drip from her hand without removing the plasters holding it in place.

Charlie Whitworth grabbed hold of the chain and, using all his weight, began to pull it from its socket in the wall.

The ring was embedded deep into the brick.

'Help me, Harry.'

Together, they pulled on the heavy chain, rocking it backwards and forwards, trying to loosen the ring from its attachment to the wall.

'It's moving,' Harry shouted.

Charlie glanced back at the computer screen. The numbers were counting down quickly, silently.

1.19.

1.18

1.17.

He pulled harder, wrenching the chain left and right. A few flakes of dry plaster began to drift onto the floor beside Sarah's head. They both tugged harder, again and again and again.

The ring embedded in the brick moved slightly, releasing even more dust onto Sarah.

1.08.

1.07.

1.06.

'The key. We need to find the key.'

Charlie dropped the chain and ran back to the desk where the computer was counting down their lives, pulling open the drawers.

Empty.

He looked around the basement, his eyes darting along the white walls, looking for the silvery glint of a key.

Nothing.

The computer clock in front of him ticked on inexorably.

0.59.

0.58.

0.57.

Harry was still trying to wrench the iron ring from the wall. 'The computer may be nothing, boss. Just switching itself off.'

But Charlie knew better. The whole situation screamed danger to him. He wanted to run up those stairs and out of this bloody basement, but he stood still, rooted to the spot.

Where would she put the key?

0.50.

0.49.

0.48.

The woman lay at his feet, her blue eyes open, the hypodermic needle still sticking out of her arm at a crazy angle, and a strange smile fixed to her face. A Mona Lisa smile. Was she happy to die?

He was wrenched away from the woman's face by the sound of Harry falling backwards as the ring finally broke away from the wall.

0.41.

0.40.

0.39.

Harry dropped the manacle on the floor and stood up quickly to grab the chain attaching Sarah's right arm to the wall. He began tugging at it, using all of his 16 stone to pull it away from the wall.

It didn't move.

The key. They needed the key.

Charlie glanced at the computer screen again.

0.35.

0.34.

0.33.

The woman's eyes stared up at him. *Where did you hide the key?* He looked down at her body, past the long hair and the white shirt to her tweed pencil skirt.

Was there something there?

He dropped to his knees and began searching through her skirt pockets, his fingers thick and clumsy, the body unyielding and unhelpful.

There was something there.

0.29.

0.28.

0.27.

He forced his hand into the other pocket, feeling the coldness of the woman's hip. His fingers touched metal: two keys on a ring. He pulled them out of her tight skirt and ran towards Harry Makepeace.

He stepped over Sarah's prone body and grabbed her arm, holding up the manacle.

Where did the key go?

A small hole on the metal around her wrist. He inserted one of the keys. It wouldn't turn. He glanced back over his shoulder.

0.23.

0.22.

0.21.

'Get out, Harry.'

'What about you?'

'Get out!' he shouted, his fingers fumbling with the other key.

Harry hesitated.

'Get out!'

He could hear the blood rushing through his head, feel the sweat on his temple dribble past his ear. The key wouldn't go in.

Calm. Keep calm. Think.

His fingers felt like sausages on the end of his hands – clumsy, flabby sausages.

Finally he inserted the key in the small black hole.

Nothing.

It wouldn't turn.

Harry was waiting for him at the bottom of the stairs.

0.18.

0.17.

0.16.

He twisted the key as hard as he could, hearing a slight click as the teeth slotted into the barrel of the lock.

The manacles fell apart and Sarah's arm fell to the floor. He picked up her body and slung it over his shoulder. She didn't weigh much, as light as air.

He ran towards the stairs, towards where Harry was waiting.

0.13.

0.12.

0.11.

He tripped over the body of the woman lying on the floor, stumbled forward but just managed to keep his feet. Harry was waiting for him, helping him up the stairs. Out of the basement, into the light of the workshop.

Dave Hardy stood at the door with two paramedics. They rushed to help him with Sarah.

'Get out,' Charlie shouted. 'Get out!'

He ran past them, still carrying Sarah across his shoulder.

Out through the door and out into the sunlight. The wind was rustling through the trees. The sun was fighting its way through the clouds covering Manchester. The air smelt wonderful, just a tinge of diesel adding a hint of industry.

Two hands came forward and lifted Sarah from Charlie's shoulder. At first, he resisted, then realizing they belonged to the emergency medical responders, he let her go, feeling the weight lift from him.

He carried on running to the far end of the car park where the armed response team and the rest of the squad were crouched down behind their cars. Up above, the helicopter whirred noisily.

Harry Makepeace and Dave Hardy were running alongside him as he reached the safety of the cars. The two medics carried Sarah Castle past him and into a waiting ambulance.

He turned back for a second to look at the workshop, standing quiet and lonely against its backdrop of trees.

His chest rose and fell as he gulped in air, fighting to recover his breath.

Perhaps he was wrong. Perhaps it was just the computer switching itself off.

On the left a bird sang from its perch in a tree. The quiet buzz of traffic from the A6 added a drone of accompaniment to the bird's song. The helicopter still whirred noisily overhead, drifting forwards and backwards.

Then the workshop dissolved in an explosion of light, followed a moment later by a loud boom and the wooden roof rising up into the air for a moment before settling back on the stone walls.

Chapter Seventy-Two

'We got her. We nailed the bitch.'

Charlie Whitworth threw his arm around Ridpath's shoulder. He could smell the beer on the man's breath and see it flecked on the end of his moustache.

He put on a brave face and smiled broadly. 'Great news, Charlie. Well done.'

The rest of the team were jubilant, standing in a corner of the pub, pints in their hands and smiles on their faces.

'It's a great result. John Gorman is over the moon. What you having? A pint of Holts?'

Charlie Whitworth had called him earlier to say they were all going to be in the pub. 'Come on down, have a few pints on me.'

'I've got some good news too.'

'You've worked out what happened to Alice Seagram's body...'

'How did you know?'

Ridpath could hear Charlie laughing on the end of the phone. 'I'm a detective, remember. And besides, the booking sergeant at the local nick rang me to get my OK. You're charging Don Brown?'

'Just a holding charge at the moment. There are some loose ends I need to tidy up.'

'It's a good collar. Come down the pub for a few – I'm buying, and you know how rare that is.'

So here he was, surrounded by the whole Major Incident Team.

'What are you having?'

'Just a half for me, I'm driving.'

'Bugger off, you'll have a pint like the rest of us.' He turned to the barman. 'Another pint for the girl on my right. Dave, you ready for another?'

'Of course, Charlie, great to see your wallet has finally left the old folks' home,' Dave shouted across the bar.

Ridpath signalled to the barman to make it a half and turned back to speak to his boss. 'Who was she?' he shouted over the raucous laughter.

Charlie covered his ear with his hand. 'What?'

'Who was the killer?'

'A psychiatric nurse, Lesley Taylor. Used to work at HMP Styal, but lost her job six months ago. Lived at home with her mother.'

More laughter erupted from the group as Harry Makepeace told a joke.

Charlie turned to join in.

'Why did she start killing?' Ridpath shouted over the crowd.

'Who knows? Perhaps she enjoyed it. Got her rocks off hurting people.'

'Why prostitutes?'

Charlie put his arm around Ridpath's shoulder. 'Enough with the questions. She's dead, and good riddance to bad rubbish. Take it easy, for God's sake. Tonight we're celebrating,' he shouted. Then he turned and raised his glass to the rest of the team. 'Here's to the best team of bloody coppers in England.'

'And Salford,' shouted Harry Makepeace.

The rest of the team cheered and raised their glasses. Charlie buried his face in his glass, sucking in a large mouthful of the warm beer through his moustache.

Over in the corner, Dave Hardy's phone rang. 'What? What? I can't hear you.'

He moved through the crowd and out onto the street.

Ridpath shouted to Charlie again. 'But why Sarah? Why take a copper?'

Charlie shrugged his shoulders. 'Your guess is as good as mine. Wrong place, wrong time. The woman was cruising the streets looking for a victim and she found Sarah. Can't have known she was a copper.'

Dave Hardy came back into the pub, his face ashen, as if all the blood had drained out of it.

'Quiet,' he said loudly, before shouting the word again and raising his hands.

The room looked across at him, but people continued laughing and talking. Harry Makepeace was in the middle of a story: '...and the barman said to the horse...'

Charlie Whitworth took one look at Dave and, despite the four pints of beer he'd drunk, raised his hands and shouted. 'Shut up.'

This time the room went quiet.

Dave Hardy stood there for a moment, his arms down by his side. 'Sarah's dead.'

Chapter Seventy-Three

A million thoughts raced through Ridpath's mind in a jumble of images, memories and questions... What happened? How? Her smile. Her reddening face at the briefing. Touching her hand as she gave him the thumb drive. Her voicemail. 'What?' was the only word that escaped his lips.

Dave Hardy stared at him. 'Sarah Castle died in intensive care five minutes ago. The hospital just rang me.' He held up his mobile phone as if showing them proved the truth of his words.

'But... but we saved her. She was alive. The ambulance got there in six minutes...' Charlie stammered.

Dave shook his head. 'She's dead.'

It was like a shroud had been thrown over everybody.

Her shroud.

The party ended pretty quickly. People gradually drifted away to go home, go to eat or simply go to sleep.

They found out more details. Her body had suffered multiple organ failure at Stepping Hill hospital. The doctors had attached her to a life support system and tried to put her into a coma, but it was all too late. She had died at 8.23, just two hours after she had been rescued.

Half an hour later there were only two tables still occupied. Ridpath, Charlie Whitworth and Harry Makepeace sat at one of them, and a few others from the team including Dave Hardy, silent as a morgue, at another. Charlie had spent 15 minutes telling Ridpath how they had found the killer.

'You know, we work our balls off but it's always the stupid mistakes that give them away.'

'Ain't that the truth,' muttered Harry Makepeace.

'A nosy neighbour who thought she'd watch two dykes having a snog. Would you believe it? And using the same car on all the murders. Stupid.'

Then Charlie had fallen silent, working his way through the pints littering the table with the determination of an alcoholic who had been teetotal for a year.

Ridpath nursed the half pint he had been given, not knowing what to say, but with a thousand questions buzzing around his head.

'She was a good copper.' Charlie finally broke the silence.

'The best,' said Harry Makepeace, swallowing the last of his pint.

Ridpath shook his head, 'It doesn't make sense.'

'What doesn't make sense?' Charlie looked over his pint glass.

'The profiler said the perp was male, he'd done it before, and the crimes were always carefully planned and executed.'

'Don't they all say the same thing?' Charlie raised his glass to his mouth and took a long swallow of the dark beer, finishing it in one. 'He was wrong,' he said finally. 'They usually are.'

'It doesn't make sense. Why would it be a woman? Women are rarely serial killers.'

Charlie looked across at him. 'Well it was. When we broke in, she was there on the floor, a needle sticking out of her.'

Harry Makepeace continued. 'She must have heard us breaking in and took her own life. She deserved to die. Saves the courts the hassle of trying her, and they won't be using my bloody taxes to keep her banged up for the next 40 years.' He took a long swallow of his beer. 'Anyway, nowt left of her now. Explosion took everything.'

'And the car. Why make such an obvious mistake?'

Charlie lifted his head from his pint. 'They're criminals, murderers, not infallible. They make mistakes like the rest of us.'

'But—'

'Enough, Ridpath.' Charlie's voice was tinged with anger. 'Forget it. She's dead.' He pinched the bridge of his nose, shaking his head. 'I can't get the picture out of my head. Sarah manacled to the wall, barely alive. We should have got there earlier, should have been quicker. Sarah would—'

Harry patted his boss's arm. 'You can't think like that, guv'nor. We did the best we could. We couldn't have done any more. We didn't kill Sarah, that bitch did. She was the one who tortured her to death, not us.'

'You're right, Harry. It doesn't help, but you're right.' He stood up. 'What are you havin'? It's my shout.'

He didn't ask Ridpath what he was drinking.

Chapter Seventy-Four

Ridpath didn't stay long in the pub. He could sense the atmosphere had changed; he was an outsider, no longer part of the team. When he said he was going, neither Charlie nor Harry tried to stop him.

Outside, he took three deep breaths, started up the car and raced home through the quiet streets of Manchester.

Polly was waiting up for him. 'I heard,' was all she said. 'Did you know her well?'

Ridpath shook his head. 'We were working together on Alice Seagram's case. She helped me at the graveyard and with a few other things.' He sat down next to his wife. 'But I knew nothing about her. Who she was? Where she came from? What she liked? Didn't have a clue. We just worked together.'

'You've only been back on the job for a few days, Ridpath, don't blame yourself. It was just one of those things. She was in the wrong place at the wrong time.'

So that was the story, was it? The wrong place? It all seemed too pat, too coincidental, for him. It wasn't the MO of the killer. He picked up prostitutes in red-light districts, not women on suburban streets.

She leant over and kissed him on the forehead. 'I'm off to bed. Don't stay up too late.'

'I won't.' She knew him so well, understanding he needed to be alone right now with only a glass of Laphroaig for company.

At the door, she turned back, 'Don't forget the hospital appointment tomorrow, Ridpath. It's the most important thing for you to do. You can't bring Sarah Castle back, but you can make sure you look after yourself. Eve and I are counting on you.' A slight nod of her head and she was off.

God, he loved that woman. He went over to the bar in the corner and poured himself a large Laphroaig.

His mind turned to Sarah. Her youth, the way she reddened so easily, wearing her heart on her sleeve. Her brightness, the sharpness of her mind. Why had she rung him the day he saw James Dalbey? What did she have to tell him? He supposed he would never know now. A secret that would forever remain a secret.

He took another sip of the whisky. Despite Charlie's belief, the case didn't feel right – there were too many unanswered questions. Why Sarah? Why pick her up in the middle of suburbia? She wasn't like the killer's other victims. Not a street-walker, no history of drug use. Not from out of town.

The profiler had said the killer was a man who had murdered before and who was meticulous in his planning.

But the kidnapping of Sarah didn't fit in with the pattern of the others. It was easy to follow on CCTV, Lesley Taylor's white BMW a clear target.

Was it just chance the woman had seen Sarah being taken?

Probably. Arrests of serial killers often happened by chance rather than through police work. Look at the Yorkshire Ripper, arrested by two coppers in a routine traffic stop because he had false number plates on his lorry. Or Denis Nilsen, caught when the bodies of the young men he dismembered blocked the drains.

He took another sip of Laphroaig.

But this case, it didn't make any sense. He could feel something was wrong; he just couldn't put his finger on why.

Chapter Seventy-Five

The following morning Ridpath had a slight headache. He had sat up until two in the morning drinking Laphroaig and thinking about the case. He had looked at it every way but still didn't understand.

Polly had already gone to school with Eve, but not before having a word with him.

'I've put your clean underwear out. The appointment is at 9 am, Ridpath – make sure you're there early. I've been thinking.'

Ridpath looked at her over the rim of his coffee mug. 'It's bad for you.'

'I've been mothering you too much, stifling you. I'll stop, Ridpath, I've decided you have to take responsibility for your own health from now on. I can't keep being this woman who spends her life nagging you to do something. So I'm going to trust you more. You're a grown-up, you can take responsibility for yourself.'

'Like me,' said Eve putting on her shoes and tying the laces.

'Just like you, sweetheart.'

She kissed him on the head. 'Tell me what the doctor says tonight.' She checked her watch. 'Shit, is that the time? The old witch, Mrs Hardacre, will be telling me off for being late again.'

'I didn't know Mrs Hardacre was a witch, Mummy.'

His wife ushered her daughter out of the kitchen 'Don't say a word to any of your schoolmates, Eve – that's not for public consumption.'

'So Mrs Hardacre being a witch is a secret. Does she have a broomstick?'

Ridpath heard the door closing with a bang.

He sipped his coffee. Today was going to be busy. After the doctor's, he would follow up on Don Brown's case, take a formal statement and make sure all the paperwork was up to date. He'd have to hand over the actual preparation of the case to another police team, but he would make sure they had all the evidence they needed plus a watertight statement admitting guilt. Whether or not they went to trial would depend on the Crown Prosecution Service.

His phone rang and he picked it up absent-mindedly. 'Ridpath.'

'I'm glad you answered, I need you to do something.' It was the rich tones of Margaret Challinor.

'I'm just going out to—'

Before he could finish she carried on speaking. 'We have a problem. The inquest into the Alice Seagram case is set for Monday...'

'We know what happened now. The inquest should be a formality, shouldn't it?'

'There's a problem. We still haven't discovered her body.'

'But we know where it is. TRACE, near Preston. That's where Don Brown took it.'

'But we still have to find it.'

Ridpath thought for a moment. 'I can go up on Monday with a forensics team. It should be fairly straightforward to find out what happened to it.'

'That's the problem.'

'What?'

'The whole area is closed off for a month from next Monday. Some experiment they're conducting. Nobody's allowed in.'

'But you're the coroner, can't you order them to keep it open?'

'I've already tried. They've said no – scientists coming from all over the world apparently. I could get a court order but...'

'But...'

'They've said we can come today. I've arranged a forensics team from Preston run by a man called Davis. Do you know him?'

'He's good, meticulous.'

'Great. You have to be with him, of course.'

'I guessed. When is he going to be there?'

'In two hours. You have to leave now.'

Ridpath thought for a moment. Polly would kill him for missing the appointment at Christie's again. He would have to make it up to her somehow. 'I'm on my way. But where is it? Don Brown didn't tell me.'

'I'll email the address for your satnav. They are expecting you at ten.'

Ridpath checked his watch. 8.45. He would have to drive quickly. Preston was almost an hour away. 'I'm leaving now.'

'Thank you, Ridpath. I'll remember this.'

He put the phone down and rushed upstairs to change into his suit. He hoped Polly would forgive him. She would understand, wouldn't she?

Chapter Seventy-Six

The TRACE facility was heavily guarded; an eight-foot tall security fence surrounded the site and was topped off with three vicious coils of barbed wire. A thick strand of cable and the ubiquitous sign of a lightning flash of live electricity were attached to the fence.

One narrow road led into the facility, blocked by a red and white painted barrier, watched by a single CCTV camera and guarded by a burly man in uniform. A single white sign with the words University of Lancashire painted on it in black letters was the only indication of who or what owned the land.

Ridpath stopped at the barrier. He had driven up the M61 as quickly as he could without attracting the attention of the motorway police or of the cameras monitoring the road. The last thing he wanted was to be pulled over for speeding.

The security guard donned his hat and approached the car. 'Can I help you?'

'Tom Ridpath, the coroner's officer. I have an appointment with a Mr Downey.'

'You're in the book. Park behind the security building over there. Please do not leave your car until Mr Downey comes for you and do not go past the red sign in the car park.'

The security guard lifted the barrier and Ridpath drove round the corner to see another building which, up until now, had been hidden from view. He parked in the area reserved for visitors and waited.

The area looked like the rest of rural Lancashire; wood-land on the left skirting the bottom of a hill. Drystone walls separating areas into fields. The luscious green of grass and trees undulating off into the distance.

It could have been any other farm where animals grazed, lambs frolicked and wild rabbits bred to their hearts' content. Except this was a place where experiments were carried out to monitor the rate of decay of animal bodies, where insects fed on remains and wild rabbits were electrocuted if they came anywhere near.

A man in a white coat carrying a clipboard stepped out of the admin building and approached the car. Ridpath opened the window.

'Mr Ridpath?' he said, looking at his clipboard.

'Detective Inspector Ridpath, actually.'

'Hmm.' The man made a note on his clipboard. 'The forensics team hasn't arrived yet. But you can wait in admin if you like.' He indicated the building he had just come from.

Ridpath stepped out of the car. 'You are...?'

'Patrick Downey, facility manager.' The man held out his hand.

Ridpath looked at it for a moment before shaking it. Had this man been handling dead bodies this morning? A shudder went down his spine.

'I have to ask you what this is about. The coroner,' he checked his clipboard once more, 'Mrs Margaret Challinor, didn't explain much.'

'We are looking for the body of an Alice Seagram, one of the victims of the Beast of Manchester—'

'Her body wasn't in her coffin,' he interrupted, 'I saw it on the news. But what's that to do with us? We do not test human remains here. This facility only conducts tests on animal bodies – pigs mainly.' He made another note in his clipboard. 'Actually, in the UK, there are no body farms, as the Americans like to call them,' he sniffed twice. 'We are dependent on them for all our information on the effects on the human body of environmental factors.'

He said the last sentence with a note of regret.

'I am aware of what your establishment does, Mr Downey, but we have information that a body may have been left here without your knowledge.'

'Impossible. I've been the manager of this facility for the last 20 years. No human remains or cadavers have ever been used as long as I have been in charge.'

'Our case occurred ten years ago.'

'Then it's impossible, Inspector, I would know if any bodies had been placed here and I would have rejected any such proposal from one of our scientists without the express permission of the university authorities.'

Ridpath realized he was getting nowhere, so he tried a different tack. 'Do you keep records of everybody who comes to your facility, Mr Downey?'

'Of course, Inspector. Every delivery of a carcass to the facility is recorded before it is moved into the cold store. Obviously, we have to keep track for the scientific records, we can't just dump them willy-nilly in the grounds.'

Ridpath was fed up of being treated like an idiot by this man, but he kept his temper in check. 'Could I see the records?'

The man hummed and hawed for a moment.

'If I could see the records then we may not even need the forensics team to search the facility. Particularly when you have such an important experiment taking place in a couple of days.'

Ridpath watched as Downey weighed up the problem. Finally, the man's shoulders relaxed. 'OK, come this way. The records are confidential but I'm sure the university would approve if it meant minimal disturbance to our work.'

They walked to the admin building. Inside it had all the charm and warmth of a mental asylum. Downey was obviously proud of his facility, giving Ridpath a guided tour. 'On the left are three state-of-the art labs; beyond them are the insect and mammal buildings. Obviously, we need ready supplies of flies, insects, mice and rats. We can't rely on nature.'

'Who would?'

'On the right, we have the cold stores where we keep the animal bodies, mainly pigs, before using them for the experiments.'

'Let me get this right. You are looking at the decomposition rates of bodies?'

'That's just one of the research areas we pursue. Environmental effects on carcasses, insect pupae and their role. The effect of heat and cold on rates of decay. One of our researchers is looking into the effect of predation on animal cadavers. In other words, how long it takes rats, in our case, to discover and devour a pig's carcass.'

'Charming. Quicker than humans at a barbecue?'

'You may joke, Inspector, but our work has a valuable role in the solving of many crimes.'

He opened a door. Ridpath half expected to see a row of pig carcasses being attacked by horseflies. Instead, there was a row of filing cabinets.

'Now what year were you looking for?'

'March 2008 – the 22nd, to be precise.'

'Good. I like precision.' He unlocked a cabinet on the left and shuffled through a series of files before taking one out. 'Here we are. There was a delivery that day.' He opened the file. 'The delivery was from Manchester. A pig's carcass. Number 246834. The driver's name is printed here, a Mr Donald Brown. See, there's his signature.' He pointed to a scrawled signature.

'But who sent it?'

Downey checked along the line. 'This company. We get deliveries from them occasionally for research.'

As Downey reached for another file, Ridpath peered over the man's shoulder to see the name.

Prospect Limited. Where had he seen that name before?

Downey spoke again. 'You're in luck, Inspector. For some reason that particular pig's carcass has never been used for research. It's still in the cold store.'

Chapter Seventy-Seven

The forensics team under Davis had finally arrived at 10.30 and he had put them to work immediately examining case number 246834.

The pathologist came out of the cold store within ten minutes.

'Is it Alice Seagram?'

'All I can tell you is it's the body of a young woman. She seems to have undergone some sort of post-mortem in the past, displaying the classic Y section. After being frozen for ten years the features are degraded and there seems to be evidence of acid being applied to her body. Her fingerprints may be unusable, but her DNA should be OK. Once we have her back in the lab, we'll be able to give you an answer pretty quickly.'

Ridpath had rung Mrs Challinor. 'I'm think we've found Alice Seagram's body.'

'Well done, Ridpath. After a truly shitty week, it's the best news I've had for a long time. I'll get on to the family straight away.'

'Can we postpone the inquest?'

'Impossible. The warrants to give evidence have already gone out.'

'Gorman and Whitworth will not be happy.'

'Their happiness is the least of my worries.' There was a moment of silence. 'Why do you want to postpone the inquest?' she asked suspiciously.

'I can't talk over the phone. Can we meet tomorrow morning?'

'Why not this evening?'

'I need to recheck something in the files of the 2008 investigation.'

'Of course, ten o'clock at the Coroner's Office tomorrow morning.'

'I'll see you then.'

'This is all extremely cloak and dagger, Ridpath. Can't you tell me what's going on?'

'Sorry, Mrs Challinor, I need to be sure.'

Downey was hovering nearby, so Ridpath lowered his voice.

'Can I call you back, Mrs Challinor?'

'See you tomorrow, Ridpath. I hope it's good ne—'

Ridpath switched off his mobile.

'I was thinking about the 2008 delivery and realized we had a similar delivery two weeks ago.'

'Who sent it?'

'The same company who sent the pig's carcasses. See. Prospect Limited.'

'Who delivered it?'

Downey tried to remember. 'The researcher himself, I think. It wasn't a busy day for deliveries.'

'What was his name?'

'I don't remember.'

'Think, man.'

'I can't remember the name of every researcher who turns up here. But we have the record.' He produced a new file marked '2018'. Inside, a document showed another pig's carcass being delivered to TRACE two weeks ago. A signature was scrawled across the bottom of the page in a blur of blue. It could have been anybody.

'Can we find this delivery?'

'Of course, it's in the cold store next door.'

Ridpath called Davis to join him and both of them were shown to case number 578459 by the facility manager.

A blast of icy air hit them as he opened the door and stepped back. According to Downey, the delivery was in the second drawer from the bottom on the far right-hand side.

Davis went first, pushing past the frozen bodies of pigs, covered in a hard white rime, hanging from hooks in the ceiling. The pigs swung gently to and fro as Ridpath ducked past them

On the left the assorted bodies of other animals fought for space on a metal bar: two mongrel dogs, a group of ginger cats, a fox, three badgers, all still enclosed in their frozen fur, eyes like glass marbles. Next to them, the two larger, skinless bodies of what looked like cows, ghostly in the frozen air.

'It's over there.' Davis's words came out hard and visible as two clouds of white frost. Ridpath felt his ears begin to tingle beneath the thin covering of the Tyvek cap. They couldn't stay here long.

Davis opened the drawer. Inside were blue body bags stacked one on top of the other.

'It should be the third one down.'

Ridpath rubbed his hands together in their nitrile gloves trying to put some feeling back in them. With Davis's help, he removed the top two bags, placing them on the floor.

'Is this it?'

Davis nodded.

Ridpath reached out to pull down the zip on the bag. A white cloth stared back at him.

He pulled the cloth away to reveal a woman's face, the right side crushed and broken, the edges of the bones rimed in white.

'I think we've just found another victim,' said Ridpath, his breath forming clouds of white vapour.

Chapter Seventy-Eight

Ridpath's mind was racing. The killer was clever – too clever. Deflecting attention onto an innocent man in James Dalbey and now finding a fall woman in the shape of a psychiatric nurse, Lesley Taylor. Although from what Charlie Whitworth said, it seemed she may not have been that innocent.

He accelerated into the outer lane of the M61, passing a slow-moving white van and then moved back into the middle.

His mind flashed back to that first day on patrol with Sergeant Mungovan. Chasing after James Dalbey, running through the streets of Chorlton, fighting on the floor of the lock-up, the great feeling of triumph as his fist smashed into the man's temple.

How could he have been so wrong? How could what seemed so true have been such a lie?

The traffic increased considerably as he neared the M60, coming to a virtual standstill, cars and lorries edging forward and then stopping.

What he needed now was the siren and lights of a police car to force his way through. But he'd had to give them back nine months ago. It seemed an age and half a lifetime away.

As he stopped in traffic, waiting for it to start moving, a busload of questions ran through his mind.

Who was the other woman they had found in the ice store? Could it be Irene Hungerford, the sex worker missing from Moss Side? He could release pictures of her, but it would be better to use DNA for a definitive identification.

Even without an identification, the woman's body at TRACE showed two things. Firstly, the killings in 2008 and the recent murders were linked. And secondly, Lesley Taylor had not acted alone: she had been guided by the same man who had committed the murders in 2008.

He knew who the Beast of Manchester was, and it wasn't the man who'd been locked up for the last ten years in Belmarsh Prison.

How could he prove the murders were committed by the same man?

He remembered something in the police files. Something said by James Dalbey on the day he was arrested. It was in his interview with Charlie Whitworth and John Gorman. What was it? He needed to check the files of the police investigation in 2008.

The profiler had been close to the answer. His profile had given them more clues than any of the police realized at the time. He was a man, he was clever, he was obsessed with water and he was ruthless.

However, the answer to one question eluded Ridpath and the profiler had come no closer to answering it.

Why?

Why had he killed the women? What perverted pleasure did he obtain from it? And how had he managed to set people up to take the fall for his crimes?

He found himself gripping the steering wheel, his knuckles white against the black leather. No women would suffer again. Not here. Not in his city.

The traffic started moving.

Ridpath put the car in gear and edged home. The answer was waiting for him there. All he had to do was check the files.

Thirty minutes later, he parked the car in the driveway, noticing Polly's Polo wasn't in its usual place.

As he opened the door, he expected both her and Eve to rush out to welcome him back.

Nothing. The house was dark. Empty.

He switched on the lights and rushed into the living room. On the mantelpiece next to the mirror was a short note written in capitals with a thick black marker pen.

I'VE HAD ENOUGH.

Chapter Seventy-Nine

He stood there staring at the note, reading it again and again.

I've had enough.

Just three words, but they took all the breath out of his body.

He rushed upstairs, checking the bedrooms. Polly's was empty and the suitcases were missing from the top of the wardrobe. Her favourite jeans and all her work clothes were gone. He ran into Eve's room. Her school clothes were no longer there and the travelling case in the shape of a hippo on wheels wasn't in its place in the corner.

He rang Polly's mobile.

No answer.

Then her voice. 'Hello, you've reached Polly Ridpath's phone. I'm busy right now but I'll get back to you just as soon as I can. Unless you're a cold caller, then I won't get back to you at all and you can bugger off. Byeeeee.'

He flopped on Eve's bed as if all the bones had been removed from his body.

She had finally gone.

Seventeen years they had been together. She was serving in her father's Cantonese restaurant, her kooky green hair and black fishnet tights a stark contrast to the peonies, red lanterns and Chinese characters decorating the walls.

He had gone there with two friends before a night on a pub crawl.

'Chinese food lines the stomach, so you can drink more,' one of his friends had said.

So there they were. She approached them with her order pad.

'Number 24 is off and I wouldn't eat number 37,' she said without looking at them.

'Why wouldn't you eat number 37?' he asked.

For the first time her brown eyes stared at him. 'Because it's off.'

'Oh,' was all he could say.

She spoke with a clear Manchester accent with no hint of her Chinese heritage.

'Your English is good, where do you come from?' his friend asked.

Her eyes rolled. 'Chorlton. Your English isn't great. Where do you come from?'

'Bury.'

'That explains it.' The pen hovered over the notepad.

'How about the spring rolls?' he said.

'We've run out of springs...'

'So they're off?'

She nodded.

'What would you recommend?'

'The restaurant down the street.'

'Are you the rudest waitress in Manchester?' his friend asked.

'Not yet, but I'm trying hard. I'm in training. Came third last year in the "Rudest Waitress in Manchester contest". I'll do better this year. The bitch from the Flaming Dragon has hung up her notepad.' She scratched her green hair with the pen and fixed me with her brown eyes. 'So do you want to eat or do you want me to practice my one-liners on you? Eating is better, but less fun for me...'

They ordered.

'Three specials,' she shouted across to her father without making a note in her pad. 'Now what would you like to drink?'

'Three Tsingtaos.'

'Three beers from China for the Englishmen,' she shouted again.

'Why do you have a notepad but never use it?'

'Same reason you have an appendix.' She turned to go.

He didn't know why he did it. But just as she was walking away from the table, he asked, 'We're going to be at the White Lion later on. You want to meet us there?'

She turned back slowly. 'So this is the "let's hassle the kooky Chinese waitress with the green hair and see if she's stupid enough to be taken in by it" moment? It happens at least once a night, usually with lads out on the lash, but normally it comes after the beer, not before.'

He stared down at the red tablecloth. 'Sorry, shouldn't have asked.'

'And I shouldn't have bothered to explain.'

She left them, returning only once more to deliver their food.

But that night she turned up at the pub and they had been together ever since.

Until tonight.

The doorbell rang. *It was her, she was back.*

He ran down the stairs two at a time and wrenched open the door.

Charlie Whitworth was standing on his doorstep. 'You've been a naughty boy, Ridpath.'

He stood in the doorway. 'I don't know what you mean, Charlie.' He could smell the alcohol on the man's breath.

'I don't know what you mean, Charlie,' the DCI mimicked. He waved a piece of paper in front of his face. 'I got home and found a summons to appear at the inquest on Monday into Alice Seagram's death.'

Mrs Challinor had been quick. Or more likely Jenny Oldfield.

'John Gorman's got one too. He's beyond angry. You were supposed to keep us informed of what the bloody woman's up to.' A sober-looking Dave Hardy appeared at his DCI's shoulder.

'I told you before, Charlie, I'm no stoolie. The coroner is doing her job. And I've done mine. I found the body of Alice Seagram.'

For a second, Charlie seemed to sober up. 'Where?'

'At a university research facility near Preston.'

Charlie clapped his hands slowly. 'Aren't you the good little detective? Mummy's good little boy.'

'James Dalbey couldn't have arranged for it to be taken there in 2008. He was under lock and key.'

Charlie's face went redder. 'Not another one. James Dalbey murdered Alice Seagram. He smashed her over the head with a hammer and then slit her throat, before finally dousing her body in sulphuric acid while she was still alive. Don't you get it? He's guilty.'

'He's not. And I'm going to prove it. Now go home, you're drunk.'

He went to close the door but found the DCI's foot wedged in the gap.

'Listen to me, Ridpath. You think you're coming back on the team. Not a cat in hell's chance, mate.'

Dave Hardy put his hand on Charlie's shoulder. 'Come away, boss, it's time to go home.'

Charlie's finger appeared under Ridpath's face. 'As long as I'm there, you're never coming back. Understand? You're finished, Ridpath, and your career.'

Dave Hardy pulled his boss away from the door. The DCI stumbled backwards down the path, turning back at the gate to shout. 'You're finished. Finished.'

Ridpath stood there for a moment and then shut the door. In ten minutes, he had lost his wife and his career.

'Way to go, son,' he said out loud before sinking to the floor, 'Way to bloody go.'

Chapter Eighty

The following morning, a dull, overcast Sunday, Ridpath turned up at the Coroner's Office in Stockfield just after ten o'clock. The door was already open and Mrs Challinor was at her desk.

Didn't the woman ever go home?

He had spent a sleepless night at his house. At first, he tried ringing Polly's mobile but kept getting the annoying answering machine.

He had finally checked the police interview with James Dalbey and it confirmed his suspicions. There was a hand-written note next to Dalbey's explanation of how he had come to be in possession of the van.

> Checked 12/03/08. Van hired over the phone by a man from Prospect Limited on 7 March. Picked up by Dalbey in person morning of 10 March. Mileage records show it was driven 20.8 miles. Distance from hire firm to Chorlton 7.4 miles.

The note was initialled 'CW'. Was that Charlie? Why was there no follow-up?

But Ridpath knew why. Because they had already charged a suspect who admitted the murder. Why rock the boat with more pointless and time-wasting investigations?

He could almost hear John Gorman's voice. 'Leave it alone, Charlie. We've got better things to do.'

At least the link was now proven between the murder of Alice Seagram and of a prostitute in Manchester just two weeks ago. The link was a company called Prospect Limited. He had immediately checked them on the Companies register. Of course, no such company was listed.

He was back to square one.

Mrs Challinor was going through a pile of documents on her desk. 'Good to see you, Ridpath, and good work finding Alice Seagram.'

He walked in and slumped down in the hard chair in front of her. He spent the next hour telling her everything that had happened, including Charlie Whitworth's late-night visit.

Margaret Challinor stroked her bottom lip. 'It seems like we have a few problems, Ridpath. The first is the inquest tomorrow. At least, we have Alice Seagram's body. Dr Davis will confirm her DNA before then.'

'We can't postpone?'

She shook her head. 'Too difficult. The Ministry of Justice is sending an observer and so is the High Court. If we delay, it will only give the national newspapers time to pick up the story, and the last thing I need is a mob of braying journalists in my court. But more importantly, we need to take the family into account. We can't let them down any longer. They've waited ten years for this to come to court. So no postponement, not anymore.'

'And the second problem?'

'We know somebody else killed Alice Seagram, not James Dalbey, but we don't know who it is.'

'I've told you who I think it is.'

'But do you have any proof? Any evidence?'

Ridpath shook his head. 'The murders in 2008 and this year were committed by the same man. A company called Prospect Limited links them together. But other than a signature, we have no evidence.'

'He could just say it was forged. There has to be verifiable evidence.'

'After ten years, we're unlikely to find it. And the explosion wrecked any evidence we may have found in the workshop.'

'It's all very convenient, isn't it? Just as the police get close to the killer, somebody is found to take the fall. First it was James Dalbey and now this nurse, Lesley Taylor.'

'I don't believe in coincidences, Mrs Challinor.'

'Neither do I, Ridpath. We also have a third problem. The body of the murdered woman you found at TRACES. According to Dr Davis, she was scalped before she died...'

'Not a nice way to go.'

'Dr Davis is looking for links to the disappearance of the sex worker in Moss Side. The DNA results haven't come back yet. He's not getting a lot of help from Greater Manchester Police.'

'They already have their killer – it's Lesley Taylor, and she's dead.'

'So we have no real evidence of the involvement of another person, other than the word of James Dalbey.'

'The family believe him.'

'That's not enough to get him out of jail.'

'Do you believe he's innocent?'

She nodded. 'But whether I believe it or not doesn't matter. We have to prove he's innocent.'

Ridpath stared at her. 'We're stuffed, aren't we?'

'We have one thing that may save us. The truth.'

'You've just said we have nothing to prove the killer's guilt or James Dalbey's innocence.'

'But we have the inquest, where my job is to find the truth.'

'It's not enough, Mrs Challinor. It's never enough. We need evidence, hard documentary evidence.'

And then, as if looking down at himself from above, he heard his words again, 'Hard, documentary evidence.'

Of course, why hadn't he thought of it before? There was one simple way of showing who the killer was.

He stood up quickly. 'I have to go, Mrs Challinor. I'll call you this evening.' He grabbed his jacket and rushed out of the building.

This was his last chance.

He knew how to prove who the killer was.

Chapter Eighty-One

He hadn't slept last night. Not the best preparation for an inquest. He shaved, only nicking himself once, put on his best suit and drove along the M60 to Stockfield.

That morning, he had rearranged the appointment with Christie's for Tuesday with a mixture of charm and persever-ance. At least he could tell Polly when he met her.

If he met her.

He rang Polly again before he left the house, hearing her voice once more on the answering machine but never talking to her directly. Would she ever speak to him again?

The front door of the Coroner's Court was open and, for once, Jenny was actually in reception.

'Good morning, Ridpath. I see from the empty coffee cups and Subway wrappers you and Mrs Challinor had a busy weekend.'

He had returned to the Coroner's Office last night so that he and Mrs Challinor could work out a plan of action. After three hours, they finally thought they had a chance.

'It's 50/50, Ridpath. It all depends on how he behaves. We might be able to pull it off.'

'We have to try, Mrs Challinor.'

'You know this goes against all procedures for a coroner's court?'

'How?'

'Unlike other types of court case, coroners are not required to find someone "guilty" or "not guilty", or to blame anyone; our job is to record the cause and manner of death.'

'But if we do that, he'll go free. And who's to say he won't begin killing again a few years from now?'

'We could give our evidence to the police.'

'How long would that take? John Gorman and Charlie Whittaker have closed their minds. They already have their killer.'

She thought for a moment. 'It's about time I stuck my head out. You know, the clerk from the Ministry of Justice will be observing.'

He nodded. 'Is that bad?'

She made a moue with her mouth. 'Let's hope he's left his axe at home. If I screw this up, my head will be on the block.'

'We'd better not screw it up then.'

It was their only chance to finally catch the killer who had been terrorizing Manchester for so long.

It was their last chance.

He had wanted to stay at the Coroner's Office with Margaret Challinor on Sunday night as she went through all the papers, but there wasn't much he could do.

She noticed his discomfort. 'You don't have to be here, you know. You've done your job, now it's my turn.'

'That's all right, I prefer to be here.' He was telling the truth.

'Go home, Ridpath. You're making me nervous. I can't concentrate.'

'Isn't there anything else I can do?'

She shrugged her shoulders. 'You could pray, but I've a feeling you're not a God-fearing man.'

He shook his head. 'I was an altar boy when I was young but then I saw the light and became a devout atheist.'

'Even when the cancer came you didn't turn to God?'

'Because the cancer came, I would never turn to God. How dare he put my family through such pain? And you surprise me, Mrs Challinor, I wouldn't have put you down as a God-botherer.'

She brushed a grey hair off her forehead. 'I'm not. It's just, the older I get the more I ask myself: what's the point of being here? Why do we live?'

'To punish the bad guys...'

'It's not enough, Ridpath.' She stared at the papers on her desk. 'Go home, I have work to do before tomorrow.'

So finally he had gone back home and opened the door, hoping against hope Polly would be there.

But silence and emptiness were all that greeted him.

Now he was back at the Coroner's Office again. 'Good morning, Jenny. Is Mrs Challinor in?' He went to walk past to knock on her door.

'Been here since seven. But I wouldn't disturb her – the inquest is set to begin in 30 minutes. She likes to prepare alone. I would grab a coffee while you can. And no, I'm not going to make it.'

He went out and bought a coffee at Starbucks with what was laughably called a Danish but was really just undercooked puff pastry.

By the time he returned the doors to the courtroom upstairs were open. He saw three of the journalists from the last press conference sitting to the side in the public area. Mrs Challinor's strategy had worked. There seemed to be no national television coverage of the inquest. Perhaps they would turn up later.

The family arrived as he stood by the door. Mrs Seagram already close to tears, her husband as belligerent as ever by her side. Tony Seagram approached Ridpath.

'So you found my sister's body?'

Ridpath nodded.

'When can we get it back?'

'As soon as the pathologist releases it.'

'You know, my mother is organizing another funeral.' Then his tone changed, becoming much darker, almost sneering. 'Imagine that – I dare you, Inspector Ridpath – burying your daughter twice.'

Despite himself, Ridpath thought about Eve and losing her. *What would he do?*

Tony Seagram looked over his shoulder at the rapidly filling courtroom 'If this is the whitewash I think it's going to be, you lot will never hear the last of it. I'll drag you and your precious coroner out into the relentless glare of the media. Your corruption and incompetence are going to be exposed.'

'The inquest will reveal the truth.'

'Like the court case did ten years ago? Didn't work for James Dalbey. Last time I checked, he was still locked up.'

'Mrs Challinor will do her job.'

'Aye, I've no doubt. But for whom, Inspector Ridpath? For whom?'

The man moved back to join his mother and father sitting behind tables in front of the coroner.

Ridpath waited beside the door. A man and a woman both dressed in gowns and wigs pushed past him and took their places at the tables in front of the coroner's desk. They both deposited heavy files on top of the highly polished surface, chatting to each other all the time, with one of them pulling out her laptop.

They were followed soon after by John Gorman and Charlie Whitworth. Neither spoke to Ridpath and neither man looked at him. It was as if he didn't exist in their eyes. They sat down together in the viewing area, behind a flimsy pink rope strung between two brass stands, both looking straight ahead, neither talking to the other.

A tall man, dressed in an expensive dark suit, with thinning hair and half-moon glasses arrived next, sitting close to the two detectives and pulling out a sheaf of notes from his briefcase. He looked like an undertaker about to interview a recently bereaved family. He pursed his thin lips and sniffed the air of the court.

Who was he and what was he doing here? Ridpath was tempted to go over and ask him, but just as he was about to walk across, the pathologists, Lardner and Protheroe, arrived. The former was dressed in his usual tweed suit and tie. Protheroe was quieter than usual, subdued.

It was Lardner who approached him.

'Good morning, Ridpath, I hope we can get this over and done with as soon as possible. I've got three customers waiting for me back at the mortuary.'

'I'm sure they'll be happy to wait a little longer. They're not going anywhere.'

'Waste of time. It's all down to that man Seagram's work and the bloody press.'

'The inquest will determine the truth, Dr Lardner, not the press.'

'But the only reason we're here is because of them. I admitted I made a mistake on the timing of the death, that's why we performed another post-mortem. It doesn't change the fact James Dalbey killed Alice Seagram.'

'The inquest will decide, Mr Lardner.'

As he said those words, the jury began to take their seats on the right. Four men and three women. All white and all fairly prosperous in appearance. When were they selected? Obviously Jenny was very good at her job.

Finally, Mrs Challinor walked in. He expected some fanfare, as in the high court, but there was nothing. She simply sat behind her desk, opened her files and began speaking.

Chapter Eighty-Two

Her tone was relaxed and informal. 'Today we open the inquest into the death of Alice Seagram and the subsequent post-mortem.' She pointed to the empty witness box on her left. 'There will be a jury present at this inquest. They have already been sworn by one of my officers.' A quick glance down to the papers in front of her. 'Representing the police we have Mr Alex Chambers.'

The barrister stood up and bowed his head once.

'Representing the pathologist, Dr Harold Lardner, is Ms Stacey Hardisty.'

She also rose and bowed to the court.

'A gentle reminder to my learned colleagues. This is not a court of law. I will ask each witness questions as I see fit. My learned colleagues will have their opportunity to question the witnesses when I have finished. Carol...'

The senior coroner stepped forward. Ridpath could see her hair was decorated in an elaborate bun, and her suit was a severe shade of black.

'Please call the first witness. Chief Superintendent John Gorman.'

The short man strode to the witness box and took the oath on a Bible held by Carol Oates. As Margaret Challinor began questioning him, he ran his finger around the inside of his shirt collar, as if giving himself more room to breathe.

'Please state your name and occupation.'

'Chief Superintendent John Gorman, at present head of the Major Incident Team for the Greater Manchester Police, based at HQ in Newton Heath.'

'Thank you, Chief Superintendent Gorman. You were in charge of the investigation into the disappearance of five women, four of whom were murdered, in 2008?'

'I was. Through the efforts of my officers we managed to rescue the final victim, Freda Scott, before she could be murdered by James Dalbey.'

Margaret Challinor raised an eyebrow at the mention of the name but carried on anyway. 'This series of murders was commonly referred to as the "Beast of Manchester" case?'

'The tabloid press did give it that name. It was not something I encouraged amongst my officers.'

'Oh, why not?'

'The name suggested someone who was out of control, a beast, but James Dalbey was very much in control, a psychopath.'

'James never killed anybody,' shouted Tony Seagram.

The coroner fixed him with her blue eyes. 'Mr Seagram, we appreciate the concern of the family regarding this case. However, if I have another outburst, you will be removed from my court, do you understand?'

'But he keeps referring to James as the killer. James wouldn't hurt a fly, never mind murder my sister.'

'I asked if you understood me?'

His mother, sitting next to him, patted his arm. Tony Seagram nodded once and looked away.

'What were your reasons for believing James Dalbey to be guilty of the crimes?'

'He had opportunity to murder all four girls. He could not account for his movements when they disappeared. He knew victim number four, Alice Seagram. He confessed to killing her in a police interview. And he was caught in possession of the keys to a lock-up where the fifth victim was imprisoned.'

'You say he confessed?'

'That is correct.'

'A confession later rescinded...'

He smiled at the reporters. 'Criminals often rescind confessions. It's to be expected.'

'In the same confession, didn't he also talk about a man who had given him the keys to the lock-up?'

'An invisible man. We could find no trace of such a man.'

'So you investigated this "invisible man"?'

'Of course, if Dalbey had an accomplice we wanted to find him. But, despite our investigation, we could find no evidence of his existence. Nor has any proof of his existence come forward in the last ten years. I think it is significant that since we have locked up James Dalbey, there have been no further murders by the Beast of Manchester.'

Mrs Challinor frowned. 'May I remind you, Chief Superintendent, that the absence of something is not proof of the existence of something else,' she admonished him, brushing a grey lock of hair from her eyes. 'Just a few more questions... Your men found the fifth victim, Freda Scott, alive and manacled to a wall in a lock-up garage, after James Dalbey had been chased there. Is that correct?'

'That is correct. We arrested him in the lock-up and released her. Unfortunately, she committed suicide three years later. A consequence, I'm sure, of her experience at his hands.'

'Did you question her after her release?'

'We did. Understandably, she wasn't coherent; the affair had been a terrible shock to her.'

'Did she identify Dalbey as her assailant?'

'She did and she didn't.'

'I don't understand, Chief Superintendent.'

'She described a man of the same age and height as her assailant, but she never saw his face as he always wore a mask – a black mask.'

'So it may or may not have been James Dalbey?'

'From the other evidence, I believe it was him.'

Mrs Challinor frowned again. 'One last question, Mr Gorman. Did you apply any pressure on the pathologist, Dr Harold Lardner, to revise his time of death?'

The chief superintendent looked surprised. 'Of course not. And I resent the inference the police would ever put pressure on an independent forensic witness to change their findings. In fact, Dr Lardner approached me with a revised time of death. I did not ask him.'

'We will be asking Dr Lardner later.'

'I'm sure he will confirm what I have just said.'

'Thank you, Chief Superintendent.' She turned to the barristers at their table. 'I have no more questions. Mr Chambers, do you have any for this witness?'

The barrister stood up and smiled. 'Just a few, Mrs Challinor, for clarification,' he added as an afterthought. 'Chief Superintendent Gorman, did you ever find any evidence of another man being involved in the killings?'

'No.'

'No fingerprints in the lock-up?'

'No.'

'No DNA on any of the murder weapons?'

'None, other than those of James Dalbey.'

'No fibres, hairs, shoe prints or any other physical evidence of another man?'

'None whatsoever.'

'So this man who, according to James Dalbey, committed all these murders and ordered him to go to the lock-up, didn't exist forensically?'

'Not at all.'

'Did any other witnesses testify to seeing him with Dalbey?'

'No. We spent over 400 man hours looking for him but could never find any trace of his existence. Dalbey said they met in secret, nobody ever knew.'

'The unknown man?'

'You could say, Mr Chambers, I could not possibly comment.'

'Finally, Detective Superintendent, you never found the bodies of the other victims of the Beast of Manchester.'

John Gorman's face blanched and, for the first time, he looked uncertain and anxious. 'No, we never did,' he finally answered. 'Dalbey refused to tell us where he had hidden them.'

'Thank you, Mrs Challinor. I have finished with the witness.'

She turned to Gorman. 'You may leave the witness stand, Chief Superintendent, but you remain under oath. It seems a good time to break for 15 minutes. We return at 11.15.'

Chapter Eighty-Three

On her way out, Margaret Challinor indicated to Ridpath he should follow her to the office. Once inside, she closed the door. 'It's not going well, Ridpath. The barrister has him well coached and the jury is not buying the existence of the other man at all.'

Ridpath sat down in the bentwood chair in front of her.

Margaret Challinor remained standing. 'We have to speed it up. The longer we take to get to the key point, the harder it will be to get him to make a mistake. Are you ready?'

Before he could answer, there was a light tap on the door. Without waiting for Mrs Challinor to respond, it opened and the tall man in the expensive black suit entered.

'I just thought I would introduce myself, Mrs Challinor. My name is David Merchant from the Ministry. I do hope you were warned in advance that I would be observing the proceedings of this inquest.'

Margaret Challinor held out her hand. 'Pleased to meet you, Mr Merchant. This is my officer, Detective Inspector Thomas Ridpath.'

The man from the ministry shook Ridpath's hand. His touch was cold and clammy, like a dead squid.

'The Ministry did inform me somebody would be coming. I hope you enjoyed the journey up to Manchester.'

'Enjoy is not a word I would use in conjunction with Virgin Trains. Their service leaves a lot to be desired, even in first class.' The man's voice was educated and from the Home Counties, the thin top lip hardly moving as he spoke.

'But at least you are here.'

He pushed his glasses up to the bridge of his nose. 'The morning has been *interesting*, Mrs Challinor.' He stressed the word interesting as if it were the strongest obscenity.

'Really, Mr Merchant, how so?'

A pink tongue came out to lick the thin top lip. 'It was almost as if this was a court of law, not a coroner's court, and you were more interested in discovering who the murderer was, rather than the circumstances of the death.'

'Sometimes witnesses take us into interesting territory, Mr Merchant.'

He smiled a thin smile. 'I often find it is the line of questioning that takes us into interesting territory rather than the witness, don't you?'

'I couldn't agree more, Mr Merchant, but our job is to find out the truth, is it not?'

The smile again. 'It is, but within carefully defined boundaries, Mrs Challinor. Boundaries delineated by the chief coroner and his officials at the Ministry of Justice. I wouldn't want you to' – here he paused for a moment and pushed his glasses back up to the bridge of his nose – 'overstep those boundaries and expand the role of the coroner. That wouldn't be appropriate, would it? Anyway, I just thought I would come in and have a chat. I'm sure you need time to prepare for the next stage of the inquest.'

He stepped back to open the door, stopping just before he left the room. 'Just so you are aware, the Ministry has tasked me to make a full report of the proceedings, Mrs Challinor. I hope the rest of the inquest is…' – a pause and a lick of the top lip – 'less *interesting*.'

He left the room, closing the door gently behind him.

'Bastard,' said Ridpath. 'Have you just been threatened?'

Mrs Challinor nodded. 'Done with all the subtlety of the Lord High Executioner.'

'What are you going to do?'

'My job, Ridpath. And my job is to find the truth. Is your witness ready?'

'As ready as he'll ever be.'

'We'll call the pathologist next. Wait for my signal.'

Chapter Eighty-Four

'I'd like to call Dr Harold Lardner as the next witness.' Margaret Challinor made a note in her legal pad as the pathologist walked to the witness box.

Jenny Oldfield came forward. 'You have decided to affirm?' she asked.

Dr Lardner nodded and held up his hand.

'Do you solemnly, sincerely and truly declare and affirm that you will tell the truth, the whole truth and nothing but the truth?'

'I do.'

The coroner jumped straight in as soon as he had finished.

'Your name is Martin Lardner and you were the pathologist who performed the post-mortem on Alice Seagram?'

'I was.'

'Dr Lardner, we have heard testimony from Chief Superintendent Gorman that it was you who requested to re-examine the body of Alice Seagram.'

'That is not exactly correct.'

A buzz went round the coroner's court. John Gorman looked surprised.

'I'm sorry, I don't understand, Dr Lardner.'

'It is true I requested to revisit my post-mortem on Alice Seagram, but I didn't re-examine the body, I revisited my notes.'

Margaret Challinor's eyes lit up. 'Is that normal? To re-examine notes from a post-mortem?'

The doctor was calmness personified. 'Not normal, but not unusual.'

343

'And on re-examining your notes, you decided to broaden the estimate of the time of death.'

'That is correct. I felt I had been too narrow in my estimate. The weather was unusually warm for the time of year and the body had been placed in the open before it was found. Based on those two facts I revised my findings.'

'Was this before or after you learnt James Dalbey had eaten dinner with the victim's family that night?'

Dr Lardner scratched his head. 'I don't need to remind you the evaluation of time of death is not an exact science. After re-examining my notes on the post-mortem, I felt I had been too restrictive in ascribing a time of death to between 4 p.m. and 8 p.m. on the day in question.'

Mrs Challinor took off her glasses. 'Could you answer the question, Dr Lardner? Was this before or after you found out where James Dalbey was that evening?'

The doctor smiled. 'I misunderstood you, Coroner. I only found out about James Dalbey's dinner with the victim's family two days after I revised my findings.'

'Liar.' The shout was from Tony Seagram.

'I have warned you once, Mr Seagram, there will be no more outbursts in this courtroom, am I clear?' She stared at him; waiting for a reply.

He nodded once and looked away.

'Dr Lardner, do you own a company called Prospect Limited?'

He smiled once more. 'Prospect Limited? Never heard of it.'

'Apparently, neither has Companies House. And yet it was this company that placed Alice Seagram's body at a research facility called TRACE, in north Lancashire. Have you heard of TRACE?'

'Of course, most pathologists have heard of its existence.'

'Have you ever been there?'

The smile vanished. 'Once or twice.'

'Did you go there two weeks ago?'

He smiled again, looking towards his barrister. She stood up on seeing the discomfort of her client. 'I'm sorry, ma'am, I don't see what this has to do with my client and his examination of Alice Seagram ten years ago.'

'I shall attempt to enlighten you, Ms Hardisty. Her body was discovered in a cold store at TRACE on Saturday. It had been left there ten years ago by a Mr Don Brown, working under the instructions of the undertaker, Frank O'Shaughnessy.'

Mrs Seagram began sobbing loudly. Her son put his arm around her, whispering into her ear.

'I fail to see what this has to do with my client, Dr Lardner. He has already stated clearly he has no knowledge of the company mentioned and there seems to be no documentary evidence linking him to it in any way, shape or form. Perhaps, we should be asking Mr Brown these questions rather than my client.'

'Thank you, Ms Hardisty, we will get to Mr Brown in good time. However, I accept there is no evidence linking him to Prospect Limited.' She turned back to the doctor. 'Thank you, you may step down, but please remember you are under oath in case we need to call you as a witness again.'

The doctor smiled, stood up and smoothed down his tweed trousers. 'Of course, Mrs Challinor.' He then walked back to his seat next to Protheroe.

The coroner examined a note on her desk and turned towards Ridpath who was standing at the door. 'Could you bring the next witness into court?'

The two barristers looked towards each other; Stacey Hardisty stood up. 'I must object, Mrs Challinor, there is no other witness down to appear before the court.' The barrister held up a piece of paper.

'This is an emergency witness, Ms Hardisty. There was no need to inform anybody of his appearance.'

All eyes turned towards the entrance to the court as Ridpath appeared first, followed seconds later by a man wearing an ill-fitting suit, two sizes too large for him, carrying a beige folder under his arm.

'Mrs Oldfield, please swear the new witness in.'

Jenny held the Bible out and the man stepped forward to place his right hand on it. 'Do you swear by Almighty God you will tell the truth, the whole truth and nothing but the truth?'

'I do.'

'Your name?' asked Mrs Challinor.

'Patrick Downey.'

'Your occupation?'

'I am the manager of TRACE, an experimental research facility attached to the University of Lancashire.'

'And what research do people do at TRACE?'

'Mainly forensic science. Rates of decay of bodies. The effect of wild animals and insects on bodies deposited in the open, and other primary forensic research.'

'Do you use human bodies for your research, Mr Downey?'

'Never. There are no body farms in the UK at present. We use animal carcasses, mainly pigs.'

'And yet you had a human body found on your facility on Saturday, didn't you?'

Another buzz went round the court. The three reporters scribbled frantically in their notebooks.

'In fact, we found five bodies over the weekend at our facility. Four from 2008 and one which was only deposited with us two weeks ago.'

Margaret Challinor spoke directly to the court. 'A pathologist will confirm later that this last body is that of Irene Hungerford, a sex worker from Newcastle who disappeared in Moss Side. The police are currently investigating that disappearance.'

Charlie Whitworth looked across at John Gorman. The senior policeman nodded to the coroner, his chin jutting out.

'Mr Downey, I want you to look around this court today. Do you remember the man who brought this body to your facility?'

Theatrically, Downey scanned the court before reaching out with his arm and pointing. 'Him.'

Chapter Eighty-Five

Dr Lardner stood bolt upright. 'I've never seen this man before in my life,' he shouted.

'Remember you are still under oath, Doctor.'

'I don't know who this man is and why he is accusing me of taking bodies to his facility.' The doctor stopped for a moment, realizing he was shouting. A smile crept across his face and he frowned, the voice softening. 'I have never seen you before, and the last time I visited TRACE was four years ago.'

Ms Hardisty jumped up. 'I must object, Mrs Challinor. You have ambushed my client, accusing him of being involved in some sort of body-snatching.'

'Oh, I'm accusing him of far worse, Ms Hardisty. I'm accusing him of murder.'

'But this is far out of your remit, Coroner.'

'My remit, Ms Hardisty, is to uncover the truth about unexplained deaths in East Manchester.'

'But this inquest is into the death of Alice Seagram in 2008.'

The coroner opened the file in front of her. 'If you check your order of inquests for my court this morning, you will find the next one is into the death of Irene Hungerford. We have simply reached that case far earlier than expected. And as Mr Downey is down as a witness for the case, it seems expedient to use his evidence now if it helps the court to find out the truth regarding the investigation into Alice Seagram.'

The barrister glanced back to David Merchant who was scribbling furiously in his notebook.

'This is most irregular, Mrs Challinor – the coroner's role is to ascertain the facts behind a death, not to ascribe guilt or innocence—'

'Do not tell me my job, Ms Hardisty. In my court, the Act of 2009 gives me a wide range of latitude on how I exercise my powers.'

'But... but—'

'Please sit down, Ms Hardisty.' The coroner turned back to Patrick Downey. 'You have made a serious allegation against a senior pathologist who claims he has never met you before.'

In the witness box, Patrick Downey stretched to his full height. 'This is not an allegation,' he said forcefully.

'You can prove it?' asked the coroner.

'I can.' He opened the folder he had carried into the court and produced four photographs, passing them to Jenny Oldfield. She placed the pictures under a scanner next to the coroner.

'These are time- and date-stamped images taken from CCTV of Dr Lardner delivering the body to the facility two weeks ago.'

The images suddenly appeared on the three video monitors in the court. A man, clearly Harold Lardner, at the wheel of a car waiting for a security barrier to lift. A second shot of the car moving forward under the barrier. A third shot from above of the pathologist signing a book in the TRACE administration building, his head down. Finally a clear shot of Harold Lardner leaving the facility, accompanied by Patrick Downey.

'I have given the security film taken by CCTV to the coroner's officer, Detective Inspector Ridpath.'

The jury all turned as one to stare at Ridpath standing by the door, only turning back when Margaret Challinor began speaking again.

'And you can confirm that the man in these pictures is Harold Lardner?'

The pathologist jumped out of his seat. 'It's all lies – pictures can be doctored. Lesley Taylor was the killer. The police found her body at the workshop in Poynton. She killed herself.'

'There were two other security guards on duty that day. They can confirm that the person who brought the body of Irene Hungerford to TRACE was Dr Lardner, can they not, Mr Downey?' Margaret Challinor's voice was calm.

'They can, Coroner.'

Both Charlie Whitworth and Ridpath stared at Harold Lardner.

A sneer spread across the man's face as he slowly scanned the court. 'You microbes. You small, insignificant people living your small, even more insignificant lives.' He pointed directly at Mrs Challinor. 'How dare you or anyone of your sex judge me? My wife died, why should any of you live?'

Both Charlie Whitworth and Ridpath moved at the same time as Lardner jumped towards the coroner. Ridpath brought him down while Charlie wrenched his arms behind his back and fastened a pair of handcuffs on him.

'You're nicked,' he whispered in his ear. 'We never told you how Lesley Taylor died.'

Chapter Eighty-Six

Two weeks later

'Are you ready to go to Leeds, Ridpath?'

He adjusted his position in the seat in front of the coroner, trying to get comfortable in the bentwood chair. 'As ready as I will ever be to go to Yorkshire.'

'You don't like Leeds?'

'Well, it's full of Yorkshiremen, what more can I say?'

Margaret Challinor smiled. 'You'll enjoy the coroner's officer course, most people do.'

'Aye, well, at least it'll be a change of scenery from here and headquarters.'

The coroner brushed a lock of grey hair off her forehead. 'How are they treating you?'

'Frostily. They weren't too chuffed I didn't tell them what I found in TRACE.'

'But we weren't certain who was involved until we saw the pictures.'

'Still, loyalty means a lot to John Gorman.'

'What's happened to him?'

'Oh, he'll be quietly allowed to retire early with a full pension. The force doesn't wash its dirty linen in public.'

'But he committed no crime…'

'Other than arresting the wrong man and allowing a serial killer to commit at least three other murders. Greater Manchester Police can deal with stupidity and incompetence, but failure is a different set of handcuffs. The victims are quietly retired and then forgotten.'

'And DCI Whitworth?'

'Charlie? He's angling for Gorman's job, but I don't think he'll get it. Charlie's a survivor, always has been.'

'Has he forgiven you yet?'

'Well, he's moved from calling me dickhead to tosspot, so I guess we're progressing.' Ridpath scratched his head. 'And he did get the collar.'

'Lardner confessed everything to DCI Whitworth back in the station?'

'And added four other women we knew nothing about. He'd been killing ever since his wife died. Experiments, he called them. Poor women.'

'He was nothing but a cold-blooded killer. There is never any excuse, any justification for what he did.' Margaret Challinor was slowly clenching and unclenching her fist. 'He set up two people to take the fall for his killings. It was premeditated. Whenever he felt the police were getting close, he found someone to take the blame.'

'James Dalbey and Lesley Taylor. But what I don't understand is, why place some of the bodies in a cold store?'

'I don't know. Trophies? A reminder of what he had done. Souvenirs of his intelligence and power over the police and the rest of us. He's not talking any more so we'll never know.'

A shiver ran down Ridpath's spine. 'Sarah Castle rang me when I was visiting Dalbey. She said she had discovered something about the murders. I wonder if…'

'…if she guessed it was Lardner? We'll never know.' She closed the file on her desk.

'What about the man from the Ministry of Justice?'

'David Merchant?'

'That's him, Mr Charming.'

'He compiled a report for the minister and the chief coroner. I have to go to London next Wednesday to explain my conduct of the inquest.'

'And?'

'I'm not sure. I think I'll be rapped over the knuckles and told to get in my box. It means they'll be watching my every move for the next couple of years.'

'The law is an ass.'

'But you know what? I'd do it all again in a heartbeat if it meant taking animals like Lardner off the streets. And you, Ridpath? What you are doing?'

Ridpath thought immediately of Polly and Eve. 'It's half-term so I'm finally meeting up with my wife and daughter.'

'You're still separated?'

'It'll take time. I have to build up their trust again.' He laughed ruefully. 'We're going to watch *Girls vs Gangsters 2*. I didn't even know there was a first film. Anyway, I'm being educated on female empowerment. But I don't care, I'm just happy to be with them.'

'While I'm glad your wife has decided to take you out of the Neanderthal era, I was actually asking what are you going to do about my offer?'

Ridpath blushed. How stupid could he be? 'I'm sorry, I haven't thought about it yet. I just want to do the job for three months and then decide.' He realized immediately his answer sounded terribly offhand and ungrateful. 'I'm sorry, Mrs Challinor, I don't mean any offence, it's just... I've always been a copper. It's all I've ever wanted to be. I—'

She held up her hand. 'Don't worry, Ridpath. We'll decide after the three months is up.' She pulled across three files from her in tray. 'Now, while you're on the course, I suggest you read these files. They are ongoing investigations and we're miles behind, letting the families down with the slow progress on their case.'

He reached forward and took the files. 'I'm grateful, Mrs Challinor.'

'I'm sure you are, Ridpath. But your gratitude is the least of my concerns at the moment. These families, however...' She pointed to the files.

He stood up. 'I'll get on to it straight away before I leave.'

As he was leaving her room, Mrs Challinor called him back. 'I would go and see *Girls and Gangsters 2* before you start though. You might learn something about women.'

Ridpath looked at the clock above her head. It said 5.15. Shit, late again. He rushed out of the door. 'Bye, Mrs Challinor,' he shouted over his shoulder.

He was going to meet his wife and daughter. They were the most important people in his life.

Nothing else mattered.

Nothing.

From now on, he would try to let them know that every hour of every day.

The phone call had come in from Christie's that morning. The results were good; he was still in remission. Another bonus hour, another day, another month, he could spend with his family, watching Eve grow tall and strong and independent.

If she took him back, he wouldn't make any false promises to Polly this time – he knew himself too well when the momentum of a case swept him away – but he had promised himself to look after his health and attend the hospital appointments. It was the least he could do.

As he rushed to grab his coat and jacket, he remembered her words when they had talked on the phone.

'You're an idiot, Ridpath. But you're mine and Eve's idiot. The only one we've got.'

For the moment, he'd take that and work on getting them both back to where they belonged.

Home.

It was where his heart was.

Chapter Eighty-Seven

At the same time as Ridpath was rushing out of the Coroner's Office in Stockfield, another man, smaller and more slightly built, was leaving prison.

'Here are your possessions, Dalbey. Please check and sign for them.'

He opened the wallet. Inside were seven pounds and a few coins. He picked up the watch next to it and slipped it over his wrist. A watch that continually lost time, but Dalbey had always kept it as it was the only thing he still had from his father.

He signed the form in front of him. The officer checked the signature and pressed a button beneath the desk. The door slid back on unoiled castors, making a loud noise of metal against metal.

All it needed was a little oil – some care and attention and it would work perfectly.

He looked at the officer, ready to tell him, but the man was already writing something on the form, no longer aware of his presence.

The long corridor with another door at the end stretched in front of him. He stepped forward, one step at a time, towards the door. Behind him, the gate scratched and squealed itself shut.

Why didn't they use some oil?

He could do it for them; he wouldn't mind.

On his left, another prison officer behind a glass screen waved at Dalbey. Saying goodbye? Wishing him all the best? Or just glad there was one less prisoner to worry about?

Dalbey didn't know, and he didn't care anymore.

The door opened in front of him, silently this time. He stepped over the threshold and breathed in the diesel-scented air of freedom.

He glanced back at HMP Belmarsh, his home for the last ten years. The home of books, men, rancid smells, continuous noise and his own private hell.

The people who put him inside for such a long time were going to pay. He had spent a long time planning his revenge.

Ten years.

Now the time was ripe to pay them back.

He pulled up the collar of his jacket and buried his face to protect himself from the cold wind.

The old James Dalbey had been murdered in prison just as effectively as if someone had thrown a noose around his head and pulled the lever to release the trapdoor.

The old James Dalbey had trusted people.

The old James Dalbey had loved his mother.

The old James Dalbey had tried to be a good man.

They would pay for the death of the old James Dalbey.

All of them.

He stuck his hands in his pockets and shuffled over to the bus stop where they had told him he could catch transport into town.

Ten years was a long time to plan revenge.

Ten years to savour it on his tongue.

Ten years to ensure all the details were correct.

Ten years.

Ten long years.

Time to make them pay.